Praise for *There Was a Time*

'These fabulous, often funny stories have the authentic, freewheeling atmosphere of a time when all bets were off.'
Daily Mail

'A wonderful read, packed with incident, colour and detail.'
Telegraph

'The book captures the anxieties, heightened emotion and community spirit that marked this epoch-defining chapter in the nation's long and colourful history.' *Yorkshire Post*

There Was a Time vividly evokes life in a Lincolnshire village in 1940. Elegantly written and with beautifully-drawn characters, this absorbing story, amusing and poignant by turns, tells of the impact of the last War on a small, close-knit community.'
Gervase Phinn

'He writes beautifully – poignantly and with humour.'
Telegraph & Argus

'White depicts unique, worried, caring individuals who it is not difficult to warm to and who are memorable.'
Lincolnshire Life

By the same author

Frank White

There Was a Time

HODDER

First published in Great Britain in 2017 by Hodder & Stoughton
An Hachette UK company

This paperback edition published in 2018

1

A CIP catalogue record for this title
is available from the British Library

Paperback ISBN 978 1 473 65043 5
eBook ISBN 978 1 473 65042 8

Typeset in Sabon MT by Palimpsest Book Production Limited,
Falkirk, Stirlingshire

Printed and bound by CPI Group (UK) Ltd,
Croydon, CR0 4YY

Hodder & Stoughton policy is to use papers that are natural,
renewable and recyclable products and made from wood grown in
sustainable forests. The logging and manufacturing processes are expected
to conform to the environmental regulations of the country of origin.

Hodder & Stoughton Ltd
Carmelite House
50 Victoria Embankment
London EC4Y 0DZ

www.hodder.co.uk

For J.V. and The Five

My sincere thanks go to Nick Sayers, my publisher at Hodder & Stoughton, for his insight, his understanding and his kindness, and to my wife, June, but for whom the manuscript of this work would have remained mouldering away for ever on the shelf.

I also owe my gratitude to Karen Geary, Cicely Aspinall and Alice Morley who have worked devotedly on the publication, publicity and marketing of this book. I owe them a great deal.

Frank White, Marshchapel, 2017

Contents

Author's Note

During the third and fourth weeks of August, 1939, we were in Wales – at Red Wharf Bay, Anglesey. We were in Mr Evans' cottage, which sat, isolated and self-absorbed, hiding its face behind festoons of ivy, five strides from the beach. When we arrived, on the Saturday afternoon, we found a bunch of pansies on the doorstep, left there by Mr Evans himself as a greeting. Thereafter, during the whole fourteen days, not a single cloud dragged its shadow across the scene, and only once did we see another human being. A hypnotic stillness, a warm and benign silence, pervaded everything, both day and night.

At the front of the cottage was a small garden, all dry, brown lawn, from the far side of which seven broken stone steps took you down to the sand. You sat on the wall there and watched the tide, creeping in from the misty horizon, slide and slither across the beach. It came with a kind of irritable, searching eagerness, frothing over every inch of that vast bay. It paused, splashing and surging for a brief time, and then retreated at the same speed, either satisfied or frustrated.

The pale brown outcrop of rock at the tip of the headland to the west was apparently the headquarters of a flock of seabirds. They came fluttering and wheeling around it, at precisely noon each day, to report. On most days, just as the tide receded, a mongrel dog, part greyhound, part something else, trotted purposefully, tongue lolling, across the beach from east to west. Where had he been? Where was he going?

On the second Wednesday afternoon two men appeared close to the eastern headland and dug in the sand for two hours. I'd brought my father's binoculars but still couldn't see what they were after. No doubt they were fishermen digging for bait.

On the eighteenth of August I had my twelfth birthday, but I remember nothing about it. I do remember, however, that on our last full day, when the tide was in, I sat on that wall and watched my older sister, in her green swimming costume, float about on her Lilo, seeking the last tone of skin-tan and smiling at thoughts that were none of my business. My parents sat in deckchairs, my mother knitting and my father dozing. From time to time a sequence of flashes, bright reflections of the sun, sparked among the trees which clad the eastern headland, as if someone wished desperately to convey a message.

Next morning, the driver of the hired car that had brought us here and was now taking us home, sang for two hours with hardly a pause. He had a gentle, affecting tenor voice. As he sang, his fine greying hair fluttered gently and his fingers tapped the steering wheel. 'At seventeen, he fell in love quite madly with eyes of tender blue...'

On September 3rd, a few days later, at noon, on leaving All Saints church, Newton Heath, Manchester, where I was a chorister, I walked to the place where my father had an allotment. On my way the information reached me that, during Matins, while we in the choir had been singing

Psalm 18 ('The earth trembled and quaked; the very foundations of the hills shook...') war had been declared.

My father was in his greenhouse, side-shooting tomato
plants, and I gave him the news. He'd been one of those
first 80,000 professional soldiers who'd gone to France with
the British Expeditionary Force at the beginning of the
First World War and he'd fought on through Mons, Marne,
Aisne, First Ypres, Festubert, Loos and the Somme, until
wounds ended his war. He knew better than most what
the news meant. He sank on to the wall of the greenhouse
trough and tears welled up in his eyes.

The evacuation of the schools had taken place over the
previous three days. Like the irresistible siren strains of the
Pied Piper, it had emptied the streets of children. I was one
of the very few who stayed behind. On a bright, cloudless
morning, I went to the local primary school to see the
evacuees off on their way.

Three red, Manchester Corporation Transport
Department double decker buses waited at the kerb while
their conductors stood together some distance off, smoking
in silence.

On the pavement, huddled together, jostled the evacuees,
over a hundred of them, all aged eleven or under, with
their cardboard gas mask boxes slung by string over their
shoulders, their name tags pinned to their chests, and paper
carrier bangs dangling from their hands, containing
clothing, no doubt, and emergency provisions for the
journey.

Among them, fussing, straightening children's caps,
fastening buttons, staring into children's faces, milled their

parents, some fathers, many mothers. At the periphery, and sometimes elbowing their way into the crowd, half a dozen agitated teachers with lists in their hands and tense faces, called out names and tried to shepherd this group or that out of the crowd, but the noise was such that for a while no one appeared to hear them. Onlookers, with arms folded, stood at their garden gates, and shopkeepers had come to their doors, to watch it all.

The din, the confusion, went on for a good ten minutes longer until, mysteriously, in little spasms, as if someone with a volume control was slowly turning down the knob, silence began to spread. Last minute doubts, uncertainty and reluctance, were fading and a sad sense of inevitability was setting in.

For a while no one seemed to move. Then, galvanizing themselves again, the teachers, with outspread arms and loud shouts, began to gather their charges, parting them from the tearful hugs of their parents, lining them up in three shuffling columns, and feeding them at last on to the buses.

Many younger ones were crying. Others moved as if in a trance, baffled and uncomprehending. Others, older boys, unwilling to show emotion in the sight of their mates, grinned, rocked their shoulders, and refused to look back. Two sisters had been selected for different buses. They themselves didn't seem to care, but their mother screamed and ran about hysterically until she saw them sitting side by side.

A boy I knew, thin, long-haired Jim, a ragged lad whom I sometimes found trailing after me for no reason, saying nothing, had neither father nor mother with him. But I had the distinct impression that he was enjoying this, looking forward, glad to be going. On the platform of the bus he turned to offer me a cheerful smile and a wide wave goodbye.

From both decks of all three buses, the children gazed out. With drawn faces and fluttering hands, the parents gazed back, mouthing last messages. Others, whose children were on the other sides of the buses, crossed the road and waved from there. And at last the buses drew away.

'Tarra! Tarra! Tarra!' called the parents, with crumpled faces and wet eyes. 'Tarra, love, tarra, tarra tarra...!'

And the buses, like a squadron of battleships in line astern, sailed out of sight down Briscoe Lane.

For a while yet the parents lingered, sometimes conversing in quiet voices, sharing their misery, sometimes merely standing there unable to move away. But at last they all drifted off, leaving me sitting on the low wall under the privet hedge. Just as I got up the caretaker of the school came to close the gates. I watched him fix them firmly together with chain and padlock. Then I tramped away.

Thereafter for many months I had the days to myself. I wandered. I wandered into every corner of the city, on trams, on buses and on foot. I hovered around factories and mills and watched people work. I watched people come and go, I talked to them, I listened to them and I sat for hours in Piccadilly Gardens draped about with the almost tangible mood of war which at that time hung over everything. I felt it keenly then, as a boy and, if I turn to it now, as a man, I can feel it still.

It was with me for every moment as I wrote *There Was a Time*.

Frank White

There Was a Time is my small but deeply felt tribute to that recent generation of British people who endured uniquely stressful times with such courage, faith and comradeship.

Introduction

A given place at a given time: an east coast English village at one of the most potent moments of the Second World War – the six months from June to December 1940, when the people of Britain faced the grim prospect of invasion.

A village consists of its people and, necessarily, the lives of several characters are followed. This, therefore, is a broad, well-populated canvas, coloured by incident and emotion.

The anxieties of the times created a mood never experienced before and never experienced since. Its stresses transformed states of mind. Its upheavals and the heightened emotions it generated transformed lives.

This work sets out to capture the texture and sense of those times. Early chapters introduce the various characters. Thereafter their stories, woven in with the rest, unfold.

I

Mr Geiger and an Early-Morning Walk into People's Lives

Saturday, 1 June 1940

If you approached the village from Somercotes in the south, the first property you saw, there on the right-hand side of the road, two hundred yards beyond the gates of Pretoria Estate, was Mr Geiger's bungalow, built in the late 1920s of pale brown brick, unobtrusively set against a background of mature beeches. Mr Geiger had cultivated his front garden as a typical English country tangle of herbaceous plants, many of which were now in vigorous bloom. Mr Geiger was a retiring man. He was known to be a book dealer, but not a very talkative one. He was rarely seen about, never seen in the pub, but pleasant enough when cornered, and perfectly harmless. He'd lived here alone for years, but, of late, a woman had been seen moving in and out of the bungalow. This had caused some speculation in the village.

It was a warm afternoon after a morning of heavy rain. Wraiths of vapour hovered over the drenched garden. Shortly after three o'clock two Austin cars drew up at the gate and out of them, two from the first and one from the second, stepped three men, two in navy-blue suits and one in dark grey. With one of the navy-blues – a man in his fifties by the name of Lowther – leading the way, they went up the garden path. As they did so, a joke must have been made, for they all smiled.

The one in grey walked around the bungalow to the back door in case anyone bolted. He lit a cigarette and leaned against the wall there to smoke it.

The other two went to the front door. Lowther rang the bell and Geiger, small, frowning, puzzled, opened it. He had large, almost transparent eyes and was wearing a brown cardigan, too small for him, and baggy trousers.

'Franz Geiger?'

'Frank – Frank . . .' Geiger said, with some irritation. 'What is it?'

'You call yourself Frank.'

'Yes, I do.'

While this was going on, Lowther's companion moved suddenly forward, pushed roughly past Geiger and, stepping into the hall, opened an inner door and entered the living room, knocking something over as he went. It was a sweeping brush that had been propped up in a corner.

'What's happening? What're you doing?' Geiger asked, alarmed. 'What is it – what is it?'

Lowther identified himself. 'I'm Chief Inspector Lowther, Special Branch, sir. I have a warrant here for your arrest under Emergency Order 18B – wartime detention of aliens. Do you understand? Would you like to see the warrant?'

Geiger raised his arms as if to ward off catastrophe. 'Oh no – no . . .'

'Will you step back, please.'

Pushing Geiger aside with the flat of his hand, Lowther himself now went through the inner door into the living room. There was a woman in there, standing stiff and nervous in front of the fireplace under the gaze of Lowther's companion who was hovering, motionless, against the far wall. There wasn't much light in here and the air was laden with cooking smells.

Geiger came running at Lowther's heels. 'There's a mistake – I'm a naturalised British citizen! I have nothing to do with 18B – it's a mistake – I'm British.'

In the room were two leather armchairs, a sideboard bearing some photographs and a footstool.

'Someone's got it wrong – you don't want me. You've got the wrong person . . .'

Geiger was pulling at Lowther's arm, but Lowther was paying no attention to him. He was looking at the woman. She was about thirty, with good legs and short yellow hair, dressed in a simple, puff-sleeved, red-and-white gingham frock. The material reminded Lowther of a tablecloth his wife occasionally used. He realised that the woman was trembling. She was clasping and unclasping her hands and staring at Lowther with her nostrils pinched and her mouth open.

'This is Fraulein Hertz, I suppose,' Lowther said.

'What're you doing here?' Geiger was rocking backwards and forwards. There was terror in his eyes. 'What're you doing here! I'm not an alien. I've lived here for twenty years . . .'

Lowther ignored that also. 'Good afternoon,' he said to the woman, peering closely at her. Her gaze met his and her lips moved, but no sound emerged.

'Does she speak English?'

'I'm teaching her . . . Why're you here? Tell me!'

'You are Franz Geiger?'

'Yes – I've told you. Yes! And I'm British – wait, wait . . .' Geiger made quickly for the sideboard. 'I'll show you my naturalisation papers.' But Lowther held out a hand to restrain him.

'Not necessary. We know about that. You call yourself Frank.'

'Yes, yes . . . That's how people here in England – my friends – know me.'

'Then tell me, why didn't you change your name officially when you were naturalised? Most people do. If people want to be British they want to sound British. Why not you?'

'But it was my business!'

'What d'you mean?'

'When I came here after the last war I was already running my business. I'd traded under my name for a long time. That's how people knew me – Franz Geiger. It was just my business. Look, look . . .'

Shaking so much he seemed hardly to have control of his hands, Geiger pushed past Lowther to the sideboard and opened a drawer. Rummaging there, he produced a letterhead. 'See . . . See . . . "Franz Geiger, *Specialist Books*" . . . You see. That's how I'm known. For years, for years . . .'

Lowther was not interested in the letterhead. He was looking again at the woman. 'Sit down,' he said to her. She continued to stand and so he turned to Geiger. 'Tell her to sit down. She looks as if she might collapse.'

'Yes, well, she knows about this sort of thing – yes, yes!'

'What sort of thing?'

'She's a refugee. She thought she'd escaped from this sort of thing.'

'She's been here how long?'

'Since June 1939.'

'Well, for God's sake, tell her to sit down.'

But before Geiger could speak to her, the woman, obviously understanding perfectly, went and sat on the edge of one of the chairs. But not for a second had her terrified gaze left Lowther's face. She had sat down clumsily and was unaware that the pale flesh of her left thigh was exposed. Tears had appeared in her eyes, her hands were clasped on her knees, and, cowering there, she suddenly looked like a pathetic young girl.

'She's been questioned,' Geiger said. 'They've questioned her already.'

'Yes. Is she a relative of yours?'

'She's the daughter of a friend.'

'Is she a Jew?'

'No.'

'Then what's she doing here?'

'They know all that! She told them all that . . . She had to get out . . . she's an intellectual – a teacher . . .'

'Our information is that she claims to be a Communist.'

'Yes, she is. Communists're being shot in Germany. She's a good woman. She wants to be naturalised like me. She's a good woman. I can vouch for her.'

Lowther smiled. 'And who vouches for you?'

'What?' Geiger's head jerked back. For a moment he was silent. 'This is a mistake,' he said at last, pacing to and fro. 'A terrible mistake . . . What can I do? What can I do?'

'Just get your things together, Mr Geiger.'

Geiger's lower lip had begun to tremble. 'But you can't arrest me – you can't . . .'

'Just get your things.'

'But my business, my house . . . I want to speak to someone – take me to see someone.'

'Please,' said Lowther, 'just do as I say.'

'But why – why! What've I done?'

'They'll explain all that where you're going.'

'But I want to know now!'

'I can't tell you. I'm only the arresting officer. But you had four boys staying with you last summer, just before the war.'

'Boys? Yes, they were my sister's boys.'

'Hitler Youth.'

'What? No! They came for a holiday. Hitler Youth? What're you talking about?'

'According to your neighbours they were walking about doing the Nazi salute.'

'My neighbours told you that?'

'It was their duty to report it, Mr Geiger.'

'But they were boys – boys just playing about!'

'They were Hitler Youth, Mr Geiger. Young Nazis. What does that say about your sister, their mother? What does it say about you?'

'That's ridiculous. Nonsense, nonsense! And my neighbours told you that? My friends – my English friends?'

'Who can trust anybody, Mr Geiger? Who can trust you? We're fighting for our lives. That's what 18B's all about. We want people like you out of the way.'

'You're saying I'm a Nazi?'

'You're the only one who knows that. Don't worry

– where you're going you'll be with a lot of your own sort.'

'My sort? My sort! I tell you I'm a British citizen! I'd fight for Britain if I was young enough, I'd—'

'You fought for Germany in the last war.'

'But I was conscripted!'

'Yes, well, never mind. Go and do your packing, Mr Geiger. And the lady. You can bring two suitcases each.'

'Two suitcases? But my house, my business—'

'I can't help you with those questions, I'm afraid.'

For a second, Geiger looked like a cornered animal. His eyes darted this way and that. At once, the other navy-blue suit stepped towards him and, suddenly shrinking, Geiger began to cry.

'I'm afraid there's no escape,' Lowther said. 'You and the lady get packed up. Now, please.'

'I'm British!' Geiger's face was awash with tears.

Fraulein Hertz, sitting there stiff and silent in her chair, now looked into Geiger's tortured face with tears running down her cheeks.

In the pub and in the shops during the next few days, opinion was divided. Some were convinced that the quiet, retiring man who had rarely spoken to anyone, that little Jerry, was indeed a spy, an enemy in their midst. Others, who had seen more of him, thought him no such thing. But that was war for you. You couldn't afford to risk anything.

Half a mile along the road from Mr Geiger's bungalow stood The Grange. Here lived Commodore Grainthorpe and his man, Fotherby. The morning routine at The Grange was invariable. Fotherby's alarm clock roused him at quarter-past five. While still in bed, he reached for a cigarette and lit it. Then he got up. He found his way into the shreds of his tattered dressing gown and passed into the bathroom, where he turned on the taps for the Commodore's bath. He fingered the water and made small adjustments until the temperature was just right, stepped to the lavatory, closed the lid and sat down on it to finish his cigarette. The taps spluttered. The water in the bath steamed. His overnight growth of beard itched at his chin. He scratched it. When his cigarette was smoked, he opened the bathroom window and dropped the corked tip down into the garden, where he would later hoe it out of sight under the roots of valerian.

John Fotherby was in his middle fifties, short, brisk and with a head of thick fair hair still untouched by greyness. He stared away, beyond the lawn, the shrubberies and the wood, into distances of field and sky, and then, in order to judge the strength of the wind this morning, he watched small leaves of ivy flutter at the edge of the window sill.

On top of the bathroom cabinet lay a wooden ruler. Taking this to the bath and dipping its end into the water, he saw that he had drawn four and three-quarter inches. When five inches exactly had been achieved, he turned off the taps. With measured pace, he went downstairs to the hall, where, hanging against the wall, there was an arrangement of framed prints and photographs, all of ships ancient and modern.

From a bracket was suspended a large bell, ten inches across at its mouth, into the metal of which was moulded the inscription 'HMS *Iron Duke*'. Alongside this were two shiny brass hooks from which hung a bosun's call and a small pewter megaphone, once used, perhaps, to call fore-topmen down from the upper yards.

Also fixed to the wall was a polished brass charthouse barometer and matching clock. Fotherby tapped the one and stood gazing at the other. At half-past five precisely, he gripped the elaborately plaited rope that hung from the bell's clapper and drew forth three sharp peals, because half-past five a.m. happened to be three bells in the morning watch, the time at which the Commodore liked to surface. The sound shattered the silence of The Grange like an explosion in a greenhouse. Fotherby himself winced a bit, and the alarmed chattering of birds in the garden could be heard.

But there was more to be done. Reaching now for the bosun's call and taking a deep breath, Fotherby blew the shrieking, ascending notes of 'Attention'. Shadows draping the walls shuddered. Then he put the megaphone to his mouth, directed it towards the stairs and shouted through it. 'D'ye hear there! Wakey-wakey, lash up and stow! A thousand and twenty millibars, falling. Sky clear. Force two-three, sou'-wester. Rig o' the day – try number fours, Burberry and golf cap!'

With that, Fotherby returned to his room. Adjusting his alarm clock to give himself another hour, he threw off his dressing gown and got back into bed.

By now, in his own room across the landing, Commodore Grainthorpe, RN (Retd), a man in his early seventies, was already on his feet. He was standing in his pyjamas at his opened window, plump, round, almost bald, breathing deeply and smiling out at a challenging, but hopeful and interesting, world. In the distance, there could be seen, under the low sun, a dark triangle of sea. The Commodore put on his dressing gown and went to take the bath Fotherby had drawn for him.

Within half an hour, the Commodore had embarked on his walk.

The Commodore's number fours consisted of grey flannel trousers, pullover and blazer. It was not a particularly warm June morning, but the Commodore preferred to carry his Burberry raincoat folded neatly over his arm. He liked to wear his flat cap at a sharp angle over his left eye. This gave him, he believed, a rather dashing, careless air that he felt appropriate to him. He carried his slender cane at the trail, but now and then he paused to poke it gently into clumps of vegetation under the lane-side hedges, in the hope of discovering interesting specimens of wildlife. On occasion, he had actually done so: a hedgehog or two, scuttling voles, mice, frogs and, once, a weasel with young. In a leather-bound notebook, in his neat, microscopic handwriting, he kept a record of his findings in the manner of Gilbert White.

Tucked under his left arm he carried the telescope – finger-worn, dented here and there, but still optically excellent – that had served him and, indeed, been virtually part of his anatomy, a kind of semi-detached limb, for forty years.

This morning, he had elected to follow his southern circuit. This would take him through the beeches of Wyber's Wood, around the perimeter wall of Binbrook's Pretoria

Estate, across the railway at the signal box, and so up the gradual rise to the summit of Fire Beacon Hill.

In Wyber's Wood, rabbits darted and squirrels dashed. Here, out of the sun, festoons of cobwebs, heavy with dew, lay like fine silk sheets draped across the undergrowth. Something hissed away from under his feet, but although he poked and prodded, sight of whatever it had been eluded him. However, as he emerged on to the footpath at the far side of the wood, another movement attracted him.

Eighty yards or so away, down the incline to his left, at the bottom of the meadow, a male human animal suddenly pushed through the privet hedge and, keeping to the shadows there, hurried furtively away along the perimeter of the field. Grazing cattle nearby raised their heads curiously to watch him go and, moved by similar sensations, the Commodore extended his telescope and put it to his eye.

The man was in army uniform – battledress and glengarry. His hands were hidden in his trouser pockets, his back was bowed, and he seemed deeply preoccupied – certainly he had no idea the Commodore was watching him. He waded up to his knees in tall grass and clumps of weeds.

Do I know him? the Commodore wondered. But he couldn't make out the man's face. Then where had he come from, this soldier?

Beyond the hedge through which he'd so suddenly appeared lay the back gardens – littered with chicken coops, greenhouses, cold frames and compost heaps – of Sycamore Cottages, a row of five whitewashed dwellings, glowing under the sun, on Littlecotes Lane. Nothing moved down there, save plumes of smoke from two chimneys. As the Commodore watched, a breath of wind snatched at them, rolled them over and shredded them. Gusting force four, he thought.

At that moment, over there in the kitchen of 5 Sycamore Cottages, young Mrs Veronica Heath stood at her window gasping with alarm. A moment ago, she'd let the soldier out of her back door and now she could clearly see, up there at the edge of the wood, a solid figure with splayed legs and upraised arms, peering away through a telescope.

'Oh my God – it's the Commodore and he's seen Nigel!' Shocked and trembling, Veronica ran out of her kitchen and went to sit on the stairs, where she rocked backwards and forwards for several minutes.

Veronica, just twenty-two, firm-fleshed but substantial, whose body radiated femininity as a fire radiates heat, was fully dressed and alone in the house, but she put her hands to her breasts as if to hide them. Pressing her thighs together and lowering her head, she cried with frustration. Through the thin wall, the muffled sound of an alarm clock was heard from next door. It was time for her neighbour, Mr Baker, to get up.

The Commodore folded his telescope and walked on. The footpath hereabouts was deeply rutted. Wyber's tractor had churned it up on some recent rainy day and the ground had dried as hard as concrete. The Commodore had to watch his step.

Excavated into the bank at his right were old badger setts. He probed and found nothing. He walked on, casting his gaze from left to right, taking in the scenery as he took in life in general, with interest, indeed with curiosity, but with a smiling detachment, like a man in a landscape of someone else's dream. Fotherby had polished the Commodore's brown brogues to a mirror finish, but they were dusty now. The pathway met, and then began to follow, the boundary wall of Pretoria Estate. Once again, the Commodore was under the canopy of trees. The dawn chorus had concluded and the sound from overhead was of bickering territorial shrillness.

Here, the estate wall was no more than elbow height and beyond it Pretoria House itself could be seen – the largest property in the village, late Georgian, splendid yet self-absorbed. The Commodore paused to contemplate it. Swallows were fluttering about its chimneys and exploring the high angles of its gables. Was Maureen about yet, with her brood of evacuees? the Commodore wondered.

There were three of those evacuees in Pretoria House, two sisters aged nine and eleven and a young girl of five, all of whom skipped happily about its spaces, its large, high-ceilinged rooms and its long corridors.

The sisters were still fast asleep in the great bedroom overlooking the knot garden, sharing the bed in which Alfred Milner had once slept before his days in South Africa and his dubious involvement in the events leading up to the Boer War.

The five-year-old – Jenny, or Tidgy as they all called her – had the room next to Maureen herself. A few moments ago, just as sunlight had found its way into her room and touched her face, Tidgy had climbed out of bed. Now, in her flimsy blue nightie, tousle-haired, eyes still closed, arms outstretched before her, she was tripping and fumbling along the landing towards Maureen's door. Her tiny feet flopped into the warm softness of the carpet. Coming to Maureen's door, she put the thumb of her left hand into her mouth and, with the knuckles of her other hand, gently tapped.

Maureen Binbrook had been described as motherly. This was because she was on the weighty side, with thick but not unshapely legs, softly fleshed arms and an ample bosom. Perfectly adapted for a damn good romp, her brother Lance had said to her more than once. But, in fact, Maureen was neither a mother nor a romper. She had lost her profoundly loved fiancé during the First World War and since then had remained single, living with their eccentric and difficult father who had died only recently, doing her best to curb his excesses and helping with the management of the estate.

To all appearances, she was an energetic, sensible and disciplined woman, sometimes a bit stern. But the children had found another side to her. She now lay flat on her back in her small bed in the posture of one exhausted. Perhaps she'd felt overheated during the night. She had pushed the bedcovers down to her waist. Her arms lay straight at her sides and she looked as if she could sleep for ever. All the same, at the first gentle tap at her door her lips moved and she spoke. 'Come in, darling.' Tidgy, failing to close the door behind her as always, fumbled her way to the bed. Climbing in, she pressed her head to Maureen's soft breast and tried to wrap her legs around her.

'Go to sleep, dear,' Maureen said, pulling the covers up around them both. Neither of them had opened her eyes.

A quarter of a mile further into his walk, at the stile into the top field, the Commodore met Michael Philbin, the railway signalman, just coming off duty from his box along the line. Philbin happened to be one of the Commodore's tenants. He was in his mid forties, lean, with limbs like long, articulated twigs and a large, sharply chiselled face. He took off his shiny-peaked cap and drew his finger around inside its brim, as if to remove something that had been irritating him.

He was an Irishman and his greeting came in a soft, agreeable brogue. 'Nice morning, Commodore.'

'For the present, yes. But the barometer's falling.'

'Is it now?'

'The wind's getting up, and see –' the commodore pointed away to where clouds were gathering over the horizon '– a front. Rain. Squalls. About ten o'clock I'd say. You're late, Mr Philbin. I usually meet you in the wood.'

'They routed a special up from Dover. I waited to see it.' Philbin had come to this village four years ago. Last year, he had married Nancy, a forty-year-old widow, a quiet, but smiling and cheerful woman whom the Commodore had got to know quite well through his visits to the post office. She worked there for dizzy Mrs Williams.

'It was full of soldiers from Dunkirk,' Philbin said. 'Nine out of ten of 'em were asleep. The rest had faces like masks – like masks.'

'I can imagine. They've had a hell of a time of it.'

'I tell you, the Jerries'll be here within a month. They'll be goose-stepping up the lane there.'

The Commodore smiled and shook his head emphatically. 'Never. They'll have to sink the navy first, and I promise you, Mr Philbin, they'll not manage that. How is Nancy?'

'She's fine.'

'I'm glad to hear it.'

'And I think I'd better get on. She'll be wondering where I am. Enjoy your walk.' Philbin strode away and the Commodore climbed over the stile.

Indeed, the wind was freshening. It plucked at his cap. He plodded on and came at last to the litter of large stones at the summit of the hill. Thick with lichen, half hidden in the grass, they were all that remained of an old fire beacon, erected here a century and a half before when another generation of Englishmen had expected invasion.

Placing his Burberry over one of them, the Commodore sat down. A confusion of gulls wheeled overhead for a moment and then, as if at a word of command, made purposefully for the village. The Commodore was now within a mile and a half of the North Sea, visible to him between headlands for an arc of fifty degrees, north to south. From here, at another time, he might have been able to see an occasional ship – a battered coaster labouring into a nor'-easter or an oil tanker bound for the Humber. But everything was being convoyed now along bearings beyond the horizon and five minutes' scanning through his telescope revealed nothing.

With the telescope still to his eye, he turned landwards. From the church tower the flag of St George was fluttering boldly. A motor van drove past the postman, who was trudging along the lane beyond the wood. Smoke was puffing from one of the many chimneys at Pretoria House – so things were obviously moving there now. Maureen would be up and about. Yes, and there was young, pretty Veronica Heath from Sycamore Cottages who worked for Maureen – there she was, just walking around the corner of the house. The Commodore watched as she let herself in at the side door. He liked Veronica. She was a nice, quiet girl who spoke to you with a wonderfully open and smiling expression on her face.

But the sky over Pretoria House was now grey. The front was bearing down faster than the Commodore had anticipated and he was beginning to feel cold. Getting to his feet, he put on his Burberry and looked at his watch. It was half-past seven – time to go home. 'Hands to breakfast.'

He was back in the lane for eight o'clock. Opposite his point of exit from Wyber's Wood, across the lane there, lay Saddler's Row. These houses were identical to Sycamore Cottages on Littlecotes Lane, but there were more of them – eight – all very neat behind small front gardens. The end three – numbers 2, 4 and 6 – were owned by the Commodore himself, having been included in his purchase of The Grange fifteen years before. The rents he received from them amounted to something or nothing, and he could never bring himself to make any changes. But as he walked past, he glanced at roofs, guttering and downspouts to see if any repair bills were likely to be in the offing.

His tenant, Michael Philbin, the signalman, lived at 4 Saddler's Row, and the postman, seen earlier through the Commodore's telescope, had delivered him a letter. It lay beside him on the kitchen table as he sat over his breakfast cup of tea.

'Well it's entirely up to you.' Nancy, his wife, was sitting across the table from him. She reached out and tapped the back of his hand. Full of morning brightness, newly made-up in her discreet way with pale pink lipstick, her brown hair trimmed quite short but loose and shining about her smiling face, she was ready for her day at the post office.

'You mean you wouldn't mind?' Philbin asked, frowning.

'Why on earth should I? Would *you* mind?'

'Two men living in the same house with a woman?'

'Ah, I see.' Nancy laughed. 'That's a bit insulting, you know. You don't have much faith in me.'

'It's not you I'm worried about, Nancy. No, never.'

'Then what's the matter? Is he like that?'

'Brendan? He's a man.'

'You don't trust him.'

'You don't understand.'

'Then explain it to me. How long have you known him?'

'Years – at home and then in Birmingham.'

'Then he's an old friend. Don't be so mean, Michael.' Nancy reached for the letter and cast her gaze over it. 'Yes – three or four weeks at the most, he says. It's not a life-time, is it?'

Philbin was looking down at his hands, thoughtful and uneasy. 'That's not the point.'

'Well, what is?'

'I don't want him, Nancy.'

'Because of me?'

'No – no. I didn't mean all that. It was rubbish. No. I've got other reasons. I don't want him.'

'Well, all right. In that case it's the end of the matter. Don't have him. Write and tell him.'

Getting up, going around the table, Nancy took his face in both her hands and kissed him lightly. 'I'm off to work. And what's the point of me making tea for you if you leave it?'

Further up the lane, the Commodore came alongside the gable wall of the Black Bull, a long, low structure standing alone and backed by fields now turned dull green under an increasingly leaden sky. There was a small Morris car parked at the corner of the pub's forecourt. The Commodore paused to look at it. It was very shiny.

Above his head as he did so was the window of the larger of the pub's two letting bedrooms and in there a woman in her late thirties, Mrs Rimington, with elaborately coiffured hair dyed blonde and an ample, decidedly rompable figure, was sitting on the stool before the dressing table, drawing on a stocking.

'This is the time to tell you,' she said, 'that it's got to stop.'

'What?' Lance Binbrook, that 44-year-old brother of Maureen's at Pretoria House, was still sitting up in bed with a cigarette between his fingers. His movements had suddenly frozen. Wreaths of smoke curled around his delicately featured face, with its fine nose, high cheekbones and carefully nurtured military-style moustache. His bare shoulders had drooped and, for a moment, he was speechless.

Mrs Rimington glanced at him. 'Well?'

'You're pulling my leg.'

'I'm nowhere near your leg.'

'But you can't mean it. It's ridiculous.'

'I do mean it, Lance.'

'But why?'

'I'm convinced he's got someone watching me. One of these wretched private detectives, I suppose.'

'Nonsense.'

'So I'm calling it a day.'

'But you can't do that to me.'

'I'm pretty sure I can.'

'Look, the solution's perfectly simple. We stop meeting here. We dodge and weave.'

'We've been dodging and weaving for six months.'

'You're worrying for nothing, Femella. I'm sure of it. What makes you think he's spying on you? I've never noticed anyone's eye at the keyhole. I've never seen anyone peeping around corners at us. Have you?'

'No. But I sense it. Anyway, Lance, the fact is I think I'm fed up with you. I'm sorry.'

'Rubbish. We've had nothing but fun.'

'Well, it's palled.'

Lance, naked save for a short vest, got out of bed. Puffing at his cigarette as he went, he came close to her.

'Don't touch me!' Mrs Rimington exclaimed, fending him off with a stiff arm.

'But I want to persuade you, my dear.'

'You can't.' Fully dressed now, Mrs Rimington stood up. 'Just pass my coat, will you? It's hanging on the door behind you.'

'So you mean it.'

'Yes. I'm afraid so.'

'There's nothing I can do?'

'No, my dear. There's not.'

'Why on earth should you spring it on me like this?'

'Because I think I'm rather enjoying it, you know. Look at your face.'

'You rotter.'

'You deserve nothing better. I hope you have enough money to pay for this room.'

'Well, as a matter of fact . . .'

Mrs Rimington went into her handbag and found her purse. 'There's a pound note. Will that cover it? If it doesn't, I don't care.'

'Look, I'm sorry about last night,' Lance said. 'I'm afraid I didn't feel very energetic. Don't let it—'

'But when *did* you feel energetic?'

'That's not fair. Anyway, I'm sorry . . .' He reached for her.

'Don't bother, Lance. I'm off. I'll give you a kiss. Just your *cheek* – your cheek . . . There. That's it, my darling. I'm off. Goodbye. Look after yourself.'

Leaving Lance to stand there, bare-legged and deflated, Mrs Rimington stomped down the backstairs, went out through the side door and got into her Morris car. She drove past the Commodore, just as he was walking through the gateway to The Grange.

In his drive, the Commodore met young Arthur Swift, the paper boy.

'Hi!' Arthur said, pointing to the Commodore's left ankle. 'Did you know your turn-up's down?'

'So it is. Never mind.'

'Look, it's started to rain,' Arthur said, holding out a hand to feel the drops.

'So it has. You're going to get wet, Arthur.'

'That's all right. I've only got the *Daily Mail* to deliver to 15 Front Street, then I'm done. I'll leg it.'

Arthur legged it away.

Always on the lookout for the Commodore after his walks, Fotherby was there to open the door. 'You cut it fine,' he said, gazing beyond the Commodore to where rain was falling in torrents on to the limp leaves of shrubbery.

'Has there been any post?' the Commodore asked as he stepped inside.

'No.'

'Nothing from the Admiralty?'

'Of course not. How many times do I have to tell you? They don't want you at your age, man.'

'One never knows at times of emergency. There's a definite possibility.'

'Rubbish. They wouldn't trust you with a cutter in Plymouth Sound. And I don't blame 'em.'

'You've not shaved this morning, Fotherby.'

'No.'

'Well do so. And mend that tear in your waistcoat. Pull yourself together.'

'I am pulled together. Give us your coat.'

'Is breakfast ready?'

'It's always ready, isn't it? Here – your *Times*. Read it and pipe down.'

'Thank you.' The Commodore turned away. 'Where're my victuals?'

'Where d'you think? And by the way, only one egg this morning.' Fotherby's tone changed. 'Look, Commodore,' he added with sincerity, 'I'm sorry about that, but it can't be helped.'

The Commodore turned back for a moment to face him. 'Don't worry, old chap. We must all make sacrifices. We'll grin and bear it.'

'Are you all right this morning?' Fotherby asked, now peering into the Commodore's face with concern. 'You look a bit pale.'

'I'm fine, old chap. I hope there's plenty of bacon.'

'I can always fiddle that,' Fotherby said. 'Go in and I'll bring your coffee.'

2

Arthur Does Some Business;
Three Cheers for Death

It rained all that day, but from the next day onwards for several weeks there was an unbroken spell of glorious weather with barely a cloud and soaring temperatures. The new Prime Minister, Winston Churchill, told the nation that although the rescue of a third of a million troops was something like a miracle, worthy of rejoicing, Dunkirk was in fact not a victory. The Battle of France had been lost. The Battle of Britain would now begin. In a BBC broadcast, Anthony Eden, Secretary of State for War, had already proposed that men who were not actually available for the services might still, at a time when the nation was in grave danger of invasion, wish to help to defend the motherland. A new civilian corps of fighting men was to be created and it was to be called the Local Defence Volunteer Corps. Men were asked to come forward.

Forward went Fotherby. In his earlier years he had served in the Royal Marines, latterly as a sergeant. He was therefore immediately given that rank in the LDV. Since the Commodore was being ignored by the navy, he, too, went forward and was made a private. Well aware that he was actually too old to enlist in the corps, he considered it wise to accept that lowly station with good grace. For a while, men mustered and drilled in their suits because no uniforms were available, and with walking sticks or broom handles for rifles because there were no arms to be had. But the Brocklesbys at the Manor House had influence and when uniforms and rifles did at last appear, the village contingent was amongst the first to receive them.

At the village crossroads they were building a concrete pillbox to command the approaches. Someone had dumped piles of barbed wire on the edge of the cricket field, then gone away and left them there. Notices advising against careless talk or recommending young women to join the WAAF had been posted on telegraph poles, and the brick air-raid shelter next door to the village hall, long ignored in the absence so far of raids and left to the ravages of nature, had been cleaned out and whitewashed inside.

Every morning, two flights of Hurricane fighter planes flew low over the village and out to sea.

That air of confident optimism which had hung about people's heads like a halo during the early days of the war – that conviction that it was only a matter of time before invincible Britain drove Hitler and his hordes from the face of the earth – had been blown away by the icy wind from Dunkirk. In people's eyes now you could see unmistakable signs of anxiety. On 10 June, Mussolini, Italy's puffed-up, ranting dictator, convinced that the British were on the point of capitulating and anxious to share in the bounty that would be released on their defeat, allied himself to Hitler and declared war on Britain.

We move on to the afternoon of Sunday, 30 June. The church clock stood at half-past two and the thermometer that hung in the porch of the Black Bull (at the moment closed for business) recorded 78 degrees Fahrenheit. The sun was ferocious and there was not a breath of wind. The flag on the church tower hung exhausted and in the yard below not a leaf moved. Main Street was deserted, save for old Fred Withers shuffling homewards from his daughter's house, where he'd taken Sunday dinner. Every dwelling along the road there, gasping for breath, had opened its windows and, as he walked by, Fred was able to hear quite clearly several jokes and several bursts of applause from wirelesses tuned in to the BBC.

On the allotments, four sweating men, stripped down to their vests, sat in desultory conversation in the shade of a potting shed. Even the kids were weighted down to stillness. Girls, one or two in swimming costumes, others in bonnets and thin dresses, had abandoned their skipping ropes and their tennis rackets and lay on their backs on the village green with their knees up, piping messages to each other or absently plucking blades of grass. At the far side of the green, boys sat in a pow-wow circle, muttering. Now and then explosions of laughter erupted among them.

We now move into the Black Bull, where the barmaid, Mary Acton, stood knocking at the locked cellar door. 'Charley!' she shouted. 'How long're you going to be?' Mary, with a plump round face and a smooth, round forehead, worked behind the bar with the landlord, Charley Cartland, who was now being very silent down the steps behind the cellar door.

Sundays were of special significance for these two. After closing at two o'clock, Mary had hurriedly emptied the ashtrays, mopped the floor and cleaned the back fittings. She had then retired to Charley's private bathroom in the upstairs flat. She had taken a quick bath, put on fresh make-up, brushed her hair – all in the space of twenty minutes – and then slipped naked into Charley's bed. Ten minutes had hummed by. Then another five. Growing impatient, puzzled and tense, she had put on her dress and gone down.

Standing there at the closed and locked cellar door, she shouted, 'You know she expects me home before three!' She was speaking of her twenty-four-year-old daughter, Eva, generated in her by a soldier under bushes in a Liverpool park during the last war. She had been eighteen at the time, on a visit to her paternal grandparents. The soldier was called Tom, but that was all she remembered of him.

'And you know what she'll do if I'm not there. She'll come hammering at the door!'

From down in the cellar, Charley's muffled voice came to her. 'Go on up. I'll be with you in a minute.'

'What on earth're you doing down there?'

'I'm just swilling out.'

This was not true. Charley was scooping black-market sugar from a canvas sack into one-pound paper bags.

'Why d'you have to do it now?'

'I've told you – I'll only be a minute.'

'Well, hurry up! Or I'll go home! I mean it!' Mary went back to the bedroom. She had left the room door open and stale cigarette smoke from the lunchtime session downstairs had drifted in, so she opened the window and stood for a moment looking out. Two foxes trotted across the yard. They'd been at the dustbins again.

Young Arthur Swift, the Commodore's paper boy, whom we've already met, was just climbing back over the wall of Pretoria Estate, at a point where overhanging trees hid him from view. He sneaked along the ditch and then climbed the fence on to Littlecotes Lane. He was wearing corduroy trousers. Landing on the other side of the fence, he bent down and carefully patted his legs between ankle and knee. He had things hidden there.

Grinning to himself, he walked on down the lane. With the satisfying sense of casting away his boyhood, Arthur had first stepped into those long corduroy trousers on the morning of his thirteenth birthday. This was the age when all local lads went through that rite of passage. These corduroys of his had not been new. They'd been passed down to him by a neighbour whose son had grown out of them. A year or so of someone else's wear, and several months of Arthur's own, had left ravages. Strips of leather had been sewn to the turn-ups and a patch of different material had been inserted unobtrusively into the seat. However, his blazer, just a little short in the sleeves, was his own. Despite the heat, he had fastened it tight across his chest, with all three buttons, because he had something hidden under there as well.

In the hedge beside him, insects hummed. Over the fields heated air shimmered. Then, as he went on down the incline of the lane, his eye was attracted to the doorway of 5 Sycamore Cottages. We have been here before, during the Commodore's walk. We met Veronica, sitting on her stairs, alarmed at the thought that the Commodore had seen something he ought not to have seen. Now, a large, sausage-shaped object, light brown in colour, poked out of the doorway of Number 5, and for a moment Arthur was baffled by it.

But then David Heath, Veronica's husband, appeared in his sailor's uniform and Arthur realised that he was carrying the sausage over his shoulder. It was his hammock. With his bell-bottoms flapping around his ankles, David walked slowly down the garden path to the gate, where he stopped and turned to look back. He waited. After a moment, his wife, Veronica, in a pink frock, emerged carrying a green suitcase.

At the gate, she and her husband came together. Hammock and suitcase were put down and Veronica and David embraced. In a motionless tableau, they clung tightly together for several seconds. Then, drawing away at last, David shouldered his hammock, picked up the suitcase and set off down the lane for the village.

Once again becoming perfectly motionless, Veronica watched him go. A second later, Arthur had reached the place where she stood. He greeted her with a smile. 'Hello, Veronica!' But she was barely aware of him. Her gaze was fixed on her husband, and there were tears in her eyes.

Arthur broke into a trot and came to David's side. 'Give us your hammock,' he said. 'I'll carry it for you.'

'Thanks, Arthur. It's a bit heavy,' David said, sliding it from his own shoulder to Arthur's. 'Can you manage it?'

'Course I can.' And they walked on. Arthur felt inclined to talk, but there was an absorbed and very private expression on David's face and so he said nothing. In silence they passed the pinfold and then the field where Wyber's Jerseys were lying in the shade under the giant chestnut. But then

David himself spoke. 'You sure it's not too much for you?' he asked.

'It's easy,' Arthur said.

'It's all we ever get a chance to sleep in, in the navy – hammocks. Pick up your bed and walk.' David smiled.

'Have you had a good leave?' Arthur asked.

'Yes . . . Yes, it was fine.'

'How long did you get?'

'It was embarkation leave – fourteen days.'

'What's embarkation leave?'

'You get it when you're going foreign.'

'I thought you'd been foreign. Somebody said you'd been to Norway.'

'Aye, we were at Narvik during the battle, but that's still Home Fleet. Home Fleet always comes back to Scapa or Portsmouth. Foreign means foreign.'

'Oh. So where will you be going?' Arthur asked.

David smiled. 'You don't ask that sort of question in the navy. It's anybody's guess. But now the Eyeties're in the war we think it'll be the Med.'

'They don't have any tides in the Mediterranean,' Arthur said.

'Is that so?'

'At least, that's what I read. When will you be coming back?'

'And that's another question you never ask. We get open-ended commissions. It'll be a year at least. But it could be two – three . . . Who knows? I'm in destroyers. The flotilla sank a couple of Jerries at Narvik. I suppose they think we can sink the Eyeties just as easy.'

'And I bet you can.'

'Well, we'll have a damn good try, Arthur.'

They had now reached the corner where Littlecotes Lane met Main Street. David stopped in his tracks. Turning, he gazed back along the lane to where Veronica still stood at her garden gate, a pale pink brushstroke in the shining landscape. He waved to her and her own arm passed through the air above her head in slow arcs. Arthur imagined he could still see the tears in her eyes.

Several seconds passed and David did not move again. Perhaps he was trying to fix in his mind this last glimpse of his wife and home. Then he smiled. 'Right, Arthur. That's it.' They continued on their way along Main Street, past the Black Bull.

'Look, David,' Arthur said, 'I've got an errand to do. I won't be a tick. Can you wait here for me and I'll hump your hammock to the station for you?'

Leaving David sitting on the wall there, with his hammock and his suitcase at his feet, Arthur ran across the road to the back door of the pub and hammered at it. Nothing happened. He hammered again and at last Charley appeared in the doorway.

'Oh it's you, is it? What've you got?'

From inside his socks and under his blazer, Arthur produced four shining trout.

'What d'you call these?' Charley asked, taking them, weighing them in his hands. 'Where's the giants you said you could get?'

'They're above the weir. But I couldn't chance it today, Mr Cartland. When I got there Maureen Binbrook and the girls were messing about on the grass, so I had to go further up the river. That wasn't easy, either, because you can be seen from Home Farm. But so what?' Arthur prodded the trout. 'They're not tiddlers. They'll weigh a couple of pounds when you've filleted 'em.'

Charley went into his trouser pocket and offered Arthur a sixpenny piece.

'A tanner! They're worth more than that! It's not easy to corner trout. You have to do it at the right time and know the right places. You've got to have the knack. Give us a bob.'

'Oh, all right.' Charley produced a shilling. 'But if you can't get me better than this lot don't bother. And keep your mouth shut.'

Arthur went back to where David sat on the wall and together they walked on.

They found the tiny station deserted. Flanked by hammock and suitcase, they sat side by side on the bench on the dusty platform. Across the line, on the other platform, Mr Sergeant, the porter, walked slowly up and down past the open door of the waiting room. From hoardings came the messages, GUINNESS IS GOOD FOR YOU, SKEGNESS IS SO BRACING and, once again, CARELESS TALK COSTS LIVES.

The train came and Arthur helped David to bundle his gear aboard. David closed the door, leaned out of the window and smiled down at him. 'Thanks, Arthur.'

'You've got the compartment to yourself.'

'Yes. I'll probably crash my swede for a while.'

'Well, don't miss your stop.'

The guard blew his whistle and David reached for Arthur's hand. 'Cheerio, Arthur. Will you go and have a look at Veronica now and then for me? She gets lonely.'

'If you want me to – yes, I will.'

'Well, thanks again . . .'

The train began to move, but David was reluctant to let go of Arthur's hand. He clung to it, as if to the last touch of all familiar things, and Arthur had to walk and then run alongside the train for thirty yards or so. 'Cheerio, cheerio . . .' David kept saying.

At last he let Arthur go, but he still leaned out of the window, waving and waving until the train finally rolled away out of sight.

Charley at the pub was now free to join Mary in his bedroom. It was usual at these moments, as Charley came to her, for Mary to make it clear that she retained her dignity, and that some effort had to be made to get at her. Naked though she was, she lay hunched up like a foetus, covered from head to toe by the bedclothes.

Charley knelt at the bedside and rested his hand on the curve of her hip. There was an unaccustomed stiffness about her.

'What's up?' he asked.

A muffled note of disdain came from under the covers. 'Huff!'

'What're you huffing for?'

'You said one minute. You know how long it's been? I might as well get dressed and go home right now.'

'Oh no, you might not.' Charley drew the sheet from over her face and kissed her cheek. 'Me little beauty,' and his hand slipped down to her breast.

'Stop it.'

'No.'

'There's no time, Charley.'

'Course there is.' He embraced her, quickly, roughly.

'Stop that! You know I don't like it when you go like a bull at a gate. Oh, Charley, what've you been doing?'

'I told you. Swilling out the cellar.'

'No, you weren't. You can hear the water in the pipes when you're doing that. You were messing about with all that stuff you've got down there.'

'There's no stuff down there. Only the beer.'

'That's a lie. You're a crook, Charley. You're a black-market spiv. Why d'you do it? It frightens me.'

'I'm sorry, Mary, but after ten years in the army, three of them in the trenches for no purpose whatsoever it seems, because they're at it again, I don't intend to fade away at forty-seven. They're rationing the beer. How else am I supposed to get by?'

'They'll run you in one of these days.'

'They have to catch me first.' Charley stood up and began to undress. 'Move up my little beauty and let me in.'

But Mary's prediction had been correct. At that moment her daughter, Eva, came hammering at the front door, angry and shouting. 'Mother! Where are you? Mother! Mother!'

Later, we learn more of Eva.

All the Commodore's walks had been planned to include a bit of a climb at roughly their halfway points. Puffing plods up hillsides were good for his ticker, he believed. This morning, having climbed to an elevation of two hundred feet, he was sitting on the crumbling trunk of a fallen tree and taking in the view. His hands were folded on the top of his cane and his chin rested on his hands. Against the sky, thirty yards from him, a kestrel appeared from nowhere and hovered there, fluttering. He watched it, waiting for it to stoop. But then his focus shifted. Beyond the kestrel, far away against the pale blue sky to seaward, a faint tracery of vapour trails could be seen – white swirls, ellipses and slashes, like the careless marks made by a baby with a piece of chalk.

He put his telescope to his eye. Tiny dots drifted and darted in slow gyrations, like motes in a beam of sunlight. Now and then flashes of reflected sunlight winked. Two small black puffs appeared whose meaning the Commodore couldn't make out, and then a long spiral of black smoke wound slowly down towards the sea. A terrible battle was being fought by desperate men in aeroplanes. Ferocious, screaming, noisy killing was happening before the Commodore's eyes – and yet, although he listened hard, not a sound could be heard.

He watched for perhaps three minutes and then, suddenly, it was all over. The sky was empty. One by one the vapour smears faded, like plumes of breath on a cold morning.

The Commodore lowered his telescope and looked down at his gnarled and shrunken hands. Young men must fight and old men could only watch.

He sat quietly for five minutes, affected by what he'd seen. But then the thought of jays slipped back into his mind. A pair had nested that year in the copse nearby and he was hoping to catch a glimpse of them this morning. The vision of a jay's rainbow flight was, in his opinion, a special privilege. He got up and walked towards the copse.

By doing so, he missed sight of the damaged Heinkel bomber that was about to crash in the fields a little over a mile away. Darkly green with camouflage, flashing its proud black and white crosses, it came in low from over the sea.

At the beach, with a drunken leap, it climbed a few feet, lost momentum, dipped its nose, tilted its wings and levelled out again. Its engines had stalled and the sound it made was that of a high wind in trees. But, as it passed barely ten feet above the oaks in Covert Wood, its port engine came to life again, coughing and spluttering. The port wing lifted and for a moment the aircraft looked as if it was about to begin a pirouette. But the engine died again and remained dead. Levelling out once more, swaying gently like a carefree dancer, the plane skimmed over the ridges of a ploughed field.

About ten feet from its tail, an underside section of the fuselage had been ripped away and there was a neat stitching of bullet holes across its starboard wing. At the far side of the field, the plane scraped over a stone wall. It was not a high wall and part of it fell away, but it managed to take a grip on the edge of the gap in the plane's fuselage and the entire tail section was torn off. Up it went, over and over, and from it fell a body, already lifeless. The body bounced twice, and then skidded along the ground, loosely flapping. It came to rest in a sitting position against the side of an old enamel bath, a makeshift water trough from which, only a moment before, a cow had been drinking. The legs somehow managed to wrap themselves around each other like twisted ropes.

Meanwhile, the main section of the plane had gone on

to gouge a deep rut through a field of Brussels sprouts. There were two cherished walnut trees standing side by side at the edge of the field, and against them the aircraft finally came to rest, with a howling thump followed by a long, hopeless sigh.

The silence that followed was like a shocked holding of breath. After a moment or two, a cabbage white butterfly began to flutter around the shattered wreckage. The front part of the plane, mostly Perspex and like a twisted cold frame, had been wrenched away, leaving a large gap. A minute passed, and then, out of this gap, miraculously alive, crawled a man. His flying helmet had been ripped off and his face looked as if it had been dipped in flour and then splashed with blood. His legs had no use in them and his right arm trailed. He dragged himself along, moaning and grunting, by his left elbow. In that left hand he held a small canvas wallet.

Reaching a distance of about ten yards from the plane, he rolled over and searched himself for something. It proved to be a cigarette lighter. Urgently, he tried to set fire to the wallet. It would not oblige. Lying back, exhausted and frustrated for a moment, he opened the wallet, took out some paper and lit that. When he was convinced the paper was actually burning, he lay still again, groaning and perhaps dying. Then he began to crawl further away from the plane, gasping with exertion and anxious to put distance behind him.

From inside the plane other noises were now heard. Someone else had survived and was calling out, trying to scream but choking over it. 'Werner . . . Werner . . . !'

The man suddenly emptied like a sack. With his face

buried in the grass, he lay there for several moments, obviously making a desperate decision. Then, slowly, he crawled around and dragged himself back towards the plane.

He now saw that, in burning his secret papers, he had set dry grass alight. Going to it, he patted at it with his damaged bare hand. Satisfied that the flames were dead, he continued to crawl towards the plane. Reaching it at last, he heaved himself back inside and disappeared. Another minute passed. Voices could be heard and slow, painful movement.

While this was going on, John Potter and his thirty-year-old son Henry, from nearby Longbottom Farm, came running along the lane. They'd heard the noise, looked out and seen the crash from their kitchen window. Ready to encounter any Jerries who might be on the loose, John had brought his shotgun with him.

Coming to the gateway of the field, from where all could be seen, the two men stopped dead and stared, motionless and appalled. 'Christ!' said Henry, staring at the mangled wreckage. 'What a bloody mess. Nobody's alive in there. I don't think you need your gun, Dad.'

But even as he spoke, the wounded airman's head and shoulders appeared around the jagged edge of metal. With infinite slowness, more of him appeared. He was dragging a comrade behind him, heaving with all his might.

At that moment, as father and son gaped, open-mouthed and astonished, there came a sudden, shattering roar and a blinding flash as an enormous, explosive sheet of flame engulfed the plane. The man's efforts to douse the burning grass had failed. In flickering little rushes, now dying into smoke and now glowing again, wafted by the gentle breeze, flames had reached spilt engine fuel. The blasting heat of the explosion wafted across the field and touched the Potters' faces. 'Jesus!' gasped Henry. 'Get back – there might be bombs in there!' And the two of them ran headlong back towards their house.

There were no bombs. They had been jettisoned out at sea. The plane burned on, sending a dense, curling plume of black and grey smoke into the calm sky. And now, along the lane, at a safe distance, others had come to join the Potters, to stand and watch.

Presently, Constable Bowker arrived from the village on his bike. He found a gathering of eight people of both sexes, including two young boys, all from houses round about, all standing silently in shocked contemplation of the still-burning funeral pyre. 'Hell,' he said. 'Was there anyone in it?'

'Mr Potter says two.'

Mrs Hooper, still in her nightie under her coat, had tears in her eyes.

'What a horrible death,' said Mr Robinson.

'Poor souls,' muttered old Mrs Palmer.

The constable, holding on to the handlebar of his bike, stiffened, so angry that the bike rattled. 'Poor souls! What the hell're you talking about! They're bloody Germans!'

A tremor went through the sad little crowd. They looked quickly at one another. 'Yes, but Harry—'

'But nothing! Are you English or not? Are we fighting a war or not? Ten to one, that plane there's been shot down by one of our lads – and good for him. Bloody good for him. Sod the Germans. Are you ready? Three cheers for the RAF. Are you ready? Well come on! Hip, hip . . .'

And away the cheers echoed, over the black corpse of the Heinkel with its incinerated occupants, away over the village, and away towards the sea – a chorus of exultation.

Just after twenty past six on a Saturday evening, the stopping train from town drew into the station. It was a little late. From it stepped one passenger, a short, lively-faced man, quick in his movements, intent. He stood for a moment on the platform, gazing about, but with a detached kind of indifference to what he saw. Then he asked the porter how to get to Saddler's Row, and walked off briskly.

He was carrying two suitcases. Strapped to one of them was a canvas wrapper covering what appeared to be a bundle of sticks. He climbed the bridge over the line and walked out through the yard onto Main Street. At the corner of Littlecotes Lane an army lorry was parked at the kerb and two soldiers were sitting on the wall having a smoke. As he passed, they raised their heads to him and nodded. He glanced at the back of the lorry to see what it might be carrying, but nothing could be made out because everything was covered with sheets of tarpaulin. Otherwise the village seemed deserted.

At the corner of Wyber's Wood, poking up out of weeds, stood a poison-gas detector. This was a four-foot pole topped by a flat shelf. Pasted to this shelf was a square of vivid yellow paper that would change colour should the enemy resort to such infamy. From a wireless set somewhere came whispers of dance music. Briefly, distant male voices could be heard. The LDV were digging a defensive trench at the far side of the wood.

He crossed the road to Saddler's Row. At number 4,

Nancy Philbin was at her kitchen table, deep in concentration. Her fountain pen was between her teeth and she was using her hands to sift through wads of papers. When someone came knocking at her door, she winced at the interruption, but got to her feet at once and hurried to answer it.

'Hello – you must be Nancy.' He grinned and rolled his head and sent in her direction potent waves of self-assurance, familiarity.

But she didn't know this man. Her uneasy smile had a frown in it. She stared at him, too much taken aback by his manner to register what he'd said. 'I'm sorry?'

'Brendan.'

'Pardon?'

'I'm Brendan Kelly. I wrote to Michael.'

Now she remembered. She flustered. 'Oh yes . . . yes . . .' And, at last, she realised that he was carrying suitcases.

'Where is the old darlin'?' Brendan laughed. Leaning to one side, he sent his voice into the house: 'Michael!'

'Shush – please – please. He's asleep in bed. He's on nights.'

'Oh. Sorry about that. D'you think I could come in?'

'Yes, yes – of course. I'm sorry, I wasn't expecting you . . . I didn't know . . .'

They went into the little parlour. Brendan put his suitcases down and looked around. He was smiling, but in his eyes was that same cool indifference with which he'd greeted the village on his arrival. 'Very nice. Very cosy,' he said.

He went to look out of the window. Douglas Russell, the young vicar, was just walking by beyond the garden wall, his top half leaning forward and his thin hair flapping, making very purposefully for somewhere. A dog was just emerging from Wyber's Wood across the lane. The clock on the mantelpiece ticked, Brendan said nothing, and Nancy stood staring at his back, trembling and perplexed because hadn't her husband written to tell this man that he didn't want him?

'I think I like this village,' Brendan said at last. 'I think I'll be all right here.' He turned to face her. 'I'm a bit peckish. Couldn't do me a bit of bread and dripping or something, could you?'

'Yes, yes . . .' She was flustering again. 'I was just doing the forms for the Ministry.' She pointed to the litter of papers on the table.

'What Ministry?'

'I work at the post office – the shop – it's all this new rationing they've brought in – tea, jam, cheese . . . It's the registration papers. I never get a chance to do it at work and Mrs Williams is past it.'

'And who's Mrs Williams?' Brendan grinned. 'Calm down, Nancy. I'm an easy-going fellow. We're going to get on a treat.'

'I'll go and make you something to eat.'

'Hang on a bit. Let me look at you. Yes. He's done well for himself. Sit down for a minute.'

Uncomfortable under his gaze, Nancy did so. Behind his smile there was something that made her feel quite nervous. But he seemed to be doing his best to put her at her ease. 'I won't be here long enough to trouble you, Nancy,' he said. 'All I ask is time to find somewhere else in this nice village. Is there any work going for a grafter?'

'There's Evers' factory at Somercotes.'

'What do they do?'

'They used to make ploughs and harrows and things like that. They're doing war work now. Half the village works there. They make parts for aeroplanes.'

'I was thinking of something more in my line. What about farm work?' He laughed. 'Work to suit a peasant like me.'

'Yes. If that's what you want. Things were bad before the war, but the farms're doing well now. They're getting subsidies from the Government. You could try Mr Wyber – they've been here for generations. And you could see Mr Britton at Binbrooks' estate as well . . . and the Brocklesbys at the Manor. But Evers' pays better wages.'

Brendan sagged in his chair. But he smiled again. 'I'm whacked. Dripping would do nicely. I like it.'

'I'm afraid I've got no dripping. But I've got a bit of ham left.' Nancy stood up. 'Will that do?'

Suddenly, the door opened and Michael Philbin stood there in his pyjama bottoms, naked from the waist up, bleary-eyed, still half asleep and utterly downcast. 'Brendan?'

Leaping up, Brendan fell on him, embracing him, swaying backwards and forwards with him. 'Michael me laddo!' It went on for several seconds. Then, stepping back, he looked Michael up and down. 'You're fatter! It's this lovely wife of yours overfeeding you. And am I glad to see you!'

But Michael remained stiff. His face was tense and he drew a rigid arm through the air. 'I told you we didn't have a bed for you! Didn't I tell you that?'

Brendan laughed. 'Oh you don't worry about trivialities

like beds, Michael, boyo.' Turning aside, Brendan released the straps from the suitcase, removed the canvas wrapper and tipped it onto the floor. It unravelled to reveal a folded camp bed.

'There you are. I'll sleep like a top on this. I'll sleep like a virgin. All I need is a blanket and Bob's your uncle. You can let me have a blanket, can't you, Nancy?'

Michael and Nancy were staring, speechless, at each other. Then Nancy moved. 'I'll go and make you a sandwich,' she said, leaving them alone.

She failed to close the door properly and Brendan went quickly to draw it to. 'So, Mick,' he said turning around. 'You've got it good, haven't you, old mate?' He grinned. 'Together again, eh?' He went to rest his plump hands on Michael's shoulders. 'You and me.' His hands were warm and his eyes were laughing. But Michael's shoulders were limp.

3
Another Visitor;
Clifford Wants to Go Home

At the station next morning, another stranger arrived, a woman in her thirties, good-looking, perky, with a neat pageboy hairdo. She had been promised that someone would be waiting for her, and as she crossed over the bridge she saw him. He was standing at the station entrance, smiling.

'I'm Lance Binbrook,' he said. 'You must be Mrs Delgrano. Hello.'

'Peggy,' she said, confronting him squarely. 'I prefer that.'

His gaze passed over all parts of her. She impressed him and it was obvious in his eyes. 'Oh well, Peggy, then,' he said. 'I'm delighted to meet you.' He reached for her hand and held it for a moment longer than was necessary. He took her arm. 'This way, Peggy . . .'

Beyond the station gates stood a scarlet-coloured Rolls-Royce Phantom II, not brand new but sporty and still resplendent. He opened the rear door for her, but she hesitated.

'Why can't I sit in the front?' she asked.

'But of course you can, if you wish – certainly, come along . . .' and he opened the door to the front passenger seat. 'There you are.'

As she moved past him her full breasts under her red

coat brushed against his arm, and as she got into the car there was a flash of stockinged thigh. 'Lance,' she smiled, watching him as he came and sat beside her, looking into his face. 'What a nice name. It makes me think of knights in shining armour.'

'Does it?'

Lance contemplated her – her small, pretty face, her little knees, her neat hair. Under his gaze she turned away to stare through the windscreen. She folded her hands primly in her lap. But her head was high and on her face there was the look of a woman quite aware that she was being admired.

At a sedate pace, Lance drove along Main Street towards the estate. Just beyond the gates of The Grange, young Susan Pepper, late for school, ran red-faced and wild-haired along the pavement under overhanging branches of beech, lost a shoe, and hobbled on one foot to put it back on. In the yard of the Black Bull, Charley was busy sweeping up shards of glass from a broken beer bottle. He looked up to wave a hand as the Rolls went by. At Saddler's Row, Mrs Thurlow cleaned the outside of her parlour window with slow, pausing wipes of the chamois. But mingled into the sunlight that lay heavily over the scene, and tincturing it with that tremulous, vague air of melancholy, was the inescapable sense of war.

'Oh look there!' Peggy exclaimed, giggling merrily as they came alongside the field beyond the Black Bull. 'Is that the LDV?'

'Yes. They call them the Home Guard now. They got two or three old American rifles the other day – and see, others have got their own shot-guns. It's going to be rather dangerous in these parts from now on.'

'You look like a soldier yourself, you know, with that moustache.'

'Do I? I was one – once.'

'I could tell – I could tell.'

'I was in the Coldstreams during the last war.'

'Well, I like soldiers.'

'Really? What about ex-soldiers?'

'Well . . . I suppose it depends.' She opened the buttons of her coat and wafted air towards herself with both hands. 'What a summer we're having. It's the sort of weather you feel like taking all your clothes off.'

Lance drove on past the field where Fotherby and the Commodore were parading with a dozen or so other Home Guard.

As the Rolls emerged from the shade of trees along the estate drive and the façade of Pretoria House came into view with its numerous Georgian windows and its great porticoed entrance, Peggy Delgrano gave a little impressed 'Mmmm . . .'

She turned and looked at Lance's profile. 'Aren't you lucky to live here,' she said. Her gaze, thoughtful and steady, lingered on his face.

'I was barred from the place until recently,' Lance said. 'Never set foot in it for years.'

'Why?'

'My father kicked me out.'

'Why?'

'Oh, it's a long story.' The car was passing into the shadow of the house. 'Anyway, here we are.'

Inside the house, Maureen had gone into the kitchen, where Veronica Heath was chopping carrots. They had decided to feed their visitor with a chicken delivered that morning from Home Farm and, despite the opened windows, the smell of its roasting filled the air.

Maureen stood for a moment watching Veronica work. She was fond of the girl. She liked her quietness, her gentle manner, and there was something about her that made you feel in a peculiar way tender, sympathetic, towards her, although Veronica was perfectly competent and sensible. She had worked here, living in for six years, since leaving a children's home at fourteen. That had been in Maureen's father's day, when the house had always been full of visitors and a staff of ten had been kept fully busy. Now, apart from cleaners and occasionals, Veronica was Maureen's only regular help. When Veronica had married David Heath, Maureen had been delighted to give her a very nice wedding and to set her up in one of her cottages, on Littlecotes Lane, within easy walking distance of the house. And now, looking down at her as she chopped away, Maureen felt that old, comfortable warmth for her. 'How's it coming, Veronica?' she asked.

'All right, ma'am.'

'It's only just occurred to me that Mrs Delgrano might not actually like chicken, Veronica. Some people don't.

If that's the case, what else might we have to offer? Something that wouldn't take too long.'

'I suppose it'd have to be a salad, ma'am. We have a bit of cold roast beef, but not much.'

Standing with her legs apart and her body erect, her arms slightly bent at her sides, in that calculated attitude of hers, Maureen could look formidable. If she spoke in a certain tone she could also sound formidable. A look could come into her eye. After all, she had managed to control her father for the last years of his life. But Veronica understood her employer. Behind Maureen's defensive posturing was the woman who had been more than a mother to her, to whom she was devoted, whom, in every essential sense, she loved.

'Just let me know what the lady wants, ma'am,' she said. 'But I think most people like chicken and I don't think they can get it these days.'

'Will you bring some coffee? Leave it until about five minutes after she arrives and—'

Maureen was interrupted by the explosion into the kitchen of the two evacuee sisters. They had been looking out impatiently for the Rolls. 'Mam's here!' they piped. 'Mam's here!' Taking the girls with her and collecting her other evacuee, little Tidgy, on the way, Maureen, who had put on a smart green dress for the occasion, went to stand in the doorway under the canopy, at the top of the steps between the pillars, to greet her guest.

Out from the Rolls, assisted by Lance with his hand at her elbow, stepped a laughing, swaying woman with l oose brown hair and an attractive, cat-like face. She began to slip off her coat and Lance at once went to help.

She prodded at him, he prodded back, they giggled, and a tremor went through Maureen's sensibilities, because that kind of silly horseplay was not without some kind of implication. After five minutes of driving with her from the station, was Lance at it again with a married woman?

'Mam! Mam!' The two sisters – Carla aged nine and Francesca aged eleven – ran to Peggy Delgrano and there were hugs, kisses, rapid chatter and much excited shuffling about on the gravel.

While gazing at this touching spectacle of family reunion, Maureen became acutely aware of little Tidgy. She was standing at Maureen's side, dressed in her frilly Shirley Temple dress. Maureen looked down at her and saw that she was watching the proceedings out there with clouded eyes and parted lips.

Tidgy's mother had also been sent an invitation to visit her daughter today, with an offer to pay her rail fare if necessary, but Maureen had received no reply. Indeed, she had received no reply to any of the letters she had been writing to the woman for the last three months. What did this mean? It was a troublesome question. Could it ever be that a mother could bring herself to abandon her child? Was that ever possible? And after hearing nothing from her for so long, ought not Maureen to notify someone of the situation? Wasn't the onus on her to do something, say something? But that was a question she was dodging for the moment, putting to one side.

Tenderly, she stroked Tidgy's head. 'There, my darling,' she said. 'I'm sorry your mother couldn't come – but never mind, you've got me, haven't you?'

Tidgy looked up, smiling. 'Yes,' she said.

Peggy Delgrano, with a daughter hanging from each arm, came up the steps. She was wearing a flouncy yellow frock, not long at the skirt and just high enough across the chest to hide her cleavage. Maureen greeted her with an uninhibited smile. 'I hope you had a pleasant journey.'

'Yes, thank you. It took longer than it should, but what d'you expect, there's a war on.' Peggy bent down to stroke the fine fabric of Carla's dress. 'Did you buy these frocks the girls're wearing?'

'Yes. I hope you like them.'

'Of course I do. They're smashing. Thank you, thank you.'

Behind Peggy stood Lance, with Peggy's coat over his arm and that certain grin on his face.

Maureen extended a hand. 'Well, come in, Mrs Delgrano.'

'I like to be called Peggy,' she said.

'Very well, Peggy. Do come in.'

Maureen led the way into the great hall. Standing still for a second, Peggy gazed around at the gallery, the massive staircase, the dark landscapes and the dull portraits hanging from the walls. Nearer to hand was a large still life of fruit and flowers caught at that moment in a beam of sunlight from a high window.

'I could just eat that orange,' she said.

'Are you hungry? I hope you like roast chicken.'

'I could eat a horse.'

'I thought in about half an hour's time.'

But Peggy's daughters were clamouring at her elbows, pulling at her and tugging. They wanted their mother to see their bedroom.

'Will that be all right?' Peggy asked.

'Of course. When you come down we'll have coffee. I'll be in that room there.'

The girls ran over to the staircase. 'Come on, Mam, come on!'

Peggy went after them, her flouncy frock flouncing about her shapely knees. Like a fluttering yellow butterfly, she passed through another shaft of sunlight and disappeared along the landing.

'Lance,' said Maureen, turning to him.

'Yes, sis?'

'Would you put her coat away and then leave us to talk?' She went to him, took hold of his hand and gave him a little dry kiss on the cheek. 'Please, darling, do not complicate my life for me.'

'I don't know what you mean, Maureen.'

'I think perhaps you do. I'm speaking of Mrs Delgrano.'

The room Maureen had indicated was her personal sitting room, furnished with three cretonne-covered armchairs, a table bearing Spode and Meissen figurines, a work basket on legs, two bookcases, a radiogram, a smaller coffee table and a tasselled footstool. On the mantelpiece were photographs of her dead lover, her dead father and her brother, for whom she had the instincts of a concerned mother. Lance was a troubled soul. He had come back from the last war damaged in a way she could not understand. He was sometimes a tribulation to her and almost always a worry. But her affection for him was boundless.

Peggy came down at last to find Maureen helping Tidgy with her knitting. The child was trying to learn. Her effort

– an unevenly worked length of many colours intended as a scarf for the doll Maureen had bought her – was draped across her knees.

Peggy had no sooner entered the room than Veronica came in, pushing the coffee trolley.

'This is Mrs Delgrano, Veronica,' Maureen said.

'I'm Peggy,' said Peggy.

'I'm sorry, Peggy,' Maureen said. 'Yes, she prefers to be called Peggy.'

Peggy and Veronica exchanged smiles, briefly contemplating each other as women newly met usually do, with momentary detachment behind smiles and a keen appraisal of clothing, hair and face.

'Will chicken be all right?' Veronica asked.

'Peggy will have chicken,' Maureen said.

'It'll be ten minutes. Shall I take Tidgy?' Veronica asked.

'No,' said Maureen. 'Leave her with me.'

And Veronica went out.

'Sit down, Peggy, please. There, opposite me.'

'What a lovely bedroom they've got,' Peggy said. 'Francesca wrote to say she was happy, but I'd no idea you were looking after them so well.'

'They're delightful girls. I'm so fond of them. You must miss them terribly.'

'I can put up with that so long as they're happy.'

They talked, at ease with each other and smiling frequently. Tidgy, sunk deep in the other armchair, still trying to knit, exclaimed 'Oh heck!' and gave up. She cast her needles aside and flapped her dangling legs.

Peggy gazed about this elegantly fitted room, where

reflected sunlight flashed from many glinting facets and where her high heels were deep in carpet. She looked at Maureen's fleshy arms and at her beautiful, lustrous green frock. She looked at the expensive figurines on the table, at the costly curtains, and at the gilded chandelier. Held for a moment in the air of tremendous reassurance and wealth that pervaded this great house, and comparing it with the air of the poor, gloomy backstreet where she belonged, she suddenly thought again of Lance and the smiles he'd given her.

'May I ask how Mr Delgrano is?' Maureen suddenly asked.

'I wish you wouldn't.'

'Pardon?'

'I'd rather not think of the creep.'

'I see.'

'I was married to him for five years. He was Spanish. A waiter in town. He opened a restaurant on Market Street, went mad spending money and when they came after him for it he buzzed off back to where he'd come from. I'd rather not hear the word Delgrano.'

'Oh dear. That must have been a terrible blow.'

'Well, he left me broke, living in a house I had to give up, didn't he? And me with my two girls.'

'Oh dear. How did you manage?'

'I went back to work. I sew blankets for the army and navy.'

'That must be hard.'

'Perhaps it is. But I'm good at it and depend on nobody. I'm my own woman.'

'Then I admire you.'

A moment later, the door was flung open and in barged Peggy's two daughters. 'Dinner's ready, dinner's ready!'

Lance drove Peggy back to the station that evening to catch the six-fourteen.

'Why didn't you want to stay the night?' he asked.

'Because I'm working in the morning. Next time, perhaps.'

'I'll look forward to that.'

'Yes,' she said. 'So will I.'

Along the road, they passed Michael Philbin and Nancy and Brendan Kelly walking towards the Black Bull. This was because Brendan had insisted that Michael and Nancy should take a drink with him. Brendan was not short of money, apparently. His wallet was thick with pound notes.

From the moment of his arrival in the best room of the Black Bull, he made his presence felt. His laughing face cast its light across every other face in the room, drawing forth smiles and nods of acknowledgment.

'They look like decent people in here,' he said to Michael and Nancy. 'What the hell's wrong with you two? Cheer up!'

Towards the end of the evening, Brendan got to his feet and gave them all 'Delaney's Donkey' to much applause. Michael watched him from under lowered brows, sickened and angry.

On the following Friday evening, the vicar, Douglas Russell, paid a second visit to a house on Saddler's Row – number 10, three doors down from the Philbins. Its newly painted green door was opened by Mrs Thurlow, a tiny grey-haired woman, who tried to give him a little smile. She was wearing pink house slippers, one of which had a hole in its toe, and a pinny over a long-sleeved grey frock

'Hello, Vicar,' she said, and despite her effort to smile it seemed to Douglas that she was not particularly welcoming.

Such moments as these could be awkward. People suffered their pains in their own way. Sometimes Douglas could help, sometimes he was not wanted, and it could be difficult to read the signs.

Tentatively, he asked, 'I've heard the sad news, Mrs Thurlow. Would you like to see me?'

There had been a kind of stiffness about her. Now it drained away. She nodded. 'Come in,' she said.

Late-evening sunlight filled the little front room. In an armchair under the window sat Mr Thurlow, the lady's second husband, a man of fifty-seven, still in his blue overalls. He had spent the day at his workbench at Evers' factory and he looked very tired. He gave Douglas a nod and made an effort to rise, only to sink back again with his hands limp on the arms of his chair. Since Mr Thurlow never came to church, Douglas barely knew him and beyond a quiet 'Good evening', he could think of nothing to say to him.

Mrs Thurlow motioned Douglas to the second armchair in the room and sat down herself on a stiff-backed dining chair against the wall. It was Douglas's Christian duty to be here at this moment, difficult though it was for him, and he had heartfelt sympathy for the lady. But this was another occasion when he was acutely aware of the depressing inadequacy of words.

'It's an awful blow, Mrs Thurlow,' he said, 'I'm so desperately sorry.' And, indeed, how banal it sounded. The words hung in the air, hollow, empty, for seconds on end.

Mrs Thurlow's eyes filled with tears. She looked across the room to the mantelpiece on which, in a chromium-plated frame, stood a photograph of her son, Jim. He was in army uniform, with sergeant's stripes on his sleeves, and smiling happily. Three weeks ago, his mother had received a telegram from the War Office informing her that he was missing after Dunkirk, and, quite understandably, she had feared the worst, because the worst was what 'missing' generally implied. Douglas had sat here with her, holding her hand, doing his best to reassure her that there was still hope. In the confusion of Dunkirk, he'd said, how could anyone have been sure of anything? There was an excellent chance that Jim had been taken prisoner. At any moment now she might well receive news to that effect. Hadn't that happened to Mrs Foster earlier in the war? At this very moment, Douglas had said, Jim might well be thinking of his mother, just as she was thinking of him – a prisoner of war, but very much alive and well. They had prayed together, Douglas and she, and it had seemed to help.

But another telegram had arrived for her and hope was now gone. She sat, quite lifeless, staring at the picture with her hands in her lap. Several of her fingers, tortured by arthritis, were twisted into claws and her lisle stockings were in concertina folds around her ankles. A pain of profound sympathy for her struck at Douglas's heart, but he could find no more words for the moment. Sometimes silence was better.

Mr Thurlow, Jim's stepfather, sitting there on the edge of things, looked into space and made no movement.

Before the war, when he'd been an out-of-work farm labourer, this had been one of the village's poorer households, with only hard chairs to sit on, oilcloth on the floor and a bare electric light bulb dangling from the ceiling. But now, with money coming from his employment at Evers', there were these two armchairs, a carpet and a collection of cheap ornaments on a new little sideboard.

Douglas said, at last, 'He was a good son, Mrs Thurlow. God will—'

Again, it sounded so abysmally empty, and Douglas was relieved when Mrs Thurlow interrupted him.

'It's all right, Vicar,' she said, as if sensing his difficulty and putting a stop to it.

He looked down for a moment, but still wishing to communicate something of his sympathy, he said, 'I know how very upset you must be—'

But of course he didn't know, and once again she stopped him. She raised her head, looked again at the picture of her son, and smiled.

'It's all right, Vicar. It's just the same feeling I had when his father was killed in 1916.'

'Yes . . . Yes . . .'

'You mean well, Vicar. But it's all right. It's fate, you see. Jim was nearly six when his father was killed and I knew when he decided to go in the army himself as a lad of seventeen that this would happen, sooner or later. Jim's dead, like his father. I'll never see him again.'

Tears still shimmered in her eyes and as she spoke, one large drop trickled down her left cheek. She wiped it quickly away with a bent finger.

'But he died for his country, didn't he? Like his dad.

He was twenty-nine. His father was only twenty-four. They died for their country, didn't they? It breaks your heart, but I'm proud of him. He did his duty. And I know he was a good soldier, because people have told me. And he's had his mates here and they told me themselves that everybody liked him. He was my son, Vicar – my lovely lad. And I'm proud of him.'

Douglas watched another tear roll down her cheek. 'You're very brave, Mrs Thurlow. Yes, he died for his country. He will not be forgotten. He will be in our prayers on Sunday. Everyone will be sad to hear you've lost him.'

Mr Thurlow moved in his chair. He gave a little cough, uncrossed his legs and crossed them again.

There was a long silence in the room, but from next door voices could be heard from the wireless. Douglas went into his pocket for his prayer book, on the point of suggesting that they might pray now, as they'd prayed, in vain, on his last visit. But Mrs Thurlow, obviously understanding his intention, and equally obviously not wanting it, got to her feet.

'Would you like a cup of tea, Vicar?'

He declined. The mood in the house made it clear that nothing more was required of him, if, indeed, anything had been required of him in the first place. His best course of action was to go.

He stood up, smiling gently. 'I wanted you to know that I feel for you,' he said. 'If ever there's anything I can do to help – anything – please let me know.'

'There's nothing, Vicar,' Mrs Thurlow said. 'What can there be? But thanks.'

As she showed him out, she seemed relieved to bid him

good evening. Faith was a fragile thing. Douglas sensed that behind Mrs Thurlow's tears he'd seen the sad signs of its loss.

He walked back through the village. Local road signs had been taken down – one indicating the way to Somercotes and one pointing in the direction of Fulstow – so as to give no help to invading armies or furtive spies. The sun was setting over the distant hills and shadows from trees and houses stretched across the whole width of the road. Douglas barely looked up. Thoughts that had been generated at the Thurlows' still preoccupied him.

Just as he passed the yard of the primary school, something snatched at his attention from behind. He turned and realised that he'd heard the tapping of Eva Acton's excessively high-heeled shoes. There she was, thirty yards or so away, trailing after him again. Eva was the daughter of Mary Acton, barmaid at the pub. Sadly, Eva was not entirely all there. Her make-up, bizarrely exaggerated, vivid red and black and white, gave her the look of something from a circus. She was wearing her customary very short skirt. Her legs were almost black with several layers of imitation-silk stockings and she was, as ever, carrying her gas mask in its little cardboard box, slung by its string over her shoulder, when everyone else had long since discarded theirs.

For some reason, Eva had developed a fascination with Douglas. She often appeared from nowhere and dogged his footsteps like this. He affected not to have noticed her, which had proved to be the wisest thing, and walked on, past the village hall and so to the gates of the church. Eva tapped after him, even on to the granite flagstones of the churchyard, but he knew that when he took the footpath to the vicarage she would halt by the vestry door and stand there to watch until he disappeared from her sight.

In the vicarage hall, he paused, still troubled by his thoughts. But, at last, he pushed open the door and went into the shadowy drawing room. A large chestnut beyond the window always filtered any sunlight that tried to get into this room, and now, with the fading of day, he could barely make out the shape of his wife, Gloria, who sat with her new baby in her arms, cooing over it.

'Don't you want the light on?' he asked.

'Hello, dear,' she said, vaguely.

He drew the blackout curtains, pressed the switch and saw that she was gently tapping the baby's cheek. She didn't look up.

'She's been so good today,' she said. 'She's been so very, very good. Haven't you, my darling?'

'Eva's in the offing again,' Douglas remarked, and Gloria didn't seem to hear that, either.

'Eva's lovelorn, poor thing,' Douglas went on. 'I've been to see Mrs Thurlow. Her son is dead after all, I'm afraid.'

'Mmm?'

'He was twenty-nine.'

'Mmm?'

'He was just a year or two younger than I am myself, Gloria.'

'Yes.'

She had lifted the baby to her breast and opened her blouse. 'You're hungry, aren't you, my little darling.'

'He was close enough to my own age,' Douglas said. 'And here I am, Gloria. Here I am.'

She looked up at last and gave him a smile that indicated she'd taken in virtually nothing of what he'd said.

He left her and went up to their bedroom to brood. He stood by the window. Out there, the blackout had decreed that all was now quite dark. Where, in peacetime, two bright lights had always been visible away across the fields – there at Wyber's Farm and there at the Manor House – all was now a velvet black under the pale stars. War had darkened the world. And yes, here he was, under the eyes of God, asking what He wanted of him.

Next morning, Douglas officiated at an important wedding. Amanda Brocklesby was marrying Flight Lieutenant Julian Roland, DFC, Royal Air Force. The flight lieutenant had resisted nuptials on the grounds that marriage during wartime was too risky. The theme had often been debated at length, in the mess and at standby between frantic sorties over the Channel, and he'd definitely been persuaded against it. 'I could be killed,' he'd said to Amanda. 'It wouldn't be fair to you. Especially if we had children.'

But such arguments never held out for long with lovers – and certainly not when an assertive, persistent young woman like Amanda was involved. She'd been prepared to let the engagement run for three months for the sake of normal proprieties, but beyond that Roland had had no hope of remaining single.

The Brocklesbys farmed in a big way hereabouts. Their home, the Manor House, had been here long before the Binbrooks had appeared on the scene. Built in Jacobean times, of old mellowed red brick under lichen-covered pantiles, set among carefully trimmed lawns and very much

conscious of its own dignity, it was the family's pride and
joy. A romantic line drawing of it headed their private
notepaper and photographs of it appeared year after year
on their Christmas cards.

Important guests had been invited to the wedding, including
many of the county set, and it was essential that the occasion should be as brilliantly splendid as wartime conditions
allowed. A choral wedding was, of course, obligatory, and
since the church choir consisted of only twelve persons,
men and boys, choir members from other parishes had
been invited to augment it. 'Blood-alley' Cox, 'Middle-
stump' Watson and the rest of the boys, locals and incomers
alike, received two shillings and sixpence as their fee.
Arthur Swift, now head boy, who was called on to stand
on the rood-screen steps and sing solo, had managed to
squeeze four shillings out of them, because he'd been
particularly asked for.

Arthur had always possessed a beautiful, strong treble
voice. In excerpts from the *Messiah* at Christmas and from
St Matthew Passion at Easter he had always been a hit. It
was Amanda herself who had asked for him and had he
but known that, he could have demanded much more than
four shillings.

At this time, just as his voice was surely on the point of
breaking, it had assumed a new, deeply affecting quality,
a certain tender melancholy as though nature was already

sad that at any moment the sound of it would disappear for ever. Without any trace of self-consciousness, perfectly aware of his own appeal – and cunning with it, lingering on certain notes and tremulous on certain words – he sent his voice soaring into all the high spaces of the church, echoing against the vaulted ceiling and falling gently on to the women's fancy hats and the men's morning-suited shoulders. Accompanied by the organist playing with one hand and the vox angelica. Out, he sang, 'God be in my head, and in my understanding' and knew that he was bringing forth tears because he could see them glinting like fireflies along the pews. It was money for old rope.

In the vestry, as he was changing for home, a person who was helping to organise the wedding, an agitated, flushed-faced young woman whose eye make-up had begun to run, came flustering in and asked him would he sing again for them at the party on the Manor House lawn.

'How much?' he asked, feeling no compunction about it. They agreed this time on ten shillings, for which, unaccompanied, he happily gave them 'I'll walk beside you through the passing years', The 'Londonderry Air' and, to ring the changes, 'Run Rabbit Run', standing in his rather threadbare corduroys on a trestle table in the larger of the two great marquees.

With applause ringing in his ears, he went home to his parents' cottage on Front Street. His mother, the village seamstress, a nervous, fluttering woman in her thirties, thin and always anxious to finish some piece of work or other, was at her sewing machine, treadling away at speed with her head down, feeding cloth under the buzzing needle.

'Where've you been, love?' she asked.

'The wedding. I told you.'

'Did you? Whose wedding?'

'Amanda Brocklesby's – she's married an RAF pilot. Heck, you should see his moustache. It's like a Messerschmitt 109 flying across his face.'

'D'you want something to eat?' His mother still sewed without pause. 'Are you hungry, son?'

'No. I just had a turkey leg and a plateful of trifle with sherry in it. Here, Mam.'

Onto the sewing machine at her elbow, he put the ten-shilling note he'd received half an hour before

Now she did pause. The buzzing ceased. She looked up at him. 'Ten shillings.' It was as much as she could earn in four days at this machine. 'Where did you get that? What've you been up to now, Arthur?'

'I sang 'em a few songs, that's all. Honest. Money for old rope. It's yours Mam. I've got another four bob in my pocket.' Listening to all this was Arthur's father, blind since 1915 and out of work. He'd been dozing in his chair.

'By hell, Arthur,' he said, 'you're a lad an' a half.' His dark, dead eyes looked in Arthur's direction and a smile came on to his face. He hadn't shaved that morning. The darkness around his cheeks and chin made him look even older than he was, and he was fifty, fifteen years older than his wife. He'd had his legs crossed. The slipper had fallen from his raised foot and he began to feel about the carpet for it.

'Hang on, Dad,' said Arthur, going to pick it up. 'There,' and he put it into his father's outstretched hand.

Just before dusk every evening, in his police house on Church Lane, Constable Harry Bowker got up from his chair in front of the wireless, gave his wife Helen a kiss on the forehead and left her to her crocheting. It had become a habit for him then to go upstairs, open one of the bedroom doors and look in on his seven-year-old daughter, Susan. She was a restless sleeper and was usually only half covered by rumpled sheets with her nightie up around her neck. Tenderly, he put things in order and gave her a little kiss on the forehead. Then, first calling into what he called 'the station' – two rooms (one a cell) tagged on to the side of the house – to report by telephone that he was about to do so, he set off on his nightly beat from end to end of the village. His twenty years in the force had left him with the patina of his profession – a detached, rather aloof way of looking down across the world and a watchful, rather severe expression. He was still in his early forties, although, with his ample stomach and with the brim of his helmet forbiddingly low down over his eyes, he could look years older.

The bats were out around his head, twisting and turning against the stars. His rubber-soled shoes made hardly a sound in the heavy, solid silence and nothing moved. As he passed the willow garth that bordered the Binbrook estate, he heard gentle sounds like softly padding footsteps, as of some invisible person walking at his side. He paused for a second, but then realised that what he could hear was the sound of cud being chewed in the field beyond the hedge.

Halfway down Front Street, beyond the black humps of vegetation in Mr Norton's front garden, he saw movement and, with his professional instincts aroused, sensing that someone might be prowling, he stopped and stared. But then he recognised the stooping shape of Mr Norton himself.

'Good evening, Mr Norton,' he called. 'A bit late for gardening, isn't it?'

'Just getting a bit of mint for the spuds,' said Mr Norton.

The constable hadn't gone more than a hundred yards further when he saw someone else, moving towards him in the centre of the road – a small shape no higher than Bowker's own hip. Catching sight of him, the figure stopped and stood as still as a spider alarmed by some sudden movement, hoping not to be noticed. It was a boy of about six, whose face gazed up at him, featureless, like a piece of white paper. There was a chill in the night air, but the boy wore nothing but a jersey and short trousers.

'What're you doing walking about at this time o' night, son?' He got no answer. The boy simply lowered his head and began to whimper. Bowker bent down to look more closely into his face.

'Is it Clifford? It's Clifford, isn't it? Aren't you Mrs Robinson's evacuee?'

Suddenly, the boy made to dart around Bowker's legs, but Bowker's long right arm baulked him. 'Where d'you think you're going, lad?'

'I'm goin' home.'

'Have you been sleepwalking? You're going in the wrong direction. Mrs Robinson's house is that way – on Back Street.'

'No, no!' the boy exclaimed, bursting into tears. 'Home! Home!'

All Bowker could do was take hold of the boy's hand and walk with him to see Lucy Thomas. Lucy was the wife of a solicitor and expert in income tax who spent most of his week away at his office in town. Lucy herself was a school governess, a well-intentioned busybody, and an assistant billeting officer. She had just been preparing for bed and came to the door with a cup of cocoa in her hand and her greying hair combed down about her shoulders.

'I'm sorry, Lucy,' Bowker said, 'but I found him in the road. He was off home, thirty miles away. He won't go back to the Robinsons – and I'm not going to make him. And I can hardly put him into the cell for the night.'

'You'd better come in.'

They went into her drawing room, littered with papers and books. A cat came and rubbed itself against Lucy's bare leg.

'Wrong place for 'em, you know, Lucy, the Robinsons. That man's a drunken sot and she's got a hell of a temper. If I had my way I'd take those two of her own away from her – they must get hell.'

Lucy rolled her head. 'Yes, I know. They're far from suitable, far from suitable . . . but what else could I do? They sent us more evacuees than we asked for, and Mrs Robinson hung about so long that we couldn't say no to her. They get seven and six a week to take an evacuee, as you know, and it can attract the worst sort of people. It's so hard to know who to refuse sometimes. We get cases like this, where the kids're unhappy, and we get cases where the kids're terrors and drive people mad. Mrs Driffield tells me her evacuees didn't know what the bath was for. Oh dear . . .'

Tears bubbling from Clifford's eyes had washed dirt from his cheeks in white channels. His close-clipped red hair was matted and it was very likely that he had lice. He stood in his red jersey and his stained grey short trousers with his arms dangling loosely at his sides, looking up from one to the other of them with a creased, pathetic face and tears still bubbling up. 'I want me mam,' he said.

'Leave him with me, Harry,' Lucy said. 'I'll have to see what I can do with him in the morning.'

4
Soldiers, and Veronica Has
a Visitor

Harry Bowker had no opportunity next morning to enquire what had happened to the boy, because he was called on for other duties. An army convoy was making for the village. He'd been told to stand by to help them find their way to their precise destination hereabouts. Women doing their shopping at the post office and in Fuller's butcher's shop next door asked one another what Constable Bowker might be doing, standing out there by the letter box at the kerb with his hands behind his back, shifting his weight from foot to foot, because he had been there like that for twenty minutes. He kept glancing at his watch and gazing away along the road to Somercotes.

At shortly before half-past nine the puttering of a motor-cycle was heard from that direction and into view came an army rider with a leather jerkin over his battledress top and a round crash helmet like a chamber pot on his head. He stopped at the constable's feet. They exchanged a few words. Then, in slow ponderous movements, perhaps aware that he was being watched and concerned for his dignity, Harry Bowker spread his legs and climbed on to the pillion. Holding on to his helmet, sitting upright and perhaps a bit nervous, he was ridden away, back along the Somercotes road and out of sight.

Five minutes later, the convoy itself, with the motorcycle leading the way, came banging and groaning through the village. There were eleven lorries, four of them carrying troops and the others loaded with tents, sections of prefabricated timber huts and all kinds of tools. They were led into Littlecotes Lane, past Sycamore Cottages and on up the hill. Three-quarters of a mile beyond – there on the downwards slope – the convoy stopped. Harry Bowker swung himself off the motorbike, and down from the leading lorry stepped a small, agitated officer of Pioneers. Tapping his stick against the palm of his hand, he said, 'Is this it?'

'This is it,' answered Harry. 'I wondered where the hell you were. I was waiting at the post office for ages. He says you got lost. How did you manage that?'

'I was given the wrong map reference. We need to get into that field there. Open the gate.'

The man's manner irritated Harry and in any case he didn't like the bouncing little twerp. 'I'm a policeman,' he said. 'I don't take orders from the army.'

The officer pointed his stick at the motorcyclist who, it seemed, had been shooting his mouth off to the constable about the officer losing his way. 'You – open the gate. Jump to it, man!'

Bumping, grinding, bouncing, the lorries drove in procession on to the field. They travelled across country through hedges and ditches for several hundred yards until the officer considered them to be in the right place. From here expanses of scrubby grass sloped away down to the long line of yellow beach. The officer flapped his arms, the troops leaped down from the lorries, and work began at once.

As the convoy had passed the primary school on Main Street, shaking the floor and drowning the voices of the teachers, a degree of alarm had broken out amongst the kids because one of them, Nelly Walters, whose father was an air-raid warden, constantly on the qui vive for such an event and perpetually talking about it, suddenly shouted, in a voice that rang through the entire building, 'It's the invasion!' It took several minutes to calm the classrooms back to their work.

The school was a single-storey, high-windowed building with the date 1907 carved in stone over its doorway, sitting beyond a dusty tarmac playground. Behind it grew five tall Scots pines whose lower branches had fallen away. Their remaining arms and their bushy heads, after years of growth under the prevailing southwesterly wind, leaned over the roof and gave the peculiar impression that it was their business to protect the school and all in it.

Most mornings, if you walked by at about ten o'clock, you would hear a rhythmical measured chanting like the beat of distantly marching feet: 'Seven-sevens-are-forty-nine, eight-sevens-are-fifty-six, nine-sevens-are-sixty-three . . .' And at half-past ten, the kids would burst out of the doorway and swarm into the yard to hoot and scream and kick up the dust in gritty clouds for ten minutes of break.

From the ages of five to eleven, Arthur Swift had spent his days in those classrooms. He was bright enough to have

passed his scholarship and now he went by bus every day
to and from the grammar school at Louth. After tea, he
did his evening paper round and then, assiduously, he
finished his homework. After that, he carried on his business as an odd-job man, washing people's windows, doing
a bit of gardening, mowing people's lawns. For three days,
these things had kept him too busy to do much else, and
it was only on the Friday that he was able to go and see
what was happening down near the beach.

He delivered the evening's last newspaper and went by
way of Langworthy Lane. Here, there had been built a
small estate of privately owned semi-detached houses with
gardens, crazy-paved pathways, sundials, rockeries and
circular flower beds – an outpost of suburbia, incongruous
in that setting. Arthur noticed that the ground-floor bay
window of number 10 had been put in again. Number 10
was the home of the Benson family. They were Quakers
and had the reputation in the village of being good people
who would help anyone in any way they could. The son
of the house, Nathan, had declared himself a conscientious
objector, which of course was one thing. The fact that he'd
got away with it because of his religion was another. This
was the second time the glass of his window had been
replaced by sheets of plywood.

Arthur climbed to the top of Fire Beacon Hill and sat
down on one of the fallen stones there. Down the slope
towards the beach, fields of wheat had been trampled flat.
Across them in neat rows a number of bell tents had been
erected. At one point, soldiers were gashing a trench, like
a deep wound across the face of a smooth meadow. A
clump of young ash trees had been sawn away. Fences had

been flattened and hedges had been grubbed up. At the place where boys had gathered crab apples, and there, where Arthur had gathered horseradish for Charley at the pub, timber huts of various sizes were going up on sectioned wooden foundations. The piece of disused land where the boys had played football was full of parked lorries and more soldiers were laying concrete there.

Arthur was shocked. That scene had been part of his world, a world that he'd imagined would be there for ever, never changing, fixed in his mind like the image of his father, like the walls of his room at home, like the solid church tower. Its destruction made him feel uneasy – and a bit afraid.

He got up and turned away. He decided to go back home by way of Littlecotes Lane, and as he came alongside Sycamore Cottages he remembered the promise he'd given to David Heath. He walked up the path of number 5 and knocked at Veronica's door.

Veronica had never before confronted Arthur on her doorstep. She gazed at him with creased forehead and parted lips, pondering why he should be here now. 'Hello?' she said, and it was more a question than a greeting.

'Hello, Veronica. You look nice.'

'What is it, Arthur?'

'David asked me to come and see you.'

'What? When? Why?'

'When I saw him off at the station. He said will you go and see Veronica for me.'

'Oh . . . did he?' Veronica looked past him along the lane. She seemed a little tense. She was expecting someone else. She looked at her watch. 'It's nearly eight o'clock.'

'Is it?'

'You'd better come in.'

Another tiny room, with proportions similar to those of Mrs Thurlow's parlour on Saddler's Row. Its space was almost filled with a green tapestry three-piece suite. Chairs and settee all had hard wooden arms, but there were a number of frilled deep-red cushions arranged tastefully, as well as cream-coloured antimacassars, each embroidered with a large red rose by Veronica herself. There was pale green wallpaper and on a low table a vase containing blooms from the garden at Pretoria House. Underfoot were polished floorboards and in the centre of the room a small, round rug, pale cream like the antimacassars.

There was a faint smell of scent in here, emanating from Veronica herself, and the femaleness of it all, the neatness of it, touched the senses even of Arthur, who was not normally susceptible to decor.

On the table was a photograph of David in his sailor's uniform.

Veronica was wearing a bright blue rayon summer dress with short sleeves, and neat court shoes. Her brown hair had been curled with curling tongs and there was a red ribbon through it.

'You look very nice,' Arthur said again, uttering his thoughts as always without inhibition.

'Thank you. But you're a fibber.'

'No I'm not. Are you going out?'

'No – no.'

'Well I'm all right, then.' Arthur sat down, choosing the settee because it seemed the most comfy, and having sat down, expected Veronica to do the same, but she didn't.

'Would you like a cup of tea or something?' she asked, hovering there.

'No thanks.' But Arthur had spotted things on the mantelpiece. He got up and went for a closer look at a porcelain figure of a woman in a crinoline. It was Chelsea. Arthur picked it up. 'It's clever how people can do faces as small as this, isn't it?' he said. 'It's real. She's got blue eyes.'

Veronica joined him by the hearth. With a little smile, picking them up gently with her stubby little fingers, she showed him the three other, smaller figures that stood on the mantelpiece – a dancer in fifth position, a lady in black evening dress with gilt trimmings and a young girl sitting on a log of wood with a basket full of fruit.

'Maureen Binbrook gave me the lady in the crinoline when David and me got married. Just after he volunteered for the navy. We saved up for the others. Aren't they nice?'

Hanging from the wall over the mantelpiece was a large Wedgwood server.

'What's that?' Arthur asked.

'You serve food on it.'

'Who for? A giant?'

'But doesn't it look nice there? Maureen gave me that as well. David hung it up. He's clever with things like that. He's a carpenter, you know. Before he joined up he worked at Pretoria House. He did some doors, made them himself just like the originals, and he did this floor and see – isn't it excellent?'

Arthur looked down and nodded. 'How is he? Have you heard from him?'

'Oh yes, he writes to me all the time. Sometimes I get several letters at once. He writes them at sea, Arthur, and so they're all posted together when he gets into port somewhere.'

'He's in the Mediterranean, isn't he?'

'Yes, I'm sure he is. But he can't say, Arthur. His letters're censored. If he writes something he shouldn't they blank it all out with some kind of black ink. It goes through the paper and makes it difficult to see what he's written on the other side of the sheet. But he managed to mention Alexandria without them noticing. And yes, Alexandria's in Egypt. He sent me a photograph of himself on his ship. He looked very well.'

'So he's all right, then.'

'Yes, I think so.'

'I bet you miss him.'

Veronica seemed about to show tears for a moment. A little spasm touched her face. But she smiled again. 'Yes, Arthur,' she said. 'I do.'

Arthur went back to the settee. Veronica still stood looking down at him. 'Why don't you sit down, Veronica?'

'What? Well yes . . .' And she sat on one of the chairs, still half facing him.

Again she looked at her watch.

'I thought you might've been going out with that frock on,' Arthur said.

'No. I don't often go out these days. It's not the same when you're on your own. A woman, I mean.' Her fingers began to entwine themselves. There was a kind of mistiness about her, a misty kind of nervousness, to which Arthur responded with a puzzled, youthful sympathy.

'David said you get lonely. D'you fancy a game of cards or something?'

'I haven't got any cards. But I'm all right, Arthur. Thanks. I'm all right. Really.'

'D'you want any gardening doing or anything?'

'I don't think so, thank you. Mr Baker next door does the gardening. It's "Dig for Victory". He's made a cold frame in my garden. He's growing cucumbers in it. And he's got the garden planted with potatoes.'

'Well if you want anything doing, I don't charge much.'

'I'll remember that.'

Silence fell. Arthur could think of nothing more to say and nor could she, apparently. Arthur looked again at the figurines on the mantelpiece, at the blue server above it, at Veronica's nicely made-up face, at her bright blue frock, and again sensed her perfume in the air. It came over him in this silence, in the stillness of Veronica's little smile, that this was about it. 'Well I'll be going, then,' he said.

She got up at once. 'Yes . . . But thanks for coming, Arthur, thank you.'

'That's all right.'

'I'll tell him you've been.'

'Will you? Good. Tell him I didn't let him down.'

Arthur made his way towards the door. He paused. 'Did you know you've got soldiers over the hill here?'

'Yes. Sometimes you can hear them.'

'They've wrecked everything in sight. It's a mess . . . It's the invasion, Veronica. They think the Germans're coming.'

Veronica shuddered. 'Oh God . . . I'm scared. Everybody's scared. It's terrible—'

'No, it's not. We'll spifflicate 'em. Do you realise,

Veronica, we've never lost a battle yet? And William the Conqueror was lucky. King Harold's army was dead beat – they'd just whacked Harald Hadrada at Stamford Bridge and marched three hundred and odd miles. You think the Jerries'll beat the English? We beat 'em last time, didn't we? You seen the paper tonight? We've sunk two U-boats in the Atlantic.'

'But the Germans're everywhere now. In Norway, France – we're surrounded, Arthur.'

'So what? We've got the sea round us. Don't worry, Veronica, they'll not get here.'

'Well, I don't know about that . . . It's frightening.'

'We'll be all right,' Arthur said. 'We'll be all right, Veronica. You can take it from me. I'll come and see you again.'

'Will you? Yes, all right, Arthur.'

'You can hear Tommy Handley tonight on the wireless if you get fed up.'

'Yes. I'll do that.'

'My dad likes him . . . Well ta-ra, Veronica.'

As she closed the door behind him, Veronica gave a little sigh of relief and sat down for a moment on the stairs, clasping her hands together.

It was now just coming up to half-past eight. The taproom of the Black Bull was busy. It was early for the regulars to have arrived, but one or two were there, together with about a dozen Royal Engineers from the beach. There had been gloomy talk about the invasion in here as well this evening. But that had given way to a game of darts. With his elbows on the bar, the landlord, Charley, looked on.

He had his eye on a full pint glass sitting precariously in a pool of beer on the edge of one of the small round tables. Its contents trembled at the movement in the room and he felt sure that at any moment one of those flailing khaki-clad arms would catch it and fling it to the floor. But he didn't care. The lino down there was already wet. Big army boots occasionally slithered.

Charley had found an additional source of beer. An enterprising farmer over Covenham way had contacts somewhere. He'd told Charley his beer came from a monastery, but that seemed unlikely. Anyway, it was good enough to drink. Since it was illicit there could have been no excise duty paid on it, but it was still dear enough and, into the bargain, Charley had had to carry it himself, barrel by barrel, in the boot of his Morris 12 at dead of night. However, he was eking things out with measures of water. Twice he'd had complaints that his beer tasted a bit thin, but he'd adjusted things after that.

The glass on the edge of the table was picked up and emptied. Its owner brought it to the bar and Charley refilled it, together with two more emptied glasses. Then he decided it was time to go to the other bar in the best room and see what was happening there.

Behind that bar, Mary was sitting on her stool, sipping half a pint of shandy and reading the evening paper, circulated out here from town. '*Mutiny on the Bounty*'s on at the Gaumont,' she said. 'Why don't you take me out sometime, you skinflint?'

'Who can I trust with my till?'

'What about Peter – he's done it before.'

'I'll think about it.'

'No you won't. You daren't let anyone near that damn cellar.'

Charley helped himself to a whisky from the back fitting. There in the best room sat just four people – Fred Robinson, who was already halfway to his normal state of dribbling drunkenness and, as usual, would soon have to be frog-marched into the taproom out of the sight of decent people; Walter and Lorna Booker, who sat deep in conversation under the window; and Private Nigel Lawrence, twenty-two years of age, who, as Charley watched, got up and brought his half-pint glass to the bar. When we last saw Nigel it was during the Commodore's early-morning walk.

He was of medium height and slender. There was a sense of refinement about him – in his eyes, in his complexion, and in his general air. The rough, hairy fabric of his battle-dress seemed crudely inappropriate on him. The fingers that held his glass were long and fine and they moved with a kind of nervous diffidence. He had large eyes and small, delicate features, and what was left of his yellow hair after the army barber had been at it still retained its natural flowing waves.

Mary, smiling at him because she liked him, got up to serve him. He wanted another half-pint of bitter.

'You seem to do well for leave, Nigel,' Charley said.

'Yes.' Nigel gave Charley a nod. 'I'm at Newark. I can get home easily on a twenty-four-hour pass.'

'You've got a cushy number then, have you? Having a great time of it?'

Nigel gave a wry smile. 'A great time? In the army? Surely you're joking.'

Charley did not share Mary's fondness for the man.

'Come on, lad,' he said. 'You're one of thousands. You've got to make the best of it like the rest.'

'Have I really?' With another cool nod, Nigel took his drink, paid his money and went back to his seat.

'He's a disagreeable bugger,' Charley snapped, turning away, taking a quick swig from his whisky glass. 'A bloody great baby.'

Mary sat down again, sipped her shandy, thought for a moment and decided not to let that go. 'Don't be cruel. He's lovely.'

'Come off it, woman. He looks like a tart.'

'No, he doesn't.'

'Oh, but yes he does. He looks like a bloody great school-girl dressed up in uniform.'

'He can't help his looks.'

'I bet he's got knickers on under them pants.'

'Don't be crude, Charley.'

'Well . . . he gets up my wick. He might be a cissy, but at least he could make an effort to be a man.'

'He's very sensitive.'

'Balls.'

'I told you not to be so crude. Nigel is an artist.'

'And balls to that as well.'

'He's an artist. They shouldn't've put him in the army.'

'Rubbish. It's just the place for him. Give him some backbone. How the hell he's going to go on when the bullets start flying, slapping about round his head, God alone knows. That'll larn 'im.'

'You're a hard man, Charley Cartland. You've got a heart of stone.'

'Good.'

'Can't you tell, he's depressed. First his father dies, and then, three months later, his mother. It must've been awful to cope with that. And then no sooner has he finished college than they drag him off into the army. Have you seen any of his paintings?'

'Course I have. I let him hang some in here. Some nitwits actually bought one or two.'

'Well don't you think he's clever?'

'That's no bloody excuse, woman. When there's a war on, men go and fight. I did my bit, didn't I? For what good it did me. And what about his pal – thingy – Veronica's husband . . . David Heath? He was in here not all that long ago. You saw him. Did you hear *him* moaning? No, you didn't.'

'But David Heath volunteered.'

'Yes. That was daft, but at least it showed he was a man. That feller isn't.'

'Nigel's different.'

'Is he? Yes, he's a tart. D'you think he's depressed because he's having a period?'

'That was nasty. Shut up – he might hear you.'

But Nigel had heard nothing. There were other things on his mind. Draining his glass, then putting it down, he got up, put his glengarry onto his head at the correct angle, and went out.

Nigel walked about for half an hour. As shadows began to fall, he slipped into Wyber's Wood and made his way along the bottom of the meadow – where we first saw him under the gaze of the Commodore. Veronica Heath, in her blue frock, which Arthur had so much admired, and her nice court shoes, smelling pleasantly of Californian Poppy scent, was standing in her kitchen waiting for him.

Blackout curtains were being drawn across the village's windows. Younger children were already in bed and older children were drifting home, tired and mucky after their games, to whatever supper could be provided for them on the ration.

Sitting in their parlours, people listened to the news, rather tense and grim-faced. There had been more sinkings at sea. The Battle of Britain was at its height. Everyone knew that their country's survival depended on its being won, and the only way of knowing how it was progressing was by comparing the number of aircraft shot down. Today there had been seventeen British and twenty-seven of the enemy. There was no doubt in anyone's mind that should the air battle be lost, invasion would follow, and the prospect of that was intolerable.

The anxieties of war had drawn people very much closer together. There was comfort in being with others who shared the same worries, with people who would have to face the worst with you, to confront the unthinkable, if that should be their fate. Women, suddenly stopping whatever they might be doing, went next door and asked if their neighbour would like to come round for a cup of tea, then, to take their minds off things, talked for half an hour about something and nothing. Of an evening, leaving their children to sleep, neighbours got together for a game of cards or, again, simply for the reassurance of being with other people.

At twenty to ten each evening, men and woman gathered

at the bus stop near the school, waiting for the bus to take them to the night shift at Evers' factory. When the bus had groaned away into the distance, the village grew deathly quiet. Even the tolling of the hours from the church clock had been stopped. If the bell tolled again it would be to mark the beginning of the invasion. This evening, when Constable Bowker did his rounds, even that eternal sound from wireless sets had stilled. Only the whisper of the breeze through leaves went with him.

5
The Lancashire Rifles

The army proper now arrived at the station. Michael Philbin leaned out of his signal box to watch the train as it passed.

There were two companies, A and B, of the 1st Battalion Lancashire Rifles, regulars, veterans of the disaster in France, where many of their comrades had been left behind, wounded or dead. Even now they were not fully up to strength. There were just under three hundred of them in five carriages of an LNER train. Their drill was impeccable. In the engine, the driver and fireman leaned out to watch it, and the guard, eating the remains of a sandwich, stood on the step of his van to do the same.

First out, from the leading coach, was Regimental Sergeant Major Pelham, straight-backed and crisp. He slung his rifle, brushed cigarette ash from the front of his battledress blouse and marched smartly to the rear end of the train. Down to meet him from the last carriage came Major Bates, six foot two in height, as slender and square-edged as a plank of oak, uniformed alike in battledress and steel helmet. Sunlight reflected from the polish on his pistol holster and from the hard toecaps of his great boots.

The sergeant major stamped to attention before him and with a wide sweep of the arm saluted him. 'Sah!'

The major merely nodded.

The sergeant major about-turned and marched smartly away. Having reached a position halfway between the beginning and end of the train, he halted and stamped through a right turn. He was not a tall man or a very heavy one, but his voice had the rich timbre of a Russian bass. 'Carry on!'

NCOs had been standing by in the coaches waiting for the order. At it, all doors along the length of the train were pushed quickly open and out onto the platform came the men. Numbers of them gazed about at the tiny station, at the sky, and at the distant countryside to be seen away down the line. But others showed no such curiosity. Most of these soldiers had in their time travelled by rail, on foot, by lorry and aboard ship to places whose names could hardly be remembered, in Britain, India, France and Africa. What was the difference? They were here because they were here. No one knew how long it might be before they could smoke another cigarette, and so they offered them around, lit them, sometimes with lighters made from old cartridge cases, and smoked. While doing so, they formed chains and without much conversation brought on to the platform, from the corridors and the luggage racks, their great piles of kit.

Major Bates stood towering over Mr Young, the stationmaster, handing him the travel warrant. 'We'll be gone in five minutes,' he said. 'There was an officer to meet us. Where is he?'

But his question was answered as he spoke. With some difficulty, the Officer of Pioneers, the one who'd had to rely on Constable Bowker to find his way to this village, was elbowing his way through the men, flapping his hand over his head to attract Bates's attention.

Bates waited for him to come close, looked him up and down, and said, 'Bates, first LRs.'

'Yes – Broughton, Sappers. Sorry I'm a bit late.' Broughton straightened his cap. 'I've fetched a wagon for the officers.'

'Thank you,' said Bates, 'but the officers will march like the rest. I take it you've got transport for the kit.'

'Yes – yes . . . in the yard there.'

Bates looked around for the sergeant major and found him standing at his elbow. 'Load the kit,' he said, and the sergeant major marched away.

Like a stream of ants bearing fragments of leaf to their nest, the troops shouldered their kit and carried it out to the lorries.

'Tell me the route,' Bates said.

'Shall I drive ahead?'

'Good God no. Tell me the route.'

'Out of the station yard, left to the corner, right for a quarter of a mile, left up the hill and you'll see us.'

'How far in total?'

'About two and a half miles to the camp.'

'How much space is there outside the station for parade?'

'Enough, I think,' said Broughton.

'Well, you press on.'

'Right. I'll leave you to it. Just one thing – you'll be short of water for today.'

'Why?' Bates was not pleased.

'The main collapsed. But we hope to have it piped through by this evening.'

'Christ. Well hurry it up, for God's sake.'

'Yes – we're doing our best. Well, I'll get on. I'll see you later.'

As the men swarmed back into the station after loading the wagons, and as the wagons groaned away out of earshot, Bates went to speak to his officers. They were grouped together by the waiting-room doorway, smoking cigarettes. 'Put your helmet on,' Bates said to Captain Lockyer.

'Certainly, old boy.'

'Don't "old boy" me.'

'Terribly sorry.'

There was undisguised insolence in Lockyer's stiff smile. The other seven officers looked away, shuffled their feet uncomfortably and then glanced at Bates's face to see his reaction. There was anger in his eyes, but he said nothing. This was not the moment. 'We'll parade outside the station,' he told his officers. 'Sort your men out. Sar'nt Major Pelham!'

Once again, the sergeant major was at his elbow. 'Sah?'

'Fall them in – in the yard out there.'

In a moment the troops had vanished from the station. Bates stood there on the platform alone. From the waiting room, Mr Young and his porter watched him as he went into a breast pocket and took out a tin of Zubes. He had a sore throat and in a moment he would need his voice. Sucking a Zube, flexing his leathery cheeks, he cast his gaze across the posters: GUINNESS IS GOOD FOR YOU, SKEGNESS IS SO BRACING. Then, noticing that the station staff had their eyes on him, he nodded. 'Thank you,' he called. With that he went into the yard.

Already, people from nearby houses had come out to see what was happening. A group stood at the corner of the yard. Others stood at the pavement on Station Road beyond.

The men were formed up, standing easy, some smiling, some chatting, some quietly thinking their own thoughts.

'Are we marching at ease, sir?' asked Regimental Sergeant Major Pelham.

'Certainly not. We're going to do it properly. Let these people see who we are.'

'Good idea, sir.'

'Where's Lockyer?'

The sergeant major sniffed. 'He's where he should be.'

'Take your place, Tom.'

And the sergeant major marched away, ten paces.

Major Bates came to attention. In the ranks, sinews stiffened. Heads were raised, and Bates's voice echoed back from the station wall. 'Parade . . . Parade . . . 'Shun!'

Hobnails crashed against tarmac. Wraiths of dust wrapped themselves about men's legs.

'Parade . . . Slope . . . arms!'

One concerted, ferocious slap startled the onlookers and everywhere in the ranks powdered Blanco puffed white from webbing.

Bates held them waiting. Every eye was on him and a dozen of their names sounded in his brain like roll call after battle. 'Atherton, Crawford, Brighton, Chapel, Mitchell, Ramsbottom . . .' They had been through trial and sickening frustration together, these men and he. In France with the 6th Brigade they had only twice been given a chance to show their mettle. On both occasions they'd fought deadly actions, only to be retired by inexplicable orders and marched shamefully away. At Dunkirk, they'd wept. For weeks thereafter there had been complete demoralisation. The desertion rate had quadrupled. There had been no heart left in them.

Now, re-equipped, together once more, their pride was returning. It was in their eyes as they waited for the order. The old toughness was burgeoning in them, their old comradeship, that old-sweat cynicism that was part of the professionalism and cameraderie of this ancient regiment. There were very young ones here. Most of them had joined the colours during the slumps that had ravaged the cotton industry in the late thirties. But, old or young, they were men – army – British soldiers, and Bates was proud of every last one of them.

'The Lancashire Rifles will move to the right in column of three! Parade, right turn! By the left . . . quick march!'

Eyes fixed firmly to the front, their rifles bristling, their arms swinging smartly to the regulation height, their hobnails crunching with the rhythm of a strongly thudding heart, the companies wheeled out of the station yard and marched on along Station Road.

No such thing had ever been seen in this village before. Some onlookers clapped their hands. Others cheered their soldiers. Others, touched by something in the expressions on their soldiers' faces, shed tears.

At Pretoria House, Maureen happened to be passing along the upper landing. Casually she glanced through a window and caught sight of them, away beyond the fields, like a thin stream of peaty brown water defying nature and trickling slowly up the hill on Littlecotes Lane. 'Children! Children!' she shouted. And they came running – Francesca, Carla and Tidgy.

Maureen lifted Tidgy into her arms so that she could see out of the window. And now Clifford, the red-headed boy Constable Bowker had found in the lane, came dashing up the stairs. Maureen had been delighted to take him into her care. 'What is it? What is it?' he clamoured.

'Look!' said Maureen 'See – see . . . Soldiers!'

Lance was in the house. 'What's all the fuss?' he asked, coming to stand at Maureen's side just as she was lowering Tidgy to the floor.

'You've missed it. The army's here.'

'What unit?'

'How am I supposed to know?'

'Can I borrow the Rolls this evening?' he asked.

'No you can't. I've told you, I'm laying it up for the duration.'

'Then what about your little MG?'

'Where d'you plan to go?'

'Just up to town. I'll need a fiver.'

'Tell me where you're going. You know what the petrol situation's like.'

'Nowhere in particular.'

'Oh Lance!' Maureen shook her head and sighed. 'Oh all right. But do remember about the petrol.'

Clifford was looking up into Lance's face with some curiosity. He was wondering about Lance's moustache.

Lance smiled and touched his head. 'I pity you, Clifford,'

he said. 'You're surrounded by women like I am – and it's
hell, isn't it?'

For some time, small, slight Douglas Russell, the vicar, had
been in a dilemma. But he had now made up his mind. He
would do what he must do. Already, he had taken steps.
It was in fact a fait accompli, and only one painful thing
was left to do. To compose himself to it, he walked around
the village for half an hour. Amongst weeds in the ditch
at the side of the road near the school, the Home Guard
had piled a heap of old railway sleepers, a rusted kitchen
range and a litter of bricks, all in readiness to block the
road should German parachutists drop in. Young boys had
rearranged things to make a den under the sleepers. There
was a notice over the entrance to the den scrawled in
childish letters: *Privit keep out*. As Douglas walked on,
two army lorries drove by, showering him with dust. He
glanced around, wondering whether Eva Acton was going
to appear, as she so often did when he was about, but Main
Street was deserted.

Presently, he realised that the walk wasn't helping him
and so, at the corner of Back Street, he turned about
abruptly and made his way homewards. He entered the
churchyard. Even then, however, he did not take the path
to the vicarage, but pushed open the vestry door and went
inside. With his footfalls echoing on the old red tiles, he
crossed the nave, went up the three steps to the chancel
and sat down on the vicar's seat, resting his hands on its
arms and absently stroking the large, carved lambs' heads
that generations of his forebears had worn quite smooth.
Colours from the high stained-glass windows, brought

down to him by sunbeams, dappled his head and shoulders, and in the air was the sweet scent of lilies from the array of blooms at the foot of the screen.

He buried his head in his hands and remained like that for some minutes. Presently, he stood up. He took two or three decisive steps towards the nave, but then suddenly hesitated. Hovering uncertainly for a second, he changed his mind and, drifting around the rear of the choir stalls, went to sit on the organist's stool at the console. Once again he sank into deep thoughtfulness. Without his being aware of it, the fingers of his left hand stroked the organ keys, soundlessly because the electricity for the bellows was not switched on. There he remained for perhaps five minutes. Then, getting up again, he walked to the altar step, knelt down and prayed silently. When he got to his feet now there was a new expression on his face. All lingering doubts had gone.

He walked to the vicarage. Out of sight behind the house, under the trees, the lawn was being mowed. Since the vicarage lawns were large and since they extended all around the village hall, which had been built on vicarage land, the parish council had provided funds for a two-stroke mower and for someone to do the mowing. There was much noise. But in his preoccupation, Douglas was not aware of it. He went straight into the drawing room.

It seemed to Douglas that Gloria was perpetually feeding her baby. Without wishing in any way to upset her, he had asked whether that was the normal procedure, but in fact had managed to upset her very much. He knew nothing about such things, she'd told him, looking as if she might cry again, and so he'd brought the subject up in a roundabout way with his mother during a conversation on the telephone.

'A baby should be fed every four hours,' his mother had told him.

'And how long would the feeding go on?' he asked.

'Twenty minutes.'

'No longer?'

'Hardly.'

And so Douglas had wondered whether Gloria's constant nursing wasn't perhaps more for her own emotional benefit rather than for the nourishment of the child.

And again, as he came in from church this morning, there she was, with her full white breast exposed and the baby in her arms.

His mood was fixed and, bracing himself, fighting all other doubts, overwhelmed with sympathy for his young wife but now utterly determined, he said, 'I have something to tell you, Gloria.'

'Yes?' The baby's tiny fingers were clutching at the flesh of her breast and she was smiling at the contact.

'I'm convinced that my calling is to minister to the forces. I'm desperately sorry, my dear, but I must do what God wants of me.'

She looked up, frowning. 'What d'you mean?'

'I'm still a young man. It isn't right that I should be here, safe, when others are fighting and dying.'

The sound of the lawnmower was coming closer to the French window and Gloria hadn't heard him properly. 'What d'you mean! What d'you mean?'

'I intend to offer myself as a chaplain to the services – to the Royal Air Force.'

Alarm suddenly sparked in her eyes. 'But you can't do that . . .'

'Believe me, Gloria, I've thought about this for weeks. I've discussed it with the Bishop—'

'What – what? I can't hear you!' Gloria tried to waft the increasing sound of the mower away with a hand. 'What're you saying? What're you saying?'

'I'm sorry, my dear, but I must do it. I've made up my mind.'

'But what about me?'

'I've spoken to my mother. She'll be delighted to have you until all this trouble's over.'

Gloria was still straining to hear him. 'Your mother! What d'you mean, your mother? Are you saying I'll have to leave here?'

'Well yes, I'm afraid so. Someone will have to replace me.'

'How can you do this to me? I can't live without you . . . How can I live without you!' And now Gloria's face had crumpled. She was crying piteously.

Douglas went down on his knee and took her hand. 'Oh my darling, I know what this means to you. But how many other people—'

'What – I can't hear you – I can't hear you . . .'

Douglas, still barely aware of the mower, aware only of the pain of this moment, squeezed her hand. 'Oh my dear, I'm so sorry . . .'

'You're leaving me – you're leaving me! I'll die!'

'No my darling, you're brave, you'll come to understand . . .'

'What? What?'

'I need your support, Gloria. We must be at one in this. Mother will look after you.'

But he got no further. The noise of the mower filled the room and Gloria, her face flooded with tears, gave a little scream. 'No – no!'

Douglas went to touch her cheek, but with a sudden shake of the body, a sudden scream of rage and frustration, Gloria pushed him away, jumped to her feet and ran to the French window.

The sound of the mower had been so loud in here because the window had been open. But instead of closing it against the din, she opened it wide and, sobbing, screamed weakly into the garden. 'Stop it – stop it – stop it!'

Holding on to the handles of the mower was Arthur Swift. At once, he saw the lady appear in the opening of the window, saw her distress, saw that she was calling to him, and switched off the engine.

'Yes, Mrs Russell?'

'Go away! Go away! Go away!' she cried, crumpled and tearful and trembling.

'Oh, right,' Arthur said, only now noticing that Mrs Russell was holding her baby low across her chest and that her naked left breast was bulging out of her blouse. The moisture left around the pink nipple by the baby's sucking glowed palely in the sunlight.

'Go away!'

'Right, Mrs Russell. OK. Can I have me two bob, please?'

6

The Borrowed-Time Brigade

Late afternoon and an army wagon from the camp on the beach stopped outside the post office and its driver and his mate stepped down. Rattling the doorbell on its spring as they went, they entered the shop. Nancy was just serving Mrs Peters from Church Lane with a few groceries off the ration – tinned beans and some flour. As the two heavy-booted soldiers clomped in and brought their unaccustomed khaki, their substantial presence, to the counter, the ladies' conversation stopped. It was as if the soldiers had brought a sudden, blasting change of air into the shop with them.

'Morning, love,' said one of the soldiers to Nancy.

She nodded. 'Yes? What can I get you?'

The soldier looked at Mrs Peters, at her things on the counter, as if to ask, 'Aren't you already serving?' But Mrs Peters and Nancy both spoke at once.

'It's all right.' The ladies were clearly just a little intimidated.

'What've you got in the way of fags, love?'

'Only the Turf.'

'Oh hell!' The two soldiers exchanged grimaces. 'Nothing under the counter?'

'No,' said Nancy. 'I'm afraid not.'

'Oh well, give us the Turf – just two tens.'

'It's a bit quiet round here, isn't it?' said the other soldier. 'What the hell d'you do for a bit of fun?'

Neither lady answered.

The soldiers took their cigarettes. 'Thanks, love – and for God's sake try to get your hands on some Woodbines, won't yer? Ta-ra . . . Keep your chins up, ladies!'

And the soldiers went back to their wagon.

'I'll tell you what, Mrs Peters,' Nancy said, 'with the army here, there's going to be a bit of bother with the girls, don't you think?'

As it happened, down the road at her home, Mary Acton was thinking the same thing. Her daughter, Eva, having coloured her legs for the evening with liquid stocking make-up, was standing on a chair while Mary tried to draw straight lines with a crayon to simulate seams.

'You've got to go up to my knicker legs!' Eva complained.

'Leave your knicker legs out of it,' Mary said. 'And where d'you plan to go tonight, madam?'

'Nowhere.'

Eva always went nowhere, yet every person in the village knew her, recognised her crazy make-up and her mincing walk a mile off.

'Well, keep away from them soldiers,' said Mary.

Eva shook her backside. 'I want it up to my knicker legs.'

'Did you hear me – keep away from them soldiers!'

Mary had felt quite comfortable about Eva for a while now because her obsession with the vicar had concentrated her daughter's mind. She had occupied most of her time in following him about, attending all his services, and just sitting in the field behind the vicarage staring blankly through the trees in the hope of seeing him. But he'd gone now, and Eva was what she was, and Mary was profoundly worried.

'Just stay away from them soldiers! Stay away from them!'

Yet, within an hour, Eva was sitting on the high bank at the far end of Littlecotes Lane with her knees up, just across the lane from the entrance to the camp. She could be seen from the window of the guardroom.

'There she is again,' said the orderly sergeant, and his two corporals came to take a look. 'Christ,' one of them said, 'what a clown. Who the hell does she think'll want to poke that?'

He and the sergeant laughed, but the other corporal didn't find it funny. 'Poor kid's not quite with it,' he said. 'She's asking for trouble.'

The fourth of August was the twenty-sixth anniversary of the outbreak of the First World War. The date had never passed without the Borrowed-Time Brigade's notice, and the fact that another war happened to be raging made no difference. They mustered again on that afternoon. Lance was one of the brigade's three members. The other two were Clive Molyneau and Phipps Pickmere, both of roughly Lance's own age.

This exclusive association had been established during

a drunken debauch at a field hospital at Ypres on 12 November 1918, twenty-four hours after the Armistice. At the time, all three of them were suffering from wounds, both physical and mental. In their drunken conversation they'd discovered that they had something in common. Their battalions – Lance's Coldstreams and the other two's King's Liverpools – had just been wiped from the face of the earth near the Forest of Mormal. Why and how, by the grace of God, when all their comrades had gone, should they still be alive, to breathe and drink and laugh?

'The fact is,' Molyneau had said, 'we shouldn't be here. We three are living on borrowed time.'

They met on this date and on two or three other dates each year, usually at an hotel in town where the staff knew them well. They drank rum and had tea at the army hour of 4 p.m. The meal was always the same – no entrée, no dessert, only an unappetising bully-beef hash, specially made by the hotel chef to an old trench recipe. Then they retired to a room upstairs and, between spurts of banter, played an hour or two of pontoon for shillings. Molyneau had instituted this tradition (most of the ideas were his). All proceeds, plus ten pounds from each man, went to a war widows' charity. This was one cause about which Maureen had no reservation and she made certain that Lance was able fully to stand his corner.

Molyneau was a big man, with heavy shoulders and large, clumsy hands. His wound had been in the neck. Pink, shrivelled flesh marked the spot. He wore a sober grey lounge suit and a regimental tie. He had a craggy face and a long, bent nose, but bright and lively eyes. He'd won the

Military Cross as a young captain at Guillemont. He had a calm, smiling air about him. Like the other two, he was unmarried. He lived alone in an otherwise empty house on the Lincoln road out of town and spent a lot of time riding about the countryside on his horse, chatting from on high to men working in the fields and to women whose doorways he rode past.

He and Pickmere were close – indeed intimate – friends and had been so ever since Pickmere had served under Molyneau as a platoon commander in the King's. Pickmere preferred to dress more colourfully. He had on a dark blue linen jacket, grey and white check trousers, a pink shirt and a brilliant white cravat with long, fluttering ends. He had never left his widowed mother's house, where he occupied three self-contained rooms out of his mother's sight. He smoked his cigarettes with elegant gestures of the hand and arm, and spoke in a clipped and rather exaggerated accent. His men had very often had cause to be amused by him. Some had despised him for what they correctly suspected him to be. But he had nerves of steel and all of them had cheered when they'd heard he'd been given a mention in despatches.

This close friendship between Molyneau and Pickmere had awkward moments on occasion – in fact most of the time. This was because Molyneau could present a cold front towards Pickmere, a cool air of indifference, which was very irritating because Pickmere never knew whether he was performing or not – and he frequently was.

'It was Trônes Wood,' Molyneau was insisting, pausing with an ace in his hand for a moment and then placing it down on top of a king to show that he was entitled to collect their stakes again.

'It was not,' said Pickmere. 'It was Montauban.'

'I assure you, I'm right, old dear. Crocker got it in the arse on the same day, which caused some speculation. What the blazes was he doing up a tree? Of course we never knew because he'd no sooner rejoined than he was finished off. That was in the October. It was Trônes Wood.'

'It was Montauban.'

'It was Trônes Wood.'

'Oh shut up, for God's sake!' Pickmere could be petulant. He threw down his cards.

'I'll pay nineteen,' said Molyneau, looking at Pickmere's displayed cards. 'I see you have fifteen there. Too bad.' He gathered the cards together and began to deal again. He glanced at Lance. 'So, you're back home now. How d'you find things there these days? How's your sister? How long is it since we met her?'

'Don't ask me. A hell of a long time,' said Lance. 'And please don't remind me of that evening – it mucked things up for me.'

'Yes. Smythe was a bounder. I never trusted him. Where the hell did you find him?'

'He was in the battalion until '17. They put him on the staff.'

'Yes, a typical staff wallah. A snake in the grass.'

'Oh I don't know,' said Lance. 'He was all right. What the hell was my father doing with that silly woman, anyway? He really was a nincompoop. He very nearly buggered everything up for us, very nearly lost us everything.

Good old Maureen. She had him by the short hairs, thank God.'

'I remember your father well. Queer old bird,' Molyneau said.

'I suppose he had his points,' Lance conceded. 'But I'm damned if I ever knew what they were. I'd not seen him for three years before he died.'

Pickmere spoke. 'In my room when I stayed with you on one occasion,' he said, 'I found a note on the back of the door: "Please do not laugh or converse in my hearing, it upsets my digestion."'

'Yes,' said Lance. 'His digestion was important. Twist . . . again . . . Oh hell, you've bust me.'

They played a hand in silence and then Pickmere said, 'My mother's decided to have a ten-foot-deep air-raid shelter dug under the terrace.'

'Still no good against a direct hit,' Molyneau remarked.

'Who wants your opinion?' Pickmere snapped. 'I've asked you, are you coming to Brookdale with me this evening? Why won't you answer?'

'I'll see.'

'Oh puff!' Pickmere slapped the table. 'And I've got pontoon so it's my deal. Give me the cards. Give them to me! Are you coming to Brookdale?'

Molyneau smiled gently at him. 'I'll tell you when I'm ready.'

'Oh, piss off!'

'Deal the cards, dear, there's a good chap.'

They played two more hands. Pickmere took out cigarettes, gave Lance one and pointedly refused to offer them to Molyneau.

Ignoring the gesture, Molyneau said, 'By the way, I've been in touch with the army, you know.'

'Oh? Why?' Lance asked.

'I thought there might be something for me.'

'And was there?'

'They suggested the Home Guard.'

Pickmere laughed. 'They won't have you either. Why didn't you tell me you'd been in touch with the army?'

'Do I have to tell you everything?'

'You're a swine.'

'And there was something else they mentioned,' Molyneau went on, turning to Lance. 'How would you fancy coping with unexploded bombs?'

'Not at all.'

'They've got a special unit. Full course of training at Slough.'

'I detest Slough,' said Lance. 'Have we finished that bottle of rum?'

'Yes, we have,' said Pickmere. 'He's drunk it all. And, quite frankly, I think I've had enough of him this evening. I do believe I'll go home.'

'Yes – if you chaps don't mind, I'd like to break it up myself,' said Lance. 'I have an arrangement.'

'Who is it this time?' Molyneau asked. 'What's her name?'

'Peggy, if you must know.'

'I had an aunt called Peggy. She liked absinthe. What does your Peggy like?'

'Sherry, as a matter of fact.'

'Well, give her my love.'

Pickmere sat back, looking at Molyneau with angry eyes

and waving his arms about. 'Are you coming to Brookdale? Yes or no, you sod?'

Molyneau merely smiled at him again.

Lance met Peggy Delgrano at her bus stop. She had done a day's work but still shone.

'I've booked us a room,' he told her. It was at the hotel he'd just left.

'I said I wanted to go to the pictures, didn't I? If we dash we'll catch the last house.'

'Yes, of course. But I meant the room for later. Yes?'

She was as coy as Molyneau had been. 'We'll see.'

But after James Cagney and Myrna Loy she was amenable. BBC wireless was relayed into the hotel bedroom. As they undressed, quiet, romantic music was like a gentle whisper in the air. 'Leave it on,' said Peggy, and so, as they came together in the bed, Anne Ziegler and Webster Booth sang 'Lover, Come Back to Me'.

'What's the matter?' Peggy asked, drawing away.

'Nothing, dear. I'll be all right in a minute.'

And that proved to be the case.

With their arms linked, Arthur took his blind father on the ten o'clock bus down to Evers' factory to see Mr Evers. While the two men talked, Arthur waited in the outer room. After a few minutes, Mr Evers put his head round the door. 'Your dad will be about ten minutes . . .'

In rather less than that time, Mr Evers delivered him back to Arthur's care. He was very pleased with himself. 'I can do it, son,' he said. 'You just sit at the bench and they give you the frame and you just screw bits on. I can do it, easy.'

'Good old Dad!' Arthur put a kiss on to his father's whiskery cheek. 'Oh, that's great.'

'After twenty-five years, Arthur, I'm working again. Wait until your mother hears . . . Five pounds a week, lad! Five pounds. We've never been so well off in our lives . . .'

Arthur's mother cried at the news. 'And did you thank Mr Evers?'

'Of course I did! But I can do it, Sally. In a week or two I'll be as fast as any of 'em. You watch.'

Arthur was easily as delighted as his father. Next morning, when he delivered the Commodore's *Times*, he told Fotherby. 'My dad's got a job!'

He told Constable Bowker when he met him on the road and told Nancy again when he went back to the shop after his round.

'Yes, so you said before, Arthur.'

Two girls from the Women's Land Army had come down from Brocklesby's in one of the farm vans. They came giggling into the shop in their green jumpers and khaki jodhpurs and Arthur considered telling even them the good news and he knew neither of them. But instead he pointed out that one of them had a bit of her shirt dangling out from under her jumper.

'Thanks, kid,' she said. 'But mind your own business. Have you got Mrs Brocklesby's paté yet, Nancy?'

'No,' said Nancy. 'And I don't think it's ever going to come.'

As he went out of the shop, Arthur turned back for a second. Quite loudly, he said, 'And you've got cow dung down the back of your gaiters.'

For four days Commodore Grainthorpe had been ill, immobile and exiled to a shivering dimension between the sheets, where consciousness had consisted of brief, vague interludes of hot lemonade, nasty medicine, aches and sneezes. On the fifth day, something wakened him. It was Fotherby, shaking his arm. He opened his eyes and said, 'How many have we shot down today?'

'Don't know,' said Fotherby. 'But twenty-six yesterday. We're winning. Sawbones is here to take a look at you.'

Sitting at the bedside was Dr Green, sneezing too, almost as old as the Commodore, with a shining bald pink scalp, grey moustache and thick grey eyebrows. He was a plump, paunchy man and had plump, pink, tennis-ball hands. He was wearing grey pinstripe trousers and in his shapeless dark grey jacket, which lay across his sloping shoulders like a shawl, he gave the impression of a large, swaddled baby sitting there rocking to and fro. He had sneezed his rimless glasses off.

'I've caught this damned flu, Commodore,' he said, covering his face with a large red handkerchief.

'Well, go home, Doctor,' the Commodore said. 'I'll come and visit *you*. I'm feeling infinitely better this morning. Is it morning? Where's Dr Green?'

'What d'you mean? I'm Dr Green.'

'I mean your son. I normally see him – don't I?'

'They've requisitioned him. They've sent him to a hospital in Bristol. He specialises in obstetrics.'

'Does he? That makes me feel a bit queer. What was he ever doing with me? Why Bristol?'

'God knows. It's this damned war. There must be an epidemic of parturition there.' Dr Green blew on his glasses, wiped them with his red handkerchief, and put them back on. 'Now I'm on my own, run off my feet, jiggered, and I've got about ten more people to see.' He got to his feet. 'Well, sit up – let's take a look at you.'

'I feel much better.'

'So you said. Open your pyjamas.' Dr Green put his stethoscope to the Commodore's chest. 'Mmm . . .' he muttered. 'Lean forward. Lift your pyjama jacket.' And he listened to the Commodore's back. 'Yes, there's not much congestion there. Did my son give you some medicine?'

'It's here,' Fotherby said, taking a half-full bottle from the bedside table and showing it.

'Yes,' said the doctor, glancing at it. 'It usually does the trick.'

'So I can go below today, can I?' the Commodore asked.

'Tomorrow. Give yourself another day in bed.' Dr Green nodded across the room. 'What might that be – on your tallboy there?'

It was a carved wooden figure, fifteen inches high. 'A Samoan deity of some sort,' the Commodore said. 'He's called Wa-wa-sloppy or something like that. I picked him up in Pago Pago in 1915.'

'He's an ugly little devil.'

'Yes – but he's supposed to bring good luck, mostly by way of shoals of fish, I think, and good coconut harvests.'

'Mumbo-jumbo. That sort of thing's not good for you at your age. Messing about with the occult can be dangerous.'

'But it's only an ornament, old chap.'

'Yes, well, watch it.'

'Oh give him a drink, Fotherby,' said the Commodore. 'There's brandy on the hall table.'

'Daren't,' said the doctor. 'When people smell alcohol on your breath they lose confidence in you. But go on – I'll have just a small one on my way out. Good day, Commodore.'

Fotherby led the way downstairs and poured quite a large measure for him.

'Too much – too much . . .' But the doctor took it. 'I'll just sip a drop.'

'The Commodore,' Fotherby said. 'You sure he's all right now?'

'The man's as fit as I am.'

'I was a bit worried about him.'

Dr Green sipped at the brandy, sipped again, was on the point of handing the rest back and then decided to drink the lot. 'Thanks,' he said. 'I'm jiggered. Mrs Havers next on Church Lane . . . Yes.' He gave Fotherby the empty glass. 'I'll be off.' As Fotherby let him out, he paused for a moment, thinking of something. 'Where was I? Yes . . . Just keep giving him the medicine . . . Good day.'

Fixed to the windscreen of his car, a venerable Wolseley, was a sticker saying *Doctor*. The car crackled slowly out of the drive. It turned northwards and proceeded along Main Street for about twenty yards. Then, with a little screech of brakes, it came to a dead stop. 'Damn!' Dr Green exclaimed.

Going through the noisy and jerky motions of a three-point turn, he drove on in the opposite direction and came at last to his own home. It was a large, square, featureless building almost opposite the green where, nowadays, there was a circle of barbed wire enclosing a heap of wooden boxes – something to do with the army.

As the doctor entered the house, his wife, Pat, called to him from the top of the stairs. 'What've you forgotten now?'

It startled him – emptied his mind for the moment. 'Hang on . . .' he said, frowning. 'I can't remember . . . Oh yes.' And he went into the surgery for atropine from the locked cupboard. It was for Mrs Havers' eyes.

Fotherby poured more brandy and took it up to the Commodore. The old man was just getting out of bed.

'Belay there,' Fotherby said.

'I'm getting up.'

'No you're not.'

'But I feel fine.'

'He said another day.'

'He's an old dead-eye.'

'Just get back. I'll let you up this evening.'

'Oh, will you!'

'Get back in. And here, a tot for you.'

'It's food I want. I'm starving.'

But the Commodore got back between the sheets and took the brandy. 'Thanks.'

'I'll bring you a sandwich. Then tonight I'll make you big eats.'

'Did I ever tell you I once caught typhoid in Surabaya?'

'Yes. Eighteen or nineteen times.'

'Did I tell you I went down to six stone?'

'It varies from six to eight.'

'What sort of day is it?'

'So-so. A bit cold for the time of year. I'll make a fire for when you come down.'

The Commodore's pyjama jacket was still open. His white, hairless chest had lost some of its flesh, Fotherby was inclined to think, and his cheeks had sunk a little. 'I'll have to feed you up again,' he said.

The Commodore raised his glass to him. 'Cheers, old friend,' and sipped his brandy. 'You've looked after me. Thank you.'

'Thanks're not called for. You look after me. Drink your brandy and crash till teatime. I'll pipe you at one bell in the second dog.'

Indeed, at six thirty that evening, big eats it proved to be. Somehow, Fotherby had managed to get hold of a sirloin, complete with eye, large enough to feed four, and almost half of it was carved into slices on the Commodore's plate, together with peas and carrots and French beans. When he'd eaten every last morsel, the Commodore asked, 'By the way, did any of that come from the pub?'

'Why?'

'Well, you know I disapprove of the black market.'

'Yes – only once it's passed down your throat. Anyway, Charley's packing it in, he tells me. He doesn't need it any more. He's got plenty of beer now and you can hardly get in the place – all these Lancashire Rifles. They can't half shift it. He's had to take on another barmaid.'

'Oh. I see. Then no more sirloin?'

Fotherby laughed at the Commodore's disappointed expression. 'Just leave it to me.'

'I'm replete,' said the Commodore, pressing his hands to his stomach. 'In fact, a bit bloated.'

'Well go through to the library. There's a fire in there.'

At a few minutes before nine o'clock, Fotherby himself came into the library, smart and shiny in his Home Guard uniform.

The Commodore was just mixing himself a gin and bitters. 'How many parades did I miss while I was ill?' he asked.

'Two. But they didn't miss you. And I noticed you hadn't cleaned your rifle after I told you to.'

'I did.'

'You're just bloody hopeless, that's what it is. If you don't look out I'll tell them how old you are and they'll kick you out . . . I'm off.'

'Good. Give me some peace.'

'Well don't drink too much pink gin. It mightn't go with the medicine.'

'Bugger off, Fotherby. Oh – wait.'

'What now?'

'Before you go, find Lord Haw-Haw for me.'

'Why d'you want to listen to that twerp?'

'He amuses me.'

Fotherby switched on the wireless. As he tuned in, there came a sequence of whines and hooting oscillations and, finally, bouncing, jaunty, military music. 'That's the station,' Fotherby said. 'It's just a bit early for him, I think. Anyway, some of us have duty to attend to.' And out Fotherby went.

The Commodore sat for a while sipping pink gin and thinking, as he often did now, of former times. While laid up in bed the past few days, with his high temperature, drifting in and out of consciousness, he had been plagued – indeed vaguely disturbed – by fleeting, shadowy images of faces, now smiling and now wet with tears. The trouble was that some of them were so misty that he couldn't tell whether they were mere dreams or fragments of lost memory. They were all women's faces. He had recognised his mother for a moment and also Julia . . . Yes. It had been Julia, surely. How strange. He tried to call her to mind again, but waking thoughts of her were just as elusive. She came like a wraith, flickering for an instant, her face in darkness now, so that he recognised her only by the feelings that arose in him. After near enough fifty years even those feelings themselves were hard to define – a trace of sadness, a trace of longing, a trace of . . . he didn't know what it was. But for a second he did see very clearly a long row of poplar trees standing black against the setting sun. Where had that vision come from? Ah yes . . . They were to be seen from the garden of her house. Had they parted there? But he couldn't remember. He smiled to himself, his head lolling forward and just a trickle of saliva on his lips. Then he took another drink.

His mind now was full of other images, all rolling into one another, of ships and men and charts and voice pipes and crashing six-inch guns and battle ensigns and green sea cascading over plunging bows – his life, his life. That was what he'd wanted, that was what he'd had. Yet that sad little sensation from his dreams still nagged at him. 'You bloody old nitwit,' he told himself. He picked up the poker and shifted coals in the fire to stir up flames. Then he realised that he could hear the voice of William Joyce,

Lord Haw-Haw, from the wireless. He took another mouthful of pink gin.

'This is Jarmany calling, Jarmany calling. Jarmany calling . . .' Lord Haw-Haw declared in his sickening singsong tones. 'Here are Reichssender Hamburg, Station Bremen, and Station DXB on the thirty-one-metre band. You are about to hear the news in English.'

'Well I can tell it isn't Greek!' the Commodore snapped at the wireless.

'Jarman bombers have inflicted severe damage on military targets and airfields in Kent, Sussex and other regions of the Home Counties,' Haw-Haw went on. 'Forty-two British fighter planes have been shot down, for a loss of only twelve Jarman aircraft. Britain is being forced to her knees in preparation for the imminent invasion, plans for which are complete and ready to be implemented at the appropriate moment. It is estimated that Britain, like her erstwhile ally, France, will be cowed and conquered within weeks of Jarman forces stepping foot on its shores.'

'Rubbish!' the Commodore muttered. But he continued to listen. Reception on this wavelength was never very good. From time to time the voice faded to a whisper. At other times, frying-pan cracklings were all that could be heard. But Haw-Haw went lilting on. 'The Jarman blockade is having serious effects on the supply of foodstuffs to British shops. Plutocrats and all Jews, with their money and criminal dispositions, are able . . . crackle-crackle . . . whatever they wish, but ordinary British housewives, especially in the north of the country, which has always been considered unimportant, are finding it impossible to get even the essentials . . . crackle-crackle . . .'

Though he was neither plutocrat nor Jew, the Commodore, with his stomach still full of black-market roast sirloin, was touched by that. He grunted and shifted in his chair.

'At Liverpool and Hull,' Haw-Haw went on, 'the wives of merchant seaman whose ships have been sunk by Jarman U-boats are attacking men of the Royal Navy whose protection of merchant shipping has been cowardly and negligible. It is reported by our agents that . . .' The voice faded for a moment.

'. . . RAF fighter pilots, who have been forced again and again into battle without rest, are suffering so much from exhaustion that the battle cannot go on much longer. They are falling asleep at their controls and large numbers of them have crashed into houses, killing women and . . . [fade] . . . At British airfields, where Jarman bombing has been incessant, personnel have gone mad. It is reported that several senior officers have been shot for dereliction of duty and that gangs of RAF men are roaming the country, pillaging.'

Unable to endure any more, the Commodore got to his feet and stopped Haw-Haw in mid sentence. 'The damned buffoon!' he said.

He found a taper, dipped it into the fire for a flame, lit a cigarette and sat down. It was idiotic, he thought, to let the man get to you. Yet, in a way, that was what had happened. There had been stirred in the Commodore a ridiculous anxiety that there might be more than a grain of truth in some of what the buffoon had been saying. He certainly knew about the black market . . . But the Commodore shook his head and chastised himself. Of course not. It was rubbish – mere propaganda, designed to create alarm and precisely that same anxiety he himself had felt for a moment. And yet, how many Englishmen and women would have been taken in by the fool? The man was not so much a buffoon as a clever swine. And he was an Englishman at that. The sickening, craven traitor. He should be dragged out by the scruff of the neck and shot at dawn.

Before his illness the Commodore had been reading *The Old Curiosity Shop*. Rising again he took it down from the shelf. Good old Dickens. Good old England. He switched on his reading lamp and, sinking into cushions, stretched out his legs.

Meanwhile, Fotherby was on duty with the Home Guard. The night watch was seen as crucial since spies and saboteurs would naturally prefer to move about under cover of darkness. The platoon mustered at nine o'clock on the square in front of the post office. People thereabouts had long since lost interest in the spectacle and, in any case, at nine o'clock the BBC broadcast its most important news bulletin of the day and few were prepared to miss it. They were all indoors, listening in behind blackout curtains. Only Swindell's goat, tethered to a stump on the grass verge, paid the Home Guard any attention.

In all, the unit had on its roll forty-three men, drawn from the local area. The majority of these had full-time jobs. A number were on shifts. On any given evening, some would be taking essential rest and others would actually be at work. The arranging of rosters to accommodate all these variables had given the commanding officer many hours of brain-twisting work. He was Stephen Welsh, a thirty-nine-year-old Territorial captain from Somercotes. Earlier this year he and his Territorial unit had received orders to join the British Expeditionary Force in France. He had been perfectly ready for that and took it as a bitterly disappointing blow when, at his pre-embarkation medical examination, he had been declared unfit for foreign service. The rest of them had marched away without him. He had a mild form of diabetes, apparently. Neither he nor anyone else had suspected that he was anything but perfectly fit. He lived with his wife and daughter in a bungalow close to his father's farmhouse and worked hard all day long. He was bony and strong and full of nervous energy. He made a good soldier and had a degree of conscientiousness that even Fotherby was bound to admire.

On parade this evening, sixteen of them lined up in the square. They numbered off and split into eight sections of two. Three sections marched off down the road towards Somercotes and Evers' factory. Others went to patrol towards Fulstow. Fotherby and Captain Welsh took the village. It was a clear, starry night after a day that had been bright but cool, under a nor'-easter blowing off the sea, and now, as Fotherby had said earlier, it was quite cold. 'We ought to've brought our greatcoats,' he said.

'Too cumbersome. They get in the way.'

The two men were groping and tripping their way along the footpath that bordered the back gardens on Church Lane. In one of the houses a small dog barked and yapped and then suddenly squealed to silence. The breeze hissed in overhead branches and the scarecrow windmill on top of its stick, which Fotherby himself had set up for Joan Feathers in her garden, rattled round in sudden spasms.

Pausing, raising his head, holding up a hand, Captain Welsh said, 'What's that?'

'It's Mrs Williams's whistling kettle.'

Welsh relaxed. 'Yes. So it is.'

Fotherby prodded the muzzle of his rifle into clumps of weeds, expecting nothing and finding nothing.

The captain considered it necessary to search Mr Holt's garden shed because the door was not padlocked and was open to the world. All it contained was a collection of old junk – seed boxes, plant pots, thrown-out bits of furniture and scuttling mice. 'Well you never know,' he said.

They returned to the path and continued towards the far stile. But, once again, after a few strides, growing tense, Captain Welsh paused. 'What's that?'

In the blackness by Foster's greenhouse some blacker thing was moving.

'It looks like a man,' said Fotherby.

'Challenge him.'

'Challenge him? Why? It'll be old man Foster.'

'Challenge him!'

And so, not very willingly, Fotherby obliged. 'Who goes there?' he shouted.

The response was quick and angry. 'Who the bloody hell d'yer think!'

'Yes, it's Foster,' Fotherby said. 'Who else'd be messing about near his greenhouse?'

Foster hadn't finished. 'I don't know what the hell you're supposed to be doing, prowling round here at night. People don't like it. Sod off!'

Captain Welsh merely turned away and walked on. 'They don't understand,' he said. 'They don't understand.' But

Fotherby had irritated him. He paused again and faced him. 'You ask who could be messing about near a greenhouse? Well, think, man. Think. Haven't you listened to anything I ever said, Sergeant? Have I been wasting my breath all these weeks? Think! Does he grow anything in that greenhouse?'

'I suppose so. Tomatoes, probably.'

'Well there you are, man. Food! Good God. And haven't they told us this is just the sort of place enemy spies make for? Near the coast – the invasion – troops to spy on.' The captain suddenly remembered something. 'Have any flashing lights been reported lately?'

'No, sir. Not to me. I'd have told you. The last time we reported a light it was a lad playing about with a torch.'

'I can't seem to get through to you people,' the captain said, sighing. 'From a bedroom here a U-boat could see signals miles out to sea . . . People seem so damned complacent. Don't they realise what danger we're in? I despair sometimes.'

They crossed into the lane by the stile and pushed through the hedge into the copse behind the school.

'Hell!' the captain exclaimed, tripping and almost falling headlong. 'Watch your step. Someone's dumped an old mattress.'

Ten minutes later, having found nothing, they emerged from the copse onto the cricket field. The little pavilion was securely locked and bolted and, along all the way back to the lane, across the waste ground and through the thicket, there was not a movement to be detected anywhere.

Coming to a standstill under the overreaching black

branches of a cedar on the lane, the captain produced a packet of cigarettes. Fotherby struck a match, cupping it in his hand against the breeze, and they lit up. Puffing out smoke, they walked on. All was silent for a while. Then, at the corner where the lane met Front Street, they heard running footsteps behind them. It was young Private Roman. 'We've found someone,' he said, 'on the allotments.'

There, just inside the gate to the allotments, Private Black was discovered poking his rifle into the stomach of a ragbag of a figure, five foot six inches in height. His body was draped with a shapeless raincoat and his chin with a flowing beard. On his head was a battered trilby. As the captain and Fotherby drew near he began to wave his arms about and make inarticulate noises.

'What's he saying?' the captain asked. 'What language is that?'

'It's English, sir,' said Private Black. 'But he's got a hell of a stammer.'

The man had grown still during this exchange. Now he became animated again. He bounced about and his eyes shone white in the darkness. 'I-I-I-I've d-d-d-done no h-h-h-harm,' he was saying. 'N-n-n-no h-h-h-harm, no h-h-harm.'

'He sounds a bit like a Liverpudlian to me,' Fotherby said.

The captain stepped close, leaned down over the man. 'Name!' he demanded. 'Who are you? Where're you from?'

'N-n-n-nowhere . . . I d-d-d-don't know . . . I c-c-c-come here every s-s-s-summer.'

'He's just a tramp, sir,' Fotherby said. He gestured at the privates who stood by with their rifles at the port. 'Let him go, lads.'

'No!' The captain was irritated again. 'How d'you know he's a tramp? Eh? Tell me – how d'you know, man!'

'Well look at him.'

'So you think a German spy would be walking about in lederhosen with an alpenstock, do you?'

'Course not! But it's obvious. The man's a tramp. Let the poor sod go.'

To silence him, the captain pushed an open palm towards Fotherby's chest. 'Keep out of it.' Then he turned back to the man. 'Name!' he demanded again.

The man stammered hopelessly, grew impatient with himself, stamped his foot and stammered again.

'What was that?' the captain asked.

'I think he said Brewster, sir,' Private Roman said.

The captain put his face close and tried his schoolboy German: '*Warum sind Sie hier?* God, the man stinks. Where did you find him?'

'He was in one of the sheds.'

'I-I-I-I've d-d-done no h-h-harm. I w-w-was just s-s-sleeping . . . l-l-l-like last year. In the sh-sh-sh-shed.'

The captain reached out a hand. 'Show me your identity card, your ration book – anything you've got.'

The man screwed up his face, rocked from side to side. 'No . . . n-n-no . . .'

'He's not a full shilling,' Fotherby said.

'It's easy to feign stupidity, Sergeant. I told you to keep out of it. Search him.'

Fotherby stepped forward and the man raised his arms quite willingly.

'Hell!' Fotherby said, digging something out of the man's raincoat pocket. 'What's all this?' It was a chicken bone mangled together with some crusts of bread. 'Have you been in the dustbins?'

'I-I-I-I'm not a th-th-thief . . . S-s-s-somebody gave it to m-m-me.'

Fotherby put the disgusting mess back.

'What's under the raincoat?' asked the captain.

Fotherby was hesitant.

'I told you to search him.'

'But the man might be lousy. I don't much care for lice or fleas, Captain.'

'Do it, Sergeant!'

Fotherby groped about the man's body. 'A holey pullover,' he said, 'and about three shirts.'

'I-I-I-I'm not a thief. S-s-s-someone g-g-g-gave it to m-m-m-me.'

'Take your coat off,' the captain demanded. 'Strip him.'

'Hang on, sir,' Fotherby protested. 'Is that called for?'

'I won't tell you again, Sergeant! Let him do as I say. Take your coat off.'

'N-n-n-no!' the man wailed, appealing pathetically to Fotherby. 'N-n-no!'

'Just do it, lad,' Fotherby said. 'Just do it.'

Taking off his coat, the man let it fall. Poked at by Private Black's rifle, he began to undress. Off came his ragged jumper. Then off came one of his shirts. As he drew it over his head, something fell from its breast pocket to the ground.

'Pick it up,' ordered the captain.

Private Roman did so.

'Give it to me.'

Between two sheets of greasy cardboard held together by a bit of string were some papers.

'What's all this?' the captain asked, unfolding the papers and peering blindly at them in the darkness. 'Your lighter, Sergeant . . . Ah . . . This is English,' he said. He read aloud, "It was them people you lived with in Rochdale . . ." What's this about Rochdale?'

'P-p-p-private . . .!' exclaimed the man.

'Oh yes?' The captain read on. "Our Betty was not to blame. She was . . ." What's all this?'

'Oh come on, sir,' Fotherby tried again. 'As he says, it's private stuff.'

'No. This could be to fool us. It's just what you'd expect.' The captain confronted the man again. '*Warum sind Sie hier? Antworten!*'

'W-w-w-what?'

'You've been set up with these papers.'

'W-w-w-what?' Stripped down to his vest by now, the man was shivering, embracing himself. 'P-p-p-put my l-l-l-letters back, s-s-s-sir . . . P-p-p-please!'

But the captain had now found a creased and greasy photograph of a woman in a headscarf, smiling. 'Who's the woman? Who's the woman?'

'Put 'em b-b-b-back, s-s-sir . . .'

'Take your trousers off.'

'Oh now, for God's sake, Captain!' Fotherby exclaimed, and the captain turned on him.

'D'you think I like this! D'you think I'm enjoying it! It's my duty – my duty. For God's sake, let me do it!'

The man stood there shuddering, thin and insubstantial as a skinned rabbit, with his trousers around his ankles. He had tiny buttocks and short legs. Even in the darkness, grime and filth could be seen around his knees and feet. In the cold air his penis had shrivelled to a bud. His head was bowed.

'The poor sod's crying,' Fotherby said.

The captain had suddenly become quite still.

'He can't be hiding much now,' Fotherby went on. 'Can he, sir?'

'No . . . no . . .'

Unable to contemplate the pathetic sight of the man any longer, the captain turned away. 'Here,' he said to Fotherby, 'give him his stuff back. Tell him to get dressed.'

'Come on, lad,' Fotherby said, picking up one of the man's shirts, putting the papers back into its pocket and handing it to him. 'Get dressed and bugger off.'

'No,' said the captain.

'What?'

'We can't be sure, John. We can't be sure . . . I can't take the responsibility.'

'Well what the devil're we going to do with him?'

'Hand him over to the police. Constable Bowker can lock him up for the night until someone can check him properly.'

The man gasped with alarm. He jumped about again, held up his hands, pleading. 'N-n-n-no . . . I'm n-n-not a th-th-thief.'

The captain stared at him. 'Why're you frightened of the police?'

'These people are like that,' Fotherby said. 'No identity card, no ration book. He's a tramp. They pilfer – they pilfer. Let him go.'

'I can't, John. I can't risk it.'

'No! N-n-n-no!' The man was quite beside himself, shaking and whimpering. 'No – p-p-p-please! N-n-n-no!'

'You see,' the captain said. 'Why should he react like that?'

'Get your coat on, lad.' Fotherby picked up the man's raincoat for him on the end of his rifle. 'Here. Get it on.'

'N-n-n-no, n-n-n-no!'

'Do as the officer says. Come on. Left, right, left, right . . .'

And all four of them escorted the little figure down Front Street and on through the silent night towards Constable Bowker's police house.

On the way something appalling happened. An army lorry, its way lit only by two thin, flat beams from shrouded headlights, came at speed down the hill from Fulstow. As it drew near, the man suddenly stepped aside and threw himself in front of it. It hit him with a soggy, squelching sound and he was thrown aside in a slow arc, flapping through the air like a ragged bird.

The lorry skidded to a halt. Its soldier driver, paralysed with shock, stared out open-mouthed from his cab. But his co-driver jumped down at once and raced to the body.

Captain Welsh and Fotherby came to stand on either side of him.

'He jumped out!' he said. 'He was there, right in front of us. Jim couldn't do a thing.'

Not now concerned in the least about lice or fleas, Fotherby knelt by the body and put his ear to the man's chest.

'Is he dead?' the soldier asked.

'I've never seen one deader,' Fotherby said. 'And there's not a mark on him. Not a mark.'

For several seconds there was silence. Moonlight lit the

man's white face and glowed in the fine hairs of his mottled grey beard as though they were strands of silk.

'Who was it?' the soldier asked.

'Who was it?' Fotherby echoed. 'It was no one, son. Just a tramp. Just a tramp.' He got to his feet. When he turned around he saw that the captain had his hands to his face. He was crying.

7
Butter, and a New Vicar

Maureen's preoccupation with her evacuees had for some time distracted her from other matters. One of her troubles was that she'd had to lose young Clifford, the red-headed refugee from the Robinsons, caring for whom in recent times had given her such pleasure. Bright, loving and appealing, he'd been a delight to have about the house, and she'd developed a tender affection for him. As she'd watched him walk away, clinging to his father's hand, she'd shed tears. His loss had depressed her and she'd spent rather more time than she ought lavishing attention on the girls. Things around the house, therefore, had deteriorated without her noticing and it was left to Veronica to point them out.

The place was not very clean. There was dust everywhere, even in those parts of the house that were nowadays kept in daily use. The portraits on the landing of Cecil Rhodes and Maureen's father had been allowed to become grey and streaky. Certain rooms didn't seem to have been aired and on opening their doors musty smells greeted you.

'Mrs Johnson's all right, ma'am,' Veronica told her. 'It's the other two. They don't seem interested any more.'

'Really? But they were always so reliable. Oh dear. I'll have to speak to them.'

In all her experience of dealing with staff in the past she had found that that technique of hers – a certain firmness coupled with encouragement and congratulation on work well done – had always been the most productive. People responded to it with smiles of pride, even with gratitude, and she could not remember when it had last failed. But clearly it had failed now, no doubt because she had left her daily cleaning women to it and hardly spoken to them for weeks. What was required, therefore, were two kicks up the backside. Of course, she was perfectly capable of this, but first she had to prepare herself.

She took a glass of sherry, adopted a rigid posture and a severe expression, and went into the kitchen where the two ladies were taking their morning break, drinking tea.

Leaning forward with her heavy arms on the table, encircling her teacup as though she were protecting some precious treasure, was Mrs Newton, her hair tied up and her face bearing its usual expression of rather aggressive self-preoccupation. But she was quite relaxed. 'Hello,' she said, as Maureen entered the room.

Further down the long, white-scrubbed table, sat her colleague, little, mousey Mrs Leggett, who, taking Mrs Newton's lead, also said, 'Hello.' She took bossy Mrs Newton's lead in most things. She had a tiny triangular face under a great mass of curly hair that trembled as she moved, and her voice was like little tinkles from a piccolo.

Both women were wearing the blue overalls Maureen had provided and Mrs Newton was smoking.

'Ladies,' Maureen said, 'I'm sorry to interrupt your rest, but I'm afraid I have something to say to you.'

Her tone must have presaged things because both ladies

grew quite still. 'Yes?' Mrs Newton asked, frowning. A fly landed on her bare arm and she was not aware of it.

'I'm afraid the place is a mess. It is not clean.'

A sudden shock went through Mrs Newton. She stiffened. 'What?'

'In fact, it's dirty.'

Mrs Newton sat back with her hands turned to fists on the table. 'Dirty? *Dirty*? What're you saying?'

'Just go and see for yourselves. Look at the skirting boards everywhere – look at the carpets. Look on the stairs. Work has been dodged, I'm sorry to say. You've let me down.'

'Oh no we haven't,' Mrs Newton snapped, in a tone Maureen had not expected.

'But I'm afraid it's true, Mrs Newton. Do as I say. Go and see for yourselves. It's a terrible mess. I have no complaint with Mrs Johnson. She works well. But I'm afraid your rooms and the landing have barely been touched for weeks.'

'Well I'll be . . . ! Did you hear that, Elsie? You hear what she's saying when we work like slaves?'

'Look,' said Maureen, 'perhaps to some extent it's my fault . . . Yes. But I must say I'm disappointed in you. You're normally so good! However, I'm afraid I can't allow things to go on like this. I want to see a hundred per cent improvement, ladies, starting today. When you've finished your tea I want you to go back to the girls' bedroom. I'll give you an hour. Surely that should be long enough. Then I'll come and inspect your work. Thereafter, I hope to see the changes that're needed.'

Mrs Newton had swelled. Her heavy bust had blown up.

Her face had turned fiery red. 'Oh,' she exclaimed, 'do you! I see! Who d'you think you're talking to?'

Maureen had never met this rebellious attitude before. It took her aback for a second. But she confronted it boldly. 'Yes. I'm sorry to have to bring it up, we've been good friends, but things have deteriorated. I want things doing as they've always been done in the past. I'll make it my business to see exactly what effort you've made before you leave each day.'

'Is that so?'

'Yes. As I say, I have no wish to be hard. And I'm sure we can recover things. We must pull together.'

'D'you know there's a war on?' Mrs Leggett piped up.

'What does that have to do with it, Mrs Leggett?'

'Well, there it is . . . there's a war on.'

'Look, Mrs Leggett – Mrs Newton – what's going on outside these walls is irrelevant. You're paid to keep the place clean, and I intend to see that you do so.'

'She's coming the heavy,' Mrs Newton said, turning to Mrs Leggett. 'That's it. She's coming the heavy, Elsie.'

'I wouldn't have used that expression myself,' Maureen said. 'But I'm sure I've made my point. All I want is to see things as they were. You were so good, ladies. But I will not tolerate slackness.'

'Well fancy that!' said Mrs Newton. 'You hear her, Elsie? Slack, she's calling us. Slack! Well I'll be damned. Are we going to sit here and take this from her? After all we've done for her?' Mrs Newton angrily crushed her cigarette out in the ashtray. 'Ungrateful sod . . . Have you ever heard anything like it? Look at her. Are you going to take it lying down, Elsie? Can you hear what she's saying? Are you going to stand for it when we've worked like dogs? Are you? No, you're not. And neither am I.'

She glowered across into Maureen's face. 'Right then, missus, if that's how you feel, I'll tell you something. You can please your bloody self what you tolerate.' Rising slowly to her feet, she unbuttoned her overall, revealing a green dress. Two large red printed flowers blossomed across her bust. 'You can stuff your bloody job. Stuff it. You come in here and stand there like that and throw your weight about . . . Well, you can stuff it. Are you ready, Elsie?'

'Aye,' said Mrs Leggett. Now she, too, stood up and began to remove her overall. 'I don't like being spoken to like that.'

'Give her your overall, Elsie. Here – give her mine as well.'

Both overalls were draped over Maureen's arm.

'Hang on a tick,' said Mrs Newton. Reaching for her cup, she emptied it. 'Right. That's it. Oh – and here . . .' Picking up a yellow duster from the table, she put it on top of the overalls on Maureen's arm. 'Do it your bloody self. Right, Elsie. Follow me.'

Elsie did, and within a few seconds the two ladies had gone, leaving Maureen standing there shocked and baffled. She sank onto a chair at the table, hardly able to believe that such a totally unexpected thing could have happened.

The pantry door had been partly open. Veronica appeared around it.

'Oh!' Maureen was surprised. 'I didn't know you were in there.'

'I'm sorry, ma'am.'

'Did you hear all that?'

'Yes. I couldn't help it.'

'I'm dumbfounded, Veronica. I really am. Why? I thought they loved working here.'

'Well, yes . . .'

'Was I wrong? They were so different just now . . . They didn't seem like the same people.'

'Well I know they've been talking about leaving for a while.'

'Have they? Why? What've I done wrong?'

'Nothing, ma'am. I don't think you've done anything. I think it's just that they don't need the money any more.'

'Oh, is that it? Why?'

'Well, Mr Newton's working now, isn't he? And Mr Leggett got a job as a chargehand at Evers'.'

'I see.' Maureen sighed. 'As Mrs Leggett said, there's a war on . . . It's changed everything, Veronica. I just made their minds up for them, did I? I shouldn't have . . . I shouldn't have come the heavy. What're we going to do now?'

Veronica had no answer.

'Oh dear,' said Maureen.

'By the way, ma'am, I see we've run out of butter.'

'How can that be?'

'I don't know. There was some in the pantry this morning. But Mr Lance likes so much on his toast, doesn't he? That's all the ration gone. Shall I see if Mr Britton can let us have any from Home Farm?'

'No – I'll go myself. I feel like some air. I'll take the girls . . .' Maureen looked down at the blue overalls now on the table. 'I suppose they'd better go to the laundry,' she said. With another sigh, she got up, left the kitchen, and went to sit for a while in her little room while the girls screamed and played under the window outside.

At Veronica's mention of Lance, Maureen's mind had turned to her brother. She wished he were here – wished she could just be with him for a while, just to look into his eyes, to talk to him, because he was another worry to her. But of course he was out somewhere again, in town to be sure. Something was going on between him and the girls' mother – Mrs Delgrano, Peggy – Maureen was certain of it. Why did he do these things? Oh Lance . . . Oh Lance . . . And the disturbance of the last few minutes was still troubling her. It was painful to realise that people she'd thought had rather liked her had, in fact, cared nothing for her after all. She'd given them work when they'd needed it, and that was all there'd been. Gone from them was every shred of the respect that Maureen had believed herself entitled to. It was chastening.

But she could not sit here all day, depressed and withdrawn. She got up, opened the window and called out to the girls.

'We're going to see Mr Britton. Just go and have a little wash.'

She changed into her brown brogues with the fancy scalloped tongues but left on her Jaeger tweed skirt and white silk blouse. It was a warm, still day. There had been no rain for almost a week. This was proving to be the best summer she could remember in years.

With Francesca and Carla running ahead and Tidgy clinging to her hand, she left the house by the side door. The leaves of the large hostas, growing in the two tulip-shaped urns on their plinths at the top of the steps, were wilting. Perhaps Mr Sobell, the gardener, would come along and water them.

Formerly, the gardens out here had been so extensive and demanding that four men had been needed to keep up with them – but that had changed now, like many other things about the place.

On the death of her profligate father, who had spent a fortune on his obsessions and lost a fortune on wildly unwise investments, Maureen had been shocked to discover that the estate was indebted to a degree far more than she'd expected. Perhaps because he'd not lived long enough, debts were still outweighed by assets and there was no question of bankruptcy, but the financial constraints on Maureen were still severe. On advice from her accountant and agent, and with the cooperation of the bank, she had agreed a plan that would, she fervently hoped, in six or seven years' time achieve her heartfelt determination to balance the books.

Quietly and privately she had sold some of her father's African collections, some of his paintings, his objectionable books and his disgusting erotica – which had raised a sum that had truly surprised her. She had closed more than half the house, draped the furniture with dust sheets and closed the doors and locked them, intending that no one should enter them again until better days. After several weeks, their windows had grown cataracts of dust like old eyes and she'd had to let people in to clean them. But immediately that was done, the doors were locked again. Staff had been paid off and had gone without rancour – including Bevan, her father's butler, and Mrs Groves, the housekeeper. (They had actually got married and gone to Lord Moston in Dorset.) And out here, where she now released Tidgy to run after the other two girls, out here under the warm sun, the gardens had been reduced to an area small enough for Mr Sobell to manage easily enough alone. She could see signs of him. From the dell beyond the rockery a round, unruffled column of smoke was rising straight into the sky. Mr Sobell loved to light fires.

A young hedge of rosemary marked the new, reduced boundary of the gardens. Taking advantage of the Government's wartime encouragement to turn land over to food production, Maureen had handed the rest of the gardens to Mr Britton at Home Farm, and where there had once been rose beds and shrubberies and winding paths there now bristled the green heads of celery and cabbage. Francesca waited, holding open the old wrought-iron gate for Maureen to pass through. 'Thank you, dear.'

From here the footpath went on for a hundred yards between wheat fields, and then joined the lane to Home Farm, an old brick building, quite large, with thick grey thatch, three chimneys and five bedrooms. In the wide yard between the house and the stable block, chickens squawked away from the girls, who wanted to take a close look at them. Mr Britton was just entering at the far side of the yard, leading a huge, fully harnessed shire horse by its bridle. He was pleased to see Maureen, greeted her with a smile and came over. 'Hello, ma'am. What can I do for you on this very nice morning?'

He was only a little taller than Maureen herself, but thick and solid and still young – only thirty-five. He was wearing an open-necked check shirt, grey corduroy trousers, big boots and leather gaiters. His sun-bleached brown hair was longer than the short back and sides of the day, and he had a good-looking, small-featured face, brown and smooth-skinned.

For a moment, Maureen felt a little intimidated by the great size of the horse, which jerked up its head and took Mr Britton's arm with it. The tufts of hair about its ankles trembled, the massive muscles of its shoulders flexed and the chains of its harness jangled.

'Don't worry about Hero,' Mr Britton smiled. 'He's just saying hello. He's shed a shoe. I'm waiting for the travelling farrier. He should be here any minute.'

'We once had a blacksmith in the village,' Maureen said. 'But that was before your time, of course. Yes – Mr Godber. When he died, his son lost interest in the work and turned the place into the garage on Hillside. Of course, cars were becoming the thing then.'

'Oh I know Jim Godber, of course. He looks after our tractors. What can I do for you?'

'Well I'm afraid we need more butter.'

'Why didn't you phone? I'd have sent some up. I've told you, I can send you as much as you want – every Friday.'

'Well the thing is, Mr Britton, I'm doing my best to stick to the ration.'

He laughed. 'Oh now, ma'am . . .'

'Well, I mean . . .'

'With a great herd of Friesians and another great herd of Lincolnshire red poll, who can expect you to go without butter? I'll find someone to handle Hero and then I'll get some for you.'

Mr Britton turned away, but she stopped him.

'It's all right – I'm in no hurry. See to the horse. I take it your mother's at home?'

'Yes. I think you'll find her in the kitchen.'

'Then I'll talk to her. Bring me the butter when you're ready.'

As Maureen crossed to the farmhouse door, she paused and stared away at Mr Britton's broad back. There was an air of the forlorn about the young man nowadays, she felt, a sense of sadness behind his eyes. Two years ago, his wife Eileen, a timid little thing, so shy that she could never really look you in the face, the mother of Mr Britton's two young sons, had shocked everyone who knew her and run off with a seed salesman, taking the boys with her. What scars that sort of thing must leave on people's hearts . . .

Mr Britton, instinctively aware that he was under observation, turned his head, saw her gazing at him, and waved an arm.

Mr Britton's widowed mother had come to live with him after the departure of his wife. Neatly dressed in a pink frock and a little pinny, she was a lady who took care of her appearance. Even indoors she was wearing a nice pair of white shoes with Cuban heels. She was ironing at the kitchen table and invited Maureen to sit down facing her.

'Shall I make you a drink?' she asked.

'Thank you, no. It's all right. You carry on.'

'I see the three girls are with you,' said Mrs Britton, nodding at the open door beyond which the girls were running about in the yard and making a lot of noise.

'Yes. Where do they get the energy?'

'Where's the little boy – Clifford?'

'I've lost him, I'm afraid. I thought he'd be happy with us, but ah well . . . His father came for him. A nice man, but it was a wrench to part. I'd got very fond of Clifford.'

'Well, you can't expect much else, really, can you? After all, however so humble, home's home. Kids can tolerate a lot so long as they're with their mam.'

'Yes, I suppose so.'

'In any case, there aren't many evacuees left in the village, are there? Most of them've gone.'

'Yes,' said Maureen. 'The majority went home for Christmas last year and never came back. There'd been no bombing in town, of course. Evacuation seemed a waste of time I suppose. I had two teenage boys. Very boisterous. They were only with me for two months before they vanished. Then I was lucky to get Tidgy. Carla and Francesca came much later. The lady they were with, Mrs Brougham on Front Street, was taken ill – she actually died, poor thing – and I think they wanted to go home then. I was asked to look after them for just two or three days in May – but here they still are.'

'You enjoy them.'

'Yes, I do. I know they get homesick now and then, but the older girls' mother, Mrs Delgrano, does see them. She's been over four times. Yes . . . She works, you see, and so I suppose that affects the situation at home. And Tidgy seems quite happy with me.'

'I'm sure they all are.' Mrs Britton was using an electric iron plugged in to the light socket. She worked with some dedication.

'You like ironing?' Maureen observed.

Mrs Britton held up a neatly folded shirt. 'What can be nicer than to put something on that someone's ironed for you with loving care?'

'Loving care isn't always what comes back from the laundry,' Maureen smiled.

Mr Britton appeared in the doorway. 'I've got your butter.'

'I'll be off then, Mrs Britton,' Maureen said, getting up from her chair. 'Thank you for our little talk.'

As Maureen went out into the yard with Britton, there came sounds of hammering from beyond the stables. 'What might that be?' Maureen asked.

'It's that Irishman I told you about.'

'Did you?'

'Yes, I told you I'd set him on. A pal of Michael Philbin's. You know Michael.'

'Do I?'

'A signalman in the box at Baguley Fold. Another Irishman. Nancy — the one who works in the post office — she's his wife.'

'Oh, I know Nancy.'

'Well this man's a pal of theirs.'

'What's his name?'

'Brendan — Brendan Kelly. He's damned good with the plough and an excellent worker. He saw old Langland's cottage and said he could do it up for us.'

'But it was falling down.'

'True, but he tells me he worked as a builder for Birmingham Council, building council houses, and reckons he can fix it. So I'm letting him have a go. If he can do it, I told him he could live there. That's all right with you, isn't it? The place was worthless. If for fifty pounds he can make it worth three hundred, what can we lose?'

'Oh, well, I leave it to you, Mr Britton. Can I go and see?'

'Yes. I'll come with you.'

There was a new door on the old cottage and new window frames. As Maureen and Britton stepped inside, Brendan faced them, standing with a saw in his hand. 'Hello there,' he said brightly. The floor was littered with wood shavings, sawdust, planks of wood, bags of nails and screws.

'Hello,' Maureen responded, deciding at once that she liked this cheerful, buoyant little Irishman.

'Want to look at my handiwork?' Brendan asked.

'Yes,' said Maureen. 'Yes, please.'

Since, because of the army, the beach and thereabouts were out of bounds to them, as indeed was the green, the children had to find their entertainment in the village itself. All through August, while the summer holidays lasted, all corners rang to the noises of their play. Cries of 'Howzat!' and acrimonious debates about leg before wicket echoed from the boys' corner of the cricket field, pierced the air and, slowly fading, crept quietly through open back doors to the ears of mothers washing their children's clothes, scrubbing away their grime and sweating over the boiler.

From where the girls were gathered, little rhythmical songs punctuated the afternoons – 'A house to let, apply within, Mrs Smith goes out, Mrs Jones comes in' – as skipping ropes slapped the ground and girls in thin frocks with flapping ribbons in their hair jumped and bounced and giggled. Children came and went from the shops, sometimes happily for things for themselves – the *Dandy* or *Sunny Stories* or something off their sweet ration – and not so happily when running errands. They darted about on their bikes, wrestled on the grass verges, laughed and shouted in their den in the ditch on Main Street, and skipped home, sweating, every now and then for a drink of water.

But, on the first Monday of September, the schools reopened. Some kids went back to their classrooms in the village. Older ones went by bus to the secondary school at Fulstow, and others went by bus to the grammar school at Louth. And suddenly the village was deathly quiet under a sun rising lower and lower in the sky each noon. All you heard now of the children was that 'four-fours-are-sixteen, five-fours-are-twenty, six-fours-are-twenty-four, seven-fours-are-twenty-eight . . .' if you passed the school. There was, on certain mornings, a little, almost sad, hint of autumn in the air.

Flocks of birds, coming like dark clouds from the west, descended on the village. Chirping and screaming, they gathered along telegraph wires and on the roof ridges of cottages for a last rest before flapping away into the vastness of the North Sea. Weeds and tall stalks of grass at the roadside were turning brown and brittle. The freshness of sycamore and chestnut leaves was fading and they were growing rather stiff and wizened, like the hands of old men.

Further south, the air battle of Britain was reaching its climax. On the nine o'clock news one evening, people heard that Hitler had vowed to bomb London to destruction and everyone knew that the enemy was assembling large numbers of barges in preparation for the invasion. It was a great reassurance to see soldiers about the village and to know that they were there, guarding the coast. On the wind, sometimes, you could hear their bugle calls, especially the plaintive notes of reveille coming muted and frail out of the morning mists.

Down there on the beach, from north to south, as far as could be seen, stretched an unbroken chaos of concrete dragon's-teeth tank obstacles, deep ditches, pillboxes and echelons of jagged metal rods, designed to tear the bottoms out of those barges. Higher up the slope a minefield, over a hundred yards in depth, had been laid. (One of these mines went off one night, spontaneously, throwing up a fountain of sand and alerting the camp. Answering to shouts and bugle calls, a thousand men came running to their posts.) And then, after the mines, came another fifty yards or so of coiled barbed wire, slowly growing rusty under the salt breeze.

Corrugated-iron Nissen huts were arranged, again in echelons, on those old stamping grounds of Arthur Swift and his pals, and there was more barbed wire enclosing the camp as a whole. Over the guardroom near the gate flew the Union Jack. Next to the guardroom was the commanding officer's office, with a bare wood floor and the regimental crest expertly painted on the outside of the door.

The front of the Lancashire Rifles extended from opposite the beet factory at Tetney to opposite the stump of the old windmill at Somercotes, just beyond Evers' factory. To the north of them were the 2nd North Yorkshires. To the south were the 1st East Staffordshires.

By now, the other two companies, C and D, of the Lancashire Rifles had been here for three weeks. They had brought their colonel with them. He now sat at his desk, wading through a heap of papers from Division. They seemed to him to be delivering nothing but trivia, silly new orders and ridiculous, unnecessary changes to orders that already existed. But it was usually like that. He was thoroughly bored with it and wished he could just throw the lot into the waste-paper basket. An orderly knocked and poked his head around the inner door. 'Major Bates, sir.'

'Send him in.'

The colonel was grateful for the interruption. He pushed aside the papers and, merely to stretch his legs, stood up as Bates came in. Lieutenant Colonel Roper was not a tall man – barely five foot ten. Side by side with Bates, his second in command, he might look rather like a younger brother for, though the scale was different, the structure and the outline of their bodies were similar. No spare flesh, traceable bones under the tight skin of their faces and similar staccato movements. But in fact, at forty-three, the colonel was older than Bates by seven years and had commanded the battalion since 1937.

'Morning, sir,' said Bates, standing there with his cap under his arm.

'Jack . . . Sit down.' The colonel stretched, sighed, and sat down himself. 'What is it?'

'The new PTI's turned up. There's a platoon at it already.'

'About time. After that fiasco at La Bassée when we were run around in circles for three days we know damn well that stamina makes the difference between life and death. After sitting about here for weeks they're beginning to creak.'

'I left some charge sheets for you.'

'Signed. In the orderly room. No mercy.'

'They expect none.'

'Anything else?'

'Well . . .'

'Well what?'

Major Bates was hesitant.

'What is it?' But then the colonel thought of something else. 'Division're moaning on about demarcation now. Reams of it here . . . Let's look at the map.'

The map, a large-scale representation of the coast hereabouts, patched with various colours and decorated with forests of coloured pinheads, was mounted against the wall and both men went to stand before it. The colonel jabbed at it with a finger. 'All this is the open ground behind us. Two miles. Then the second line. Then the reserve lines and Divisional HQ. What they're saying now is that the two miles isn't enough. They're bloody well going to move back and leave us to ourselves on the beach. Meanwhile, the silly sods're telling us to sidestep at both sides while the Yorks and Staffs sidestep behind us.'

'Why?'

'Because they must have some fool up there who's never served in line. They've got the notion that the demarcations are vulnerable and that we can be outflanked by a quick rush.'

'I'd like to see anyone do a quick rush up this beach,' Bates said.

'Well, that's what they want. Anyway, there's some good news. They're bringing up more artillery . . .'

The conversation went on. A laden lorry drove past the window, shaking the floor, and there were laughing shouts from the driver to someone in the guardroom. Down on the open space by the canteen, twenty men, stripped to the waist, were doing knee bends for minutes on end. At the doorways of pillboxes, men sat on cases of machine-gun ammunition, read or simply dreamed. Sergeant Major Pelham, walking briskly with his stick tucked under his left arm, was doing his rounds of the billets, and in his surgery the medical officer was at his desk, coping with sick parade. As he very well knew, bored men often became aware of aches and ailments that were not there. 'No treatment,' he said, over and over again. 'Back to duty . . .'

'Anything else?' the colonel asked.

'Well, yes, there is,' Major Bates admitted.

'Go on.'

'Lockyer.'

'Again?'

'I'm afraid so.'

'What is it this time?'

'The same as always. He's a disruptive element. He's a bloody menace.'

'We've had all this before, Major Bates.'

'But he gets no better.'

'He has his own style.'

'Colonel, forgive me, but you can go on too long giving a man chances. You know that better than I do.'

'He's a gallant officer, Jack.'

'What he did at La Bassée was foolhardy.'

'That's a matter of opinion.'

'Well I can tell you what opinion his men have of him. They don't call it gallantry when a man leads three of them to a pointless death for the sake of his own bloody – bloody glory. They think he's an idiot, and once men get that idea they'll never follow an officer again.'

The colonel sighed. 'We've been through all this.'

'Apart from that he treats them like shit.'

'I've spoken to him about that.'

'Well it's done no good. Lockyer has nothing but contempt for them and they resent it like hell. Get rid of him.'

'He was seconded to us for six months. They'll get rid of him for us when the time comes.'

'Get rid of him now, sir. I ask that of you.'

The colonel flapped his hands. There were so many things on his mind that this was now annoying him. 'Right – right . . . I'll speak to Brigade. Will that do?'

'Thanks, sir.' Major Bates came to attention. 'Every man in the battalion will be grateful. Morning, sir.' Out he went, through the orderly room, to collect the charge sheets.

The colonel returned his attention to that wad of papers, sighed again, lit a cigarette and concentrated.

Later that day there was an air alert further down the coast. Confused sounds were heard, like the furious tearing of canvas sheets. The Staffs, and the Berkshires to the south of them, were being shot up by low-flying Messerschmitt

109s. It lasted only a few seconds, but two Berkshires were killed.

The village had not been touched. Nevertheless, the two air-raid wardens went again to check that the shelter near the church was in fit condition, and villagers went out to make sure their Anderson shelters had not flooded again.

At evensong that Sunday, the Reverend Samuel Duke, DD, climbed the six steps to the pulpit. From the little lamp that lit the pages of his sermon, a pale yellow glow reached up and touched his head with halo tints.

'Before I begin,' he said, 'I have a sad announcement to make. Aircraftman Harvey Jennings, Royal Air Force, of 12 Back Street, son of John and Sarah Jennings who are with us this evening, has been reported killed in action during raids on airfields. We share the pain of his loss and offer all our sincerest sympathy to his parents.'

Samuel Duke had come to replace Douglas Russell.

8

A Get-together

Samuel Duke was in his late sixties. For a quarter of a
century he had been rector of a populous and very busy
parish in north Manchester. During the latter two of those
years he'd been without even a curate's assistance. Calls
on his time had been constant and demands on his faith
had been taxing. He had borne the cross through waste-
lands of soulless poverty and done his best to hold it aloft
in the midst of industrial strife and despair. Over and over
again, he had watched people die in crumbling slums from
diseases generated by the very homes in which they lived
and he had, by his protests and useless campaigns, made
enemies in high places.

It had tired him out utterly and, desperate for a rest, he
had looked forward to his imminent retirement as a bene-
diction. His wife, Lettice, was rather dull, and sometimes
difficult, but always loving. They had not been blessed with
children, but Samuel had long since ceased to fret about
that. The problem now was that Lettice's attitude to retirement was different from his. The thought of it frightened
her.

When the church appealed to Samuel to stay on and take
over another parish he had refused at once, against Lettice's
wishes. But he was reminded that there was a war on and

that we must all pull together. He was asked at least to take a look at the place they wished to send him, and he would have refused even that but for Lettice's renewed resistance. 'We'll go and look,' she insisted. 'We'll go, Samuel . . . Please, please . . .'

And, to avoid the sight of more tears in her eyes, he had relented. She telephoned for train times and they went together one Monday morning.

It had changed everything. For each of them there was a moment of delight. With Lettice it occurred as they walked down the pathway to the vicarage. Its old hand-made brick, its shining bay windows under their eyebrows of old red pantiles, its comfortable nestling in a bower of trees, its tremendous sense of dignity, captivated her at once, and its beamed interior, polished wood floors, deep quiet and sense of peacefulness were irresistible. She prepared herself to demand, to beg, to bully, to do anything necessary to change Samuel's mind.

But, in fact, there was no need to go on pressing him. His decision had been made the second he stepped through the porch into the church. For twenty-five years he had ministered from a giant, black, soot-encrusted mock-Gothic cavern set among grim terraced houses, sombre both inside and out, full of sad ghosts. What he now confronted was an intimate little church whose interior glowed with sunlight, as warm-hearted as an old friend might be, all pale cream stone with great pillars along its nave, old oak pews with carved end posts, and a chancel most colourful with flowers.

While Lettice walked slowly about the vicarage, he had walked slowly about this ancient place of worship, noting the dedicatory plaques carved into the walls, touching this, touching that. He stood by the font, tracing with his finger the dim, faded carvings of the apostles and angels. He stood at the lectern and turned over pages of the great Bible. He climbed to the pulpit and gazed away into the far shadows. The ghosts in this church, he was sure, were all perfectly benign.

As they travelled back to Manchester on the train, both of them felt quite excited at their prospects of a new lease of life.

Samuel's tiredness had lifted, as if he'd been given a powerful injection of adrenalin, and he couldn't wait to make the move. What he had wanted in his retirement anyway was a retreat to the country. What more charming a village could he have chosen than this? People in the street raised their hats to you and smiled and said 'Good day'. The cottages were like picture postcards and there were trees everywhere rather than factory chimneys. Indeed, after Manchester, this ministry might itself be virtually a rest cure. The fact that he must step down in the hierarchy from rector to vicar was of no account. God had offered him the perfect opportunity to take life very much easier and yet at the same time to go on serving.

Since he was to become comforter, friend and spiritual

mentor to the people of this delightful village, his first obligation was to introduce himself to them as quickly as possible, and soon after his arrival he found a way. Next door to the church and under its auspices was a very nice, quite sizeable village hall. In Manchester, where, as in most congested cities, people tended to lead introverted, self-obsessed lives and suffer the sense of isolation that followed from that, he had striven to create some adhesion among his flock, some sense of community, and to this end he had organised what he called his get-togethers, occasions when parishioners could meet in an informal and relaxed mood. They had proved to be very successful and this seemed to him to be an ideal way of introducing himself to his new flock.

In Manchester, in order to give some focus to the occasions, he had offered food – the local delicacy, potato pie. Would that sort of thing go down well in the country? He decided that he could but try. And so, on a Saturday evening, there was held at the village hall 'A Grand Potato Pie Supper and Social'. Would people come?

Samuel need not have worried. The hall was full. Under its roof of corrugated asbestos sheeting, bolted to a framework of angle iron, most of the village seemed to be present.

At one end of the hall a section had been partitioned off as a food-preparation area. From it, a serving counter opened into the room. Busy working there were members of the Women's Institute, led by their chairwoman, Phoebe Brocklesby from the Manor, assisted by her number two, Lucy Thomas, formerly the assistant billeting officer. The ladies had rallied round marvellously in the preparation of the fare.

Because of rationing, the potato pie was exactly that
– little or no meat. But the potatoes and onions, laced with
OXO cubes at a penny a time and various savoury herbs,
were all boiled down to a succulent tenderness, moist but
still stiff enough not to dribble from paper plates. People
wanted more. For afters, there were five baskets full of
home-baked rock buns, some less rocky than others.

On the wall by the counter a brass geyser steamed and
Phoebe Brocklesby, who had provided the milk, poured
weak tea from a large, stainless-steel teapot while people,
chatting amiably, intent on enjoying themselves, queued
patiently. There was no sugar.

Most of the other people in the hall were pressed together
in a solid mass, elbow to elbow, trying to dance. In one
corner was a table bearing a gramophone and a pile of
78s. Arthur Swift had been put in charge there. When the
dancing paused, his clear voice rang out against the chatter:
'And now a slow foxtrot to Al Bowlly and "The Very
Thought of You".' In such a dense crowd, the foxtrot –
indeed any kind of movement other than a rhythmical
shuffling of the feet – was impossible, and Al Bowlly's
voice was almost completely drowned.

Along both of the long walls of the hall were pinned
examples of children's artwork from the primary school
– bent houses, contorted cats, ten-foot-tall fathers and
circular mothers with smiles like chasms.

Beneath these paintings chairs and benches had been
arranged. On one of the chairs, where his knees were
bumped by dancers, sat Dr Green. He talked now and then
to people who came to sit near him while they ate or drank,
but he was far from comfortable in such a setting.

His wife, Pat, however, slim and looking years younger than she was in a bold red dress, was dancing virtually non-stop and very much enjoying herself.

Elsewhere, Phoebe's husband, Rupert Brocklesby, lord of the manor, plump and healthy in a fine worsted suit, was standing conversing with two local men, tenants of his, who listened with respectful interest to his every word.

Samuel Duke himself, beaming and lively, mingled with his parishioners. His wife, Lettice, released from behind the counter where there were in any case too many helpers, trailed after him. She smiled now and then, but, as always, there hung about her an air of inward-looking stillness. People were not quite sure how to take her. Samuel himself was excited. He was a small man with a mouse-like face, not at all unpleasant, and, as he thrust his head forward in conversation, his nose could almost seem to twitch as a mouse's nose can twitch.

Fotherby was dancing with his intimate friend Joan Feathers, who clung to him, gazing into his face like a young lover.

The Commodore stood near the counter, watching them, smiling with amusement, trying to find suitable words to put to Fotherby when they next came face to face. 'You dance like a rhinoceros,' perhaps. But, at that moment, Samuel came and touched his elbow.

'Good evening, Commodore. Thank you for coming. People seem to be enjoying themselves, don't you think?'

Just dancing by at that moment was a young soldier home on leave, with a girl from Church Lane. Elsewhere there were several more men in army uniform – the Lancashire Rifles had infiltrated. They had not been invited, but no one was prepared to ask them to go. They were very noticeable. Two or three of them were dancing with Land Girls, but others had cornered, or were trying to corner, girls from the village. There was one sailor in fore-and-aft rig. There were happy faces everywhere.

'Yes,' the Commodore said. 'They do.'

'Have you had your pie?'

'Yes. I enjoyed it.'

'Good, good . . .' Samuel nodded. 'The ladies have done wonders with so little. But everyone's been generous. Sacks of potatoes were delivered to the vicarage doorstep and we never knew there were so many herbs and things you could use, did we, Lettice? Townies, you see. Things are so very different in the country and—'

Suddenly, Samuel's gaze was drawn away from the Commodore's face as if by an imperious shout. But it was not a shout. It was a smile – and a very odd one at that. It was on the face of a lady, Pat Green, the doctor's wife, dancing quite close by in her vivid red frock, and it was direct, emphatic, nothing like a mere greeting but in fact almost like a challenge. Odd, indeed. It stopped Samuel in mid breath, commanded all his attention and quite trans-fixed him. His expression froze. His brows lowered and he frowned. Then he looked down. He was silent for a moment.

'Where were we, Commodore?'

'I was saying that I enjoyed the pie. In the navy we called that sort of thing mashers. But it was never a patch on what the galley's dished up here.' He turned to Lettice. 'Are you settling down in the village?' he asked.

'Yes.' She found him a smile. When it came it was quite

pleasant. 'I love the country and I love the vicarage. So different from Manchester. It's a long time since I felt so comfortable.'

'Good,' said the Commodore. 'I'm glad.'

But Samuel had grown silent. He was frowning again, deep in thought. The music had stopped and the dancers were scuffling about like a busy culture on a laboratory slide. Pat Green had gone to stand by her husband who still sat looking out of place against the wall, and Samuel was gazing directly across at her, thinking, thinking. 'You know, Lettice,' he said, 'I think I know that lady.'

'Which lady?' Lettice asked.

'The one in the red dress, standing over there.'

'You mean Pat Green,' the Commodore said. 'The doctor's wife.'

'Ah – is that who she is? Pat, yes, yes . . .'

'She's been looking at you,' Lettice said, with a vague air of disapproval.

'Yes,' said Samuel. 'Yes. I'm sure we know each other. Will you excuse me for a moment, dear . . . Commodore?' Nodding to them both, he walked away.

Lettice watched him go, frowning a little herself now, and the Commodore wondered what next he might say to her. 'Yes,' he said, 'it's a nice little village. A true bit of old England.'

That peculiar smile appeared again on Pat's face as Samuel eased himself through the crowd towards her. 'Ah,' she said, 'so you've remembered, have you?'

'Is it Pat Grainger . . .?'

'Of course it is!' Pat laughed. 'But Pat Green these many years. When I heard we had a vicar called Samuel Duke I wondered if it could possibly be the same person. I'd no idea you'd gone into the Church.'

'Well, yes, yes . . .' said Samuel, flustered, growing a little red in the face. 'Pat – well fancy that. What a lovely coincidence . . . I can't believe it. Why haven't we met before? I've been here for three weeks . . . Haven't I seen you at services?'

'No. I've not been to church for ages.' Pat laughed again. 'But I might come more often now. I recognised you at once this evening, as soon as I saw you.'

'Why didn't you come and speak to me?'

'I thought that was up to you. Either you remembered or you didn't.'

'But how could I forget? How long have you lived in the village?'

'Oh donkey's years.'

'Well, well, well . . .' said Samuel, smiling, twitching his nose. 'Pat Grainger . . . Well, well, well.'

Dr Green, who had not so far been introduced, annoyed by that fact and in any case by now quite fed up with the evening, got to his feet and, very brusquely, said, 'Well then, Pat, it's time we were off to bed.' He gave the vicar a rather hard look. 'We're off.'

Samuel was disappointed. 'Oh,' he said. 'Oh, I'm sorry you have to go . . .'

'This is my husband, Samuel,' Pat said.

'Oh – hello . . . Delighted to meet you.' Samuel held out his hand, but Dr Green didn't seem to notice it.

'I'm worked off my feet, you know,' he said. 'And I expect to be called out to deliver Mrs Bone sometime tonight.'

'No, dear,' said Pat. 'She'll be another week at least.'

She turned to Samuel. The music had started again. 'Come along,' she said, taking Samuel's arm. 'You can do the waltz, can't you?' And she bore him away into the throng.

With his arm around her waist, looking into her bright eyes, Samuel felt a surge of unaccustomed joy. 'Pat, Pat . . .' he said again, smelling her discreet perfume, seeing again a young woman whose warm and friendly smile came back to him through the fog of years. 'How long must it be?'

'Oh God – don't ask that, Samuel. You know, you've hardly changed.'

'Nonsense – I'm an old man.'

'Well, don't tell me I'm an old woman because I won't have it. You ought to've recognised me at once. I kept trying to make you.'

'It was the place – so unexpected. But of course I recognised you.'

But then Samuel saw that both Lettice and the Commodore were watching him from the sidelines. The Commodore's face was quite expressionless. But there was something in Lettice's eyes that disturbed him. 'Look, Pat,' he said, 'forgive me – I'm so sorry – but I really ought to be circulating, you know . . .'

'Rubbish. Finish the dance. Tell me what happened to you after Cheltenham . . .'

With a moan, Dr Green had sat down again.

At half-past eight, Maureen Binbrook looked in, said hello to the Brocklesbys and others, and went home again to her evacuees.

Just after nine, Constable Harry Bowker broke off his rounds and came to stand in the hall doorway. The badge on his helmet glittered and for a few minutes he cast that high-headed gaze of his about the room, noting that some of the younger ones were a bit boisterous. Kenneth Young was among them. That lad wanted watching. But since everything seemed under control, he said good evening and went out again.

A few minutes later, Bert Silk, one of the local full-time air-raid wardens, in his tin hat and navy-blue uniform with the silver buttons and yellow armband, came down to make sure no lights were showing. 'Don't forget,' he said to Samuel, 'if anything happens, the air-raid shelter's only a few yards away. If we have to set the siren off, I'll be down to see you're all OK.'

One of Arthur's old schoolmates had joined him in the corner: Dorothy Kent, in a white frock and with straight blonde hair. She was fourteen now, as indeed Arthur had been for three weeks, but, unlike Arthur, she had left school and was working days at Evers' factory.

'My father works there now,' Arthur told her.

'Yes, I know. He gets off the bus with Tom Jenks when I get on. Isn't he clever?'

'Well he is. He might be blind but he can make all sorts of things – he made a smashing workbox for my mother last week and he can do his job at Evers as well as anyone . . . I think he's got eyes in his hands – you should see him read Braille.'

Arthur was wearing a new pair of grey flannel trousers and a new white shirt. Since his father had found work, finances at home were very much better, and Arthur had not yet grown out of the habit of earning a copper or two himself. He was getting two shillings to operate the gramophone this evening.

'Can I choose a record?' Dorothy asked.

'Sure.'

She chose 'There's a Small Hotel' and Arthur put it on for her.

'You want to dance?' Dorothy asked.

They joined the rest mooching around the floor, but Dorothy soon drove him back to his corner because he couldn't dance properly and was bruising her feet.

'Well, I'll walk you home later,' he said.

'Oh will you! I might not want you to.'

The sound of music and the cheerful laughter emanating from the village hall crept away between the trees, over the gravestones in the churchyard and out into the night. For a while it was counterpointed with the sound of high-flying aircraft, clearly not German because the air-raid sirens would have sounded.

On the wirelesses of people who had stayed at home, Gert and Daisy were singing songs and cracking mildly risqué jokes. On Front Street, the Fletchers, Mr and Mrs, were drinking tea with the Johnsons. The question was, should there be an invasion, what ought they really to do? Should they wait for instructions, as advised, or should they take matters into their own hands, grab what they could and take to the road?

Either option was terrible. When the Germans had invaded France and Belgium, hadn't they used rape as a means of suppressing people who'd stayed behind? But hadn't they also machine-gunned refugees who'd tried to escape along the roads? Such conversations had been staple fare for weeks. However, Mr Fletcher was still convinced that the Germans could never foul the shores of England

– what, with the finest navy in the world against them and our boys here on the beach ready to mow them down? In any case, even if they did, they would not come here. It was too far north.

Growing tired of that subject, they sat and listened to the wireless like their neighbours.

Down towards Somercotes, seeping through the walls of Evers' single-storey factory with its black-painted windows to keep in the light, came the sound of other gramophone music and the voices of the workers singing along with *Music While You Work*: 'You are my sunshine, my only sunshine, you make me happy when skies are grey . . .'

It was not until almost midnight that the Reverend Samuel Duke and his wife Lettice were able to go up to bed. Lettice was a little quieter even than usual, but Samuel was quite buoyant and chirpy.

Lettice combed her hair. What possessed her again at this moment was the sense of comfort and security this lovely old house imparted to her soul. She had been brought up in a lovely house, but could never forget the heartache of having to leave it and move with her mother into a hovel in Woolwich because her father had died and left them penniless. They had been awful years. The thought of them made her shudder. She never wanted to endure the shame, the penury, the terrible cramped discomfort of it again. Never. And, on her marriage to Samuel, it had indeed seemed unlikely that she would. The vicarages, the rectories she had lived in with him – even in Manchester – had been roomy and agreeable once you closed their doors to the world. She had been happy pottering about in them, secure enough on Samuel's small but manageable income, content to earn her comfort doing all that a clergyman's wife ought to do. But she had no money of her own, and after a lifetime of doing God's work, Samuel, not very provident and too generous, had managed to set very little aside. And what use was his pension likely to be? Where would she be now if he'd persisted in his determination to retire? Trapped in a tiny cottage somewhere, skimping again, ashamed, counting every coin, growing old and miserable like so many poor women she had known in Manchester. She closed her eyes and thanked God for His blessings.

Changing into a bell tent of a nightdress with ruches and rose-coloured embroidery about the neck, she got into bed.

Samuel folded his trousers. He was humming cheerfully to himself.

'You never mentioned you knew a woman in Cheltenham,' Lettice said.

'She wasn't a woman, dear. She was a girl – just a girl. Would you mind if I read for a while?'

Lettice turned on her side, presenting her back to him. This meant, 'No, read as much as you like.'

Samuel found his book, *Of Human Bondage* by Somerset Maugham, switched on the light at his side of the bedhead and settled down to chapter 6.

Lettice's breathing soon became steady. A fox screamed outside. A fly buzzed for a moment about Samuel's head. But then the printed words of the book began to grow misty and finally vanished from his sight. Old memories had taken possession of him.

He saw a fresh-faced, happy young girl walking beside him along the pavement of the street where both of them had lived in an age gone by. He had been fascinated by her then, thrilled at every sight of her, and as he lay there all that old excitement, all those old longings, arose in him again. He smiled to himself. His book lay open across his chest and he was dancing again with his arm about her waist, waltzing an hour ago with the very same girl. Pat Grainger – lovely young Pat with her long, slim legs, those fluttering hands, those shining eyes . . . Lovely Pat . . .

The surging emotion that thoughts of her had aroused in him suddenly sent shocks of alarm through his heart. 'Oh no . . .!'

On the following Wednesday evening, just after nine o'clock, Maureen said, 'Yes, it's checkmate. You've beaten me again.' She smiled. 'I told you I was no good at this – I haven't played for years.' She gathered the chess pieces.

Brendan pushed the box across the table for her to put the pieces away. 'You'll get better,' he said.

They were in Maureen's private room at Pretoria House. A few days ago, Brendan had been invited to the house to repair a damaged spindle in the staircase bannister. It had been cracked when Maureen had some furniture shifted about. In the old days, David Heath would have done such work, but of course he was far away now – and hadn't Maureen watched this rather pleasant Irishman sawing and chiselling in Langland's old cottage? He'd repaired the spindle, been called into the office to be paid and spotted the chess box there. He'd opened it. Ivory and jet. 'Ah! You play chess. Would you fancy a game sometime?'

There had been something utterly disarming about him and Maureen, who would normally have been reluctant to show favour to hired help, found herself saying 'Yes.'

Accordingly, Brendan had arrived this evening at nine o'clock. Maureen herself had made coffee for him. It was an hour when the house was otherwise very quiet – Lance out, Veronica gone home, the children in bed – and while they played the only sound was that of the Venetian clock on Maureen's mantelpiece ticking away the seconds.

'I'll bet you get pretty lonely, don't you?' Brendan said.

'Oh no. I'm always so busy.'

But Brendan was able to detect another little shadow in her eyes. Of course this rather snooty, pink-faced English spinster was lonely.

'Would you like more coffee?' she asked.

He said no and the little, passing flicker of disappointment on her face was not lost on him. 'But can I come again sometime? Can I call you Maureen?'

She hesitated, but only briefly. 'Yes,' she said to both questions. As she showed him out of the side door, he said, 'Don't worry, no one saw me come and no one will see me go. Good night, Maureen.'

Brendan had become an habitué of the Black Bull, and that was where he made his way now. It was just coming up to ten o'clock. He had bought himself a motorbike and the journey took him less than five minutes.

He was popular at the Black Bull. As his laughing face appeared around the door of the best room and his greeting 'Evenin' all!' was heard, it was as if a bright new light had been switched on. Heads were raised, smiles met him, and if you happened to be standing at the bar – as several usually were, chatting to Charley or Mary – you could be sure he'd buy you a drink. He always seemed to have plenty of money. Tonight, he bought pints for two bystanders and a drink each for Charley and Mary.

He had brought his tin whistle with him, tucked down his sock. He played 'Phil the Fluter's Ball' for them and was rewarded with two pints for the effort.

The room was packed. Many Lancashire Rifles were in there, one or two with local girls.

Just before ten o'clock, three soldiers in white gaiters – a provost party from the camp – arrived in an army jeep. In charge of them was Captain Lockyer. While the other two marched into the pub, Lockyer sat in the jeep to light a cigarette. Then he followed.

As the two soldiers pushed their way into the best room, other soldiers present said, 'Shit, oh Christ . . . Oh bloody hell, Fred! Piss off!'

Fred was the white-gaitered corporal. 'Let's see your passes, lads,' he said.

Lockyer, tall, smoking his cigarette, bored, stood in the doorway. The glances that met him were openly hostile – very. But one of the soldiers, grinning, raised his pint. 'Cheers, Captain Lockyer.'

'Mother's milk is it, Cooper?' Lockyer said, blowing out smoke. 'Your trouble, children, is that you've never been weaned.'

Somebody said, 'Balls!' but Lockyer only smiled. 'Take that man's name and number,' he said, about-turning and marching out.

Half an hour later the provost party arrived back at the camp. Lockyer stepped down from the jeep, waved a dismissal to the other two men and walked towards the guardroom. From it, greeting him with a salute, came young Second Lieutenant Barker.

'Good evening,' Lockyer said. 'We've not met.'

'No,' said Barker, 'I joined on Tuesday.'

'Poor sod. You're Barker.'

'Yes, sir.'

'I'm Lockyer.'

'Yes, I know.'

'What accent's that?'

'Pardon, sir?'

'Where d'you come from?'

'Bolton.'

'Ah, then you'll feel at home with this lot. I can't tell what they're saying half the time. I'm seconded from the Grenadiers.'

'I see, sir.'

'Well, good luck to you. You'll need it with this bloody awful rabble . . .' And Lockyer walked away.

Second Lieutenant Barker went back into the guardroom. Lockyer's attitude had troubled him. He was wondering at it.

The orderly sergeant looked at him. 'Yes, sir,' he said. 'Watch the bugger.'

'Pardon, Sergeant?'

'Just watch him.'

'It's an officer you're talking about.'

'Is it? Some bloody officer. You just watch him, sir.'

'You shouldn't be talking like this.'

'Well who can hear us? Look . . .' He was a sergeant with fifteen years' service. The second lieutenant was down from officer training school after only three months. 'Look, son, the man's an utter bastard. He gets men killed. He's a swine. And I'm telling you, steer clear of him.'

9
Veronica's Journey; an Air Raid

On 7 September, German bombs fell on London, killing many and creating extensive damage along the banks of the Thames. This was the first reported bombing of civilians and it was clear that the war was entering a frightening new phase.

Since they had no Anderson shelter in their garden and were quite a distance from the village's communal shelter, Arthur helped his mother to arrange a snug little retreat under the stairs – a camp bed for her and cushions, which she had made herself, for the other two. He dug out the gas masks, long since stuffed away in a cupboard, just in case.

'Don't worry, Mam,' he said. 'Under the stairs is the safest place of all. I'll leave a pack of cards here. We can have a game of snap if they decide to come.'

Arthur had given a few lawns a mowing lately and had actually decorated Mrs Foster's front parlour with wallpaper. It was thin, cheap stuff, excess stock from somewhere in town, and needed trimming with scissors before it could be used. But he considered that the job he'd made of it was excellent. Mrs Foster agreed. 'You can't see the joins,' she said. 'How'd you manage that?' It was well worth his fee of five shillings, she thought.

As always, the bulk of this went to Arthur's mother. With the rest, one and sixpence, he bought a paperback copy of *War of the Worlds* by H. G. Wells. He was an avid reader. At school he was never lower than third in examinations. Learning came easily to him and he could not understand why it didn't come easily to everyone else. He felt genuine sympathy for Grimshaw, 'Middle-stump' Watson and others who found it so hard. He did his homework in less than an hour. If he had no odd jobs on hand for the moment, he then read or perhaps went to meet the boys at the edge of the cricket field where they usually congregated. Some of them had started smoking – when they could get their hands on cigarettes. Arthur resisted that temptation. His experience of poverty at home had managed to ingrain in him a resistance to pastimes that cost too much money and only made your breath smell anyway.

Arthur had lost one occasional source of income – from his solo singing for weddings and other special occasions. Quite suddenly, during matins one Sunday – halfway through the Te Deum – his beautiful treble voice disintegrated into hoarse cracklings. He sang on, and for a few bars normality resumed. But then it happened again. His pitch had gone. The higher notes of the chant eluded him completely and he hovered there rigid in his glowing white surplice, astonished, embarrassed, almost in tears. The other boys found his cracklings, his croakings, his red-faced, open-mouthed dismay amusing and had difficulty not laughing aloud. But the organist's face, reflected in the mirror above his head, was smiling, not with humour but with the regretful acknowledgement of the inevitable. Something wonderful had vanished from the world.

And so Arthur shed his cassock and surplice for the last time, walked out of the vestry and never saw the inside of the church again. God had long since ceased to mean anything very much to him.

But people remembered his singing. During excerpts from the *Messiah* at Christmas it would be missed.

Arthur had begun to keep a war diary. One night that September, before undressing for bed, he wrote: *The Italians have invaded Egypt and captured a place called Sidi Barrani. It's just inside the border with Libya. The British retreated and I don't like the sound of that. We've not got many soldiers out there, it seems – well it's time we sent some.*

As a matter of fact, the unit of Veronica Heath's lover, Nigel Lawrence, had already been sent to Africa. Nigel, however, had preferred not to go with them.

Twice in two days the air-raid sirens sounded, each time at a few minutes after ten in the evening when the night shift at Evers' factory had just arrived. Production stopped and, shepherded by young Mr Evers, everyone went to press themselves into the shelter. Its size had not been well calculated. Someone declared that it was like the Black Hole of Calcutta in there, and more than one woman fainted on each night. It became therefore a matter of urgency to extend the shelter, but with the shortage of building workers it was not until three weeks later that work actually began.

AIR RAID SHELTER ➡

In the village shelter, meanwhile, there was no overcrowding to complain of, but the place was very damp. People had brought blankets for warmth and cushions to place on the benches and everything was soaking in a matter of minutes. Elsewhere, those who had been fortunate enough to get hold of an Anderson shelter and went down to it with their own blankets and cushions were also troubled by dampness.

Fortunately, both air-raid warnings proved to be false alarms. After an hour the all-clear sounded, but it was apparent that not enough thought had been given to shelters during the previous raid-free months. The air-raid wardens called a meeting in the village hall and allowed people to vent their anger and anxieties on them. They promised to see what could be done to improve conditions in the communal shelter, but could offer no advice as to how Anderson shelters, which were actually dug into the earth, could be kept dry beyond digging drains and putting stoves in them.

However, as time went on, and as false alarms became more and more frequent, people stopped troubling to seek shelter. It had been felt locally that the Germans would be intent on attacking Evers' factory, busy producing parts for British bombers, but it soon became apparent that, although their planes might pass over the coast nearby, and so justify warnings, their targets were actually much further inland.

When German planes did come to shoot up the army camp, they arrived without any warning at all.

Lance was having one of his downers. They usually lasted three or four days, during which he could do nothing but feel sick, cry, think of the shattered corpses of old comrades, and lie about unshaven, unapproachable.

On his return to the house after his years of exile from it, and on discovering that half of the accommodation, including his own rooms, had become unavailable, he had chosen to take over the old estate office in the basement at the rear of the building. This had previously been converted into additional accommodation for guests – a small living room, a bedroom and a bathroom. You entered down a flight of steps from the garden. The living room looked out on to a grey stone retaining wall, from between whose tiny cracks furtive ferns sent tentative fronds. It was just possible to see, at the top of the wall, the stalks of hollyhocks, now turning brown.

Lance lay about down there, deep in his depression, for most of the time lifeless. On the second day Mr Sobell came pottering about up there beyond the window in the garden at the top of the wall, and Lance wished to dear Christ he'd go away. The only face he could endure was that of his sister. Three times a day Maureen brought him something to eat and drink, asked if he was all right, got no answer, and came back in half an hour for the tray. He would have eaten nothing.

These bouts of his didn't worry her very much. She'd seen many of them. When, today, he at last emerged, he did so looking perfectly smart, shaven, smiling, his old self, only a bit thinner.

'Can I borrow the MG?' he asked, and again she had to refuse. The petrol ration was two gallons a month.

And so he had to make his way to town by train and bus. He arrived a little early; it was not yet quite dark. To pass time, he spent half an hour in a pub on Mosley Street. It was full of servicemen and their women. Pressed about by hips and softly yielding breasts, he had to fight to get his two gin and tonics and had no option but to drink them standing upright.

There were hazards attached to walking in town during the blackout. Lamp posts suddenly loomed, kerb edges caught your heels, and heaps of sandbags, piled around doorways, blocked half the width of the pavements. Dark figures could seem intimidating and it was important to see faces. Without a face, with only a shadow where a face ought to be, an approaching human could appear strangely menacing. People peered warily, looking for recognisable signs of the benign, the harmless.

The number 25 bus dropped him off at the corner of Peggy's street – a long row of two-up, two-down terraced houses. She preferred him not only to arrive in the dark but also to approach by way of the back entry. Here, it was so black that he had to use the old trench way of making progress – one arm folded in front of his face and the other outstretched ahead. But she had left her yard door open for him and, by dint of much groping and prodding, he found it at last.

She'd been expecting him, listening out for him, and as he went across the backyard her kitchen door opened. Her shapely black shadow spread its arms and he walked into them. They kissed. 'You've had a drink,' she said. 'It's on your breath.'

'Yes – but in my pocket I have half a bottle of Haig Dimple.'

Only when the door had been closed could the light be switched back on. Her kitchen was very small, painted white, and contained a table with two chairs, a line of shelves laden with pans and crockery, a sink, draining board and laundering boiler. There was a black gas cooker against one wall and in the air a faint smell of old meals. She had made him a cheese sandwich. He was not too fond of cheese but it had come off her ration and he would not have refused it for the world. He ate it and she led the way into the front room.

This was not much larger than the kitchen, but Peggy had spent money on it. There were good, double-lined blue brocade curtains and a crammed-in blue-flowered three-piece suite. The floor had been carpeted from wall to wall and there were several cushions distributed over the furniture. Above the fireplace was a large framed print of *The Hay Wain* and in the centre of the room was a small coffee table around which you had to make your way carefully in order to get to your seat.

'Excellent little place you have here,' said Lance, as she switched on the light.

'Don't be ridiculous!'

'But it is. It's very nice.'

'You live where you do and you can say that about this hovel? How can you talk such rubbish?'

Lance took his seat to one side of the sofa and placed the whisky bottle on the table. Peggy had brought two glasses. He poured, offered her a glass and patted the cushion at his side. She, however, remained standing. 'Tell

me, how would *you* fancy spending your life in this dump?
Give it some thought and let me know.'

'But you seem very comfortable,' he said.

'Ah, I see what you mean. You mean it's all right for
someone like me.'

'I simply mean that it's very nice – cosy, agreeable,
pleasant.'

'Oh stop it, for God's sake! It's a shithouse. It's a
shithouse, surrounded by shithouses. Somehow or other
you've managed to find your way into a slum.'

Outside, as Lance knew, directly in front of her window,
blocking out daylight, they had built an air-raid shelter for
the street – a brick box with a flat concrete roof, over the
door of which someone had written in chalk the subtle
advice, *Piss off*.

Lance again patted the cushion at his side and, gazing
at him for a little while longer, she came to sit next to him.

After finishing off the bottle, they went up to her
bedroom. This, too, had had money spent on it. Her double
bed had a good wooden headboard and her dressing table
was new. Lance undressed at once and got under the sheet.

Peggy undressed slowly, standing in front of the dressing-
table mirror for a while with her back to him, but then
turning. In briefs and brassiere, voluptuous and aware of
it, she paused, staring at him for some moments. Then,
going through a kind of striptease that was clearly calculated, she slowly took down her knickers, put her hands
behind her back, unfastened her brassiere and released her
full, trembling breasts.

'I can't get a brassiere to fit me,' she said, cupping her
breasts in her hands. 'That thing makes me ache.'

Getting into bed, she came to Lance's side, put her arm across his chest and purred.

Unfortunately, despite his hot desire, it was to be another night when that desire for some reason suddenly faded. It had happened twice so far with Peggy.

The alarm clock rang out next morning before six because Peggy considered it important that Lance should get away early.

He wiped sleep from his eyes. 'Good morning, dearest.'

Peggy was already sitting up in the bed. 'I've got a bit of bacon I can fry for breakfast,' she said.

'Excellent.' He reached out and stroked her breast. 'I'm sorry, my dear . . .'

'Never mind,' she said, gently putting his hand away from her.

'Still, we had a lovely romp, didn't we?' He sat up.

Peggy turned to look at him, at his shoulders and arms. 'You seem thinner than you were the last time you were here. What's been happening? Have you been ill?'

'I've just been off my food for a day or two. It's nothing. Where're my cigarettes . . .' He found them on the floor at the bedside and lit one.

'And what will you do with yourself today?' Peggy asked.

'Hard to say.'

'Is it? Have you ever actually done a day's work, Lance? Half a day? Of course not.'

Peggy got out of bed. Glancing at him once more, she went to the dressing table and, going into a drawer, found clean knickers. 'This damned thing!' she said, putting on the brassiere that didn't properly fit her. 'I work sixty hours a week. Did I tell you that?'

'Yes, you did. It must be very tiring.'

'For four pounds eight and six.'

'Yes, well, I wish I could help in that connection, I really do. But you know what things're like with me just now. Maureen is an out-and-out skinflint.'

'Well, why d'you take it? What are you, a coward? She's loaded – anyone can see that. Stand up to her, can't you!'

'The trouble is, my dear, that whatever money we did have my father managed to get rid of, the old bugger . . .' Lance took a puff at his cigarette. 'He kicked me out, you know.'

'So you've said. Why d'you let people bully you? And why did he kick you out?'

'I've told you, he was an old bugger. He made a fortune out of investments in South Africa and lost it all in Venezuela. My mother – I was very fond of her – gave up the ghost and turned it in with a stroke, poor dear. He then lost his mind and went mad on women. He went utterly berserk over Glennis Zenda, an actress person he dug up somewhere. She was about twenty-two – no older. He brought her to live at the house. I turned up one day with a few old army pals and one of the blighters, Jack Smythe, managed to run off with Glennis. Now tell me, what the hell did that have to do with me? All the same, that was it. He booted me out. To tell the truth, he'd wanted to be rid of me for years. He detested me and the feeling was mutual. Actually, we hardly knew each other. I went away to school, and at eighteen I went to Sandhurst. So in fact we were strangers. That suited me.'

Having dressed in a plain grey frock good enough for

the factory, Peggy went to draw the curtains and the faint light of dawn filtered into the room. 'Yes,' she said, gazing out. 'This is a lovely place. A little paradise, isn't it? The man who lives opposite over there opens his window of a night and pees into the street. Hurry up. Get out of bed, Lance.'

'But I don't think I'm truly awake yet. Must we continue with this late-night, early-morning routine? It's quite taxing, you know.'

'Yes, we must. So hurry up. You think I want them to see you coming and going and start calling me a whore?'

'Well no. Of course not.'

'I mean it would be different if you said something.'

'Said something?'

'Well, how long d'you expect to come in my bed like this without saying something to me? Do *you* think I'm a whore?'

'No – no – of course not, darling.'

'Then I'm waiting.' She turned away. 'Come on, I'll get your breakfast. Then I can go to work and you can go home to your lovely big house in the country.'

Heavy rain was falling and Veronica Heath covered the distance between Richmond Station and Richmond Castle in Yorkshire at a run. In the castle guardroom the Sergeant of Military Police, smiling agreeably, noted her breathlessness and said, 'Settle down, love, settle down.' He leaned his elbows on the counter and winked at her. 'You look a bit wet. What can I do for you?'

'I'm late.'

'Ah. I see. She's late, sir.'

Behind the sergeant, standing stiffly at ease with his hands behind his back, rising from floor almost to ceiling, was an officer, immaculately turned out in red cap, field uniform and leathers. He did not move. He stared fixedly at Veronica with an expression so indifferent, so icy, that it frightened her.

'What time were you due?' the sergeant asked.

'One o'clock . . . It's on this letter . . .'

Veronica went into her handbag, found the letter and gave it to him. While he read it, she took off her wet headscarf and nervously screwed it into a ball between her hands.

From somewhere close, marching feet and staccato shouts could be heard. A red-capped soldier, bulky as a barrel, with a wet trench cape across his shoulders, came to the door, looked at the officer, said, 'Seven, sir,' and vanished again.

There was a smell of disinfectant in here. The granite stones of the wall had been painted a dismal dark brown. On the counter lay a large book like a ledger, an inkwell and a ring binder. Under the window, three short Lee-Enfield rifles were clipped to a rack.

The sergeant flapped the letter under the officer's nose. 'She's here to see Private Nigel Lawrence, sir.'

The officer showed no response.

'Four-six-two-four-six-one-nine, Lawrence, Nigel. Let's see, love.' The sergeant opened the big book. Humming to himself, he flicked over the pages, found where he was going and slid the tip of his finger down a column of names. 'Yes. Private Lawrence, DLI . . . One of that lot we got, sir, when Fifty Div got posted.'

The sergeant grinned at Veronica. 'Didn't fancy the idea, did he, love?'

'He was ill – he was ill.'

'Yes. Well, he wasn't on his own, love. It gets 'em like that. We know all about it, don't we, sir?'

The officer's frightening gaze at Veronica's face hadn't wavered.

The sergeant was now flicking through the ring binder. 'Private Nigel Lawrence seems to have taken one or two other little holidays, love, now and then. You can't do that in the army, you know, can you, sir?'

'He couldn't help it . . .'

'No. There's a few like that . . . We get 'em, we get 'em.'

He glanced at Veronica's frightened face and saw tears in her eyes. 'All right, love – all right. Don't get upset. You his wife?'

'No – no . . .' Veronica had had the sense to remove the wedding ring her husband David had given her.

'Sister? Daughter? Aunty? Ah – girlfriend. Well, you should've been here at one o'clock, shouldn't you? And if you look at the clock on the wall over there you'll see it's thirty-three minutes past.'

'I know – I know. But I couldn't help it. It wasn't my fault. I had to change trains at York and it wasn't on time. I was—'

'In the army, one o'clock means one o'clock, love. Here,' the sergeant returned Veronica's letter. 'Tell you what to do: write for another appointment.'

'But I promised him I'd come . . . He's expecting me . . . I've been waiting a fortnight for this appointment.

I've come all the way from Lincolnshire. I thought – I thought—'

'Sorry, love. But this is one place where rules're rules.'

'Oh please!' Veronica begged.

'Can't help, love. If you'd been wife or family – but girlfriend . . . Sorry.'

'Oh no!'

'Write for another appointment.'

'Can't I make an appointment here?'

'Afraid not. That's another rule.'

'Oh no . . .'

Veronica covered her face with her hands. Tears were flowing freely now. The letter fell from her limp fingers. Scuffling blindly about the floor for it, she found it, picked it up and, turning, walked towards the door.

As she did so, that other soldier suddenly appeared again in the doorway. 'Nine, sir,' he said this time. Taking off his cap, he shook rain from it and stared hard at Veronica's dejected figure. 'What's the matter with her?'

But the sergeant was now calling after her. 'Wait . . . wait . . .'

Veronica turned round.

'It's all right, love,' the sergeant said. 'The officer says it's all right.'

There must have been some silent communication between the sergeant and the officer because no words had been spoken. When Veronica turned to the officer with her wet eyes to thank him he still showed no glimmer of response. Not a muscle of his face moved.

'Nine,' the soldier at the door said again.

'Heard you the first time,' said the sergeant.

But now, at last, the officer spoke. 'Take the lady's coat and scarf, Sergeant,' he said. 'Put them on the radiator. Give the sergeant your bag, miss . . . Take her up.'

The sergeant led the way up a narrow flight of stone steps built into the thickness of the castle wall and showed her into a circular room barely ten feet in diameter. In the centre of the flagged floor stood a black steel table with two chairs facing each other across it. At intervals around the wall, black steel ringbolts were embedded into the stone like tethers for mad dogs.

'Sit there, love,' the sergeant said. 'He'll be down in a minute,' and he went out, leaving the door ajar.

Veronica rested her hands on the table, but quickly drew them back. The steel was cold.

The hollow sound of someone shouting indistinct words came to her. It went on for some moments. Looking up, she saw, high above her head, a small window, eighteen inches square, with thick iron bars concreted into lintel and sill. There was a third chair in the room – against the wall near the door. Tense, trembling, wringing her hands, Veronica waited.

Heavy, running footfalls were heard. 'Halt! Left turn. In you go.'

And Nigel was standing there in the doorway. With thudding heart, Veronica got to her feet. 'Oh Nigel . . .' But at once his shocking appearance stunned her to silence. His lovely hair had been shaved away entirely to reveal the skull, quite awful in its whiteness. His body seemed to have shrunk. His face had lost its flesh. His cheekbones showed as white as his skull through tightly drawn skin and his eyes glowed out of deep pits. He was wearing a shapeless blue jacket and trousers and his wrists were clamped together in handcuffs.

At his side, grinning, stood a soldier, heavy and solid. He pushed past Nigel into the room. Dangling from his belt was a truncheon. 'Sit down again,' he said to Veronica. 'Move the chair. There – sideways on to me.'

Growling, 'Hold your hands out man!' he removed Nigel's handcuffs. 'Your boots. Take 'em off. Give 'em to me. Sit down. Sit facing her – sideways to me – let me see your hands all the time. Have you got a handbag, miss?'

'They've got it downstairs.'

'Anything in your pockets?'

'I haven't got any pockets in this dress.'

'Well, have you got anything stuffed up your knicker leg?'

Nigel spoke now. 'That's not called for,' he said.

'Shut up, Private. Have you got anything up your knickers I said!'

'No . . . no . . .'

'Well, you've got five minutes.'

Veronica's heart sank. 'Five minutes – is that all?'

'Yes, miss, you should come at the proper time.'

The soldier banged the door to and the noise of it echoed away into the far reaches of the castle. He put a key into the lock and turned it. Then he sat down on the chair near the door.

'Are you going to sit there?' Veronica asked.

'What does it look like?'

'Can't we be by ourselves?'

'No chance. You've got to keep your eye on these hard cases. Don't worry. I won't listen.'

Leaning forward with his elbows on his knees, the soldier bent his head, stared at the floor and began to whistle irritatingly between his teeth.

Veronica reached across the table.

'Are you giving him something?' the soldier asked.

'No . . . No, I'm not.'

Veronica took hold of Nigel's hand.

'You're cold,' Nigel said, wrapping his two hands about her own.

'It doesn't matter. Oh Nigel, look at you . . .'

'Never mind about me. What about you?'

With his gentle smile, with profound affection radiating from him, he gazed at her. 'How lovely you are, Veronica. Thank God you're here . . . You've not been out of my mind for a moment. I thought you weren't coming. I'd given you up.'

'I'm sorry, love. I set off so early . . . It wasn't my fault. The train was late.'

'Never mind, never mind. Oh God, Veronica, I do love you.'

The soldier's whistling grew louder for a moment and he was grinning.

'You *are* listening, you *are* listening!'

'No, I'm not, missus. Anyway, I've heard it all before. Just get on with it.'

'Forget him,' said Nigel. 'Pay no attention.'

'Well, it's not right! How can we talk? Oh my poor Nigel . . .'

Veronica touched his cheek. 'Look at you . . . What've they done to you?'

'I'm all right, Veronica. I'm fine – now that I've seen you

. . . You're the only thing I care about in the world. I thank God for you. If you're OK so am I.'

'Your poor hair. You look so thin . . . What a terrible place this is. Oh, Nigel!'

'Don't worry about me, Veronica. I'm all right, really. The point is, how are you?'

'How d'you think I am, seeing you like this in this place?'

Nigel smiled that away and changed the subject. 'It's pouring down outside. Did you get wet?'

'What does that matter? Oh Nigel – there's so much I want to say, but how can I with him sitting there? It isn't fair! Oh Nigel!'

Nigel leaned closer across the table and whispered. 'About what you said in your letter, love. Oh, God, I'm so sorry.'

She whispered back. 'No, don't be, don't be . . .'

'But what're we going to do?'

'What does it matter? We love each other. What else matters? I'm glad, Nigel, I'm glad!'

'Are you? Is that the truth?'

'Yes, yes . . . I'm happy. I wanted it! It's yours and—'

Veronica was interrupted in mid sentence. 'What's all the whispering about? Let me see your hands. Lift 'em up!'

'Oh God!'

Showing the soldier her hands and then pressing them to her face, Veronica rocked to and fro in a spasm of bitter frustration. 'Oh Nigel, we can't talk!'

'Don't let's have any hanky-panky,' the soldier said.

'Shut your mouth!' Nigel snapped.

'Don't stick your neck out, Private. You've got two minutes.'

'Oh dear!' Veronica wiped away tears and again gripped Nigel's hands. 'I love you – I love you.'

'I know.'

There were tears in Nigel's own eyes now as they sat there, clinging to each other's hands, bursting with things to say, but driven to intolerable silence and aching at the heart.

'When will you come home?' Veronica asked at last.

'I think it might be a long time, Veronica. I don't know what's going to happen to me.'

'Oh Nigel . . .!' Veronica was on the point of sobbing. 'I can't bear it, I can't live without you.'

'That's it!' said the soldier, getting to his feet. 'Let's be havin' yer.'

'It's not five minutes yet, man!' Nigel protested.

'It bloody well is on my watch. Stand up.'

They both got to their feet. For a moment they confronted each other, limp, in tears. Then, stepping close, they embraced with a desperate kind of passion, kissing lingeringly and mingling their tears.

'That's enough. Put your hands up, Private,' said the soldier. 'Put 'em up.'

And, tearing himself away from his loved one, Nigel went to him.

'Wet-eyed are we?' the soldier grinned. 'Christ, I've shit men like you.'

Nigel flushed with rage. 'I told you to shut your fucking mouth! Well shut it!'

'Or what, pretty boy? I've shit 'em, I tell you. Give us

your fucking hands.' And he clamped the manacles back on Nigel's wrists. 'Get your fucking boots on.'

With manacled wrists, Nigel struggled to slip his feet into his boots and the soldier laughed. 'I've shit 'em,' he said again. Unlocking the door, he held it open. 'Up the dancers! At the double!'

And with one last look at Veronica over his shoulder, Nigel was hurried away.

The guardroom sergeant was waiting for Veronica at the bottom of the stairs. 'All right?' he asked.

'We couldn't say anything – he was listening!' Veronica was sobbing in earnest now.

'Aye. I know, love. That's how it is here. But he shouldn't have been such a naughty boy, should he? Come on – I'll get your things for you.'

At the station, they told her that the train she needed would not arrive for an hour and ten minutes. Still bursting with the things she had wanted to say to her poor, dear Nigel with his pale, thin face, she went to buy herself some writing paper, some envelopes and a pencil.

Ordering a cup of tea in a café, she sat down at one of the tables and wrote a letter.

After telling Nigel how upset she'd been to see him looking like that, and after bitter sentences expressing her anger at not being able to have him to herself, she went on:

You said you were sorry – but that's the last thing you should be, you silly boy. I am very, very happy having your baby, and I want you to feel the same. Your baby will be the most important thing in my life next to you.

I am going to write to David and tell him what has happened. You and him were always such good friends and he loves you as much as I do, so I know he will understand. I will come to see you again as soon as I can.

There followed endearments, blotted by a tear, and advice to Nigel to look after himself, to be brave until that happy moment when he was released and could come to see her again. She ended with the repeated assurance that she would write to David and explain everything to him – indeed this very evening. *Don't worry, David will understand.*

She posted the letter, there in Richmond, caught her train and was home again at Sycamore Cottages for half-past six that evening.

But she was exhausted, not so much with the stress of travelling in wartime as with the emotional strain of the day. She sank into a chair, too weary even to get herself a drink or something to eat. From next door's wireless came the faint sound of dance music. The eyes of her figurines on the mantelpiece and the eyes of her husband in his photograph on the table watched her. For ten minutes, she sat slumped, with her arms dangling over the arms of the chair and her legs stretched out.

She kicked off her shoes and sighed. Then, as powerfully as she had felt them at the time, she felt again the almost insupportable emotions that had risen in her at the sight of Nigel's tortured face, at the sight of his manacled wrists, and at the piteous, deeply unsettling sight of his cruelly bald head. She cried out, 'Oh Nigel!'

But in her letter to him she had made a promise, and

she now felt a great urgency to keep it. She got up, took off her outdoor clothes and flung them aside. She went into her bag and found the writing paper and pencil. Then, sitting down again, resting the paper on a magazine on her knees, she began to write.

Impatient to deliver her message, she expressed it in her first sentence.

Dear David,

I am having Nigel's baby and I write to you right away to tell you what has happened, even though I know it will upset you, seeing you are so far away. It does not mean that I don't love you, because you know I think the world of you. You and Nigel have been my dear friends ever since I was a girl. But these things happen, even though they break your heart, and I'm so sorry but it just happened. I know what you think about Nigel and you and him have been so close, and I think you've always known that I've always loved him too. It is sad that it has happened this way and it wouldn't have done if you hadn't gone in the navy. We would have all been friends as always. But it's the war, isn't it? It took you away from me and you know Nigel hates the army and because of things our love has become too much to bear. I know you will forgive us but I can't say how much it hurts to write this letter.

She was aching with sadness, and now there were tears falling on to *this* letter, smudging words. She had to pause for a minute to wipe her face and blow her nose.

I'm crying, she wrote. *I'm looking at your picture and now I feel like dying, I really do. You are my true, good, brave, loving David.*

Quite overcome with misery, she could write no more. The pencil fell from her fingers. She put her hands to her face, doubled up in the chair, and sobbed.

Again, she looked up, through tears and between her fingers, at David's face, smiling at her from his photograph. 'Oh David,' she wailed. 'Oh David, I can't do it to you. I can't, I can't.'

Slowly, she crumpled the letter into a ball and held it between her two hands.

Her husband still smiled at her.

Halfway through his walk, Mr Latham, the postman, in his baggy uniform with his large canvas satchel over his shoulder, had called in at the post office for the ounce of Glacier Mints that Nancy set aside for him every day.

'These damned government circulars don't half give me some work,' he said, slapping the bulge in his satchel and then sifting through a fistful of brown envelopes. 'Here – here's one for Mrs Williams. You want yours or shall I put it through your letter box?'

'Oh post it, Mr Latham,' Nancy said. 'What is it this time?'

'Ministry of Food. Something else going on ration, I suppose.'

'Oh – more work for me.'

'How's Michael?'

'He's fine. On six until two today.'

'Give him my regards.'

Mr Latham took his mints, opened the little paper bag and offered it across the counter. This was routine. Nancy took one and put in into her mouth.

'Hear the news this morning?' he asked. 'London got bombed again last night.'

'Yes. Poor devils.'

'And Hull. The question is,' Mr Latham said, 'how long can people take it? It must be awful – awful. Well, I'd better get on.'

Easing the strap of his bag more comfortably over his shoulder, Mr Latham turned for the door.

'It's cold out there,' Nancy said.

It was. A stiff nor'easter was blowing off the sea, tearing brittle brown and red leaves from branches and scattering them about the lane, throwing kittiwakes about over Mr Latham's head. As he left the shop, Mr Latham walked past a heap of aluminium saucepans and kettles collected weeks ago in response to a national appeal. They were supposed to have been taken to be melted down and turned into Hurricane fighter planes long before now, but here they still were, being shifted by the wind.

Mr Latham, sucking a mint, went on into Back Street, through wicket gates, up and down the paths, now and then seeing a face at a little window and waving to it.

Earlier, by standing arrangement, Mr Latham had handed over the Lancashire Rifles' civilian post to a corporal dispatch rider who waited for him each morning at the corner of Littlecotes Lane, and now, in the CO's office at the camp, Colonel Roper was considering a letter from the Reverend Samuel Duke, DD, vicar of this parish.

Dear Sir [it went],

I have to bring your attention to the fact that your troops are making serious misuse of my church and precincts and in your capacity as commanding officer I expect you to put a stop to it. On Saturday evenings, a number of women of a certain sort arrive by train in the village to consort with your men. Because it is secluded and unfrequented during the hours of darkness, they are making use of my churchyard. I have tripped over them. They also make use of the tops of important family tombs. The other evening, when there was rain, I found two people actually in the church behind the organ. I cannot, and will not, lock the church because it belongs to everyone and, especially in these stressful times, people need access for prayer and contemplation at all times of day and night. This must stop. Please inform me what you plan to do.

Yours . . .

The colonel replied:

I am deeply disturbed by your letter. Please allow me to quote Kipling: 'For it's Tommy this and Tommy that and Tommy how's your soul? But it's "thin red line of heroes" when the guns begin to roll.' I understand your concern, but the time has been and will be again when my men will face a determined enemy on behalf of their country, and don't you think they are entitled to the recreation of their choice while they can get it, providing of course, they remain fit, which is something we are doing our best to ensure? They know all the dangers. But I take your point about the location. It is quite inappropriate. There are things that can be done to stop it and I give you my assurance that you will not be troubled in that way again.

Yours,

Lieutenant Colonel V. Roper, DSO, MC, Officer Commanding, 1st Lancashire Rifles

Having dictated that, the colonel sent for the MO, asked about the level of VD reports at sick parade, and ordered him to make sure adequate supplies of condoms were available at the NAAFI.

Mr Latham had also delivered a letter to Veronica. It was in response to her second application for an appointment at Richmond. It said:

Re. yours of 15th inst. I have to inform you that Private Nigel Lawrence of the Durham Light Infantry is no longer based at this establishment. I am afraid I am unable to give you any more information. Yours faithfully.

Next day Veronica received three letters from her husband, David. They were short, cheerful, loving.

We can't get these blinking Italians to come out and fight. They don't mind dropping bombs from three miles up, but we've searched the sea for them for three months and not seen hair or hide of them. We've been doing convoys **xxxxxxxxx** [censored] and I can tell you we're all right.

And, in another of his letters:

> Shore side is a bit bleak and don't worry, no women you'd
> want to chase. I really love you, Veronica, and when this
> war's over and I come home I'll not let you out of my
> sight for a minute. All we can do is keep loving each other,
> say our prayers and get on with things until the great day
> comes.

And, again:

> I love you as nobody ever loved anyone, Veronica. I see
> you in my mind all the time. They say there's no chance
> yet of getting back to Blighty, but keep your chin up. Tell
> people at home we won't let them down. We've just
> xxxxxxxx [censored] . . .

And, then, the very next day, Mr Latham brought her a
letter from Nigel Lawrence.

> I've only got a few minutes [he had written]. I've just
> come to the end of a journey during which I was mana-
> cled all the time. They've only just taken them off and I
> can't write properly. Veronica, I don't think I'll be seeing
> you for a long time. I don't know what's going to happen
> to me but xxxxxxxxxx [censored]. I am sick at heart,
> longing to see you and sick because I won't be able to for
> God knows how long. xxxxxxxxxx [censored]. If only I
> could be there with you.
>   All my love, Nigel.
>   PS. I'm yours until I die.

Nigel had written that on a troop ship at Liverpool. Still serving his sentence, he was on his way to rejoin the regiment he had allowed to go to Africa without him.

Brocklesby Gets It Off his Chest;
Bad News for Veronica

The Reverend Samuel Duke, surrounded by corn dollies, baskets full of vegetables, giant marrows and festoons of autumn blooms, presided over the Harvest Festival. It was always one of the best-attended and most joyous services of the year. All had been 'gathered in, free from sorrow, free from sin'.

As she had promised, Samuel's old boyhood friend, Mrs Pat Green, the doctor's wife, had placed herself among the congregation that evening, and afterwards she and Samuel had a short conversation, mentioning Cheltenham and the old days. They were interrupted by Mr Freiston, the green-grocer, who happened to be passing by on his way out of church. 'You do know, don't you, Vicar, that it's traditional for you to do the harvest auction at the pub on Wednesday night?'

Samuel had heard nothing about that.

'Yes, Charley's customers bring their stuff. You auction it all off. There'll be a lot of disappointment if you can't do it.'

'Then I must,' said Samuel.

'You also take some of this stuff down,' said Mr Freiston, pointing to the array of produce brought to the church by parishioners and lying on the rood steps, 'and all the proceeds go to the church's charities.'

'Oh, I see. Very well.'

When Mr Freiston had left them, Pat said, 'How will you get the stuff down there, Samuel? You don't have a car, do you? Well never mind, I'll borrow my husband's car and drive you myself. As the local doctor, he gets an extra petrol ration, you know.'

'Oh Pat – how very decent of you!'

And so, on the Wednesday evening, Pat drove Samuel – on the front seat – and a great heap of produce – on the back seat – down to the Black Bull.

The pub had a gardening club, very active now with Dig for Victory, and there was much to auction off: a monumental prize-winning marrow that was bought by Brendan Kelly for a pound, artistically arranged parcels of vegetables, house plants, home-made apple pies and various items of gardening equipment, including a wheelbarrow.

Samuel was kept busy as auctioneer for almost an hour and a half, and then he was obliged to drink two pints of Charley's beer. Thinned down though it was, it still went to his head.

Pat had preferred not to go into the pub. She waited for him in the car.

'Oh dear, Pat,' he said. 'I'm a little dizzy.'

She drove him slowly past the school, past the dark cottages on Front Street. As they approached the vicarage at the end of their journey, at the point where she would have to stop the car and let him go, she said, 'We've not really had much chance to talk, Samuel, and there's so much to say after all these years. Let me take us for a little drive.'

Ten minutes later, they came to the crest of the hill near

Fulstow, five miles inland from the village. From here, the distant sea was a thin, pale blue demarcation between the sky full of stars and the moon-silvered landscape.

They chatted amiably for half an hour, again mostly about Cheltenham in the 1890s.

It had been so very pleasant a conversation that they agreed to meet again. What harm could the meeting of old friends do to anyone – providing, of course, that they were discreet about it? And so, after that evening, they had sat in the car, up there on the hill, three more times.

On Sunday, 20 October, the Commodore decided to go to church. He had missed two or three evensongs because he'd been rather irritated by the Reverend Duke's sing-song delivery. It was too damned High Church, and it reminded him of a weird evening he'd once spent at the home of Admiral Homerton, when some mad poet had recited incomprehensible verses for five or six hours. He considered himself to have made a much better effort at Samuel Duke's job when, for years, he'd presided over Divisions – religious services – on quarterdecks at sea. But it was time he took the walk to church. In any case, heavy rain had prevented his peregrinations of late and he needed the exercise.

In the church porch he encountered Rupert and Phoebe Brocklesby, both wrapped about the ears in fur and both wearing cashmere scarves of the same green colour.

Phoebe made a fuss of him. She patted his cheek, came between him and her husband and whispered, 'Share our pew.' He had never received this invitation before. He preferred his usual place at the back of the congregation where he could nod off during the sermon if he felt so inclined, but Phoebe had caught him unawares and he meekly agreed.

The Brocklesbys' Manor House pew occupied a pompous position of splendid isolation against the south wall, surrounded by oak stanchions and surmounted by a heavy oak canopy elaborately carved. It was up two steps. One sat eighteen inches higher than everyone else and felt ridiculous. But at least, from this vantage point, you could glance around and see who'd turned up.

Maureen was there with her three evacuees, in her own family pew on the other side of the nave. She did appear now and then, despite the distance between here and Pretoria House. The Commodore gave her a little nod. Elsewhere he saw Mrs Williams from the shop, the usual villagers dressed in their best, and, to his surprise, because he'd never seen her at church before, Pat Green, the doctor's wife. He looked for her husband, but no, she was alone, with a little floppy hat on her head and her face nicely made up. She looked quite young, quite radiant. She wasn't a bad looker, the old girl, the Commodore thought. When the choir trooped in, he searched for his paper boy, that lively Arthur, but he wasn't to be seen.

Psalms prescribed in the psalter for the evening included, 'O Lord God, to whom vengeance belongeth, shew thyself. Arise thou Judge of the world and reward the proud after their deserving. How long shall the ungodly triumph?'

That, the Commodore decided, thinking of the man with the moustache across the Channel, was a good question.

At the end of the service it became clear why Phoebe

had collared him. Taking his arm as they went out through the porch, she said, 'He's rather off it at the moment, Commodore.'

'Who?' he asked.

'My husband – Rupert. Do come and sit with him for an hour – please. Try to cheer him up. Will you?'

Phoebe drove them to the Manor House herself. She had bundled the men into the back seat of the car and Rupert Brocklesby was obviously faintly puzzled as to why the Commodore should now be sitting next to him. As the car moved off, there was a quizzical look on his face. 'How are you, Commodore?' he asked, looking at the Commodore from a distance. 'Did you want me for some reason?'

'No,' Phoebe said, glancing at them in the car mirror. 'I invited him.'

'Oh. I see. Well hello, Commodore. Delighted.'

In the great inglenook in the Manor House drawing room, a log fire was crackling and flaming. The walls were panelled, the ceiling was beamed. There were leather armchairs, two polished oak tables, an escritoire bearing a reading lamp with a green shade, brass firedogs, and old framed prints, each lit by its own overhead strip light.

'Whisky and soda?'

As she mixed two drinks, a gold bracelet on Phoebe's wrist clinked against the decanter. 'More soda?' she asked the Commodore.

'No. That'll be fine, Phoebe. Thank you.'

'Well then,' she said. 'Now talk away. Tell him, Rupert.'

'Tell him what?' Brocklesby asked.

'He's been depressed of late, Commodore,' Phoebe said. 'He went to London on business the other day and it very much upset him. Didn't it? He needs someone to talk to. So tell him, Rupert. Pay no attention to me, I have things to do.'

She went into the pool of light at the escritoire, opened a drawer, took out a bundle of papers and drew up a chair for herself. They both watched her. She looked up. 'Well? Tell him, Rupert.'

'Now why on earth should the Commodore want to hear my troubles?'

'Because he's sensible and doesn't mind – do you, Commodore?'

'Not at all.' The Commodore sipped from his crystal glass. 'Excellent whisky.'

Phoebe jabbed a finger towards the decanter, which glowed with reflected light from the fire. 'Just help yourself.'

The Commodore gave Brocklesby a smile. 'What was it, Brocklesby?'

'Nothing, nothing. I can't imagine why Phoebe troubled you. It's ridiculous.'

'Oh no it isn't,' Phoebe declared. 'He bottles things up. He needs to talk to someone.'

'Rubbish!' said this squire, the lord of the manor, this master of half the village, this controller of many destinies. Why the devil should he need to talk to anyone about anything? 'It's just that I've been rather tired lately. Nothing more. My wife worries too much. I'm just a little tired.'

'Well, it's a tired time of year,' said the Commodore.

'Yes. Phoebe was wrong to trouble you.' Brocklesby yawned. 'You see – just rather jiggered.' He stretched out his legs and silence fell.

The logs in the fire shifted. An explosion of sparks disappeared up the chimney. The Commodore was warming up, beginning to feel quite relaxed in this agreeable room, and Brocklesby's tiredness was catching. He felt that his eyes wanted to close.

Across the room, Phoebe was speaking on the telephone. 'That's true. Grey skirts? Blue? Well someone ought to make up their mind . . . Yes, I'll order them, but we need to know everyone's size . . .'

Brocklesby spoke again at last. 'Phoebe's been asked to organise a local Women's Voluntary Service, the WVS, you know,' he said.

'Really. They do excellent work, I understand.'

'Much more work than some of the men!' Phoebe piped up.

'Yes,' Brocklesby went on. 'You see them at stations serving tea to the troops, and sandwiches and whatnot . . . Yes.' He nodded at his own thoughts. Then he looked into the Commodore's face. 'London's suffering terribly, Commodore. Night after night . . . In this quiet little village it's impossible to imagine what the Blitz is like. Shocking. Awful. I was there the other day.'

'So Phoebe said.'

'Yes. The devastation's unbelievable.' Brocklesby's shoulders had drooped. He held his drink in both hands and looked down at it. 'Terrible. I was being driven back to King's Cross in the taxi. Tottenham Court Road was blocked with debris. My driver had to take to the back-streets. Even there we were held up. A partly wrecked building was being searched for bodies. As I sat there they brought two out – a woman and a baby. They laid them down at the side of the road, just there where I could see them.'

Brocklesby was silent again for a moment. He took a quick sip of his whisky. Through his thin hair his scalp could be seen. The cheeks of his wide, creased face had grown loose and his eyes were clouded. 'Yes,' he went on. 'It shook me, I can tell you. They were lying there . . . her legs were all bare, the poor woman. They hadn't cared at all. She was dead – oh yes, she was dead, and so was the baby, but they just laid her there. You could see her tattered undergarments. I've never seen anything so pathetic . . . Everyone was so busy digging away . . . So I got out of the taxi and pulled her skirt down for her. Her mouth was wide open, no blood, but one of her arms was twisted . . . She was covered all over with thick grey dust . . . It was terrible. Awful. I can't get it out of my mind, you know.'

'Yes,' said the Commodore. 'Yes. I can understand how you felt.'

The two men gazed quietly at each other.

Phoebe had been speaking on the phone again and so had heard nothing of this. 'Be a dear, Commodore,' she said cheerily, 'and pour yourselves more whisky. I'm so busy here. I must telephone Helen. What's the betting she's out?'

The Commodore refilled their glasses.

'You know, Commodore,' Brocklesby went on. 'There're people suffering terribly in this war. We don't see it here. We don't understand. There're people suffering terribly, dying, being maimed, and others taking beastly advantage, growing rich in the black market, profiteering in all kinds of ways . . .'

'Yes. That's always the case, isn't it?'

'It's so depressing, Commodore.'

'Have you any idea where we can get our hands on some trestle tables, Commodore?' Phoebe asked. 'No, I suppose not. Please, both of you, try not to interrupt me.'

There was a sequence of scratching noises against the door. Its handle clicked down, it opened, and in padded a very large Irish wolfhound.

'Close it, Erin,' Phoebe commanded, without looking up, and the dog obeyed, leaning against the door until the latch clicked again. Then he stalked to the thick rug in front of the shining brass fender and flopped down with a thud.

'Share prices have slumped,' said Brocklesby. 'American investors won't touch anything in Britain now. I've lost money. Yes.'

He was not interested in his drink any longer. He reached out and put it on the table. 'You know our son-in-law is in the air force – in fighters. That's another worry. God knows how Amanda would take it if . . .' He sighed. 'Yes . . . and of course this invasion. Where will they land? Have you any thoughts about that?'

'They won't land at all,' said the Commodore.

'I'm convinced they will. Not here, of course. They say Kent – Sussex. But not there, either. In my opinion they'll fool us all as they fooled us in May and as they fooled us in 1914. They'll do one of their outflanking movements and catch us unawares. Think about it, Commodore. They'll land north of here – in north Yorkshire or Durham. They'll do their blitzkrieg with their panzers down the Great North Road. We'll be entirely cut off here. We'll lose everything. There's going to be slaughter. It's going to be hell.'

The Commodore smiled. 'I don't think so. There'll be no invasion. They can't beat the navy. And, in any case, it's too late. They've missed the boat. It's the wrong time of year now. They've given up the idea. What they're resorting to now is the bomb. They're trying to bomb us into submission.'

'No, no. I wish I could believe you, but I'm afraid I can't. I know someone in the War Office. I asked him what plans they had if they came through Durham. "None," he said. Can you believe that? The Government? The people who're supposed to have everything under control. What confidence does that give you? We're going to lose everything, Commodore. It's only a matter of time.'

Phoebe spoke again. 'Oh dear. Do brighten up, darling!'

'Brighten up?' Brocklesby looked at the Commodore, looked away again, and said, 'Phoebe doesn't understand. It's all going to go. After generations of work and effort, they're going to take it all from us. They'll demolish our cities, they'll lay villages to ruin . . . and what about our women? And some Gauleiter will take this house. Some damned Nazi.'

With that, Brocklesby sank again into a gloomy reverie.

The fire crackled. The dog snored. Phoebe went on talking on the telephone. When the Commodore looked across at Brocklesby now he saw that he had closed his eyes.

The Commodore closed his own. In a moment he, too, was asleep.

Some time must have passed.

'Wake up! Wake up!' Phoebe was standing over them.

'Oh dear,' Brocklesby said. 'I'm sorry, I must have dropped off.'

'Well, pull yourselves together. It's time for dinner. You'll join us of course, Commodore.'

'What time is it? No, thank you, Phoebe, no. Fotherby will have something ready for me. I'd better be going.'

Brocklesby got to his feet, yawned and stretched. He smiled at his wife and smiled at the Commodore. 'What a nice chat we had, old chap,' he said. 'It did me good. Thanks.'

'Well, I knew it would,' said Phoebe.

The Commodore tried to remember what he might have said to Brocklesby to deserve his thanks. Very little, he thought. But Brocklesby did indeed look brighter now. He must have got it off his chest. He was lord of the manor again. 'You must stay for dinner, Commodore,' he said, in his old commanding tones.

And the Commodore had to refuse again.

Outside it was dark now. It had grown colder. A raw wind bit into the Commodore's cheeks. He pulled down his cap, twirled his stick and set off for The Grange. Venus was high, the Dog Star low.

At that moment, Eva, that wayward daughter of Mary at the pub, with her face like a painted puppet's, her mouth open and little sounds coming from it that could have expressed either ecstasy or agony, was lying under bushes at the edge of the cricket field. Her skirt was around her waist, her knees were up and opened wide, her arms were outstretched at her sides, and her left hand was spasmodically scrunching her white cotton knickers. The soldier on top of her, a little, eager man, was getting on with his business without a sound, and at least he'd had the thoughtfulness to spread his greatcoat under her. It was indeed very cold there.

Just then, a car drove by along the lane on the other side of the bushes. It was Dr Green's car, but the label declaring its ownership had been removed for the present and placed on the back seat.

Pat and Samuel were off again on one of their little drives. For discretion's sake, they rang the changes as to where they went to park up for half an hour. This evening, they drove through Fulstow and on into the Wolds. After turning off the road through an open gateway into a field, the car grew silent.

The sky was cloudy now. Under it, all was black. The breeze whistled across the windscreen and sighed in the hedge nearby.

There hadn't been much conversation between Pat and Samuel during their last two meetings, and there was not going to be much this evening. Samuel simply reached for Pat's hand, put it to his lips, kissed it, and then put its palm to his cheek. What had happened was that old love, old longings, the old excitement and passions of youth, buried under almost fifty years of time and humdrum life, had once again gripped old hearts.

Samuel placed another gentle kiss on Pat's hand. Turning to him, she reached with her other hand and stroked his thin hair.

Barely a fortnight passed before Veronica received a letter from one of Nigel's comrades. Men had exchanged their home addresses for just this purpose.

Nigel's troopship had been torpedoed off the Azores. He had been one of 343 men who had not survived.

> Nigel was a very good friend of mine [his comrade had written], and I'll miss him very much. Those of us who got away were very lucky and I only wish he could have been one of us. There was a whole brigade on the convoy. Some nurses were drowned and two navy ships were sunk.

Veronica could read no more. Tears blinded her.

Attack from the Sea; Conversation
in a Signal Box

Without any warning, two Messerschmitt 109s, almost at the end of their range, bent on one last quick hate before turning for home, roared in over the sea at fifty feet and shot up the army camp with cannon and machine-gun fire.

Reaction was swift. There were adapted Brownings and old Vickers to greet them and, as it happened, men were at rifle practice in the makeshift butts behind the canteen. As the enemy planes swept two spurting, crashing swathes of destruction across the camp, setting a lorry on fire and tearing sheets of corrugated iron from two Nissen huts, and then howled back towards the sea, a hail of bullets whined after them from machine guns and Lee-Enfields.

Suddenly, a thin stream of smoke began to trail from the port wing of the rear plane. A moment later, the wing dropped and dipped into the sea. The plane cartwheeled spectacularly twice, danced back into the air and blew up in a chaos of flying fragments.

An ecstatic cheer went up from all corners of the camp.

Casualties among the men were surprisingly few. Two men working on the transport had been killed outright by flying fragments, two had been wounded by bullets skidding along the concrete of the parade ground, and a third man had been killed outside the officers' mess, some distance away on the far side of the canteen.

'Get me a damage report as soon as you can,' Colonel Roper said to the adjutant. Then, together with Major Bates, he went to the medical hut to look at his two wounded men, Private Kenworthy and Corporal Accrington.

Kenworthy had had his left thigh shattered and Accrington had been shot through the left arm. In the absence of Captain Smith, the battalion medical officer who was on leave, the two men were being attended to by young Captain Brighton, an MO from Division. Pink-faced, rather tentative, rather nervous, he met Colonel Roper and Major Bates as they entered the hut.

Kenworthy was lying unconscious.

'How bad is he, Doctor?' the colonel asked.

'It's hard to say just now, sir. I've done my best for him. But I think his soldiering days are over.'

'Damn it. He was a good man.'

Accrington, whose face, under a spiky mop of fiercely red hair, bore its habitual inexplicable grin, was sitting on the edge of a bed with his arm in a sling. As the colonel and Bates crossed the room to him, he jumped to attention. 'We got one of the buggers, sir.'

'Yes, Accrington, we did.'

'I think it was Corporal Dobcross with the Bren.'

'How d'you feel?'

'Bloody sore, sir. But the MO says no bones shattered.'

'Good. Then you'll be able to rejoin.'

'I hope so, sir.'

'Yes. So do I. Get fixed up, get some leave and let's see you again.'

'That you will, sir.'

The colonel turned to the doctor. 'Where're the others?'

'In the annexe, sir.'

The colonel led the way through. The major and the doctor followed.

The three bodies were lying humped and hidden under yellow rubber sheets. There had been a lot of blood.

The doctor took a piece of paper from his pocket and read out names. 'Private Liddell, Private Graham and Captain Lockyer, sir.'

The colonel and the major stood for some moments gazing down from one to the other of the bodies. 'Which one's Graham?' the colonel asked.

The doctor pointed a finger. 'Through the chest.'

'Graham was in the orderly room this morning,' the colonel said. 'He brought me my tea.' He nodded at the covered body lying on another bed. 'Is that Lockyer?'

'Yes, sir.'

'Let me see him.'

The doctor hesitated. 'It was a bad one, through the head.'

'Let me see,' the colonel insisted.

The bullet had entered half an inch above Captain Lockyer's left ear. There was a neat, blood-rimmed hole there. The other side of his head had been blown away. Things had been cleaned, but that half of his face was a mangled mess of bone and raw flesh.

'What a bloody waste.' The colonel shook his head. 'All right – thanks.'

He flapped a hand and the doctor drew the sheet back over Lockyer's head. 'It was damned bad luck, sir,' he said.

'Yes.' The colonel nodded. 'If they'd done as I asked and sent him back to his regiment he wouldn't have been here.'

'No, sir. I mean how it happened. It seems he was just walking out of the officers' mess. It must have been a stray. Bad luck.'

Now, for the first time, Major Bates, standing at the colonel's side, spoke. 'These things happen. There were ricochets all over the place.' He suddenly seemed impatient. He turned away from the body, raised his head, looked at the colonel and said, 'Shall we press on, sir? We ought to go and see—'

'Hang on, hang on, Major . . .' The colonel hadn't finished with the doctor. 'Have you ordered transport for Kenworthy and Accrington?' he asked.

'I was just about to do that, sir.'

'Well get them off. And find Accrington something to eat, Doctor.'

'Yes, sir. I will.'

With that, the colonel about-turned and, with the major at his heels, left the hut.

'They made a hell of a mess of the armoury,' Major Bates said. 'You'll want to see it.'

Both men stepped off purposefully in that direction, but after only a few strides the colonel stopped in his tracks.

Major Bates frowned. 'What is it, sir?'

Clearly something disconcerting was stirring in the colonel's mind. His face was set. He stood perfectly still with his shoulders back, staring at the major with cool eyes.

'Was the doctor right?'

'What d'you mean?'

'Lockyer had just left the officers' mess?'

'Yes. So they say. Shall we press on . . .?'

'The officers' mess is a good fifty yards from the damage.'

'Yes. As the MO said, it was bad luck. This way, sir.'

But the colonel refused to move. 'Was anything else hit there?'

'Where?'

'I'm talking about the officers' bloody mess, man.'

'I've no idea. Why d'you ask, sir?'

'You know bloody well why.'

Bates frowned. 'I'm afraid I don't, sir.'

'There were men on the rifle range.'

'Yes. They got a few rounds off as the planes flew over. Maybe a hit or two . . .'

'Who were they?'

'I'm not sure.'

'Who were they?'

'A platoon of C Company, I think. As you know, there's a platoon there every morning, ten until noon.'

'And a bullet clean through the head. Very neat.'

'A ricochet can find its way anywhere, sir, as you well know. Wasn't it a ricochet that got old Nettles at Béthune?'

The colonel's cold eyes went on searching Bates's face. 'Don't be so bloody obtuse, Jack.'

'Am I being, sir?'

'Don't come it, man. You know perfectly well what I'm thinking.'

'No, I don't.' Bates preserved his frown. 'All I'm thinking, sir, is that we shot a Jerry down. All I'm thinking of is the good name of the regiment.'

That last sentence was not lost on the colonel. For a second, he glanced away. He looked towards the officers' mess and on towards the rifle range beyond. Then he looked again into Bates's eyes.

'We've had three dead and two wounded,' Bates said. 'Enemy action. But yes, we got one of the bastards, didn't we, sir?'

However, that, it seemed, was being contested. As the two officers stood there confronting each other, the RSM came marching smartly to them.

He saluted. 'Sah, them bloody shirkers, the East Staffs, are claiming they shot the Jerry down.'

'What!' The colonel was at once red-faced with anger. 'They were nowhere near their bloody front. Who's claiming? Colonel Peterson?'

'It must be, sir.'

'He's at it again, is he, the sod? We'll see about that.'

Pushing past the sergeant major, the colonel set off at pace for the guard-room and the telephone.

When he was out of earshot, the sergeant major turned to Major Bates. 'I hear Captain Lockyer's bought it, sir.'

'Yes. I'm afraid so.'

'Ah well,' said the sergeant major.

And the two men went after the colonel. They wanted to hear what he had to say to Colonel Peterson of the East Staffs.

That night, Michael Philbin was on the ten-until-six shift. He had only just arrived at his signal box, hung up his coat and stoked the stove when he heard the sound of an elaborate arpeggio on the tin whistle, thin yet exuberant and close to hand, like the bubbling song of a nightingale in the trees at the edge of the line. There was a pause. Then came the crisp, expertly and jauntily played notes of 'The Wearing of the Green'.

Switching off the dim overhead light, Philbin opened the door and went to stand on the platform outside. There, in the darkness at the bottom of the twelve signal-box steps, the shadow of Brendan Kelly swayed gently from side to side. The sound of music stopped abruptly. For a second there was total silence – and then a chuckling laugh. 'Is that you up there, Michael?'

'Yes, it's me.'

Brendan climbed the steps, took hold of Michael's arms, peered into his face and laughed again. 'Am I butting in on anything? Not got a girlfriend in there, have you?'

'Come in. Close the door,' Michael said, switching the light back on.

Raising his trouser leg, Brendan slipped his tin whistle down his sock. He was wearing a loose navy-blue overcoat cut from some kind of blanket material, rather furry, which made him look like a smiling, friendly bear. On his head was a narrow-brimmed trilby. Under the pale orange light, his round, still youthful-looking face – which, for the moment, as he gazed about, bore an expression of gentle interest – was like the face in an affectionate portrait painted by an old friend. 'Well, boyo,' he said. 'This is a veritable home from home.'

The box was not much larger than the average cottage living room. Indeed, if you overlooked the signal rack and the repeater box on the wall, it resembled one. There was an easy chair with wooden arms and corduroy cushions, just a bit threadbare. Alongside it was an iron stove always kept glowing with coal from the pile at the bottom of the signal-box steps. Next to that was a low table bearing a neat pile of magazines and a copy of the evening paper, and then a wooden bench on which were ranged half a dozen books, held upright by half-bricks that served as bookends. One of the signalmen had even brought an old cotton carpet. Its corners were inclined to curl up and someone had nailed them to the floor with tacks. On an upturned box in one corner stood a tin kettle and a Primus stove.

Brendan nodded at the books. 'You get time to read, then?'

'Sometimes, yes.'

'How d'you manage it in this light?'

Michael indicated a cylindrical tin box with a slit in its side, containing a low-wattage bulb attached to a coil of wire. 'We plug that into the socket. It's good enough.'

'Mmm. All very comfy. Very nice. Very domestic, Michael. You think you could get me a job on the railway? I've been following two horses, ploughing all afternoon.' Brendan picked up the evening paper and glanced at the headlines. 'They cocked it up at Dakar.'

'Yes. It was a mistake.'

'I see London got it again last night.'

'Yes. That's no way to fight a war. Killing women and kids.'

'The English have done a bit of that in their time.' Brendan folded the paper neatly and put it back on the table. Then, taking off his overcoat to reveal a smart grey suit and tie, he sat down on the chair. He tapped his fingers against its arms. 'Is this one of those things that slides out to make a bed?' he asked.

'Yes. It's been here for years.'

'So you can actually have a kip now and then?'

'Unfortunately not.'

'I see you've got tea-making things there. How about it?'

'All we can do is boil water. We bring our own brews.'

'Well, I won't ask to share your brew. Never mind. In that case . . .' Brendan leaned over, reached into his overcoat pocket and produced a flask, half encased in a leather cover. 'A drop of the old Irish.' He took a drink and held the flask up. 'Yes?'

Philbin shook his head. 'What is it, Brendan?' he asked. He had been tense from the moment of Brendan's arrival. Now the tension put a strain in his voice. 'What is it?'

'Nothing, lad. I've not clapped eyes on you for ages. I just thought I'd come and see what you get up to down here.' Brendan pointed at the signal levers. 'Why the different colours?'

'Red for the signals, green for the points.'

'Heavy work, is it?'

'If you're not used to it.'

'You build up your muscles.' Brendan took another drink. 'I think you operate the branch line from here.'

'We've got two branch lines.'

'I mean the one that goes to the shunting yard at Evers' factory.'

'Yes.'

'Yes, the line that passes the field at Greenbank. That's where I was ploughing today. Heavy clay, Michael. Not like the nice black stuff at home. Yet it seems fertile enough. Thousands of bushels this year. There was an ergot scare but it never happened. Yes – the branch line. You see the train going by Mondays, Thursdays and Saturdays.'

'That's right,' said Philbin. 'Stuff going up the factory on Mondays, stuff coming out Thursday and Saturday.'

'Closed vans.'

'Sometimes.'

'Where do they go?'

'Bradley, near Leeds. The marshalling yards there.'

Brendan put the flask to his mouth. 'Taste of the old country. The lights're still on over there. Dublin shines like a jewel.' Putting the flask back into his overcoat pocket, he stood up and stretched. He looked at the clock against the wall. 'Is that right, Michael?'

'It has to be.'

'I must be away for half-past ten.' Brendan went to the high desk near the signal gantry and fingered through the pages of the logbook there. Philbin resented this. He went and closed the book under Brendan's nose.

Brendan grinned into Philbin's face. 'Ah – top secret, is it?'

'No, but what d'you want, Brendan?'

'I've told you. I wanted to look at your face. By hell, lad, you do get nervous, don't you?' Brendan took a pace towards the signal-box window and looked out. He put his hands into his trouser pockets and hummed to himself for a moment. 'Lots of paperwork, then, is there, Michael?'

'We just keep a record of movements.'

'It's a busy line.'

'A lot busier now, with the war.'

'Stuff for the army, stuff from the factory for the air force . . . It must be all go.'

Michael moved about agitatedly. Then he went to sit down on the bench, leaning forward with his elbows on his knees, gazing down at the floor. 'For God's sake, Brendan,' he said at last.

'Anything special due along the line tonight?' Brendan asked.

'No.'

'You look as if you *do* need a drink, old chum. In my overcoat pocket.'

'I don't need a drink. Look, man, you're all right here, aren't you? You've got your job, you've got your cottage. You've got no enemies here. You're all right!'

'Is that how *you* feel, Michael?'

'Yes – damn it! And I won't have things spoiled.'

Brendan smiled, but at that moment a sequence of bells rang out from the console. The black finger of the block indicator swung jerkily from side to side.

'What's that?' Brendan asked.

Philbin didn't answer. Going to the console, he pressed the bell punch to acknowledge the signal and adjusted the indicator. Reaching for a strip of rag that hung from the gantry rack and wrapping it around the handle of one of the levers, he put one foot against the frame and, leaning back, hauled the lever forward.

Brendan watched him. 'That was very smooth, Michael. You can see you've got the hang of it. Very smooth. You've got a responsible job here.'

Philbin was not looking at Brendan, ignoring him instead.

'I say you've got a responsible job here, Michael. One mistake – pull the wrong lever, nod off for a few minutes – and crash. Mayhem. Isn't that right?'

'Yes,' said Philbin.

'Good money, is it?'

'Nancy and me get by.'

'Good woman, Nancy. Thinks the world of you. You're a lucky man.'

Along the line the train approached. It was a heavily laden goods train. The beat of its wheels against the joints in the rails transmitted its slow, steady rhythm to the foundations of the box. The kettle rattled and the floor shuddered. As the engine went hissing and gasping by, the night out there beyond the window convulsed into a swirling agitation of grey steam. The bright red light from the open firebox of the engine lit up the footplate with its two vague figures and spilled out on to the trackside, but was trapped overhead by heavy sheets of tarpaulin stretching from engine to tender.

'Where might that be going?' Brendan asked.

'Peterborough.'

'And what will it be carrying?'

'Coal.'

'Not very interesting,' Brendan said, turning back to the window. 'Damned lonely job you've got, Michael. Not a thing in sight. Not a star. Miles from anywhere.'

'It suits me.'

'Yes. I suppose it must.' Brendan turned now to look into Philbin's face again. 'Yes, I've not seen anything of you for weeks.'

'No.'

'Not since I left your place.'

'No.'

'You were glad to get rid of me.'

'Well, you weren't very comfortable yourself, sleeping on that damned camp bed.'

'Well you know what they say – any port in a storm.' Brendan grinned. 'You've not even been to the pub lately. Is that because you didn't want to meet me, Michael?'

'Don't be stupid. I don't go to pubs. Never did, did I?'

Brendan nodded. 'True. That's true. You found yourself a nice little retreat here, Michael. Didn't you now?'

'You always had my address. I did nothing underhand.'

'Oh now, come on. That's stretching it a bit. I certainly don't think Sarah would agree. The day after you skedaddled she came round, hopping mad. She guessed I knew. But I said nothing. I said nothing to anyone. You see, I'm a good mate, Michael. Did you ever know what happened to Sarah?'

'No.'

'Rather *not* know, eh? Well, they came over here and had a bit of a do last autumn. Started off well. Made a mess of the gasworks at Bolton. You must've heard about that.'

'Yes.'

'Then there was that bloody stupid letter-box stuff in Birmingham and Manchester. What fathead dreamed that up? Behan no doubt.'

'And Coventry last August,' Philbin said. 'Some killed. I suppose that was them too.'

'I think so. But I knew nothing about it.'

'Brendan . . .' Philbin looked into his eyes.

'Well?'

'Why did you come here?'

'Why do I have to keep telling you things twice? They rounded them up – the Garda, for God's sake. They got Donovan. As you know, I was never sure about bloody Donovan – he could open his gob – so I got out while the going was good.'

'Right, so you're here, Brendan. Who knows? *Who knows?* We're all right here, aren't we?'

'I suppose we are, Michael. But you know what they say. "Once a Catholic, always a Catholic."'

Philbin went back to sit on the bench. He sighed. He pressed finger and thumb to his eye sockets and sighed again.

'Yes, Michael,' Brendan went on, 'the bastards at home are rounding 'em up now. It's that sod de Valera, sucking up to the British, the fucking bastard. The English're scared he'll invite Hitler into Ireland and de Valera's scared the British might pre-empt things and invade. So he's giving 'em the boys. Bloody fool. What chance have the British got of invading Ireland? Bugger all. Hitler'll see to that. He'll be pissing up the King's legs any day now.'

Brendan stretched again, reaching out his arms and giving a little moan. 'Ah well, it's time I was off. We'll talk again soon.'

'For God's sake, Brendan,' Philbin said, and there was a profound note of pleading in his voice, 'leave me out. Leave me out.'

But Brendan merely smiled. He put on his overcoat and

trilby, took one more sip of whiskey, offered the flask to Philbin, received another refusal, put the flask away, buttoned up his coat, waved a hand, and went out into the night.

Half a mile away, at the far end of the path that led to the signal box, lay the dirt track down to Longshore Lane. Against the hedge there, Brendan had parked his motorbike. From here, first over humps and bumps, then on to Longshore Lane and so to Front Street and Somercotes Road, the distance to Langland's old cottage was just over four miles. Brendan travelled slowly. Otherwise his hat, tight to his head though it was, would have blown away, and so it was sometime after quarter to eleven before he reached home.

He removed his tin whistle from down his sock, had a quick face wash, combed his hair, put his hat back on and, taking his route through the shrubberies, walked to the side door of Pretoria House at just after eleven o'clock. It was unlocked. Opening it, passing through, and closing it quietly after him, he groped his way down the dark corridor. His hand brushed across the heavy door to the kitchen and his fingers followed the fluted dado rail to the door that opened into the great hall. There was moonlight in the hall. It fell like dust from the high windows. His footsteps sounded on parquet, then were deadened by carpet. He stood still for a moment, listening. The silence in this large house hummed as if the place were alive and dreaming. But then, as he walked on, he heard piano music coming from Maureen's private room. He recognised it. It was Cyril Smith playing 'Clair de Lune' on a gramophone record. He gave a little tap at Maureen's door and pushed it open.

Maureen had been listening to the music and waiting for him. She sat in her high-backed winged chair amidst the roses printed on its cretonne cover. Her greying hair, normally fastened in a tight, old-woman bun at the back of her head, had been untied. It was brushed back from her face and held by a glittering gold comb. She had made up her face with lipstick and eyeshadow and a discreet hint of rouge.

As Brendan entered, she stood up. She was wearing her green silk dress, plain but exactly right for her matronly, motherly body, and there were gold bracelets on both wrists. She stood there quite stiffly.

'You look lovely,' Brendan said.

'Nonsense.' She shook herself. But that old imperious air of hers was a perfect sham at this moment. She was staring hard at him, uncertain of him, uncertain of herself, nervous.

'I'm a bit late. You thought I wasn't coming.'

'Yes. I think I did.'

'And now I'm here I can't tell whether you're glad or sorry,' Brendan said.

'Can I get you a drink?' she asked.

'No. Just let me look at you a minute.' Brendan went to her and took her hand. It was trembling. There was something like anxiety in her eyes now. 'Yes, Maureen, you're a lovely woman.' And with that, Brendan reached out to her, drew her to him, and embraced her tightly.

There was only a very brief resistance. With his cheek pressed to hers she gave herself to him in a chaos of emotions that almost stopped her breath. Her heart thudded painfully and she gave out a little sobbing cry, impossible to stifle. After thirty years of lonely, emotional deprivation, of devoting herself entirely to others, of being a slave to this demanding house, of suppressed longing, to be held in a man's arms again filled her with an almost unbearable sensation of comfort, of heart's-ease and wonderful reassurance.

'Why're you crying?' Brendan asked.

Despite the contempt Charley had expressed for Nigel Lawrence – and perhaps to some extent *because* he had expressed it – he was quite affected when he heard of his death. 'Well at least they might've let the poor sod actually get into action,' he said to Mary. 'Something of the same sort happened to Rupert Brooke, you know. Damn bad luck.'

Nigel's few personal effects had devolved to an uncle who lived in Tetney and it was Mary's idea that some of the boy's pictures should be hung on the walls of the Black Bull's best room as a kind of memorial. Charley put them up himself, with some reverence, and they were greatly admired by most of those who took the trouble to look at them. There were local landscapes in watercolour, boldly executed and colourful still lifes, mostly arrangements of flowers, and impasto seascapes in oils.

Nigel had lived on Manor Row, six comparatively new houses built by the district council at the edge of Manor Wood in 1930. Notwithstanding the fact that they were on the main Tetney road and a good half-mile from the Manor House, they had not appeared without objections from Rupert Brocklesby, who considered it outrageous that the approach to his fine house should be blighted in this way. At that time of acute housing shortages and widespread slum clearances, councils were under pressure to build houses to rent wherever suitable land could be requisitioned, and Brocklesby's objections had been over-ruled.

As to the tenancy of these houses, priority had been given to men from the First World War, who had been promised homes fit for heroes, but in fact only two of the houses had been let to old soldiers; the rest of the occupiers, including Nigel and his parents, had been people from squalid properties on Back Street that had been demolished.

But now, when Nigel's possessions had been removed from number 3, another old soldier was indeed given its key – Arthur Swift's blind father.

The council had responded to local pressure by designing the exterior of these houses with reference to the district vernacular. They had little bay windows, pantile roofs, front and back gardens. But inside they were identical to other local-authority houses. They had two rooms down-stairs – living room and kitchen – and three bedrooms, together with a combined bathroom and lavatory, upstairs. They were solidly constructed, had cavity walls against the damp that had so much plagued country cottages, hot water, and a fully equipped kitchen. Arthur – with his now developed wallpapering skills and the help of his mother – decorated all five rooms in the course of six evenings and two weekends. Mrs Swift declared that she had moved into a little palace.

At this time of year, outdoor odd jobs were few, and so most of Arthur's time was now his own. He spent much of it in his new room at the back of the house. Under its window stood a small table, formerly used for meals, which served him as a desk for his homework. With the help of his father's dextrous hands, he had made himself three bookcases from old boxes, sanding down their roughness and staining them a dark oak. The newsagent's at Somercotes sold paperbacks and had a shelf of second-hand books you could buy for two or three pence, and Arthur was building up his library. He'd found on that shelf a set of five classic novels, including *East Lynne, Vanity Fair* and *Pride and Prejudice*. He had not as yet read any of them, but there they were in their black morocco bindings, waiting patiently in his bookcase.

With the advent of more affluent days, Arthur had thrown away his old corduroys and wore a pair of new flannels, sharply creased by his mother, and a new, crested school blazer with school tie and cap. Only his raincoat was second-hand. But his mother had renovated and adapted it very expertly.

He was persevering with his war diary. *We've won the Battle of Britain*, he wrote on 1 November.

In the House of Commons, Mr Churchill made a speech saying so. 'Never in the field of human conflict was so much owed by so many to so few,' he said, and it looks now as if the invasion won't happen. Italy has invaded Greece. Greek soldiers wear skirts and look stupid, but they're whacking the Italians all over the place. And the

British Army is driving them back in Africa. The Italians are lousy soldiers. Dad said that they're very good at marching backwards. But London has been bombed again. That's twenty-four nights on the run, and they've bombed Hull and other large towns as well. But we've not had one bomb here yet.

12

Peggy Visits Maureen and a
Stranger Visits Veronica

It was Armistice Day. There had been a sharp drop in temperature overnight and under the high hawthorn hedge on Church Lane hoar frost still coated the tangled stalks of dead weeds. Branches of oak in the churchyard twisted and contorted against an icy blue sky. A few dry leaves still clung to them, but a thick carpet of fallen foliage, growing moist and slippery under the low sun, made walking on the pavement a little hazardous. Fotherby held the Commodore's elbow to help him along.

The war memorial was a simple granite cross standing in a small patch of lawn a few strides from the lychgate to the church. Fourteen people were gathered there, nine men and five wives, most of them in overcoats and scarves, one, Fotherby himself, in his Home Guard greatcoat and glengarry.

At five to eleven, just as the Reverend Samuel Duke in his cassock and flowing white surplice was seen to be approaching from the vicarage, Fotherby said, 'Right, lads, fall in.' The men shuffled into line facing the memorial. Their medals glittered in the sunlight.

Tom Swift, Arthur's father, with his arm linking that of Fred Short, his new neighbour, had been asked this year to bear the wreath of poppies. He held it against his chest and heart. Lance Binbrook, his face pinched by the cold and his moustache looking quite black, had brought his own wreath, and so had Charley from the pub. George Lambert, also from the council houses, had lost his left arm at Passchendaele and the empty sleeve of his overcoat was tucked into his pocket.

They had all fought a war to end all wars, and as if to point out the sad irony of it there was a metal sign fixed to the wall across the lane from the lychgate. In white letters on a yellow background, and with a white arrow pointing down the lane, it said: AIR RAID SHELTER.

Samuel had brought his Bible and his prayer book with him. He had a large Remembrance poppy pinned to his breast. 'Good morning, everyone,' he said. He looked at his watch.

A few moments went by, and then, looking along the line of bright medals, he began. 'We are gathered here at the eleventh hour of the eleventh day of the eleventh month to remember . . .'

Someone in recent days had removed the lichen from the five names engraved into the granite of the memorial.

Next evening, during supper at The Grange, it was announced over the wireless that a squadron of Swordfish torpedo bombers from HMS *Illustrious* had attacked Taranto harbour and destroyed a good part of the Italian surface fleet.

The Commodore, one of the old school, had been convinced that aircraft could never be of much use at sea. The battleship was the thing. All this business of aircraft carriers and people flapping about in the air was a waste of time, merely an irritant, like midges buzzing around the heads of giants, he'd said.

Now Fotherby invited him to spread his words over his ration of ham and eat them.

'With pleasure,' said the Commodore, chewing.

Later that week – to be precise, on Wednesday the 13th of November – Samuel Duke, the vicar, left the vicarage and was never seen in the village again.

And on the following Thursday evening, at Pretoria House, Maureen answered the telephone to hear Peggy at the other end.

'Hello, dear!' she said. 'And how are you?'

But Peggy ignored that. 'Is Lance there?' she asked, without ceremony.

'No, Peggy, he isn't, I'm afraid. I—'

Peggy didn't allow her to finish. 'That's all right. Thank you. Goodbye.'

She rang again three evenings later. Maureen was just putting Tidgy to bed – reading to her from the *Rupert Bear* annual.

'Has he turned up yet?'

'No, dear. I did expect him today, but—'

Again, Peggy wished to hear no more. 'Thank you,' and the phone went dead.

She rang for a third time early on the Saturday morning.

'Of course he's still not turned up, I suppose. D'you think I could come to see the girls tomorrow?'

'Certainly, Peggy. We'll all be delighted to see you. What time will you arrive?'

'There's a train that'll get me there just after half-past ten.'

'Then I'll pick you up at the station. I'll look forward to seeing you again.'

It was another bright, cool morning. As Maureen drove past the Black Bull in her little MG, Charley was in the yard brushing dead leaves into a pile against the pub wall.

The station yard was patterned with sharp-edged wedges of black shadow. Maureen walked through them, greeted the stationmaster as he went by towards the booking office, and, drawing the skirt of her coat around her knees, sat on the platform bench to wait.

The train pulled into the other platform. A woman passenger, sitting in one of its compartments, stared at Maureen with a smile as though she knew her, and Maureen smiled back in case she did. Into its own cloud of steam, the train moved off again, and there Peggy was, just climbing the bridge over the line. Seeing Maureen, she gave a little wave.

Remembering the mood Peggy had conveyed to her over the telephone, Maureen was rather surprised to see that she was smiling brightly. She broke into a trot, wobbling on her high heels. Her green eyes shone and Maureen thought again how attractive she was. Her elder daughter, Francesca, was very like her – that broad, cat-like face and those wide-set eyes.

'Thanks for coming, Maureen. I've put you to a lot of trouble.'

'Not at all. I left the girls with Veronica. They're looking forward to seeing you.'

'There's a train back at one ten,' Peggy said. 'Will that be all right?'

'It doesn't give you long. Surely there's something later?'

'It's work,' Peggy said. 'They've put me on late turn for a bit. Have you heard from Lance since I rang?'

'I'm afraid not.'

'Well, never mind.'

During the drive to Pretoria House, the car was overtaken by a man on a motorbike; he wore a flat cap back to front and heavy thicknesses of scarves. As he sped away, he raised an arm and flapped it. 'That,' said Maureen, 'is Brendan Kelly, a very nice man. He works at Home Farm. I wonder where he's been?'

Carla and Francesca met them under the portico and, with a daughter holding each hand, Peggy led the way into the hall. Stopping for a moment, she looked about from staircase to far wall, at the pictures and at the sharply slanting beams of sunlight that, on such days as this, added a particular kind of splendour to this space.

'Come into the kitchen,' Francesca said, tugging her mother in that direction.

On the long kitchen table were earthenware and enamel bowls, a bag of flour and a set of scales. Tidgy sat with a peeler, concentrating hard over peeling an apple. At her side stood Veronica in her blue pinafore with a flounce at its hem. 'I'm showing them how to make an apple pie,' she said.

'Veronica's good, Mam,' Francesca said. 'Come on, sit down, watch her.'

'No, dear. I want to talk to Maureen,' Peggy said. 'You just carry on.' Kissing each of her daughters in turn, Peggy watched them go to sit at the table and then went to stroke their heads. 'D'you stew the apples?' she asked Veronica.

'Oh no. I bake them in the pastry. You keep the flavour better like that. But I don't have the pastry too short. Would you like a taste when it's done?'

'I'd love it.'

Behind Peggy, Maureen was standing in a shaft of sunshine from the window. 'Shall we go to my room?' she asked.

Sunlight bathed Maureen again as she poured sherry from the decanter. She was wearing her hair differently now. It was cut in a short, modern style, a bit young for her, but all the same it suited her. Peggy told her so.

'Thank you,' said Maureen, offering Peggy the sherry.

Taking it, Peggy went to the window and looked out across the garden, slumbering now for the winter. Then she looked about at Maureen's antique clock, her expensive ornaments, the silk curtains, the oriental carpet. 'It's lovely here,' she said.

Maureen stood watching her, smiling. 'I gather you wanted to speak to me, Peggy.'

'Yes,' said Peggy, and sat down.

Maureen took the chair opposite and looked at her with her head on one side, waiting.

'Francesca tells me in her letters that you've bought them bikes.'

'Yes. They can ride around to their hearts' content here without any danger. They love it.'

'Thanks. I could never afford bikes. You look after them very well.'

'Thank you.'

'They've got everything.'

'Well, shouldn't they have everything?'

Peggy gazed into her sherry, tilted the glass so that its contents lapped around its tulip curve for a moment, and then sipped. 'They don't know how lucky they are.' Then she smiled again. She assumed that bright-eyed look and asked, 'Have you any idea where Lance is?'

'No, dear. I'm afraid I never do know.'

Peggy tossed her head. 'Never mind. How're the girls doing at school?'

'Very well. I spoke to their teacher the other day. She showed me some of their work. Carla is very clever. Ten out of ten for her arithmetic, page after page. And Francesca can write so well. You must know that from her letters.'

'Yes. They're happy here. I don't think they'll ever want to come back to that dump of mine.' But Peggy brightened yet again. 'Where can I get in touch with him, Maureen?'

'Lance? But I've told you, dear, I've no idea. Of late, I've always assumed he might've been with you.'

Peggy's smile had faded. 'No, he's not been with me. Just tell me where he is, Maureen.'

'I'm telling you the truth, Peggy. I don't know.'

Peggy's tone was quite different now. 'Then he's a bastard.'

Maureen recoiled. 'Pardon me?'

'Oh don't look like that.' Peggy slapped her sherry glass, still half full, on-to the coffee table, spilling some. 'I've not seen him for more than three weeks. And he promised – he promised!'

'Oh dear.' Maureen sighed.

'I want to know where he is.' Peggy's face, a moment ago like the face of a purring cat, was now like that of a cat ready to dig its claws in. 'He promised!'

'Oh Peggy, haven't you learned by now that Lance's promises are worth nothing?'

'He told me he'd meet me at the Midland three weeks ago. I waited there an hour – an hour! He made a fool of me. Listen to me, Maureen, I'm not a kid. I'm not a nobody. He can't play around with me like that. He's dumped me, hasn't he?'

Again Maureen sighed. She put down her own sherry glass and looked into Peggy's angry face. 'I must be honest with you,' she said, 'and tell you that you're almost certain to be right. If his women don't throw him over he tends to get tired himself. And that, I'm afraid, is how my brother is.'

'So I was just one of his women, was I?'

'I'm so sorry, Peggy.' Maureen leaned towards her, reaching for her hand, but Peggy wanted none of that.

'I let him sleep with me – over and over again. I dropped a good man for him – a good man, earning good money, who loved me!'

'Well that was hardly Lance's fault, was it?'

'Of course it was his bloody fault. He led me on. He spent nights on end with me. He couldn't keep his hands off me, slobbering and groping! What did I expect? What did I expect!'

'Lance is what he is, Peggy.'

'What d'you mean – what he is? He's a bastard, that's what!'

'Lance has been a lost soul for twenty years, I'm afraid,' Maureen said.

'Well he wasn't lost in my bed, I'll tell you that. Lost soul! The pig. And half the time he couldn't get it up, could he!'

Again, Maureen recoiled. She stiffened. 'How crude that is. And yes, how disappointed you must be.' There was an edge to it.

'What exactly d'you mean by that?' Peggy asked.

'I can see very well you're angry and I suppose I can understand it, but from the way you talk about my brother, I wonder.'

'What're you talking about?'

'Do you love Lance?'

Peggy frowned for a second. 'Love him?' She raised her voice again. 'Of course I love him!'

'Yet you call him those names. Are you sure there was nothing else?'

'What're you suggesting?'

'Nothing. I'm just asking. You call the place you live in a dump. You tell me how much you like this house.'

Peggy interrupted her sharply. 'I see. You think I'm just a gold-digger. You're insulting me.'

'I didn't want to do that. But we're both grown-ups. Such thoughts in a woman would be perfectly reasonable.'

'Yes – you're just like that sod. You think I'm muck.'

'Nonsense. I'm just trying to point out that perhaps you had your own perfectly reasonable agenda, Peggy.'

'And I thought you liked me.'

'But I do like you.'

'No – no. You both think I'm just a scrounger. You've talked about me.'

'No. Never.'

'Well listen, if you think I'm the scrounger, listen – that bloody brother of yours owes me thirty pounds. He's the scrounger, not me.'

'Oh dear.' Maureen sighed yet again. 'Peggy, I'm sorry, I really am.'

'Where is he?'

'I don't know. On my heart, I've no idea. But why must we fall out?'

Peggy had begun to cry. Groping clumsily in her handbag, she found a handkerchief and put it to her face. She had nothing more to say.

An aircraft flew by low overhead and sunlight sparkled in the pool of sherry around Peggy's glass on the table.

And then Carla pushed the door open. 'Come and taste our apple pie, Mam.'

Later, as Maureen walked with Peggy to the car to return her to the station, she held out three £10 notes. 'There, my dear – what my brother owes you.'

'I don't want it.'

'Please, take it.'

'No. He can drop dead.'

While the two women were discussing him so heatedly, Lance, with Molyneau and Pickmere – the Borrowed-Time

Brigade – was sitting in the lounge of a public house fifty yards from Slough railway station. Half an hour earlier they had been released from the rude hospitality of the Royal Engineers after a crash course on unexploded-bomb disposal.

Lance and Molyneau, bareheaded, were slowly making their way down pints of bitter.

'Am I wrong,' Molyneau asked, savouring a mouthful and frowning slightly, 'or is this beer a bit sour?'

Lance took another sip. 'No,' he said. 'It's fine.'

Pickmere, unable during the past days to dress in the flamboyant way natural to him, had resorted at least to a rather ridculous-looking bowler hat. He was drinking sherry from a tall schooner. At the moment, he was presenting smiles, first to Molyneau and then to Lance, because both of them had agreed to spend a few days with him at Brookdale, his home. In thirty-five minutes' time they would be catching the train that would take them there. When pleased, Pickmere's personality underwent a transformation. All tension vanished from him, his body seemed to diminish in size and his smile became quite naïve.

'What're you doing, Lance?' he asked.

Lance was flicking through the course manual, a copy of which had been given to each of them.

They were sitting at a round table in a corner. Apart from them the room was empty. But beyond the bar, where there must have been another room, there was much noise. A loud female contralto was uttering short sentences, each followed by loud male laughter.

'What're you doing?' Pickmere asked again.

'There are four circuits listed here,' Lance said, poking the page with a finger. 'We were told eight.'

'Then the manual must be out of date,' said Molyneau. 'Anyway, it's all hit and miss, isn't it?'

Lance nodded. 'Mmm. Yes, hit and miss. How right.'

'Don't worry. We'll sort it out between us,' Molyneau said. 'We'll sort it out. We're going to make a good team. We're going to do this job right. And there's one thing for certain – if we go up, we all go up together.'

'Yes,' Pickmere said. Smiling that smile, he reached out and gripped Molyneau's wrist and Lance's wrist. In such moods his brown eyes were as soft and vulnerable as a woman's. 'Yes, we'll all go up together.'

Through the lobby of the Queen's at Cheltenham and out into the street passed two army officers and two girls, all laughing happily. It was half-past eight in the morning. At a table in the dining room, gazing into each other's faces over a bowl of daisies, sat Samuel Duke, without clerical collar, and Pat Green, wearing pink lipstick and green eyeshadow.

Pat's father had left her valuable property in this town – several houses and two thriving town-centre shop premises. It was her income they would have to rely on, because Samuel had only his pension.

The waiter came. Samuel ordered bacon, tomato and sausage. Pat ordered egg instead of the sausage. Both wanted toast and marmalade and both preferred tea to coffee.

Their bedroom upstairs looked out over streets familiar to them from their youth. Last evening, they had stood there holding hands for a while, gazing down, remembering. Then they had enjoyed a loving hour together and a sound sleep in their double bed.

Across the table, Samuel reached for Pat's hand and squeezed it. 'Is this where the heartache starts?' he asked.

'No,' said Pat, emphatically. 'Nothing but our happiness, Samuel. What else matters?'

Lovers old and young ask the same question.

On the evening of that same day, Veronica answered a knock at her door and found on her doorstep a woman in her fifties, smartly dressed in a fashionable fur-collared tweed coat, unsmiling, but at ease with herself and positive in her manner. 'You spoke to Mrs Evans.'

'Yes.' Veronica stood back. 'Come in.'

'Are you alone? Is there anyone else in the house?'

'No.'

'Good. Just hold on to this for a tick.' She slipped over Veronica's outstretched wrist the handles of the large cloth bag she'd been carrying and then took off her coat. 'Where can I hang it? No one's likely to turn up, are they?'

'No.'

'But you never know, do you? Have you got nosy neighbours? Yes, you have, 'cause they're all nosy. Lock the door, there's a good girl. And the back door, too.'

'It's already bolted.'

'That's fine. I was interrupted once. What a kerfuffle. So I always make sure now.' The woman opened the inner door and entered the living room. 'You've got a good fire going. It's damned nippy out there.' Her gaze lingered on Veronica's mantelpiece. 'They're nice little figurines.' Then she saw David's photograph on the table. 'The sailor in the picture. Who is it?'

'David – my husband.'

The woman nodded knowingly. 'Yes, I thought so. Away, is he? Mmm. I have a nephew in the navy.'

'Where d'you want to go?' Veronica asked. 'The bedroom?'

'Why the bedroom?' The woman smiled. 'Because that's where it all starts? No, love. We can do it here by the fire.' From her bag she removed a stainless-steel bowl, fourteen inches in diameter and eight inches deep. 'Have you got anything like this in the house?'

'Yes, but it's a bit smaller.'

'It should do. Here – take this and go and give 'em both a good scrub. Have you any hot water?'

'Yes. The fire has a back boiler.'

'Better than nothing. But back boilers aren't much cop. If your fire goes out, no hot water. You want to get yourself one of these electric things that go in your cistern – an immersion heater. They're not all that dear. Give the two bowls a good scrub and half fill 'em both with hot water. D'you mind if I smoke while I'm waiting?'

'No.'

The woman lit a cigarette and, while puffing at it, looked around the room. When Veronica returned carrying one of the bowls, she said, 'These cottages're a bit poky, but comfy enough. When you come back with the other bowl, bring a towel – have you got a big bath towel?'

When Veronica returned a second time the woman was warming her hands at the fire, while her cigarette dangled from her lips. 'Don't worry, I won't touch you with cold hands, love. Put that other bowl on the table for a bit and spread the towel over the carpet – here, near the fire. That's it. Take your knickers off.'

'What about my frock?'

'You can leave that on. Put your knickers down on the chair there. That's it. Just let me have one more puff.' She took one more lungful from her cigarette and threw the rest of it into the fire. 'Now just lift your frock up and crouch down over the bowl. No, not like that. Just as if you were having a wee. Good.'

Veronica could feel the heat of the fire against her thigh. When the woman passed around the back of her, out of her sight, she turned her head anxiously.

'Don't look at me. You won't see much. Open your legs – wider. I'm using the other bowl here and I need a bit more room. Shift to your left a bit, away from the fender. That'll do.'

Veronica heard a splashing of water and felt the brush of the woman's fingers against her thigh. She started.

'You've got to keep calm, love. Just breathe nice and steady.'

There came a strong smell of carbolic soap and more splashes.

'You'll just feel a little twinge. Some call it a little prick.' The woman laughed. 'Didn't you think that was funny, love? A little prick to get it in and a little prick to get it out. Never mind. Lift your frock a bit higher – and your vest.'

'Will it work? Will it work?' Veronica asked.

'Yes. Just lean forward. Further. That's it.'

Something hard, smooth, soapy, passed between

Veronica's thighs and into her without any sensation at all. She put a hand to her madly beating heart.

'Just keep still.'

Now Veronica felt it – the twinge, the prick, a little hot stab deep inside her. She tensed herself for pain, but none came.

'There you are,' said the woman.

'Is that all?'

'What more d'you want?'

'Have you done it?'

'Yes. You'll start in about twenty-four hours.'

'Oh God, I hope so.'

'You will. That's a promise. No money-back guarantees, mind you, but you'll be OK.'

Veronica glanced over her shoulder and was just in time to see the woman wrapping a vaginal douche – black spout, orange bulb – in a towel.

'Is that all you use?'

'It's not what you use, it's the way you use it. You can stand up now. But hang on – just shuffle aside a bit. Go on. You need the towel to wipe yourself. Are you all right? Get hold of the towel . . . Just wipe yourself first. There you are. You can put your knickers back on now. Did Mrs Evans tell you how much?'

'She said three pounds.'

'Well she was spot on.'

Veronica got into her knickers, pressed her frock against the inside of her left thigh where a trickle of water ran down, went to her handbag and handed over three pound notes.

'Will you rinse my bowl out for me now, love. Dry it for

me. I travel about by bike, you know. By hell you don't half get a draught up your bum in weather like this.'

When Veronica came back, she asked, 'How many periods've you missed?'

'Two.'

'It'll be OK. Yes, I like them figures you've got on your mantelpiece. Must've cost a bob or two. And that's your husband, is it? Never mind, love. They send 'em away and what the hell do they expect? We're only flesh and blood after all. But don't worry. You can let me out now. Is Geraldo on the wireless later tonight? I like Geraldo. Good night then, love.' And down the garden path she waddled to where her bike stood waiting.

This early arrival of wintry weather had inclined the village to hibernation. Even the kids preferred to spend most of their time indoors. Women calling at the butcher's shop and the post office for their rations came in puffing and shuddering and spent even longer inside, gossiping and warming up for a while before venturing back into the street. But their conversations were less gloomy.

Like Arthur, people were beginning to believe that the invasion scare was over. Winter was imminent, the RAF had won the war in the air, and newspaper and wireless commentators had been unanimous in considering the threat to have vanished. Indeed, although no one in Britain was aware of it, the man with the moustache across the Channel had abandoned his plan as far back as September. As the Commodore had said to Brocklesby, Hitler was happy to let the nation be bombed to oblivion while he perfected his more grandiose scheme to invade Russia.

In the village, apprehension had given way to resentment – resentment at the shortages of almost everything and at the smallness of rations, problems that, while those other, greater problems had preoccupied them, they had endured more or less in silence. In the absence of anyone else to carp at, they vented their frustrations on the innocent shopkeepers.

'Why haven't you got any corned beef?' 'D'you expect us to eat this bloody Spam?' 'Why did it take three days for me letter to get to Edinburgh?'

Fighting back, the butcher had had a poster painted and stuck to the inside of his window. DON'T BLAME ME.

One of the shortages was of fuel. Mr Waters, the coalman from Fulstow, sitting up on his cart, talking to his old horse as he went, wearing on his back a leather carapace like a tortoise, had usually visited the village twice a week to hump his sacks into people's coalhouses. Now, he came only once, rationing his coal and forced to stand with streams of sweat washing coal dust from his face while people asked him how the hell they were supposed to keep warm in front of an empty grate. Brocklesby's supply of logs for his fires dried up and he had to resort to using the trimmings from his woods, which were often not much more than twigs.

But then, suddenly, the mood changed. 'If London can take it,' people began to tell each other, 'so can we.' The old cheerful stoicism came back, that dogged determination, despite all anxieties, to endure, and that cheerful courage which had been expressed in words by Winston Churchill: 'Let us . . . so bear ourselves, that people . . . men will still say, This was their finest hour.'

The Women's Institute called a meeting in the village hall and a campaign was launched to collect clothing and other comforts for bombed-out families of the East End who had lost everything. Several bagfuls were collected in a single day.

A certain kind of shortage confronted the Commodore. Every month for some years he'd had delivered from his merchant in Liverpool two cases of his favourite wines. When his early November delivery failed to appear, he telephoned them. The line was dead. He tried again, later, but dead it remained.

Two days went by and then he received a letter.

Dear Commodore Grainthorpe,
    We regret to inform you that due to enemy action we are unable to supply you with your regular order. All our stocks have been destroyed.

'Yes,' Fotherby said. 'Liverpool was raided the other night. So that puts a stop to your gallop. A period of sobriety must now follow, and it could be a hell of a long one. How're you going to get hold of your poncey French wines now, when the Jerries are over there drinking it all?'

'What a disappointment. Ah well, one will survive. We mustn't let a small matter like that destroy our morale.'

'So you don't think it'll bother you?'

'I won't let it bother me. Although there is a problem, Fotherby. How the hell am I going to get your meals down without something to deaden the taste?'

'You might have something there,' Fotherby said. Then he turned to the Commodore and gave him a long stare.

'What's up?'

'I'm thinking.'

'Oh yes?'

'I'm wondering whether you deserve it. Mmm. Follow me.'

Fotherby led the way down to the kitchen, through it, and on into the corridor beyond. 'When were you last here?' he asked.

'I can't remember.'

'No. You see, you don't know your own house. That door there is the pantry. But this is where we're going.'

There was another door at the far end of the corridor. As Fotherby opened it, the Commodore's eye fell at once on a wine rack full of bottles lying on their sides. On a shelf nearby, other bottles stood upright.

'What the devil's this?' he asked. 'Sauterne, Chablis, Bordeaux – have you been stashing away your own stuff, you dog?'

'No. They're all your old empties.'

'They look full to me.'

'Yes they are – see.' Fotherby switched on the light. On a bench in there stood two glass carboys with airlocks, full of fermenting fluid. In the air was a strong smell of alcohol. There were funnels, filters, empty bottles. Fotherby had been brewing his own.

'Well I'm damned,' said the Commodore. 'How long has this been going on?'

'Three years – long before the war. You had your French muck, I had my own good, home-made English nectar. In those bottles on the shelf is last year's elderberry, what's left of it. Here, you have last year's parsley. This is a bit of last year's grape. I sent away for the grape juice. Well, what d'you think? I'll decant an elderberry for your dinner tonight. I think you might just like it – when you get used to it. I'll tell you one thing, it's as strong as Pusser's grog.'

There was frost again this evening. Veronica, whose journey from Pretoria House took her along slippery foot-paths and over a slippery stile, broke now and then into a little trot to keep herself warm. The woman had said twenty-four hours and Veronica had been praying ever since. In fact, only twenty hours had passed when, just as she turned into Littlecotes Lane and began to climb the hill, she sensed that something might be happening. She hurried on home.

But, no. A wave of disappointment swept over her. She drew the blackout curtains, switched on the light and went to the hearth. This morning before leaving for work, she had, as always, laid the kindling and a few pieces of coal in the grate ready for her evening fire. She lit it, took off her coat and went into the kitchen to brew herself some tea. She'd had her evening meal at Pretoria House.

She took her teacup back into her living room, sat down and watched the flames fluttering in the grate.

Just before eight o'clock, a sharp little period pain struck her and she realised that she was bleeding. She cried with relief and, from his place on the table, her husband smiled at her. Totally ignorant as to what might now happen to her, she went up to her bedroom, put on a sanitary towel and lay down on the bed. For half an hour she felt nothing – no more than she had felt with any ordinary period – and so she got up again. She went downstairs, switched on the wireless and listened to Carroll Gibbons with his Savoy Hotel Orpheans.

But then she felt a powerful pain all the way across the pit of her stomach. She had lost a large, almost black clot of blood and, at the horrible sight of it, she began to feel afraid. More pains stabbed at her, and now she found that she was bleeding alarmingly. Was this what she ought to expect?

But how could she know? She was alone, and in her loneliness, in the absence of anyone to turn to, she grew more and more frightened. Into her mind came a jumble of tales of women haemorrhaging and dying while trying to abort babies, and it seemed to her that blood was oozing from her faster with every minute. She lost more sickening clots and, now, with a thudding heart and little cries of alarm, she went into a panic. She stood in the middle of the room, with her hands to her mouth, while Carroll Gibbons played 'A Nightingale Sang in Berkeley Square'. She could feel the blood leaving her. She was trembling, wanting help, and felt desperately alone.

Then, convinced in her panic that she was going to die if she didn't do something, she put a towel between her legs and hobbled out of the house to knock at Mrs Baker's door.

Mrs Baker's seven-year-old daughter opened it.

'Your mother, Martha – please!'

'My God, Veronica,' said Mrs Baker, 'what's the matter?'

'I'm ill – will you go to the telephone for me? I need an ambulance. I'm very ill.'

'Oh dear, Veronica – what is it?'

'I'm having a haemorrhage. Oh please!'

Veronica reached out to the door jamb to steady herself.

'You're going to collapse,' Mrs Baker said, reaching to her. 'Yes, I'll go – I'll go now. But come on, let me get you home first before you pass out.'

At the vicarage, Lettice Duke, the Reverend Samuel's abandoned wife, was also ill. She telephoned for Dr Green, but chose a time after tea when he was resting.

'Dr Jones at Fulstow is locum for me at the moment,' he said. 'Call him. Hang on, I'll give you his number. Hang on. Damn it, where is it? Hang on.'

But Lettice pleaded and at length he relented and agreed to visit her.

There had been persistent drizzly rain all day. Now it had stopped, but as Dr Green crossed the churchyard the bare branches overhead wept on him. There was a smell of drenched earth and the doctor, unable to see where he was going in the blackout, unused to this place, had to grope his way to the porch.

Lettice had left the door open for him and, from another open door, light spilled into the hall.

He found her lying under a blanket on a chaise longue. Only one standard lamp, at the foot of her couch, lit the room, casting an arc of its light over her limp body, which seemed at that moment to be no larger than a girl's. Her thin hair was lank and, without make-up, grey-faced, she appeared to have grown older than the last time he'd last seen her – an old, lifeless child.

The doctor had draped a raincoat over his shoulders. Now he let it fall across the seat of a chair. 'What is it, Lettice?' he asked.

'I can't stop shivering and I feel terrible.' Her hands holding the edge of the blanket were like spiders.

'Yes,' he said. 'It'll be the shock. An emotional shock can bring on all kinds of things.'

The skin about Lettice's eyes was wrinkled, blotchy red, and her lips were as pale as her cheeks. 'Have you been crying?' he asked.

'I can't stop crying. I've not stopped crying since it happened.' Tears welled up in her eyes as she spoke and, fumbling, she reached for a large man's handkerchief tucked under her pillow. 'Why didn't you stop her! Why did you let it happen?' Her wrists seemed as thin as bare bone. 'Why didn't you stop it?'

'I knew nothing about it, Lettice. How could I?'

'I devoted my whole life to him. Year after year – all that time.'

Swallowing hard and leaning up on one elbow, Lettice blew her nose into the handkerchief and left a shimmering trail of mucus against her cheek. Her pale blue eyes were dim behind her tears and, for a moment, as the blanket fell away from her, the upper parts of her skinny breasts were revealed.

'It's a chill you've got, Lettice. This business has undermined your resistance. It's what I expected.' The doctor went into his bag, took out a bottle of medicine and shook it. 'Have you got a glass?'

'In the cabinet there,' she muttered.

He found a glass and poured a measure, gauging the dosage by the gradations on the side of the bottle. 'Drink this,' he said, handing it to her.

She took it in her spider fingers, put it to her lips and sipped. The taste made her shudder.

'There's quinine in it,' he said. 'It'll help with the temperature.'

'Will it help with a broken heart?' She looked at him with her dim, wet eyes.

'Drink it,' he said. 'I'll leave you the bottle.' He put it down on the sideboard.

White-faced himself, he looked about the room in that vague way of his, with his arms dangling at his sides and his round fists trembling. For a moment, he was absent within himself. Then he said, 'It's cold in here. You'd be better in bed.'

'How can I lie in the bed I shared with him? How can I?'

'Mmm.' The doctor gazed at her while she sipped away at the medicine. Strands of hair stuck to her damp forehead.

'I don't know what I'm going to do,' she said. 'I can't bear it – I can't.' She held the empty glass towards him, but her arm fell back. 'I'm so weak.'

He took the glass from her and sat down on a buffet facing her. He was silent again for a while, his shoulders hunched and his head bowed. The glass fell from his hand and he started, shocked that it had happened. Picking up the glass, looking around for somewhere to put it, he went back to the sideboard and put it down there near the medicine bottle.

A dimly lit picture hanging against the wall there seemed to interest him. He peered through the shadows at it. 'D'you know anything about ration books?' he asked.

She gave no response to that. She dabbed her face and let the handkerchief fall across her chest.

'I can't find my ration book,' he went on. He turned

back to her. 'Are you eating?' She was still not listening. 'Lettice – are you eating?'

'I can't. I can't get anything down my throat. How could they do it? We were married for forty years.'

'Forty-three in my case. Who knows what goes on in people's minds?'

'How can you bear it?' she asked, looking into his face.

'What option is there?' He came to sit again on the buffet. His face was shaded around his heavy jowls and upper lip. He hadn't shaved that evening. With his knees almost under his chin and his bulk balanced precariously, he said, 'I'm so tired I could fall asleep. I've had to make do with cornflakes and oats for three days. I didn't realise how much I relied on her. I thought she was happy.'

His mind drifted away again. The small fire in the grate flamed and threw red light over him for a second. 'What was I saying?'

Wearily, Lettice brushed the handkerchief across her eyes. 'How could they do it? How could they be so cruel?'

'It's the treachery of it that gets you,' the doctor said. 'I thought I knew her inside out . . . I'm angry – *angry*.' He thumped his thigh with his fist. 'But what was I saying?'

'I don't know. I don't know . . .' Lettice shook her head hopelessly and the heavy creases under her chin moved like deep folds in cloth. 'My life is in ruins. They want me out of the vicarage. Where am I going to go?'

'Is there nowhere else?'

'No. And he's sending me five pounds a week. Five pounds. He was supposed to be a man of God. For years I stood at his side. He always pretended to be so good, so holy. But it was all a lie, wasn't it?'

'She left me a note,' he said. 'It was very bright and breezy . . . Mmm.' He nodded himself to silence. Then he said, 'Mr Waters is in a bad way. I don't think he has much time left, you know.' His gaze came back to Lettice's strained, skeletal face. 'We have a son . . . At times like this you wonder whether you were his father. But no, no . . . I can't think that. We were very happy in those days. I thought we still were.'

He closed his eyes and covered them with his hand. For a moment it seemed as if he was about to cry himself. But he coughed and pulled down the sleeves of his coat. 'But life has to go on, Lettice. This sort of thing could destroy you if you let it. Yes . . . After all these years . . . Forty-three long years . . . It's the day-to-day things, you know. The meals, the things around the house. God knows where my ration book is . . . Life has to go on.'

The blanket had come away from Lettice's feet. They were encased in wrinkled woollen house socks. 'How can my life go on? Where can I go? Where can I live on five pounds a week?'

'It isn't all that bad, is it?' he said.

'Could you live on it? Could you?'

'Some of my patients live on less than that – with three or four children. Move into a cottage.'

'A cottage? Don't say that to me. How can you be so callous? A cottage? I couldn't bear it. He knew how terrified I was of being poor – he knew it. And look what he's done to me. I can't bear it.'

'You should stop saying that, Lettice. Gather your courage together.'

'But I'm a pauper! Don't you understand? Where am I going to live?'

'Mmm . . .' he said again. He got up and wandered off into the shadows. Deep in thought, he paused, standing across the room by the window. Absently he pulled at a dangling cord and the blackout curtains parted. He fumbled for some seconds to find the cord that closed them again.

'Lettice . . .' he said. But then he changed his mind. He went to stand and think by the fire, fingering the mantelpiece. At last, he came back to the buffet.

'Nowhere to live,' he said.

'He's left me destitute. A man of God . . . How could he? His wife . . .' Her spidery hands held the blanket close under her chin. 'I gave everything to him. My whole life.'

'Yes, yes . . .' the doctor nodded. 'Lettice . . .'

'Yes?'

'You know I've got that rambling place down the road – it needs a woman in it. My son and his wife had a sitting room and a bedroom and whatnot – all self-contained. All we shared was the kitchen. What d'you say? We needn't bother each other. All I need is someone to do the meals, answer the phone, keep the place tidy. It soon gets very dusty. People are ringing up all the time, especially this time of year. I can't manage to record them all. I've lived on cornflakes and oats for three days. It's not good. I've got no energy. I need a bit of help. And I'm damned if I know where my ration book is. What d'you say?'

Her handkerchief had fallen to the floor and she didn't have the strength to reach for it. With her two hands screwed into fists and resting against her forehead, she said, 'How can I go on living in this village now?'

'But I have to go on living here.'

'I couldn't! My life's ruined. I'm sixty-seven and I'm destitute.'

With that, she closed her eyes and grew silent.

Some moments went by.

'Lettice . . .' he said, leaning his head towards her. 'Lettice . . .'

But she wanted no more. 'Can you let yourself out,' she muttered. She had dismissed him.

'Mmm,' he mumbled again. He let out his breath, got up, picked up his bag and his raincoat. 'Take the medicine three times a day,' he said.

As he closed the outside door after him he realised that it was drizzling again. 'Oh damn!'

Ten days later a furniture van arrived to carry off Lettice's bits and pieces. On its side were painted the words: *J. Trimble & Sons. Haulage and Removals, St Albans.*

Later that afternoon, Lettice called into the booking office at the station and bought a ticket to King's Cross. Only the stationmaster was there to see her board the train in her blue coat and her little blue hat.

13
Maureen Goes to Town

Veronica was taken to the cottage hospital at Covenham, close to the church on the Louth Road, a glassy, single-storey building rather like a modern open-air school, all windows. It was an institution that had been largely funded by local collections and donations from the surrounding gentry. By the time they delivered her there it was gone nine o'clock and quite dark.

Veronica was taken to a small ward, the whole of whose outer wall was draped with two thicknesses of heavy blackout material. There was only one other bed – empty.

There was a permanent staff of nurses, but doctors were on rota from the surrounding villages. This evening, Dr Rivers was on call from Fulstow and he was at Veronica's bedside within fifteen minutes of her arrival. He was a tall, spare, almost cadaverous man with long, dark, curly hair and heavy black eyebrows. He had a rather remote, contained, concentrated air and was not given to uttering unnecessary words.

He and the ward nurse stood aside for a moment. She talked, he listened. And then they both came to Veronica's bedside.

'Mrs Heath,' he said.

'Yes.' Veronica was still trembling with anxiety.

'When did the bleeding start?'

'About eight o'clock.'

'What did you see?'

She told him.

'Mmmm.'

Veronica was lying without covers, dressed only in a flimsy cotton nightie they'd lent her. Both doctor and nurse gazed down at her. It was a cool, professional scrutiny, but behind their eyes Veronica was convinced that she detected something more. They know what I've been doing, she thought. They know.

Unable to face them, she looked away towards the large framed watercolour print of Lake Windermere that hung on the wall behind them.

'Let me take a look at you,' the doctor said.

Putting on a rubber glove and gently lifting her garment, he pressed her stomach. He took her hand and felt her pulse. Again, with great gentleness, and despite the fact that Veronica felt certain she was still losing blood heavily, he then gave her a brief internal examination.

'Mmmm,' he said again, stripping off the glove. 'Eight o'clock you say.'

Doctor and nurse exchanged glances and, once again, gazed down at her in silence for several long seconds.

But now Veronica was prepared to meet their eyes. Words formed themselves in her mind: I don't care what you think – you don't understand. I did it and I'm glad – I did it for my David.

'Will I be all right,' she asked, aloud. 'Will the bleeding stop?'

'The bleeding will stop,' said the doctor. 'Isn't that why you're here?'

For moments longer, doctor and nurse contemplated her. Then, at last, they turned away. They spoke out of earshot for a moment, left the ward, and returned two minutes later.

'The doctor will give you an injection,' said the nurse, cleaning Veronica's upper left arm with surgical spirit.

While injecting her, the doctor again treated her with great gentleness.

'We'll keep you in overnight,' he said. 'Don't worry. Good night.'

As he left the ward, the nurse ratcheted up the lower part of the bed. 'It might be a bit uncomfortable,' she said, 'but it's necessary. I'll bring you a cup of tea. But first I have to put you on a drip.' Plunging a needle into Veronica's arm, she set up the apparatus.

With the tea, she brought a pill in a little dish. 'You must take this.'

Elevated at an angle as she was, Veronica drank her tea only with difficulty. Perhaps the pill was a sedative of some kind, for within minutes of finishing her tea Veronica fell into a profound sleep.

She awoke next morning to birdsong. The blackout curtains had been drawn open and wintry sunlight filled the ward. A nurse – different from the one last night, breezy, busy, talkative – was at her bedside.

'How d'you feel?' she asked.

'I don't know. Have I stopped bleeding?'

'Well you ought to have. Doctor's here. Let's get you ready for him.'

The nurse wound down the bed and took away the blanket that had been draped over Veronica during her sleep. 'It's Dr Newton, you'll like him. Would you like bacon and egg for breakfast?'

Dr Newton nicely complemented the nurse. He was short, plump, about thirty-five, bouncy and exceedingly cheerful. His hair was the colour of polished copper and he spoke with a pronounced Scottish accent.

But when he pressed Veronica's stomach there was a heavy, brusque energy about it, and when he examined her he moved her leg aside without ceremony.

'Am I all right?' Veronica asked.

'Yes, Mrs Heath.' He laughed. 'You know, I almost crashed the car this morning on the way here. Ice everywhere. I skidded into the ditch. If I'd not had my wits about me I might be lying there next to you. Is Mr Butterfield here, Nurse?'

'Yes. Next door. He's waiting to see you.'

'Good. He promised me a brace. I'll go and collar him. Ah, Mrs Heath, look, stay with us for the morning. You can take the drip down, Nurse. Lie there and rest, Mrs Heath. You can go home after lunch – one o'clock. I'll be back then – just a quick look at you before you leave. Right, Nurse, let's get on . . .'

Veronica lay in an ecstasy of relief. 'Thank God,' she muttered to herself. 'Thank God it's done.'

Yet another nurse came in, raised Veronica up on pillows, and gave her breakfast – one fried egg and one small rasher of bacon, and a mug of tea.

Veronica was smiling. 'Oh lovely!' she said. 'What time is it?'

'Just after nine, love.'

'I can go home at one o'clock.'

'Yes. Would you like a brush for your hair?'

'Am I tousled?'

'A bit . . . Well, finish your breakfast and I'll bring one.'

'Thank you, thank you.'

With happy relish, Veronica consumed her breakfast and then, resting back with the mug of tea in her hand, gave herself over to thoughts of her husband, David. Affection for him flooded through her, mingled with that barely containable sensation of joyful release. It would have broken his heart, broken it – poor, poor David. How had she brought herself to let him down like that – her lovely, darling, beautiful David? Now he need never know. Oh what a relief . . . Now they could be happy again when this awful war was over. 'Oh David, when am I going to see you again? I love you – I love you . . .' she whispered to herself.

At one o'clock, dressed for home, she waited in the office for Dr Newton to return to the hospital after his rounds.

He pushed open the door. 'Ah, Mrs Heath. How d'you feel?'

'I feel fine, Doctor – fine,' she declared, bright-faced, happy.

'Good. You look it. Have you had lunch?'

'Yes, a nice salad.'

'Good. Let me feel your pulse . . . Tick, tock, tick, tock . . . Strong as a horse. Let me look into your eyes . . .' He drew her lower lids down, not too delicately. 'Excellent. Well then, yes, you can go home. You'll be as right as rain, Mrs Heath. Another hour or two and you'd have lost your baby, but thank goodness they brought you in in time. We think you're about twelve weeks. Talk to the nurse before you go. When your baby's ready to come we'll see you again. We'll look after you. Goodbye, Mrs Heath. Just watch your step – it's very icy out there.' And with that Dr Newton marched briskly away down the corridor.

Veronica stood up, but her legs were like columns of water and at once she fell back onto the chair. Pools of tears brimmed over and ran down her cheeks.

Maureen had been expecting it, of course. It came by post on the morning of Thursday, 28 November.

Dear Miss Binbrook, Peggy had written with cool formality, in neat, very legible italic script, *will you please put my daughters on the ten-thirty train on Sunday, 1st December. I will meet them at the station. Thank you, Margaret Delgrano.*

Maureen read it with a sinking heart. She sat in her room while rain streamed down the window. The girls could be heard shouting happily to each other as they ran across the hall and up the staircase. For some minutes, Maureen was too affected to move. She felt very much like crying.

But then she got up and went across the hall to the room she called 'the office', formerly her father's sanctum, which had been left virtually untouched. Its walls were bedecked with pictures of horses, one of them a Stubbs, and water-colours of Spanish dancers in sepia tints. There was a large mahogany desk with a set of inkwells and a stationery-holder with crested notepaper.

Resting along the top edge of a blotting pad was Maureen's fountain pen. Taking off its top and drawing out a sheet of paper, she wrote:

Dear Mrs Delgrano,

Thank you for your letter. I am very disappointed that you have chosen to take this action and I do suggest you reconsider it. Many cities have been bombed and – although I have no wish to alarm you – can you be sure that your own city will not suffer in this way? I understand that when the Blitz started children were evacuated again for their own safety, and I'm sure this applies to your own town. Therefore, is it wise to bring your daughters home just now? I am certain they'd be safer here. Perhaps you would give this some thought. I do sincerely advise you to change your mind.

I send you my best wishes,

Maureen Binbrook.

Because of the weekend, Peggy's reply did not reach Maureen until Tuesday, 3 December. It said:

I had made arrangements to pick them up on Sunday, when I said. I now have to take time off work. Will you please send them on the ten-forty-two train on Friday the sixth. Thank you.

Margaret Delgrano.

On reading this, Maureen felt a surge of anger and she wrote again at once.

I will not put them on the train by themselves. I will come with them. I ask you again to reconsider. If you change your mind, please telephone me. I think you know the number.

Maureen Binbrook.

There was no telephone call.

When Carla and Francesca were told they both cried and there was nothing Maureen could do to console them. There was nothing she could do to console herself. A true love for them had burgeoned in her over the months and her overwhelming impulse was to sit and cry with them.

The possessions the girls had accumulated here, their clothing, their books, their dolls, filled three large suitcases. And there were also their bicycles. Maureen had to ask Brendan Kelly to drive them to the station in Mr Britton's Austin, with the cycles strapped to the luggage rack on its roof.

What a sad journey. It was a dark, showery day with a lowering sky. The countryside through which the train passed was sodden and utterly colourless, quite dead, as if all human life had abandoned it. As they came into the suburbs of the town, drab houses, shoulder to shoulder, drenched with rain, shrank into themselves, and as the train passed over bridges you glimpsed drab people slouching along drab streets. The girls, sitting opposite each other in the compartment, looked out miserably and spoke not a word. Carla sucked her thumb. Francesca had hidden her face behind her high coat collar.

When the train slowed down towards the station, Maureen said again, 'Now you won't forget to write to me, will you? Tell me everything. Promise me.'

Five minutes later, the train shuddered to a stop and Maureen helped the girls down on to the platform. 'Just wait a moment,' she said. Turning away, she beckoned to a porter and he came grinning, a wiry little man whose cap hung precariously to the back of his head. 'Could you help with the three suitcases?' she asked.

'Sure, madam. Hang on, I'll get a trolley.'

'And there're two bicycles in the guard's van.'

'Did you get a ticket for 'em?'

'Yes – here.' She gave it to him. 'There's a lady waiting for us.'

'Right, well, go on. I'll follow you.'

As Maureen and the girls passed through the platform barrier, they saw Peggy Delgrano. She was standing against the far wall in front of a large pre-war poster advertising Bournemouth. She was wearing a fawn raincoat, tightly belted at the waist, and a red beret. Yet again, Maureen could not deny her attractiveness, that wholly female shape, which now came tapping towards them on high heels. But she was not smiling.

'Hello, girls,' she said, quite coolly, bending to kiss them one after the other.

They gave her restrained little smiles. 'Hello, Mam,' Carla said. Their feelings were obvious. Of course they loved their mother, but they did not want to be there and they could not understand why they were. They gazed up at her, perhaps hoping for something from her, but she offered them nothing and turned to Maureen.

'Thank you for bringing them. What do I owe you for the fare?'

'Nothing, Peggy. Nothing. Just let me ask – are you sure?'

'Yes. I am.' She nodded firmly. But then she looked into Maureen's eyes. 'You've been good to them. I won't forget that. And it's not your fault. I don't blame you. Haven't they got any luggage?'

'Yes. Quite a lot.' The porter had come to stand close by them with his trolley bearing the three suitcases and the bicycles balanced on top of them. Maureen gestured in that direction. 'It's there.'

'Oh God – all that? How am I going to get it all home?"

Maureen spoke to the porter. 'Can you find them a taxi?'

'Sure. Might have to wait a bit. I'll go to the rank and get a place in the queue.'

He pushed his trolley away and Maureen went into her handbag. 'Here, Peggy,' she said, offering a pound note. 'Let me pay for the taxi.'

'No,' said Peggy. 'I can afford my own taxis. Come on, girls.' She reached for her daughter's hands, but they were both looking up into Maureen's face. When she bent to kiss them goodbye, they both clung tightly to her.

'Bye-bye, my darlings,' she said, kissing their cold cheeks. The girls' eyes were brimming with tears and neither wanted to let go of her. Holding back her own tears, she gently eased them away. 'Come along now – go with your mother.'

She watched the three of them, hand in hand, walk away into the throng and knew in her heart that she would never see her dear girls again.

She had to wait ninety minutes for her train back to the village. The station was crowded with soldiers and their kitbags, and sailors in their flared overcoats with their steaming bags. A group of RAF men stood leaning against the wall drinking tea out of paper cups served to them by women of the WVS at their stall by the station entrance. From half a dozen locomotives, lively clouds of steam rose to the glass roof and rolled away in search of escape.

Maureen went into the buffet for a coffee. It was utterly tasteless, and in any case she couldn't get it past her dry, tight throat. Cold tears flowed freely now. Her handkerchief had become sodden and it was so embarrassing to be stared at across the table that she got up and went out into the street. It was raining, quite hard, and so she walked about in a department store. Oh Lance, she said to herself. Oh Lance, look what you've done to me now.

With an air of relief pervading the village after so many months of anxiety about invasion, people intended to make something special of their Christmas. The village shops, and shops at Somercotes and elsewhere, stocked up with every festive thing they could get their hands on. Saturday trains to town – to see Father Christmas and to buy whatever presents were available – were full. Few families in the village were so poor nowadays as to set aside for their children the meagre bits and pieces – an odd item of clothing, a couple of bars of chocolate, a few apples or oranges – that in former times had been tipped out of Christmas stockings, and popular items were dolls that said 'Mama' when you leaned them forward, air rifles (for older boys who already saw themselves as soldiers) and kits for building model aircraft in balsa wood.

Real Christmas trees were in short supply and expensive. Only the better-off could afford them, and their sale was left to Mr Godber at the garage, who had found a supplier in Yorkshire. At the post office and elsewhere, you could buy for one and sixpence imitation trees made from twisted wire interlaced with green fibre needles – effective enough when dressed. Tinsel was plentiful. There was a shortage of glass baubles, but there were boxed sets of tiny coloured candles in tin holders – dangerous but attractive when lit. Supplies of made-up decorations were soon exhausted, but Nancy sold reams of coloured paper that people could cut into streamers for themselves. Across shop windows Christmas greetings were written in whitewash. Holly, snipped from hedges all about, decorated the lintels over doors. On 9 December there was overnight snow. Under the early sun it glittered along branches, over roofs, and along the lanes. But in the afternoon the sky clouded over, rain fell and the snow slowly shrivelled away. A white Christmas now seemed unlikely, and in fact didn't happen.

Mothers and wives with men away in the forces wrote in their letters, *Oh, I hope you can get home for Christmas.* Separation at any time was bad enough, but to have them away at Christmas was just too sad a prospect, especially for young wives with children. Unfortunately, war service allowed no consideration of such things and the chances of a serviceman sitting down to Christmas dinner at home were slim.

Actually, only eight of the village's young men were serving. Certain kinds of farm work (which occupied many) and skilled war work at Evers' factory (which occupied others) were given exemption from call-up. Such working men would be present at the Christmas hearth, but those eight service wives would have to entertain their children alone – visiting their parents if they lived close enough, perhaps, but sitting and pining while the festivities went on around them.

At the best of times, young wives in the village tended to live rather isolated lives. Marriage inevitably meant children and a young mother expected – and was expected – to put husband and family before everything else. Few either worked or wanted to. An efficient housewife and mother was a proud creature, if, from time to time, a little lonely. At all times of day, prams and trolleys containing youngsters wrapped in blankets and scarves were parked outside the shops while young mothers stood at the counters with their ration books, asking what was available at the moment. A good young mother never failed to have meals on the table when children and husband came back from their day.

Most of Nancy's artificial Christmas trees and sheets of coloured paper were sold to these young women, who went home full of enthusiasm for setting up the tree and snipping away the paper into cheerful festoons.

Understandably in the case of a daughter with Eva's worrying naïvety and peculiarities, ever since Eva reached puberty, Mary had constantly worried about the possibility of the girl getting herself pregnant. She constantly badgered her with warnings, sometimes gently, but often with harangues and threats. Another girl could reasonably expect the boy to marry her; indeed, that was how a great many marriages came to pass. But who would marry Eva? It had been a never-ending worry. In fact, largely on account of it, Mary had sacrificed marriage herself. Charley had twice asked her to let him make an honest woman of her, to get hitched and come to live at the pub with him. But how could she do that? How could she expose her vulnerable daughter to it, when at the pub Mary herself had almost daily to fend off the attentions of men drunk and sober? That Eva had reached the age of twenty-four without calamity sometimes seemed to Mary to be something of a miracle.

The outlandish way the girl dressed and made herself up – 'You look like a prostitute!' – had long since passed beyond Mary's control. But, in fact, Eva's appearance had been one of the things that had preserved her. Village men had a saying, 'If you'll shag mad Eva, you'll shag anything.' Eva had become a kind of pariah. To be seen about with her would have brought ribald contempt down on a man's head. In her earlier days, boys had been content to probe at her, grope up her legs, sometimes to hit her for no reason at all, but then to leave it at that. So far as Mary knew, Eva remained a virgin.

But the village was now full of here-today-and-gone-tomorrow soldiers and ever since Eva's adored Douglas Russell, the former vicar, had left the village, Mary had always marked the calendar with the due dates of Eva's period.

'Did you come on last week?' she asked.

'Yes.'

Mary had been tired of late. Since the army's arrival her

work at the pub had been hectic. She'd increased her hours, working now every night of the week and four sessions over weekends, and there were times when she was exhausted. Perhaps because of this she had allowed Eva's reassurance to be enough, and it only dawned on her today that she had seen no visible confirmation of things. Mary bought the sanitary towels and counted them. And Eva was not very particular about personal hygiene. But Mary now realised that she had let such things go. With some alarm, she remembered that she'd done no counting and paid no particular attention to other details for weeks.

She sat Eva down and cross-examined her. 'Have you seen?'

'Yes,' Eva said.

'When?'

'Last week.' Eva sniffed and got up out of her chair.

'How long this time?'

'I can't remember.' Eva began to walk to the door.

'Where did you get the towels?'

'I didn't bother.' Eva opened the door.

'Come back here.'

'No.'

'Come back when I tell you—'

'No.' And Eva escaped up the stairs to her bedroom.

Mary sat for long moments with her hands to her face, rocking to and fro in her chair, made certain by Eva's attitude and behaviour that the girl had been lying. 'Oh God!' she said.

Quite weak in the knees, she climbed the stairs. Eva had locked her bedroom door.

'Let me in.'

'No.'

Mary began to scream and to hammer at the door with both fists. 'Let me in! Let me in, Eva!' It went on for some time, but then the door was opened and Eva stood facing her with that blank, open-mouthed, slightly puzzled, vacant expression on her face. 'I want a wee,' she said.

'Who was it?' Mary asked, entering the room, closing the door behind her and gripping her daughter by the arms.

'I want a wee,' Eva said.

'Who was it! Tell me – tell me!'

'Mind your own business.'

'You little bitch!' Mary let go of her, stood back and slapped her face, hard.

That sort of thing had not happened since Eva was a girl. She cried out. Tears came into her eyes and she tried to push her mother out of the way and get to the bedroom door.

But Mary grabbed her arms again. 'Who was it? Tell me his name! Tell me or I'll hit you again!'

'How do I know his name? Which one?'

'Which one? Jesus! How many were there?'

'How do I know? They were just soldiers.'

'Oh no!' Mary screamed. 'Oh no! You stupid bitch! You've had no period! You're pregnant! Aren't you?'

'I want a baby – I want a baby.'

'What? Oh you bloody fool! You stupid cow!'

Mary's face was livid and she was shaking her daughter so fiercely that her head was rocking backwards and forwards like that of a savaged doll's.

'I couldn't help it!' Eva had emptied like a canvas sack. She was crying piteously. Her thick mascara was running, her big nose had turned red. She was seven years old again. 'Don't hurt me, Mam,' she begged. 'Don't hurt me . . .'

And Mary herself, deeply affected by that, suddenly grew limp. The pathetic look on her daughter's face, those tears in her eyes, that dim look on her face, stabbed at her heart. Up surged all those tender feelings that had lain in Mary since the days she'd held her poor daughter in her arms as a baby, and tears came flooding into her own eyes.

'Oh Eva,' she said. 'Oh my little girl . . . Come here.' And she embraced her.

After all, something of the same sort had once happened to Mary herself.

The Lancashire Rifles abandoned their camp. With Colonel Roper at its head, and in a gesture of farewell, the battalion, a good half-mile of them, marched to drum and fife along Front Street, past the church, and made their way to the station by way of Back Street. Their music and their marching feet brought people out to watch them go. There were a few cheers and a lot of waving. Some were sad to see them go. Perhaps Eva wasn't the only one who'd fallen for the charms of one or two. But most people were glad to have them depart. Many had seen them as a nuisance, a menace. But even those who had tolerated them in and about the village of an evening were relieved because their going confirmed the fact that their presence in defence of the coast was now no longer needed.

The troops did not know it, of course, but in a month's time they were to sail for India, where they were in just the right place, eighteen months later, to join in the grim battle for Burma.

14
A Shock

As in the past, Mr Britton at Home Farm provided Maureen with a Christmas tree, although it was not a fir but a young Scots pine, six feet in height. It was set up in the large drawing room and the three of them – Veronica, Tidgy and Maureen herself – spent all afternoon dressing it. Over the years, the house had accumulated boxfuls of tree decorations: great glass baubles, miniature fairies and miniature Father Christmases in fine porcelain, sets of flashing lights and even strings of real gold and silver tinsel bought for Christmas parties when Maureen's father wished to impress with every detail.

When finished, the tree looked magnificent and all three of them sat down for a quarter of an hour simply to admire it.

This was 18 December. That night, after dinner, when Veronica had left for home and Tidgy was asleep in bed, Maureen sat in her room reading for an hour with her glasses perched on the end of her nose. At nine o'clock she closed her book and listened to the news on the wireless. Then came a talk on nutrition by someone from the Ministry of Food, but Maureen heard only a few minutes of it. Reading had tired her eyes and, settled back comfortably in the cushions, she fell asleep.

She awoke to the sound of audience laughter. It was Robb Wilton telling one of his tales – 'The day war broke out, my wife said to me . . .' – and Maureen jumped up at once. It was almost quarter-past ten. 'Oh dear!'

She went up to her bedroom, took a quick wash, made up her face, and changed into the dress he liked – the green silk she'd worn on that first night. When she got back to her room downstairs it was almost twenty-five to eleven. She poured a glass of whisky, turned off the wireless, decided that she had indeed left the side door open, and sat down, composing herself to calmness.

Thus she was sitting there smiling when, a few minutes later, Brendan came gently knocking. Entering, he stood for a while in a long navy-blue raincoat, and his brown face, so attractive to Maureen's eyes, smiled back at her. 'And how are you today, love?' he asked.

'Much the better for seeing you, my dear. But what's the matter?' She had noticed immediately that there was something unaccustomed in his normally lively and cheerful eyes, a strange sense of distance, and there was something in his posture, an unusual stillness. He simply stood there, smiling around those shadowed eyes.

'What's the matter?' she asked again.

Instead of answering, he came to her, bent over her and kissed her cheek.

'Tell me,' she said. 'What is it?'

He still didn't answer. He removed his coat. 'Raining again,' he said, sitting down, stretching out his legs. He was wearing his old brown boots with the polished toecaps.

'Yes, your hair's wet. Let me get you a towel.'

He waved her back into her chair. 'Don't move. Never mind my hair.' His gaze lingered on her face. 'You're a lovely woman, Maureen.'

'I do wish you wouldn't keep telling me that.' As always, it had made her blush. 'You're worrying me, Brendan. There's something the matter.'

He just smiled again. 'What've you been doing with yourself today?' he asked.

'We've been doing the Christmas tree. It's lovely – come and see.'

'Later,' he said, waving her down again. 'You know, I think you've lost a bit of weight.'

'Does it show? Good. I've been trying to.'

'Why? You were perfect as you were.'

'Oh do stop your Irish blarney, Brendan.'

Now she did get up. She went and gave him the whisky she'd poured for him. When he reached for it, he took hold of her wrist and held it for a second, gently. 'It's true, you know. I've really fallen for you,' he said, 'you darling Englishwoman.' He sipped. 'And you've got some damn good whisky.'

'Oh, I see. It's that, is it?'

'No – but it helps.'

They both smiled at that.

'No, Maureen, it's true. You're a real darlin'. At first sight of you I liked you, but I thought that's a stiff-backed one. That's one to watch . . . But how wrong I was. You've got a heart as big as this house.'

'Oh stop it!'

'No. I want to tell you. I love you, lass, and it's a fact. How did you manage it?'

'Just drink your whisky.' Maureen went back to her chair. 'And what have *you* been doing today, Brendan?'

'With this weather, not much. But I've finished the cottage.'

'Oh, that's marvellous.'

'Yes . . . I intended to finish it. Fit for a king now. Britton tells me you could sell it for three hundred pounds sterling.'

'Why should I want to sell it? You live there.'

He smiled. 'I've finished the main bedroom, fixed the roof, fixed the ceiling. I think you'll be very satisfied.'

'It's *you* who has to be satisfied. So you're quite comfortable there.'

'Anyone would be comfortable. I think I've made a damn good job of the fireplace.' Brendan took a sip of whisky. He closed his eyes.

'Are you tired?' Maureen asked.

'Just a bit.'

And silence fell. As he sat there, with his head back, breathing steadily, Maureen watched him intently. There was certainly something different about him this evening. What could it be? She felt very uneasy.

Suddenly, his eyes opened. He saw that she was gazing at him and gave her another affectionate smile. What a lovely man he was . . .

'Sing me "Phil the Fluter's Ball",' she said.

'What – again?'

'Yes. It amuses me.'

'Very well . . .'

Leaning forward in his chair, putting his glass down so that he could gesture with his arms, and assuming a broad Irish brogue, he sang.

Have you heard of Phil the Fluter
From the town of Ballymuck?
Sure the times were going hard with him,
In fact the man was bruck!
So he just sent out a notice to his neighbours, one an' all
As to how he'd like their company
That evening at a ball.

With a toot on the flute
And a twiddle on the fiddle-oh . . .

Maureen listened with delight and at its end applauded. 'Wonderful! It's so funny and you do it so well.'

'Let me see your Christmas tree,' he said.

'Oh yes. Come with me.'

The blackout curtains in the large drawing room were already drawn, but Maureen left off the main lights and switched on only the lights on the tree itself. The glow lit their smiling faces.

'What a beauty,' Brendan said. 'I like the fairy dancing about on the top.'

'Yes. I've had that since I was a girl.'

'What a lot of little parcels you've got dangling.'

'They're all little presents.' Maureen reached for his hand and held it gently in her own. 'There's one for you. You'll get it if you see me round about December the twenty-fifth.'

Gently, he eased his hand from hers. 'I've not finished my whisky.'

They went back to Maureen's room and sat down. Brendan's gaze clung to her face and that smiling, distant, worrying look was still in his eyes.

'There is something wrong,' Maureen said. 'Isn't there?'

'Yes, love. There is.'

'I knew it. What is it?'

'I can't stay with you tonight, love.'

'Well, never mind. There're other nights. But why not?'

He looked down at the floor and didn't answer.

'Well, Brendan?'

'The fact is, Maureen, I'm leaving.'

'What?' Maureen started and put a hand to her mouth. 'Oh no . . . Why?'

'I wish you wouldn't ask me. I have to go, that's all.'

'But what have I done?'

'You – done? Nothing, Maureen – it has nothing to do with you. How could it be your fault?'

'When – when?'

'I should've been away now, to tell the truth.'

'But why?'

He simply smiled again.

'Don't do it, Brendan. Don't go.'

'Ah,' he said, leaning towards her, taking her hand and holding it tenderly now. 'I've never felt for anyone what I feel for you, Maureen. It's true – I can't believe it myself, but it's true. You're such a loving woman – you're all heart – I've never known anyone like you. I'll never forget you, never, as long as I live.'

Maureen, so often close to tears in recent days after the loss of her two girls, was on the brink of crying now. 'Oh Brendan! What can I do? What is it you need? Tell me.'

'I need nothing, Maureen. I just have to go. Sell the cottage and forget me.'

'But I can't do that! How can I forget you? Oh Brendan
. . . don't . . .' And she really was crying.

Going to her, he got down on his knees and put his arms
around her. He kissed her wet cheek, her forehead and
then, softly, her trembling lips. 'I'm sorry – I can't stay
with you tonight. I shouldn't have come. I shouldn't have
upset you like this, but I couldn't go without seeing you
. . . I'm sorry. Don't cry. Look at me . . . Smile.'

But the tears were rolling down her face.

He got to his feet. 'Look at me. Look at me, Maureen.
Are you ready?' And, twisting his face, going into his funny
Irish accent, he sang to her again:

Oh they all joined in
With the greatest joviality
Covering the buckle
And the shuffle and the cut.
Jigs were danced,
Of the very finest quality,
But the Widda bet the company at the 'handlin' of the
fut'.

With a toot on the flute
And a twiddle on the fiddle-oh . . .

Next morning, Thursday the 19th, Nancy Philbin at the
post office had got the last paper boy off on his rounds
by twenty to eight. Mrs Williams had made her a cup of
tea and she was just drinking it before officially opening
the shop when the telephone rang. It made both women
raise their eyebrows, for a call at that hour was not at all
usual.

Mrs Williams answered it. 'It's for you,' she said. 'It's your husband.'

'What?' Nancy found that hard to believe. Michael was supposed to be on earlies that day – six until two. She had washed the breakfast things he had left on the table. He was now in his signal box down the line, two miles and more from a public telephone.

'Michael?'

'Yes,' Mrs Williams said. 'Come on – he sounds in a hurry . . .'

Nancy took the receiver from her. 'Michael . . .?' There was a note of concern in her voice. 'What's wrong?'

He had a garbled, confused and frightening message to deliver. His voice was taut with tension and he was breathing hard. 'I've only got a minute to talk, Nancy – and as God's my judge, I didn't want this to happen. I'm going – forgive me – I don't know how to say this.'

'Going? Where?'

'Don't speak, Nancy.'

'Don't speak! What's the matter? What're you saying?'

'For God's sake, Nancy, this is hard enough. Don't say anything, please – there's no time. I've got to go. I love you and always will, but it can't be helped. I've left you four hundred pounds.'

'Michael – Michael!'

'Don't speak. It's under the teapot on the table. Oh God, Nancy – I didn't want this. Listen, you're going to hear things about me you don't want to know. It makes no difference – I love you, I love you. Get out of it, Nancy. You know what people are. No, don't speak – listen, *listen*. For God's sake, get away as soon as you can, Nancy. Don't say anything to anyone – just get away. The money will buy you a house somewhere and keep you going for a bit. It's the best I could do. It's everything I've saved. I've got to go now. Get out of it, Nancy. I love you.'

'Michael – Michael!'

'Go now, Nancy – today. Please, get away. I love you, Nancy.' And the phone went dead.

'My God, what's the matter?' Mrs Williams asked, looking at Nancy's face.

Without a word, trembling, fumbling, distraught, Nancy grabbed her coat and hat.

'Where're you going?' Mrs Williams asked.

Nancy could do no more than stare at her, shake her head, and leave the shop.

Shocked by it all, Mrs Williams flopped into her chair behind the counter and couldn't move again until she heard someone rattling at the shop door. It must have gone eight o'clock. The person rattling was the Commodore, calling here on his way home from his walk.

'Morning,' he said. 'Was that Mrs Philbin I saw running down the lane just now?'

'Yes, it was. Her husband rang her and she just dashed off. She looked terrible. There must be something wrong.'

'Oh, I hope not.'

'I've never seen her like that before.'

'Really? Well let's hope she's all right. I want some stamps, Mrs Williams. I know you don't open the post office before nine, but I think you usually keep a few stamps behind the counter, don't you? And I want one more Christmas card – are there any left?'

The card was for the Commodore's old shipmate Hambley, a battered, loud, hunting, shooting and misogynistic bachelor and retired captain, now in his seventies. The Commodore sifted through cards with pictures of stagecoaches, of Father Christmas, of cricket matches on village greens, and one of a scene in an eighteenth-century inn with men not unlike Hambley boozing from tankards. But, feeling whimsical, the Commodore took a card showing an elegant, effeminate floral arrangement – one flower in a vase.

When he turned to leave the shop, the Commodore stopped to look at the noticeboard against the wall near the door. Onto it people had pinned postcards advertising items for sale, and the Commodore had always found them rather interesting. For instance, today someone was offering *Two large coils of rope, suitable for clothes lines*, and someone else *A pair of lady's patent leather shoes size five, a girl's gymslip for ages 12 to 14, a picture of Queen Alexandra in frame, a barely used trilby hat size seven.*

Lower down, a card announced: *Madam Kenworthy, at her salon at 7 Langworthy Lane, is available to offer her services by appointment.* The Commodore had seen similar announcements in Plymouth, Singapore, Hong Kong, San Francisco, Cape Town and Trincomalee, but he knew that Madam Kenworthy only did people's feet.

Then his eye caught a card that had been there for a long time and was now a bit faded, a bit dog-eared. *Mrs Swift*, then the address had been altered, *3 Manor Row. Dressmaking and alterations at reasonable prices. Call any time.* And that gave him an idea.

Since Monday, Fotherby had been away. He was spending

a few days visiting a sister in Scarborough. But he would be home this evening. Yesterday morning, over breakfast in Fotherby's kitchen, the Commodore had spotted his tattered old waistcoat hanging on the back of a chair. The man had resisted all the Commodore's pleas to have it mended – resisted, the Commodore felt sure, simply because Fotherby wished to be bloody awkward. He could be like that. Here was a chance to sort the bugger out.

Chuckling to himself, the Commodore hurried down to The Grange, ate some toast, drank some coffee, made out Hambley's card, and strolled up to number 3 Manor Row, posting the card on his way.

It was still not quite half-past nine. When Mrs Swift, Arthur's mother, opened the door to him, she put her finger to her lips and jabbed another finger towards the ceiling. 'Mr Swift's in bed – nights.'

'Oh, right,' said the Commodore, whispering. 'Mrs Swift, d'you think you could do me a little rush job?'

'Come in.'

Mrs Swift's Singer treadle sewing machine was under the window. Over its working end and passing under its needle was draped some dark blue fabric, and there was more fabric – white and red – folded on the table next to the machine.

'I see you're busy at the moment,' the Commodore said.

Little Mrs Swift had a smooth-cheeked face and smiling green eyes. 'Yes. I'm making a dress for Amanda Brocklesby.' She said it with pride. Perhaps she felt that working for the Brocklesbys entitled her to that.

'Oh, jolly good. What's happening to her husband, d'you know?'

'He's in the air force.'

'Yes, I know that.'

'They're going to some air force do . . . He was in the Battle of Britain and they're having a do. That's what the dress is for.'

'Oh. So that puts me out of joint. I wanted something doing today.'

'Well, what is it?'

'It's this . . .' The Commodore had brought the waistcoat in a brown paper carrier bag he'd found in the kitchen. He produced it. 'Look at it,' he said. 'It's Fotherby's. I wondered if you could mend the damn thing – get it looking decent.'

Mrs Swift took it, held it up. 'Oh dear . . .'

'What d'you think?'

'Well I could fix the pockets – that's no trouble. But the back . . . it wants another back sewing in.'

'Could you do it?'

'Oh yes – and I think I might have a bit of suitable material upstairs.'

'Good. The point is, he's coming back today and I'd very much like to give it to him tonight. Is there any possibility, d'you think?'

Mrs Smith pondered, looked at the partly made dress on the sewing machine, looked at the Commodore's face, and was just about to speak when there came a sudden thudding, echoing explosion – from some distance away, but very alarming.

Mrs Swift gasped. 'Is that a bomb? Is it an air raid?'

She reached out and gripped the Commodore's arm. 'It's an air raid! Tom's in bed. Tom! Tom!' she shouted, running out of the room and calling up the stairs. 'Tom!'

The commodore had not moved. He stood with the empty carrier bag dangling from his hand, his head cocked, listening.

'Tom!' Mrs Swift called again.

Several moments had passed and the Commodore was now able to say, 'No, Mrs Swift. That was no bomb. Had it been there would've been more. They don't drop them one at a time, you know. It was no bomb.'

'Then what on earth was it?'

'I've no idea,' said the Commodore.

Mr Swift could now be heard moving about upstairs. Then his voice was heard. 'Sally – what's up? What was that bang?'

He came down the stairs in his pyjamas and stood in the doorway of the room. His blind-man antennae sensed the Commodore's presence.

'Who is it?' he asked.

'It's Commodore Grainthorpe,' said Mrs Smith.

'What in hell's name was that bang, Commodore?'

'I'm afraid I don't know. Perhaps the army was up to something down the coast,' said the Commodore. 'Yes, I suspect that's the case. Blasting, perhaps.'

The three of them stood about, listening and waiting, for five minutes. Nothing more seemed to be happening, however, and so, shrugging his shoulders, saying, 'I bet I can't get to sleep again now,' Mr Swift went back to bed.

'Can you fix the waistcoat for me?' the Commodore asked. 'I mean today, Mrs Swift.'

'Oh go on. I'll have it done by teatime. I'll send it down with our Arthur.'

What had actually happened was that the Thursday-morning train from Evers' loading yard, carrying four days of their work along the branch line, had been sabotaged. A good part of it had been blown up. There had been seven wagons, loaded with aircraft parts – gun turrets, mostly. Five of these wagons had been flung into the air, scattering their loads all over the place. The engine had been derailed, but had remained more or less upright. The driver was uninjured, but the fireman had damaged his spine. The guard's van had gone into the air with the wagons, and the guard himself, who had been standing smoking on the platform at the rear of the van, had been flung out on to the track. He had broken both legs and was to remain unconscious for the next three days.

Just before one o'clock, and two hundred miles from the village, near Lancaster, Brendan's motorbike, with Michael Philbin riding pillion, turned off the A6 on to the cinder parking area of a busy transport café. They had ridden continuously for three hours. Swaddled though they were in caps and overcoats, they were both numb with cold. On his back, Michael had a rucksack that contained all the possessions both men had taken with them.

The café was quiet at that moment. Only half a dozen vehicles were parked in the yard and only eight or nine men sat at tables. Some were reading newspapers. Others were chewing or drinking, indifferent to everything else. The steamy heat in here was intense. It wrapped itself about Brendan's and Michael's heads like wet blankets.

They bought a fried-Spam sandwich each and mugs of tea. Brendan had been wearing thick leather riding gloves. He took them off and stuffed them into his pockets.

Though they sat opposite each other, neither man spoke. Presently, Brendan got up, took off his heavy outer coat and threw it onto a chair at the next table. Then he loosened his scarf. A few minutes later, Michael took off his cap, opened the buttons of his raincoat and unfastened his own scarf. Nancy had knitted it for him.

At the counter, a customer who had just arrived said something to the woman who was serving him that must have amused her. At her musical laughter, several faces looked towards her. Brendan himself gave her a quick glance, but Michael still stared down at the stained blue tablecloth.

Having eaten his sandwich, Michael lit a cigarette. When smoke came across the table to him, Brendan wafted it away and looked across the room for a moment to where someone was just rising to leave. Then he too went back into himself. His round, youthful-looking face was expressionless.

They drank their tea slowly. Outside, a heavy wagon arrived in the yard. Its engine idled for a moment and its vibrations could be felt underfoot. A moment later, two men entered the café, grinning. 'What's on the menu?' one of them said as they went to the counter.

A quarter of an hour passed. Brendan got up and put his coat and scarf back on. Draining the last dregs of tea from his cup, Michael himself got to his feet and picked up the rucksack. They went to the malodorous, muddy lavatory, buttoned up and went back outside.

In all this time, neither had looked into the face of the other. But as he hitched the bike off its stand, Brendan said, giving Michael a quick glance, 'Right then, me old mate. Let's get on with *our* bloody war.'

He started the bike's engine, revved it and climbed on to the seat.

Michael said nothing. He got back into the straps of the rucksack and got on to the pillion. Rather than cling to Brendan's waist, he put his hands into his pockets, and as the bike suddenly moved off he almost fell backwards. If he were to be flung from the bike at sixty miles an hour and be killed he wouldn't have cared.

They still had a long way to travel – Stranraer and the ferry across the Irish Sea.

Nancy Philbin had not taken her husband's advice. She had not left at once. His message had come to her like something in a nightmare, inexplicable, heart-stopping, terrifying, but unreal. She had no capacity to comprehend it.

What she in fact did, not very rationally, was run gasping and panting through Wyber's Wood and on towards Michael's signal box where, at this moment, he ought to have been working. When she came to the stile, she heard the echoing crash of the explosion, quite close, along the line towards the Evers' siding. She stood for a moment, wild-faced, her panic now made more intense by this other shock.

Running on to the signal box, she saw Victor Gibbons standing on its platform. 'Did you hear that!' he shouted down, so alarmed himself that it hadn't occurred to him to wonder what Nancy was doing here. 'The train's been derailed!'

'Is Michael there – where's Michael?'

'What?'

'Michael – Michael – where is he!'

'I don't know, Nancy – I don't know. He knocked this morning. I'm his relief. What the hell's happened? The train's been blown off the rails!'

Within a matter of hours the police were hammering at Nancy's door. She was sitting lifelessly, still dressed in her outside clothes, with mud on her shoes from the wood, numb and speechless like a traumatised child.

Two days later the facts were known to all. The story occupied the front page of the local paper and was mentioned briefly during the nine o'clock news on the wireless.

Nancy had already been escorted away and no one ever saw her in the village again. She had lived there all her life. But the brick-throwing fraternity considered it reasonable, even though she was no longer there, to smash all the windows of her house, and the Commodore was put to the expense of new glass throughout.

15
Christmas; the Borrowed-Time Brigade

Now that the risk of imminent invasion seemed to have faded, Brocklesby was feeling more cheerful. The thought that he and his family might be booted out of this marvellous house and see it occupied by some official of the German occupying forces had lain at the root of so much anxiety that for the past six months his mood had been one of almost unrelieved tension. He couldn't understand how Phoebe and so many others around him could carry on their lives so normally, behaving as they had always behaved, as if nothing at all unusual was happening. Phoebe had taken to the war almost with enthusiasm, dashing around the county on charitable work, organising her WVS, disappearing for days on end, and driving her Women's Institute into the war effort like Boadicea. He had sat for hours, immobilised by his anxieties, while she had flitted around him perfectly happy.

He had been ashamed to think that his instincts were cowardly and, unable to tolerate that, had decided that other people were simply fortunate. They did not have his imagination. They couldn't see possibilities. But now that all threat of Germans advancing across his fields had gone, he was a new man, full of energy and desperate to let it be known that he was playing his part.

He was seen out and about every day, even calling at the shops and talking to people in the lanes who had never before had a word from him. He met Fletcher, his woodsman, one morning and asked about his family, discovering that since they'd last spoken Fletcher had had a child.

Fletcher had been asked to find a suitable Christmas tree for the Manor House and was digging up a young spruce. He waved an arm at the densely packed twenty-foot-tall specimens all around. 'It'd give the kids a treat if we stuck one of these up in the village near the church somewhere,' he said.

'Could we get one out?' Brocklesby asked.

'We'd just saw it down. The tractor would shift it easy.'

On his return to the house, Brocklesby said to Phoebe, 'I've had a wonderful idea. I'm going to put a giant Christmas tree up in the village for the children.'

'Excellent,' said Phoebe.

The tree was erected a few yards from the war memorial and decorated with the lights that during Christmases before the war had been draped across the front of the Manor House. They had to be switched off after dark, but still looked festive during the gloomy December days. Phoebe herself went down to the school and led the procession of children to stand around it when the lights were first switched on.

The new vicar, who had allowed the lighting cable to be connected to the main circuit of the church, providing Brocklesby would pay the bill, joined them. He said a few prayers and they all sang a few carols.

This new vicar was Francis Lightowler, a freshly

promoted curate from Derby aged only twenty-six. He was an ambitious cleric, and as he stood in the midst of the children of this village, tall and thin and self-possessed, there was about him that rather aloof, complacent air of a young man pausing just for a moment on a stepping stone to greater things. Giving the children only a moment or two of his time, he turned to Phoebe, that doyenne of all the things, and set about charming her for ten minutes. In the sixties he was to become a bishop.

On odd occasions, Colonel Roper of the Lancashire Rifles had been happy to allow the Home Guard use of the butts. It had been an important part of their training. On hearing that the Lancashire Rifles were to abandon their camp, Captain Welsh had managed to persuade the War Office to allow his Home Guard unit to continue using the facility. As quid pro quo, he had agreed to guard the empty camp for the time being as part of the Home Guard's normal routine. This saved the Military Police a job they could well do without.

On Sunday the 22nd, sixteen of the Home Guard marched up Littlecotes Lane, with Sergeant Fotherby bringing up the rear. 'Private Grainthorpe, pick your feet up, man!' He could never resist it.

They shot off a magazine each, ten rounds, with mixed results. Jim Lavery, Britton's foreman at Home Farm, now thirty-five, had been handling a shot-gun from the age of ten and, as usual, he found the bull easily, and several inners. Fotherby, never going to let himself down in front of his men, made sure to get at least one bull.

Halfway through the session, Captain Welsh, dismayed,

said, 'Most of you don't seem to be improving much.' Then he felt it necessary to give them another lesson in sight adjustment. It didn't make any difference.

'Fall them in, Sergeant.'

And as they stood there to attention, Captain Welsh said, 'I have the rota here for Christmas Eve. I'll be doing the village with Private Holmes and Corporal Dobbs—'

'What – Christmas Eve!' Corporal Dodds protested.

'Yes, Christmas Eve,' the captain said.

'Perfectly right,' the Commodore remarked, drawing serious frowns and grunts from his comrades. 'On Christmas Eve and every eve, England expects every man to do his duty.'

The joke was not appreciated. He received three or four raspberries.

'You, Private Grainthorpe,' said the captain, looking at the Commodore, 'with Sergeant Fotherby, will patrol the Somercotes road as far as Evers' factory.'

At the factory, where shifts would be working until six on Christmas morning, the Home Guard had been given a place to rest between patrols. It was an old storage shed in the yard near the gates, and whatever might be happening the duty patrol tried to be back there at half-past ten in the evening because at that time a brew-up was provided.

On the dot of ten thirty on Christmas Eve, Fotherby, carrying the Home Guard aluminium teapot, went into the noise and bustle of the factory to collect the tea. Men and women at the benches, catching sight of him, waved and grinned. Big, twisted-nose Fred, an overlooker, that evening in charge of the geyser, filled the teapot.

'How's Tom Swift doing?' Fotherby asked, nodding to

where Arthur's father was sitting, moving his hands in steady, practised motions.

'He's bloody good,' Fred said. 'Watch him – see how nifty he is. I had a brother in the same unit as him in the last war. You know what happened, don't you – how he lost his eyesight? It was at Loos. The British let their gas go even though the wind was in the wrong direction. It blew back into their own trenches. Some mad bloody officer. Bloody fool! Fancy being blinded by your own gas!'

Fotherby went back to the shed and poured tea from the teapot into Home Guard enamel cups. 'I've brought a couple of sandwiches,' he said. 'And see . . .' He produced a flask.

'What is it?' the Commodore asked.

'Double-fermented parsnip. It'll blow your head off.'

'Good man,' said the Commodore, reaching for the flask.

In the village, families sat listening to the wireless. A music hall was being broadcast, with the Two Leslies, Arthur Askey, Tommy Handley, Nosmo King and others. There were jokes about Hitler and songs that had sunk into the nation's soul: 'There'll be bluebirds over the white cliffs of Dover' and 'We'll meet again, don't know where, don't know when, but I know we'll meet again some sunny day.'

Down the road, the Black Bull was crowded. As the troops had marched away, Charley's trade had gone down virtually to nil. He'd had to sack his extra bar staff. He'd been worried. But by now old regulars, who'd been driven out by the intolerable crush and din of a place full of soldiers, were gradually coming back, and tonight all the old faces were there. The atmosphere was very merry. Charley had drunk a good bit, and so had Mary.

In a pause, when no one was clamouring at the bar, she said, 'Do you remember asking me something?'

'What sort of thing?'

'The last time was March.'

Charley gave thought to that, then asked, '*Was* it March?'

'Yes, it was. A woman doesn't forget such things.'

'Why d'you ask? Don't tell me you've changed your mind.'

'I think I have, Charley.'

'Well fancy that. What's brought this on? What about Eva?'

'Oh don't ask! I was worried about her.'

'Yes, I know.'

'Well it doesn't matter now. She's gone and got pregnant.'

'What? Oh no. Oh hell, I'm sorry, Mary. I really am. One of them damned Lancashire Rifles was it, the sods?'

'So there's no point in worrying about her any more, is there? But it means that if I – we – come here with you, there'll be a baby coming too.' She looked into Charley's face. 'I suppose that makes a difference.'

'Does it hell. I'll be glad to have a kid about. That's one thing I've missed in my life.'

'Is it?'

'Yes it is, believe it or not. And in any case, listen, I'll

tell you something. With the army and my little sideline
I've made a packet these past few months. If you feel like
it, I can sell up here, Mary, and move on to something else.
What d'you think?'

Mary stepped towards him, reached up and kissed his
cheek.

'None o' that,' said a man at the bar with two empty
pint pots in his hands. 'Let's have a bit of service.'

'Just hang on, Derek,' said Charley. Putting his arms
around her, he hugged Mary to him.

Earlier that week, German bombers raided the town fifteen
miles away.

Lance Binbrook had come home for Christmas, but at
six o'clock on Christmas morning his call came.

Lance was earning a little these days – from the Government.
He had bought himself a second-hand Morgan, a delight
to drive, and was allowed an extra petrol ration. He was
wearing the blue overalls he'd been provided with and, next
to him, on the passenger seat of the car, was his steel
helmet.

He reached the outskirts of the town at eight o'clock
and, concerned about the safety of his abandoned Peggy,
took time he didn't really have to drive along the 25 bus
route as far as the end of her street. He was relieved to
find everything intact there.

Reversing the car, he went back towards the town centre.
He came on the first signs of destruction after three-quarters of a mile. A bomb had fallen in the yard behind a
large pub – the Angel Inn. It had blown the entire building

into a mass of debris across the road and he could make no further progress. There were several people on the pavement, watching men dig into the ruins of the building, and from among them a policeman came walking over to him. 'You'll get no further down here,' he said.

'I can see that.'

The policemen looked at the badge over Lance's left breast. 'Ah,' he said, his expression changing. 'Where're you trying to get to?'

'Mill Street, and I'm a bit late. How do I get there now?'

'Well Monsall Road's no use to you either – that's blocked. Let me think . . . Yes, Mellor Street. Go back about a quarter of a mile. Turn right at Mellor Street, then go left at Foster Street. Got that? Mellor Street and left at Foster Street.'

'Yes. Thanks.'

'We've got some people buried under this lot,' the policemen said.

'Well I hope you get them out alive.'

'Not much hope, I'm afraid. Good luck to you.'

'Thanks.' Lance turned the car round and drove away along streets of terraced houses, corner shops, chapels and small factories. There was no damage here, but in the slight breeze dense clouds of smoke were being channelled along these narrow chasms, reducing visibility to nil, and he had to stop several times until they dispersed. It was when he came nearer to the city centre that the effects of high explosive became obvious. While he bumped his groaning car over more rubble he saw a woman sitting on a pile of bricks nursing a baby. Behind her, the fronts of two houses had been blown down. High up on the rear wall a double bed, hanging there by two of its legs, dangled precariously from the remains of a bedroom floor. Wallpaper had been torn away in strips and on top of a heap of roof tiles an upright piano stood with its lid open, as though someone had just finished playing. A few hundred yards further on he came to a stop again, confronted by a fire engine and a confusion of pulsating hosepipes like a nest of snakes. He had to park his car and go the rest of the way on foot.

Mill Street was one of the main thoroughfares of that part of the town. It lay ahead of him – dead straight as far as the eye could see. At its far end, just visible as smoke drifted, it was lined with shops, but here there were more terraced houses. Many doors were open and another crowd of people stood huddled on the pavement, saying little or nothing. Some of them had cups or mugs in their hands.

Just beyond the crowd a rope was stretched across the street. From it dangled, crookedly, a sign saying DANGER UXB. All the houses beyond the rope had been evacuated.

As Lance approached, people turned to watch him come.

'Here's another of 'em,' someone said.

Lance now saw that there were police in this gathering also. Two of them, an inspector and a special constable, took a few strides forward to greet him.

The inspector spoke to him. 'You Mr Binbrook?'

'Yes.'

'They've been waiting for you.'

In the restricted area, fifty yards or so away beyond the rope, a semi-circular barricade had been erected, two sand-bags thick. In the smoky morning light, several tin-hatted figures could be seen there. Lance recognised Molyneau at once from the shape of him and from that hands-on-hips stance of his.

'You want some tea?' a woman asked.

'Aye, give him some,' a man said. 'All the others've had some.'

The woman hurried away across the road.

Two soldiers went by, carrying between them, a handle in each man's hand, a large and heavy canvas bag. Glancing at Lance, they gave him a nod.

'You've not forgotten the large clamps again, have you, boys?' he asked.

They laughed good-naturedly. 'No. Not this time.'

'In fact we've brought four,' said one of them over his shoulder.

Lance found a large mug of tea under his nose. He thanked the hand that held it. 'Can I take it with me?' he asked.

'If you want.'

He looked at her. She was a woman of about thirty with an agreeable smile on her small, daintily featured face. 'Could I ask your name?' he said.

'Why?'

'D'you object?'

'No. Why should I? It's Sue.'

'And where do you live, Sue?'

'Aren't you nosy? Across the road there – number 33.'

'Well, when we're finished, I'll bring your cup back.'

The crowd had watched this intently. Turning away, Lance followed the two soldiers with the bag. He had not gone far when he realised that the police inspector had fallen in beside him. 'It's been here since the raid we had on Saturday,' the inspector said. 'These things cause chaos. Traffic gets mucked up, people have to leave their homes – all the people from down here have been camping out in St Peter's Church.'

'Yes, chaos. That's the general idea. That's why they drop these delayed-action bombs.'

'The hole it made was as neat as pie, just as if someone had drilled it in the middle of the road. There'd have been a lot of dead round here if it'd gone off. There's about six of the things from Saturday. What kind of swines would want to bomb people at Christmastime? The army've been digging all night.'

Molyneau and Pickmere, overalled and wearing tin hats like Lance himself, also with teacups in their hands, stood together waiting for him. Nothing was said. They merely nodded and sipped from their cups.

The two soldiers with the tools were at the barricade now. At its centre, pressed up against the sandbags, stood a solid-looking box serving as a desk. On it lay a tattered notebook and some pencils. In front of the box, absently flicking through the book and smoking a cigarette, sat Staff Sergeant Quest, wearing a combined earphone and mouthpiece set. The two soldiers dropped the bag of tools at his feet. One of them spoke to him for a moment and then the two of them walked away, back along the street. As they went they gave casual waves to the three men drinking tea.

Putting out his cigarette, removing his headset and getting to his feet, Staff Sergeant Quest walked across to Molyneau, bringing a piece of paper with him.

'Major Grover and the lads're at Hulme,' he said. 'So you're on your own. But he was here earlier. He's left you some notes.' He handed Molyneau the paper.

Molyneau read it.

'What does he say?' Lance asked.

'It's a five-hundred kilogram, ten feet down. They've revetted the dig.'

'But watch it,' said Staff Sergeant Quest. 'It was shale. They've put a cross member in. They've mounted the tripod for you as well.'

'Yes,' Pickmere said, gazing along the road. 'I see it.'

Molyneau was still reading Major Grover's notes. 'They've sandbagged it, but not clamped it. He says they've attached the Q coil, but the fuse boss is damaged. The wrench won't work.'

'Then it's hammer and chisel again,' Pickmere said. 'You can do it, Lance. I'm still bruised from last week.'

'And for God's sake don't light up,' said Quest. 'There must be a gas main somewhere.'

Molyneau and Pickmere both gave the staff sergeant their empty cups. 'Are you ready, Lance, you late scholar?' Molyneau asked.

'Certainly!' Lance now gave his own cup to the staff sergeant, who almost dropped it, but then hung it over his thumb.

'Hang on to it, please,' Lance said. 'I've promised to return it.'

'Good luck,' the staff sergeant said.

'Whose turn is it to carry the bag?' Pickmere asked.

'Lance's and mine,' said Molyneau, and he and Lance went to the barricade for it, each taking hold of a handle.

Side by side the three of them confronted the long walk. 'Good luck!' the staff sergeant said again.

The police inspector, who had stood a few feet away during these exchanges, watched them go. 'How long will this take?' he asked.

'If they're lucky, less than an hour,' said the staff sergeant. 'Then we can drag it out and get rid of it for you.'

'But why did they have to wait four days!'

'It's these Rheinmetall delayed-action fuses. They can set 'em for up to a week. Policy is to leave them for eighty hours if possible. Generally, if it's not gone off in sixty hours, it's a dud. At least, that's the theory. The trouble is these fuses are temperamental. They can easily malfunction.'

'Can they?'

'Oh yes. That's the snag. They can seize up before they're due to go off. They can seize up when they hit the ground. Then any sudden shock or movement can set 'em going again. It could've gone up while we were digging the hole – easy. They're going up all the bloody time. That Q coil they talked about helps with the magnetism. But you can never be sure.'

'And what will those three be doing?'

'Screwing the fuse out. If they can.'

'Rather them than me, I think.'

'You can say that again. Jerry's got diabolical lately. They ring the changes. One goes off when the case is tapped, another goes off when the fuse is unscrewed. Booby traps, you see. Yes, it's tricky. One of our teams went up the other day in Birmingham. I knew 'em well – mates of mine. Yes, they're going up all the time.' The staff sergeant touched the inspector's sleeve. 'Those three call themselves the Borrowed-Time Brigade.'

'Why? What does it mean?'

'God knows. Something to do with the last war, I think. They were all in France. But you see those two on either side – the fat one and the thin one? Molyneau and Pickmere? Don't tell anyone, but they're raging ponces.'

'Oh. Are they?'

'Wouldn't expect blokes like that to volunteer for a job like this, would you? But they're a good team. This'll be the fourth they've done. Anyway, I've got work to do.'

The staff sergeant went back to his folding stool and the wooden-box desk. He opened the notebook, picked up one of the pencils and began to put his earphones on.

'They talk to you, do they?' asked the inspector, joining him there.

'Yes. There's a line from here to the dig. I note every move they make. It's the only way to know what Jerry's up to. They tell us what they're doing. If it goes up we know not to do it next time.'

'Look,' said the inspector, 'we're safe at this distance, aren't we?'

'Should be. But if you're a bit worried go behind the rope. Safe as houses there. Just keep your fingers crossed for them three down the hole.'

Echoing through the smoke from fifty yards away, yet to those listening as if at only arm's length, came the clanging sound of hammer against chisel against the fuse boss of the bomb. Clang, clang, clang.

People in the crowd stood frozen, some clinging to one

another's hands, cringing and wincing at every blow of the hammer. Others, unable to bear the tension, ran indoors or pressed the palms of their hands to their ears so as not to hear. Clang, clang, clang.

In the village, a little later on that Christmas Day, there was music. A Salvation Army brass ensemble from Louth (cornet, tenor horn, euphonium and E-flat tuba), on a tour of local villages, was now tonguing lustily at the corner of Church Lane: 'Away in a Manger', 'Good King Wenceslas', the 'Coventry Carol'. The sound was carried on the northerly breeze into most corners of the village, only losing itself to silence in the cold and empty spaces of the abandoned army camp. People went to stand at their doorways to listen.

16

Constable Bowker's Final Round
of the Year

New Year's Eve fell on a Tuesday, and that is as far as this story needs to go. We will follow Constable Bowker on his last round of 1940.

It had been a bright day. With darkness had come a sharp frost. By the time Constable Harry Bowker set off on his round the moon was haloed, the stars glittered as fiercely as angry eyes, and hoar frost crackled under his boots. But for that faint, wavering sound of music from village wirelesses now and then, all was quiet. He walked as far north as Brocklesby's Christmas tree at the church gate. There he lit a cigarette and peered through the shadows into the churchyard.

In the light of the moon, black gravestones enshrining long-forgotten memories of long-dead villagers leaned sometimes to the left and sometimes to the right under the weight of the years. Between the trees, the dark outline of the vicarage could be seen and, puffing at his cigarette, the constable was reminded of Douglas Russell who had suddenly disappeared into the air force and Samuel Duke who had equally suddenly disappeared with Dr Green's wife. How long would this new young chap, this Francis Lightowler with his skinny little bossy wife, survive? God's right-hand men were having a bad war in this village.

Throwing his cigarette end into weeds under the hedge and pressing it out with the toe of his boot, Harry walked on towards Front Street. Along branches overhead, frost flashed in quick little sparks. As he came to Manor Row a dog barked six times in one of the houses. The garden gate of number 4 was open. He closed it, realised that its catch was broken, and left it to its own devices.

Inside number 3, Mrs Swift was sitting back in her chair with her eyes closed listening to the wireless. Her son Arthur was sitting across the fireplace from her, reading *The Adventures of Sherlock Holmes*. Mrs Swift's sewing machine had had its cover placed over it. For once she had no intention of working in the evening. As if to emphasise that decision, the table standing near the machine had been cleared of its bolts of fabric and its bobbins of cotton. All it bore now was a small piece of coal, a section of loaf and some coins. These things were there waiting until five to midnight. At that time, in the absence of his father, again at his war work, Arthur would put these things into his pocket, go outside and hang about for five minutes. Then, as Big Ben tolled midnight over the wireless, he would walk back in again, bringing in the New Year, and with it those hopeful tokens of warmth, food and a bit of wealth. This was a tradition exclusive to the Swifts in this village. Mrs Swift had come from Yorkshire when she married Arthur's father and had brought it with her.

She opened her eyes and gazed at her son. He'd had his hair cut shorter of late and she would have preferred him not to have done it. It made his nice face look too thin and bony. His knees were bony as well, poking up under the cloth of his trousers, and he sat there reading with a distant, very serious expression on his face. When he talked these days, he did so with the voice of a young man. That lovely song of his was no more. His hands were bigger. He had begun to call her Mother now, not Mam, and had begun to hug her around her shoulders rather than simply kiss her cheek.

He became aware of her stare. 'Yes?' he asked, indeed just like a man.

'Nothing, love,' she said, closing her eyes again.

But there *was* something. She had lost her little boy.

Harry went on into Back Street. At number 8, Mr Robinson appeared to have dumped something in the middle of his garden. From here it looked like an old mattress. What a sod Robinson was. Where would he be now but in the pub, boozing himself into a stupor? No wonder his wife was half demented. And their poor bloody kids. What a life! But there were dead-legs in every village and what could you do with them?

The constable remembered Clifford, the Robinson's evacuee, who'd been driven from that house by sheer misery. He remembered the sight of him, a small white face drifting along this dark lane, hell-bent on walking to Birmingham.

From the upper windows of the houses, moonlight reflected almost as bright as sunlight. There were patches of ice on the pavement here. Harry skidded dangerously and had to resort to walking in the gutter where it was safer. Number 17 Back Street was the home of Martin Walter, now in the air force training to be a pilot in Canada. Harry had played cricket with him in the village team before the war. Martin could bowl as fast as Larwood.

He passed Dr Green's house. Now that his wife had

vanished, the constable imagined Dr Green sitting miserably alone and felt a spasm of sympathy for him. What d'you make of these silly old devils who run off with each other in their sixties? The constable shook his head.

In fact, Dr Green was not at all miserable. He'd had a slap-up meal at the White Hart Hotel in Cleethorpes, a whisky at his favourite pub in Tetney, was off duty for two days, and was enjoying a glass of very good brandy while listening to Gilbert and Sullivan on his radiogram. Pat had disliked Gilbert and Sullivan. She had disliked many things the doctor himself was fond of, and had wanted things he hated. Free now to indulge his own fancies, to eat out when he felt like it, to sit where he wished, to leave books about, to belch if so inclined, to drop cigarette ash, to make noises when he ate, he was realising now that for forty-three years his own true self had been submerged under the blasted tyranny of the blasted female of the species. And how the hell had he tolerated someone sleeping in the same bed with him for all that time, pushing at him, complaining, telling him to stop snoring? Good God, how had he allowed it? He sipped his brandy and hummed to the music. And if he felt like it, he'd get drunk tonight, damn it!

Harry Bowker was reminded of the doctor again when he came to the post office and shone his torch through the reinforced glass of the door. Against the noticeboard was pinned a card rather larger than the others. What was written on it was just about legible. *Daily woman wanted . . . Dr Green.*

Harry walked on and came to The Grange. The gates were open and open gates always annoyed him. That was why he'd tried to close the gate at Manor Row. But these great gates here were never closed and had been open for so long that rusty hinges would never again allow any movement. A little frisson of irritation went through the constable and he hurried by.

The Commodore had grown very fond of Fotherby's parsley wine and they had saved some to celebrate the arrival of the New Year. It was in a decanter on the sideboard. They sat together in the drawing room before a hot fire, for the moment drinking: in the Commodore's case, gin and bitters, and in Fotherby's case, bottled beer. On the brass fender reflections from the fire mingled with reflections from the lights on the Christmas tree on its table against the wall. The wireless, low enough to listen to but not so high as to prevent abstracted thought if that came over them, was broadcasting light music: Eric Coates's 'Knightsbridge', well known to everyone because it was the signature tune of *In Town Tonight*, a popular Saturday-evening programme. From time to time they talked. From time to time they didn't.

'You know, old chap, I wouldn't have minded in the least if you'd wanted to sit with Mrs Feathers this evening,' the Commodore said.

'Joan Feathers has her daughter with her tonight – and that bloody beak-nosed son-in-law.'

'You don't like him.'

'No I don't. I can see Joan Feathers any time.'

'Ah.'

They sank into silence again. On the wireless now Peter Dawson was singing 'Roses are shining in Picardy, in the hush of the silvery dew, roses are flowering in Picardy, but there's never a rose like you . . .' The Commodore, round and comfortable, feeling sentimental for the moment, was singing along with him.

'I know all about Picardy,' Fotherby said. He'd been on the Somme with the Royal Naval division in 1916. 'I never saw any bloody roses there.'

And the Commodore stopped singing. 'Mmm,' he muttered.

Fotherby poured more beer into his glass. The Commodore lit a cigarette and sat with it between his fingers for two or three minutes. He reached for the ashtray, tapped the long grey trunk of ash into it, and only now took in a lungful of smoke. 'When will we get some decent cigarettes again?' he asked. 'What happened to Passing Clouds?'

'Things've got worse than I expected. Why don't you go back on your pipe?'

'I suppose I'll have to. Who was it said the war would be over before Christmas? Last Christmas at that!'

'Some nitwit. They said the same in 1914.'

'I think we can look forward to years of it now, you know. Years. Can you see an end to it? I can't. There are already thousands dead in London, Coventry, Hull, Manchester, Liverpool . . . How many more will there be? The navy's doing its best – and the lads in Africa. But can you see the end of it?'

'No,' said Fotherby.

'But of course we'll win in the end, old friend. You mark my words.'

'You getting peckish?' Fotherby asked.

'I don't think so. Why, are you?'

'No.'

'You look much smarter now that I went to the trouble of getting your waistcoat fixed. But why haven't you shaved again today?'

'Why don't you drink your mother's ruin?' Fotherby said.

Harry now came to the pub. They were singing in there. The noise of it seemed to bulge the old walls and there was someone – it looked in the darkness like a woman – being sick in the far corner of the yard. Otherwise, the yard was empty. For weeks it had been populated by the Lancashire Rifles overflowing from the pub, being squeezed out through its doorway like khaki toothpaste from a tube. But there would be only villagers in the pub now. Young male locals with too much beer in their bellies could occasionally make a nuisance of themselves in this yard. Harry expressed a wish into the air that he wouldn't be called out to deal with them later, wouldn't have to leave wife and child on New Year's Eve and pedal down to sort them out.

He walked on. Coming abreast of Saddler's Row, he thought of Michael Philbin and his wife, Nancy. Poor woman. He'd been there when they arrested her and he would never forget her distress. That swine Brendan Kelly, who had wheedled his way into everyone's good books – the swine. But who would ever have believed it of Michael Philbin? There never was a nicer, gentler man in the village. Two men fighting a war of their own at a time like this. Yes, the world was mad.

Further down Somercotes Road, there beyond an overgrown garden, sat the squat square shadow of Geiger's bungalow, which had been boarded up and dead for weeks.

That man didn't deserve what he got, either. The war . . .
the bloody war . . . You don't need to be in the front line
to have your life ruined by a war.

But then, as Harry stood there, staring away across the
black garden, a sudden shock went through him. Was that
smoke he could see against the dark sky? Smoke rising
from the chimney of the bungalow? Yes, by God, it was!
And yes, now that he looked more closely, he saw that in
fact the boards had gone from the windows. What he was
actually looking at was the blackness of blackout curtains.
What was going on? Had the bungalow been sold? Were
there newcomers in the village? Were there kids in there,
playing about? Or squatters? Deciding that it was his business to find answers, Harry opened the garden gate, walked
down the path and knocked at the door. A wireless was
playing inside – he could hear music. Assuming that
because of it his knock had not been heard, he rattled the
knocker again, loudly. But indeed he had been heard, for
while he still held the knocker between his fingers, the door
was pulled open. A small black shape confronted him in
the darkness of the lobby.

Harry's uniformed figure, his helmet, must have been
recognised. 'Ah, is that Constable Bowker? Good evening!'

Harry was astonished. 'Is that you, Mr Geiger?'

'Yes, it is I! It is I!' Geiger was laughing.

'Have they sent you home again?'

'Yes, yes. It's all right. Everything's all right, my friend.
Come in, come in!'

'Thanks, Mr Geiger – but I can't come in just now. I'm
doing my rounds. But by hell, I'm glad to see you back.
What happened?'

The inner door opened, flooding out light, and Fraulein Hertz stood there, smiling.

'Quick,' Geiger said to her. 'Come . . . *die Tur*—'

The fraulein closed the inner door, shut back the light, and came to stand beside him.

'Well, well,' Harry said. 'So it's all over for both of you. I'm very glad. What happened?'

'But what does it matter?' Geiger asked. 'We're here again. They took us to prison – I in Coventry and Rosa in Holloway. We didn't see each other for weeks. We were surrounded by some terrible people and fascists – yes, fascists. Terrible people . . . Six times the authorities questioned me – six times – and Rosa the same. But I'd told them it was wrong – it was all wrong – and they saw it, Constable. In the end they saw it. We're very happy.'

'And I'm happy for you. Welcome home.'

'This is England, and I'm British, and they saw it. I love this country, Constable, and I want people to know it. Will you tell people? Tell them I'm British? Please, tell my neighbours that they were wrong and I forgive them. Come in, let me give you a drink of Scottish whisky.'

Geiger reached out and took hold of Harry's sleeve.

'I'd love to – but no, I really can't. I'd better get on. But I'm very glad for you, I truly am. Best of luck to you both. Welcome home, welcome home.' And Harry turned away.

As he walked down the path he waited for the sound of the door closing behind him. But it didn't come. They were watching him go. At the gate, he turned to look back. In the darkness of the hall their two shadows stood side by side. He imagined them smiling and he smiled back. 'Good night!' he called.

'Happy New Year!' Geiger cried.

'Happy New Year!' cried Fraulein Hertz in fervent English.

At the gates to Pretoria Estate, Harry turned about and headed back for home. Frost had nipped at his nose and his ears, and his feet were cold. In order to speed up his circulation, he increased his pace and marched on with arms swinging. His silhouette against the sky as he went past the Home Guard's field had the widely striding posture of Johnnie Walker on Mr Geiger's whisky bottle.

At Pretoria House, Lance was home. He'd brought with him Sue from town, the woman who'd given him that mug of tea, a childless widow much younger than Lance had at first sight guessed, who had lost her husband in an industrial accident two years earlier. She was twenty-six, quiet, intelligent, almost two decades younger than Lance, but unconcerned about that. They were sitting chatting amiably in the large drawing room where the Christmas tree sparkled and glittered.

Time, thought Maureen, would tell how long this little affair lasted. Sue was a very nice, smiling young woman, rather diffident, and it was obvious that she was developing an attachment to Lance. The thought that, as in the case of all Lance's girlfriends, the poor woman was destined for heartache, troubled Maureen greatly and her instinct was to speak to her, warn her. Yet in her devotion to her brother and in her anxiety not to betray him, hurt him, she found this impossible to do.

She had left them to it and gone upstairs to look at dear little Tidgy. The only light in the room came from the partially open door and she sat holding the sleeping child's warm hand. Maureen was troubled, and the problem of Tidgy was one of the things that troubled her. For months, her letters to Tidgy's mother had been unanswered. Indeed, the two Maureen had posted off in November had been returned *Not at this address*, and the notion that the child had been abandoned – unbelievable though it had seemed – had now to be confronted as a fact. She ought to have done something about it long before now – as far back as July. But the thought that that would almost certainly lead to her losing the child had been too much. She'd behaved foolishly and she knew it. The day of reckoning would have to come sooner or later. But even now she persisted in her foolishness and intended to do nothing.

Another cause for her low mood was that she had heard nothing from either Francesca or Carla, who had both promised so faithfully to write. Their mother had prevented it, no doubt. But Maureen longed to hear from them. After their loss, and the loss of Brendan, which had so much wounded her, she clung to Tidgy as the most precious thing in her life. She put the child's tubby little hand to her lips and kissed it. Then she went downstairs.

Veronica, who would otherwise have been at home alone, had been invited to spend the night of New Year's Eve at the house. She had gone to the kitchen to mull wine. The smell of it steaming struck Maureen as soon as she opened the kitchen door. Veronica was sitting there at the table, paused in her work for the moment. She was re-reading a letter from her husband that had reached her that morning. It had been delayed in the post. *Dear Veronica, I hope this*

reaches you before Christmas and that you'll have a happy
time, but not without thinking of me. I am sending you a
photo of me and some of the lads . . . Veronica looked
up.

'That's all right,' said Maureen, 'read your letter.'

But Veronica folded it and reached for her handbag to
put it away. Then she looked at Maureen again. 'It's from
David. Would you like to see his picture, ma'am?'

'Yes, I would.'

Maureen took the photograph from her. It showed David
Heath in naval tropical uniform, white shirt and white
shorts, leaning against the taffrail of a ship and surrounded
by other sailors, all laughing like himself. 'He looks well,'
Maureen said.

'Yes, doesn't he? He's very brave, my David, ma'am. His
letters are always cheerful. He never complains. He's always
trying to cheer me up.'

'Yes. I'm very fond of him.'

'He's fond of you,' Veronica said.

For days, except at meals, Veronica had seen little of
Maureen. Maureen had seemed unwilling to emerge from
her room, had been quite unprepared to talk and had
looked quite ill. Now, sitting with her hands folded on the
table, she sank again into self-absorption.

'Are you all right, ma'am?' Veronica asked. 'Aren't you
well?'

'As a matter of fact, Veronica, no. I'm not.'

'What's the matter?'

Maureen's thoughts at this moment were of the dear
Irishman she'd lost, that kind soul who had given her such
tender affection after a lifetime of loneliness – the man

she still loved, despite what she now knew about him. Her heart was aching. But she could say nothing of that. She simply smiled, weakly.

There was a sudden gust of wind against the window, bringing with it a handful of dead sycamore leaves. They tapped at the glass like angry fingers. All along the shelves, polished copper pans poked their handles into the room and from one of the hooks in the ceiling beams a bouquet of rosemary dangled.

'I'll make you some coffee,' Veronica said.

'Thank you, dear. Yes.'

'What about Mr Lance and the lady?'

'They're drinking whisky, I think. Let them wait for the mulled wine.'

Veronica took down the percolator, filled it at the tap and went for the coffee jar. 'We've not got much left,' she said. 'Mr Carter when I spoke to him on the phone told me they mightn't be able to get any more coffee at all for a bit.'

'Then we'll drink tea. It doesn't matter.'

Maureen watched while Veronica, tonight free of her pinny and dressed in a black skirt and white blouse, brought cups to the table. She continued to watch as Veronica went for the sugar and milk.

'You're looking very well yourself, Veronica.'

'Thank you, ma'am.'

'Sit down, dear.'

Veronica sat.

'You've put on some weight,' Maureen said.

'Have I?'

'Yes.' Maureen reached for Veronica's hand. 'Would you mind terribly if I asked you something?'

'Of course not, ma'am.'

'Well forgive me, dear – but are you pregnant?'

'Yes,' Veronica said, without hesitation, merely moving her fingers slightly in Maureen's hand.

'Well, I'm very happy for you. David must be delighted.'

Veronica looked directly into Maureen's eyes. 'He doesn't know.'

'Doesn't he?'

'I'm just showing, ma'am. I'm just over four months. David's been away since June, hasn't he?' Veronica slipped her hand away from Maureen's. 'So there you are.'

'Oh my dear . . .'

'It's all right, ma'am. It's all right. It was Nigel Lawrence. We loved each other.'

'But poor Nigel was killed.'

'Yes, ma'am, he was.'

'Oh, Veronica – I'm so sorry. Oh dear, what're you going to do?'

'Nothing,' Veronica said.

'But what about David?'

'Why should I break his heart when he's so far away? I can't do it to him.'

'But Veronica, he'll have to know sometime. Won't he?'

'I suppose so. But it's all right, ma'am.' Veronica now had a little smile on her face. Her head was high. There was an air of determined self-possession about her. 'It's all right.'

'Is it? You seem to mean what you say.'

'I do. You forget, ma'am, I've had months to think about it, haven't I?'

'Yes, I suppose you have.'

'You see, I've worried myself out of worry. D'you know what I mean?'

'Yes, I think I do.'

'Now I just live from day to day. I love David with all my heart. I can't upset him – never. What will be will be.'

Maureen was gazing at her. 'Yes, yes,' she said.

'Excuse me.' Veronica stood up. 'The percolator's bubbling.'

They sat drinking coffee without speaking again for several minutes.

Then Maureen said, 'Look, Veronica, we must cheer up. I've been very depressed of late.'

'I know, ma'am. I've seen it.'

'Well, as you say, you can't go on fretting for ever. I'll tell you what we're going to do. We're going to enjoy ourselves tonight. Never mind the coffee, let's find the punchbowl. Let's enjoy ourselves. And tomorrow we'll go for a drive – you, Tidgy and me. We'll put the hood up, take some blankets and damn the weather. We'll go and stay for a night or two at a nice hotel I know in Stamford. We'll blow all the petrol ration! You can eat some meals you've not cooked for a change. We'll enjoy ourselves, my dear, and come back only when we feel like it. What d'you say to that?'

*

Harry Bowker arrived home after his patrol at half-past ten, but even before he'd had time to get out of his uniform, he was disturbed by the ringing of the telephone. Phoebe Brocklesby, in her capacity as chairperson of the parish council and commander-in-chief of most things in the village, rang to tell him that a special train would be arriving at the station in an hour's time. She was rallying her ladies and would he please be certain to be at the station when the train arrived.

It had brought bombed-out people from Manchester of all places, a hundred miles and more away. There were about sixty of them, old men, young men, old women, young women and children, all carrying their pathetic bits and pieces – blankets, a portable wireless, a puppy, a budgerigar in a cage, brown paper carrier bags and bundles wrapped in newspaper. The village hall was opened and they were trooped into there. Locals had lent four electric fires to warm up the place. The geyser was steaming away and cups of tea were being handed around. Phoebe and her ladies were behind the counter at the cooker, boiling up Samuel Duke's recipe for potato pie.

The exhausted refugees sat on the benches that lined the walls. Others sat on the floor. Yet others lay on the floor. Very few spoke. Very few moved. Even the kids, tired out, were immobile.

Harry Bowker spoke for a while to a woman whose husband, so far as she knew, was lying dead under the rubble of her house. She had a bandage around her head. Then he cradled a baby while its young mother, grey-faced and tangled-haired, drank her tea. Then he tried to entertain a group of children, putting his helmet on their heads and showing them his handcuffs and his truncheon. But they could barely raise smiles. He handed out cigarettes, until only one was left in his packet. To smoke that one, and to get a bit of fresh air between puffs, he went outside.

After a moment, as he stood speckled with moonlight under the trees, he realised that one of the small boys he'd tried to entertain, in a tattered raincoat and boots far too big for him, had followed him out. 'Hello there,' Harry said.

He felt the boy's hand searching for his own and took hold of it. Looking at the watch on his other wrist, he saw that it was just coming up to midnight. 'Happy New Year, son,' he said.

From inside the hall a lone, tremulous male voice began to sing, 'Should old acquaintance be forgot and never brought to mind . . .'

After only a few bars, other voices began to compete with it, gradually growing in number until it was overwhelmed. Inharmoniously, in mixed keys, wearily, but with feeling, the refugees were singing:

There'll always be an England
While there's a country lane,
Wherever there's a cottage small
Beside a field of grain . . .

There'll always be an England,
And England shall be free
If England means as much to you
As England means to me.

Harry stamped out his cigarette end. 'Don't worry, son,' he said to the boy. 'We're going to be all right. Come on – let's go and find your mother.'

About the Author

Frank White was born in 1927 and brought up in Newton Heath, Manchester. His father was one of the original Old Contemptibles, that tiny army of British professional soldiers who went to Belgium at the beginning of the First World War in August, 1914. Frank's older brother, William, was killed at the Battle of Mareth in March 1943.

At seventeen Frank volunteered for the wartime Royal Navy and served his time in the British Pacific Fleet, latterly on the staff of the Commander-in-Chief. In later years, he worked first in journalism as assistant editor of a textile trade journal and then as publicity manager for two large companies in Lancashire and Yorkshire.

At forty-two he suffered two severe heart attacks. Uncertain of his own survival and concerned to provide a continuing livelihood for his family (he and June, his wife, had five children) he took over the tenancy of the Waggon & Horses public house at Oxspring, South Yorkshire.

In his spare time Frank had written two novels, short stories for BBC radio, essays and articles for numerous journals, as well as plays for the stage. During his time at the Waggon & Horses he was commissioned to write plays and entertainments for local town councils. He also became Writer in Residence at Lincoln Theatre Royal. He grew attached to that county and, with June, retired there in

1986. He continued to contribute material to magazines, and wrote a short book on the First World War and two full-length plays for BBC radio.

In 2013, realising that the world was no longer full of people who could write at first hand about the Second World War, Frank spent three summer months on *There Was a Time*, which he set in his adopted county.

Also by Frank White

Originally published in 1964 and now reissued,
Frank White's powerful debut novel

A Morse Code Set

'Told through a small son, *A Morse Code Set* concerns
the break-up of a marriage as a result of war . . . fluent
and well-built. This is a writer to watch.'
The Sunday Times

Freddy is thirteen years old in 1939, when
the close comfort of his family life is breached by
his father being called up to the Army. His mother is
emotionally unable to cope with the separation, and
becomes withdrawn and depressed. When Freddy's
beloved morse code set, which his father built, is
broken, it is almost as if all lines of communication
have failed. Then the father of one of Freddy's
friends offers to repair the morse code set.

Has the boy brought healing or tragedy into
the family home?

Read on for the opening of this intense novel by a
writer with an acute eye and ear for family relationships
and a superb sense of storytelling.

HODDER

HALF an hour ago, I returned from Dawson Park Cemetery, which is just off Queen's Road on the northern boundary of Manchester. It was a disturbing afternoon, and the mood it has created will, I know, linger with me for weeks.

The funeral had been arranged for two o'clock, but I was late. There had been fog and ice on the hills and the drive had taken me almost an hour longer than I had estimated. I arrived as the last prayers were being said.

The grave was in a hollow, where the ground sloped away towards the Medlock. I came round the little chapel, and, hesitating, looked down across the sooty grass and smears of yellow mud to where the minister and the solitary mourner stood together by the mound of earth.

I don't know why I expected to see more people. If I'd thought about it at all, I would have found it difficult to imagine who else might turn up. But I hadn't thought about it, and the spectacle of those two dim figures, huddled together in the rain, gave me pause. Now, the prospect of meeting Mr. Hanson – which, since there were no other people among whom I could lose myself, seemed inevitable – alarmed me, and I stepped back out of sight between the buttresses of the chapel.

It was a cold day. The rain touched my face like pinpoints. Out there in the open, gusts of wind pulled at the minister's robes and flapped Mr. Hanson's raincoat limply like a sodden brown duster. Low grey clouds scudded across the maze of factory chimneys in Clayton beyond the river, and the sense of gloom and desolation which overcame me as I stood there was so powerful that my body ached.

I had come to this funeral almost involuntarily – almost as a reflex, not troubling to consider what the act of coming implied or what memories best left dormant the occasion would revive. If I had pondered the point, I would have been better armed against this subtle pain, perhaps. Indeed, I don't think I would have gone at all. Two decades had laid down their strata of forgetfulness, and if I had stayed away this afternoon I should have been able to go on forgetting. But there I was, at her funeral, within a mile of the house, looking away over that well-known view, and those old memories came bursting back irresistibly into my mind. Those long forgotten emotions took hold of me again as though it had all happened yesterday. Despite my thirty-odd years, I was literally trembling again with the fervent misery of a boy.

I like to think that as one grows older one develops techniques for keeping one's feelings more or less under control. This may not be true. It may be, quite simply, that one's emotions are less powerful, more manageable. But whatever the reason, it seems to me that no normal adult ever feels things so keenly as a child – and to be suddenly subjected, as a man, to such an intensity of childish feeling, was an unnerving experience. These remembered sensations of boyhood came back quite unaltered, filling me with infantile bitterness and depression.

The minister, who had been reading from a card which he held close to his chest, suddenly flung out both arms over the grave. For a second, he remained there, poised tensely. Then, with a perfunctory glance towards the sky, he withdrew his arms, tucked the card away under his robes and put his hands into his trousers pockets. Mr. Hanson raised his head and looked at him. They spoke briefly. Mr. Hanson put his cap on. And then, together, they turned from the grave and came up the hill.

They passed within three yards of me, but neither of them saw me standing there. The minister, his hands still in his pockets, his head to one side, was saying something to Mr. Hanson and nodding gently. The sound of his voice, the words confused by the wind, came to me patchily as they walked by. It was over twenty years since I'd seen Mr. Hanson, and even now I saw him only indistinctly. But I recognised that face at once. Two decades hadn't changed it much. The long nose, the small chin, that peculiar curve of the forehead ... But he seemed shorter than I remembered him, slighter. This surprised me, and when they'd passed, I stepped out and looked after them. He was, indeed, an altogether small man, short and thin with sloping narrow shoulders – a figure which contrasted strongly with my memories. At the far corner of the chapel, they parted. The minister hurried inside out of the rain and cold and Mr. Hanson walked on towards the cemetery gates.

With a decided effort, I left the shelter of the chapel, crossed the pathway and walked on to the turf. The ground was spongy with contained moisture, but the grass was somehow so brittle that it crackled under my feet like a carpet of twigs. A stray dog appearing from the forest of gravestones farther down, came trotting to meet me. He circled me twice and went back the way he had come. I found myself contemplating him carefully. I stood still as he sidled round me, and observed his lolling tongue, the dark, matted fur along his spine. I have never cared at all for dogs, and find it difficult to tell one breed from another. They are creatures that mean absolutely nothing to me. And yet, for a full minute, this bedraggled animal occupied all my attention. His arrival seemed significant, and his departure was a distinct disappointment.

The fact was, I realised, that I simply did not want to complete this brief journey to the graveside. The superstitious feeling that the dog's strange behaviour was an omen, a sign to me not to do so, was in itself a reflection of that reluctance. Of course I did not want to go. I watched the dog slink away among the gravestones, and continued to search for it long after it had vanished, holding on to the thought of it in a silly effort to keep those other thoughts at bay.

But there was the grave, a stride or two from me, and a moment later I was at the edge of it, standing in clay and looking down. Even now, my gaze passed only slowly across the smooth, wet side of the pit. Little rivulets of water ran down from the pile of earth on the other bank and cataracted over the brink. On top of that mound, stuck upright in the hump of clay, there stood a spade. My first glance hardly took it in. But almost at once my eyes returned to it, and the fantastic symbolism of it quite paralysed me for a moment. But then, suddenly angry, I strode round the grave, pulled up the spade and threw it away. I was gasping and shaking, and despite the fierce cold, sweating profusely. Standing with my back to the grave, and with deliberately slow movements, as though by forcing my body to behave calmly I would somehow soothe my mind, I took out my cigarette case and matches and lit a cigarette. Then just as slowly, just as deliberately, I turned and looked down. There the coffin lay, at the bottom of that slimy pit, daubed with mud and under a sheet of rain.

For a long time I stared at it, thinking of her. But gradually I sensed something amiss, something wrong. When

I realised what it was, I felt myself start. Once again, I had been surprised by smallness. The coffin seemed minute. It could hardly have been five feet long. My amazement was so profound that, for a second, it overwhelmed all other feeling. How could I have been so mistaken?

And yet the answer was obvious. Twenty-one years ago, I was thirteen, and not very tall at that. One's childhood memories are always out of proportion, as I had learnt so disquietingly already this afternoon. One always remembers looking up, and the mind rarely has the ability to make adjustments for one's own growth. But, despite this realisation, the sense of surprise persisted. And as I looked down at that little box, it dawned on me like a revelation that I had not known her at all. Thirteen years in a lifetime is a mere nothing – especially thirteen very immature, introspective years. I had not known her. All those images which had come flooding back into my mind were incomplete – seen through the eyes of a child who understood very little. All those memories were shadows, merely, warped and misshapen by the emotions and inadequate vision of a baby. And all those upsetting sensations, which were so much a part of those memories, they too belonged to another age, another person, almost. I simply did not know her.

For one painful moment, I began bitterly to regret those years of abandonment. If I had stayed there any longer contemplating that coffin, I think I should have gone a little mad with remorse and guilt. But the spell was broken by the arrival of two gravediggers. They came out of the mist like bats, leather capes flapping about their shoulders, and at the sight of them, I turned away and walked back to the path.

Once outside the gates of the cemetery, my mind began to readjust itself. One's defence mechanisms came to one's aid. It was true, I told myself, that I had not known her except as a child knows a person. But what difference did that make? If things had taken another course, if I had come as a man to know her, perhaps I would have understood. But understanding is not always forgiveness – and forgiveness there could never have been, for her, or, I feel in my heart, for me.

As I drove past the gates, I looked back briefly through the darkening vapours to where the gravediggers were piling earth on to my mother's coffin. They worked rhythmically, tossing their heavy spadefuls indifferently into the pit. A light came on in the chapel. It was getting late. Quickly, I drove on, up the hill, under the bridge and away.

Do you wish this wasn't the end?

Join us at www.hodder.co.uk, or follow us on
Twitter @hodderbooks to be a part of our community
of people who love the very best in books and reading.

Whether you want to discover more about a book
or an author, watch trailers and interviews, have the
chance to win early limited editions, or simply browse
our expert readers' selection of the very best books,
we think you'll find what you're looking for.

And if you don't,
that's the place to tell us what's missing.

We love what we do, and we'd love you to be part of it.

www.hodder.co.uk

@hodderbooks

HodderBooks

HodderBooks